AMELIA AND THE

VIRGIN

AMELIA AND THE
VIRGIN

NICKY HARLOW

Published by
Pewter Rose Press
17 Mellors Rd,
West Bridgford
Nottingham, NG2 6EY
United Kingdom
www.pewter-rose-press.com

First published in Great Britain 2011
© Nicky Harlow 2011
ISBN 978-0-9560053-9-7

British Library Cataloguing in Publication Data
A catalogue record for this book is available from the British Library

Cover design by www.thedesigndepot.co.uk
Printed and bound in Great Britain by
TJ International Ltd, Padstow, Cornwall

Nicky Harlow grew up in Liverpool. She moved to Leeds to study Fine Art and now lives in Hebden Bridge where she lectures for the Open University. In between she has restored church statues, been a shop display artist, worked with older people in residential care and run art and writing workshops for community groups. In 2010, she was awarded the Michael Schmidt Prize for her Creative Writing portfolio by Manchester Metropolitan University.

She lives with her partner, poet and novelist, Daithidh MacEodaith, and two daughters, Abby and Ursula.

THANKS

To the many kind people who have read parts or the whole of this book and offered their valuable insights:
Daithidh for continuing advice, support and cider making
Anne McDonnell of Pewter Rose, for eagle eyed editing
Paul Magrs and Lynda Prescott
The members of the MMU 'Novel Swap shop'
The tutors of Manchester Metropolitan Creative Writing MA
The tutors and students at Leeds University Continuing Education department, Creative Writing modules – where this book began.

DEDICATION

To Dr John Livingstone, Mr Paul Chumas and the rest of the Children's Neurology Team at Leeds Infirmary for giving my daughter back her life.

PART ONE
THE JOYFUL MYSTERIES

CHAPTER 1
4PM. 7TH SEPTEMBER 1981

Amelia heard a fluttering, batting noise. A pigeon walked sedately across the skylight, its hard toes clattering on the murky glass. A shadow fell over the altar and she clasped her hands in prayer. At last, a Sign.

The Goddess had spoken to Amelia in many ways but never so clearly as during the past two days: several tennis racquets had appeared in her school locker and the coveted Our Lady of Lourdes pendant from the devotional shop at St. Gerard Magella's was found miraculously tucked inside her knicker pocket. This morning she had opened her sock drawer to discover a packet of cigarettes and a lighter. So far she had smoked four and they made her sick, but her duty to the Goddess knew no bounds. If She required Amelia to smoke, then smoke she would.

The hour had come.

Amelia had arrived home at her grandmother's house, coughing a little from the effects of the Capstans. Silently, she let herself in through the kitchen door and tiptoed upstairs to the landing. The cockloft could only be reached by inserting the brass hook on the end of a window-pole into the little loop embedded in the door in the landing ceiling. Once the door dropped down, opening like the lid of an upside down box, the ladders were coaxed out, creaking and gasping like a pair of ancient bellows. She gripped the first rung and looked up. A section of cobwebby rafter could be glimpsed from the landing, an enticing view of box-ends and suitcases.

The inhabitants of Number Eighteen Calvary Crescent crammed everything they wanted to forget in the dark space between the roof and the bedroom ceilings. Amelia's family never threw anything out. The loft housed fifty years-worth of death and disappointment. Broken dreams, failed romances, bitter memories, flawed personalities, all were rammed up there with the ladders. Forgotten but not gone. And presiding over this half century of failure loomed the altar of the Goddess. This magnificent form took up the entire width of the chimney-breast, billowed out to embrace the Suicide Cousin's medical books, the Lupus Aunt's doll collection, the Philandering Great-Uncle's navy uniform. Trunks and boxes nestled the darker recesses that Amelia had yet to explore, but for now she was content to worship, bringing as her offering yet another atrocious school report and a pocketful of wilted chrysanths, pilfered from the graveyard at St. Gerard Magella's.

She slung her school bag around her neck and climbed up, listening for a change in the whistle of her grandmother's breath or the click of the latch on the front door. The house was silent save for the steady thud of the clock in the hall. A shaft of coloured light from the stained glass window made a mosaic of green and mauve and deep blue on the landing walls, giving the narrow corridor a churchy feel. She smiled. The Goddess would be pleased at this touch.

'Oh Great and Esteemed Goddess,' she whispered, shuffling forward on her knees. 'Please accept my offertory.' She looked up at the holy raiment, the fall of silk and organza, made the sign of the cross, then took her report, opened it and placed it beneath. The dead roses were removed from the smelly jam jar and replaced with the new flowers, before Amelia clasped her hands together and said her version of the Hail Mary, substituting any mention of the Mother of God with Goddess Irena's name. She prostrated herself at the altar in the way novice nuns did when they were taking their vows. Her own Holy Orders had been taken over six months ago and she had shorn off her fringe as an act of penance. There were still tufts of yellow hair on Great Aunt Mabel's sewing box.

'It is time,' she whispered. 'I have waited many months for you to show yourself to me. I summon you, oh mighty one …'

She sensed, rather than heard, the Goddess's approbation.

Keeping her head bent low, she managed to stand up. She moved towards the Goddess's robe keeping her eyes averted, as was the custom. For those who looked directly upon this beautiful and terrible form would be immediately condemned to death. With shaking fingers, she managed to pull the gown from its wire coat hanger. Spiders dropped lightly onto her bare arms, moths exploded towards the light. Again she heard the fluttering sound and inwardly thanked the Goddess for Her generosity.

The dress was stiff with dust, the fabric felt coated and sticky. The crisp carapaces of a thousand insects pattered to the floor as she undid the hooks on the bodice. It whispered mystical secrets to her. The Goddess had held them safe for many years and now it was Amelia's Holy Obligation to release them into the atmosphere where they would mingle with other, nobler truths, before evaporating into the power of the universe.

The fluttering grew louder. Amelia prayed silently. She crumpled the dress to the floor and stepped into it. It was far too big for her. The waist fell to her thighs, the long medieval sleeves hung far below her hands. With difficulty, she managed to refasten enough of the hooks to keep the dress up. Delighted, she spun around, catching sight of her reflection in Great Grandma's old dressing table mirror. Even with the expanse of orange and white school dress peeking over the neckline, she made a magnificent bride. The veil was a more complicated affair, a wiry circle of silk lilies and roses from which there flowed a long train of organza. This had become knotted and puckered. Part of the fabric rent when she crammed it on her head and it hung down over her eyes, grey and tattered as the curtains on the outhouse window. It released a drift of ancient perfume, heady and exotic: the Goddess's incense. Amelia knelt and prayed and felt herself transported by the rhythmic fluttering and batting noise: her grandmother's soul, trying to escape the failing fabric of her body.

Four hours later, the O'Dowd family, such as it was, were arrayed around the deathbed, staring down at the rattling form.

'She's definitely going,' Marguerite announced. 'I haven't heard her sound like that before.'

Amelia glanced up at her mother, noticing the way the September light outlined the crevices in her face, making her seem older and harder. 'Will she stay here, in bed until the funeral?'

Aunt Dolores snorted. 'I bloody well hope not. I'm sleeping in the next room tonight. If I've got to share a room with a corpse, I'd rather book an hotel. I've had enough trouble with strange bedfellows, what with Ken's latest craze —'

'We'll phone the Co-op, love,' Marguerite said, briskly. 'Mum left instructions.'

Amelia wondered what the instructions could be and why they had been left at the supermarket.

'I thought she'd outlive me,' Edith wailed. 'What shall I do without a sister left in the world?'

'You're five years younger than Mum,' Marguerite whispered. 'And you've got us. We're your family.'

Amelia walked around the bed, squeezing between the adults until she was beside her grandmother's pillow. She knelt piously, and leaned her head against her praying hands. She felt Edith glance at Marguerite in proud acknowledgement. Edith had always hankered after Convent Life, but blamed poor health and the responsibility of caring for elderly parents for her lost opportunity. Amelia's mother reckoned that Great Aunt Edith had never taken Holy Orders because she was too fond of the High Life to make the vow of poverty and mean it.

'Can I be alone with Grandma for a moment?' Amelia asked, feeling the Vicks jar clatter against her hip. 'I want to say goodbye.'

The adults clucked their tongues and sighed.

'You're a credit to your mother,' Edith whispered, tearfully.

Marguerite was not so easily taken in. 'Why?' she demanded.

Amelia sniffed in what she hoped was a convincing manner.

'Oh leave the little ghoul to it,' Dolores said, already half out of the door. 'I can't bear death scenes and I could drink a pub dry. Does Mum have anything in the house except Baileys and crème de menthe?'

'Five minutes, madam,' Marguerite said. 'And I'm coming back.'

Grandma's room was a featureless cell, painted pale pink with a border of roses. Everything smelled of lavender, talc and bad breath. There was one picture, a postcard-sized view of Whitby Harbour that had been painted by a long dead Artist Uncle whose easel and paints were up in the loft. The only really interesting object was the bed, which was a carved mahogany affair with Egyptian wings over the headboard. It had been slept in by Queen Victoria herself, when it resided at the Duke of something-or-other's palace, or so the story went. Grandma said it made her feel like a princess. Marguerite said Granddad had been 'ripped off'.

Amelia waited until her mother and aunts had reached the bottom of the stairs, before taking the jar from her cardigan pocket, opening it and immediately abandoning herself to the refreshing scent of eucalyptus. She rose and looked at her grandmother. The old woman looked nothing like her usual self. Her hair had been allowed to grow long during her illness and instead of its usual neat bob, it fanned around her face, light and wispy as cuckoo spit. Her cheeks and eyes were sunken and her skin a yellowish mauve.

'The Goddess Irena offers you Extreme Ointment,' Amelia announced, taking a liberal pat of Vicks from the jar and anointing Grandma's temple. 'She forgives you your trespassing and for being cruel to your granddaughter who is now Her High Priestess. Hail Irena, full of grace, may the power be with you ...'

Grandma's breath heaved and cranked through congested lungs. A tear squeezed out from between her closed eyelids. Her gnarled fingers gripped the duvet, clutched and let go, clutched and let go. It was the first real sign of a response all day. Encouraged, Amelia continued.

'Repent of your sins and reject the glamour of evil.' She lifted her arms in supplication. Earlier, she had moved the

Goddess's dress so that it now hung from an antiquated wardrobe in the loft, the veil spread out like the wings of a terrifying cabbage white.

Maybe it was this uprooting from its usual position on the chimney breast, maybe Grandma's deathbed was just what the Goddess had been waiting for. The summons, this time, had worked. A circle of light hovered over Grandma's head, brilliantly white in the centre bleeding into a lemony yellow at the edges. The light filtered through the room, the painting of Whitby harbour vanished, as did the tea roses on the border. Grandma's flossy hair seemed to melt; her face became misty, faded. Amelia dropped to her knees, squinting in the brightness, and heard, louder this time, an insistent beat, the flutter of a moth trapped in a lampshade. She looked up and saw a pair of feet dangling through the ceiling. As she watched, the feet dropped towards her, followed by slender ankles and the hem of a white robe. Hips appeared, a narrow cinched waist, arms outstretched in welcome. Finally a head, the most beautiful head Amelia had ever seen, surrounded by a fluffy haze of golden hair. The lips were red, the eyes a deep and dazzling blue.

'Goddess,' Amelia gasped.

'Help me,' Grandma replied.

Amelia groped for the old woman's hand and clutched it. 'It's okay,' she whispered. 'The Goddess has come to tell us …'

'She's come for me.' Grandma's voice was different, foreign, as though she was speaking through a crackly megaphone. 'Help me, child. I lapsed in my faith and now the time of reckoning has come …'

The Goddess looked down. Amelia felt warm, full of love and forgiveness.

'She has forgiven you,' she whispered to her grandmother. 'Look, she is smiling.'

Grandma tried to shade her eyes from the Goddess's brilliance, but her arm was too weak to cover her face.

'Help,' she said. 'Hel …' Grandma's final breath pinned her body to the bed. The old woman's face contorted, twisted away from the awful light and from Amelia who had fallen into a prayerful trance.

The Virgin,' Grandma wheezed as her soul loosed its earthly moorings. 'The Virgin.'

Edith claimed later that she had seen a dazzling light emanating from her dying sister's room and the air rang with angelic singing. Unfortunately her account was not to be trusted as the cockloft door had shot open onto her head when she was halfway across the landing, knocking her right into the bathroom and leaving a nasty lump over her right eye. Marguerite told Edith that she was a stupid old woman who needed to lose some weight if she was to have any hope of living as long as her sister. Marguerite, Amelia knew, would never have anything to do with what she called 'religious mumbo jumbo'.

But even Dolores, marinated in spirits of her own, had embraced the tale, adding that she had seen the heavenly glow seeping through the floorboards and into the kitchen below, where she had discovered a stash of gin in the bread bin.

Amelia, the cause and sole witness of the phenomenon, had been sent to bed without any tea.

'I think I'll have to send that child to a shrink,' she heard her mother saying as she lay in the gloom of the box room, thinking over the day's events. 'I mean, it's not bloody normal, is it, for a thirteen year old girl to be going around saying she's seen the Virgin … And she stank of Vicks. She'd put it all over Mum's head. I had to take a damp flannel to her before the undertakers arrived.'

Dolores gave a high-pitched parroty squawk. 'Margie, you can't say that it didn't happen. Why, with my own eyes I saw …'

'You'd just downed half a bottle of bloody Gordon's. No wonder you could see things. Amelia spends too much time on her own. I knew I was wrong giving up the house in Eccles Road to come here. But with all the business with her brother, well …'

'Your daughter is a little saint,' Edith announced. 'I knew there'd be one in the family somewhere and it is she without a shadow of a doubt. You said she favoured me, well I had the calling, the vocation, you know, but the times were against me. I had my own pasteurising concerns …'

'I said she was a nutcase and she's not alone.'

'Shh.' Dolores cleared her throat. 'The question is, what are we going to do about it? I mean this is privileged information.

The Mother of Christ appearing to Amelia like this. The authorities ought to be informed.'

'Authorities?' Marguerite demanded. 'What authorities?'

Dolores cackled. 'Why the Pope in Rome. I'm sure he'd want to know if one of his flock had seen the Mother of God especially as, don't forget, he'll be here, in Liverpool on Pentecost Sunday.'

'Put that bottle down,' Marguerite said. 'You've had enough. Now let's get one thing straight. No one is going to 'be informed' of Amelia's ridiculous fantasy. And as for telling the Pope! Since when did you start going to Mass again? No, we are all going to forget about it. There's enough to think about with Mum ...' At last her armour cracked and she broke down.

Amelia dozed off to the sounds of reminiscence and sobbing and the smell of gin.

CHAPTER 2
9TH SEPTEMBER 1981

Whiskey. It smelled sharp, smoky, made your eyes water but none of them noticed. So, maybe the smell was just under the table, Amelia decided. It was a possibility. Under the table, she swigged at her cherry brandy. Not bad. Not exactly Vimto but not bad. Maybe a few crisps would make it more palatable; there were some sticking into the close knit of her school tights. She vaguely remembered the bowl of savouries going over, her frantic scrabble to retrieve Twiglets and Monster Munch. Most had been consumed by a shabby fox terrier, brought by some whispering cousin twice removed who'd had her voice box out in 1952. Just a few savoury snacks remained, nicely filling the cigarette burn in the Axminster. Amelia crawled forwards. If only it wasn't so hot, she would brave the wake; run the gauntlet of slobbery kisses from the relatives amassed in the parlour and escape outside. And there was the problem of the two stupid boys, more removed cousins, smoking their stolen cigarettes behind the coal bunker. The last time she'd seen them, all they had wanted to do was lift up her skirt and look at her knickers.

She lunged forwards and managed to grab three Twiglets, a couple of pickled onion Wheatos and a crisp, narrowly missing a dropsied ankle in the process. She stuffed them into her mouth and retreated once more, wondering what had happened to the dish of peanuts. Obscured from the wake by

Grandma's finest linen table-cloth, she listened to her mother making a show of herself.

'There have always been stories about wakes and whiskey, like the one the midwife told me …' Marguerite paused to make sure everyone was listening. Amelia blushed for her. She knew that her mother's breasts would be plumped up above her low-cut top and she'd be wearing that stupid grin she put on when she thought people were looking at her. Everyone quietened down.

'… when, legs akimbo, feet in stirrups, I was giving birth to Amelia.' A flutter of applause. 'The midwife's name was Colleen, an Irish woman who had lost all her children to influenza after the Great War …' More clapping. Amelia felt her mother swell in the success of the moment.

'She was far too old to be delivering babbies, of course, seventy if she was a day but she told me about the wake of her old Uncle Seamus back in 1937.'

Amelia drained her glass and lay back on the carpet, staring at the small portion of her mother that she could see from under the table. She was enjoying this kind of attention. On other occasions, the role of raconteur had been hogged by one of the many 'characters' within the family but tonight Marguerite had adopted the mantle, born to it. She began her tale with a flourish, a mock bow, and the family (all forty-two of them crammed into the front parlour) clapped and cheered for no wake could be complete without reference to an historical other.

'Now, Uncle Seamus liked a drink or two. On the night he died, he had consumed a legendary amount of ale and whiskey before being trampled by an elephant escaped from a travelling zoo. In the main street it was too, right outside Biddy O'Neil's butcher's shop. She was carving up a cow at the time and saw the whole thing. Seamus put up a stout defence, so the story went. He went down biffing and kicking. But man against elephant is no fair contest. His head was squashed flat, still encased within its legendary homburg ...'

Around Amelia, the words seemed to weave and thread, like bunting or multi-coloured strands of wool. They spun her around, danced, making her feel quite dizzy.

'... Seamus's wake ... a pub in town ... spit and sawdust ... corpse propped up ... two-dimensional face ... head flat as a pancake ... a glass or two of the hard stuff poured inside ... the sun was coming up ... the dead Seamus had drunk ...'

Marguerite paused to replenish her drink. There was a clatter of appreciative applause, a few gerronwithits. She asked for another glass of Uncle Con's Bushmills, despite Edith's earlier warning that it was 'Proddy-dog' booze, fit only for floor polish.

Amelia turned her attention to her own booty, pilfered from the drinks table when everyone was hanging around the coffin admiring Grandma's peaceful rictus. This was the first wake she had been allowed to attend and she was anxious to sample all the refreshments on offer. There had been so many bottles and jars awaiting consumption that it had been easy to remove a few interesting looking ones from the back and stick them under the table for later.

She took a sip of loyalist Bushmills, thought it bitter and repulsive, so poured herself a liberal glass of gin (brought by an elderly relative who had marked the bottle with indelible pen). This she found quite disgusting, like drinking perfume. She added the rest (about two centimetres) of a bottle of the oddly named Blue Curaçao, a couple of maraschino cherries from a mildewed jar, a liberal dose of One Cal cream soda and, glad she had mixed her cocktail in a pint glass, downed the drink in one.

Marguerite cleared her throat, swayed a little on battered Dr Scholls: 'In the morning, the widow came to take a last look … eyes puffed from weeping. She had the eldest girl with her, young Mary, who was plain as a pikestaff. At the sight of her Da, the girl began keening, threw herself at the corpse. The weight of her toppled the dead man, snapping his neck bone once and for all …'

Screeches of laughter. Relatives milled excitedly beyond the table. Legs, stout and slender, lumpy and smooth, paraded like actors, framed by tablecloth. There was a man with his trousers hitched up, sock garters on display; a woman in culottes, her massive stretch-marked calves curving inelegantly into suede ankle books and then … Knees, black-jeaned knees bending low beneath the cloth. He was singing. 'And it's no nay never, no nay never no more. Will I play the wild rover, no nay never, no more …'

'What have we here, hey, it's little Amelia …'

A face, a familiar face loomed so close she couldn't make it out. A cousin? He snuffled about, crouching on all fours beneath the table, sniffing around like a dog. She couldn't see his face, it was too dark; the only impression she had was of a thin white arm, furred with ginger. She wondered if perhaps the terrier had assumed human form.

'My n ... namesisameliasm ...' Her lips slid around the words. She giggled. The words slipped from her tongue. Slipslipslip. The man was so very very close. And the smell of whiskey and something sweet and familiar.

'You are most favoured,' he whispered.

'Gloooooooooria.' Amelia lay back. It seemed so dark all of a sudden, so very very dark.

'Indeed. Most highly favoured. You got it, Amelia ...'

Again, him. Why wouldn't he go? His voice was gruff, thick with catarrh. It was hot, so hot. Most highly favoured lady, Glo-o-o-o-ooo-ria!

'Do not be afraid. Oh Amelia, Amelia, so long it has been ...'

It was light, so light, so bright she couldn't keep her eyes open. Her body tensed. So hot. She screwed her eyes tight closed. Breath, hot breath on her neck. The Goddess! Here she was, was it her? Hot on her neck. And the pain of it, ripping, tearing at her within and without. A pressure on her chest, so heavy she could barely breathe. Most highly favoured. Do not be afraid. Hail Irena full of grace may the power ... Gloria. Those eyes, looking into hers. The Goddess? So bright, so rough upon her face.

And now?

… No nay never, no more …

The Goddess was gone. The man, or was it a boy, so thin he was, so hardly there. He crouched, his back to her. He was rocking, chuckling to himself. Amelia tried to sit up but pain stopped her. Through the forest of legs, she could make out her mother's blue jeans. She turned her head and made herself stare at them, hideous things, flares. Who wore flares? No one, not any more … Only Mum … Amelia's face was wet with tears.

'The women screamed, ran from the place as though a banshee were after them. The men, drunk and bleary eyed, hoisted the dead man onto their shoulders and made off down to the church for the funeral …'

The story was over.

Amelia managed to raise herself onto all fours, intent on crawling to her mother but Marguerite had taken the floor again. This time, she was telling of her own grandmother, the one who staged her own death scene every two weeks or so for a year. Of course, in the way of all 'boy who cried wolf' stories, she died alone, in pain with no one in attendance. This story was not as entertaining as her previous one and the relatives quickly lost interest. Any applause at the end was thin, more polite than anything.

Amelia lay beneath the dining table, looking up at the bare knots of wood in its unvarnished underbelly. The smell of whiskey was sharp and dangerous. There were so many people, relatives she scarcely knew. He was smoking, a thin loop of white smoke drifted below the tablecloth to be lost in the room above. The carpet was rough on her uncovered legs. She had begun the wake wearing tights, thick woollen tights in a shade of brown you could only get at a special shop in town. She slept or thought she did. The boy, she thought, was still there, the whiskey smell strong. And then he was pulled away, pulled out from under the table and there were voices, 'What the hell are you doing down here? For Jaysus' sake ...' fading into the night.

She awoke in the early hours with a furred tongue that felt too big for her mouth, a crashing headache. She knocked her head as she scrambled from under the table. There were people asleep on the parlour carpet, great snoring relatives, with loose teeth or no teeth, with sagging bagging skin. She looked for her mother but Marguerite was nowhere to be seen. The heap of bodies seemed indecent, somehow; wrong. She ran upstairs, made it to the toilet, retched into the stained lavatory pan.

Amelia, tucked into her own bed, dreamed she was on fire. The fire grew from inside out, her skin flamed last. Through the heat and the choking smoke, she could see her mother, waving, far away. She saw a group of relatives gathered around the dead body of her grandmother. She fought to escape the hungry flames. Some time during the night, she awoke, aware of cool fingers on her forehead, her mother's hand stroking her back to sleep. Amelia didn't open her eyes but lay, still and calm until she heard the creak of Marguerite's bed in the next room.

CHAPTER 3
10TH SEPTEMBER 1981

The following morning Amelia, still fully dressed, crawled gingerly out of bed to find blood all over her best white skirt. It was on the bed too; a long brownish stain in the shape of the letter 'I' (for Irena) had run into the grooves of Grandma's nylon sheet, giving it a striped appearance, as though someone had drawn the I with a ruler and a running-out felt tip. She studied it with interest, hazily remembering the Goddess so close, so bright.

She gasped in wonder. This was another Sign! The bleeding had stopped as mysteriously as it had started. She checked herself for injury. There was no doubt in her mind about what had happened. The pain was quite normal. It was simple. It had happened once before to a devout young girl. The Goddess had chosen her. She, Amelia Joan O'Dowd, was Most Highly Favoured and she was with child. The Goddess Irena had chosen her to bear the Saviour of All Mankind.

Her bedroom began to revolve. Everything smelled of booze: her clothes, her hair, her breath. She steadied herself against the headboard and prayed fervently for the Goddess to appear to confirm this miracle. But she must have dozed off and it was Edith, breathing nicotine and a conspiratorial air, who woke her with a plate of poached eggs on bread, set on a tarnished silver tray. Amelia threw up all over it.

Edith tutted. Today they would be dressing the body, she whispered, pointedly. It would be useful if the Blessed Virgin, Our Lady, Holy Mother of sweet Baby Jesus could be summoned to watch over the proceedings.

Together, they recited a rudimentary rosary while the egg congealed and hung-over relatives trooped out of the front door.

CHAPTER 4
11TH SEPTEMBER 1981

On the day of the funeral Amelia lurked on the stairs, listening to her mother frantically preparing for the second onslaught of guests that week.

'Tablecloth ironed … oh, bloody hell, where has that tea stain come from? Now, the best china. Christ, you'd think Mum would've washed it before putting it away. Okay, stick it in the sink. Cake stand … The fold-up one, rusty as hell. And it was supposed to be silver plated … Amelia! Where are you? Are you dressed yet?'

Amelia, clad in suitably sombre attire, borrowed from Great Aunt Mabel's mourning box in the loft, sneaked into the parlour. There were already several mourners standing awkwardly around the barley twist sideboard. One of them, the disgraced Great Uncle Con, usually referred to as "The One Who Got Thrown Out of the Seminary", had already started on the crème de menthe, which, they were all agreeing over bacon sandwiches, had been there for at least forty years. Since that priest brought it one Christmas. Amelia avoided walking sticks and boozy breath to reach the coffin.

'Ah, there she is, the little saint,' Aunt Edith announced through rattling teeth. Since the death of her sister, she had stopped eating; she wore overlarge clothes to exaggerate her weight loss and her old dentures that no longer fitted. 'Did I not tell you, Con, of the Vision?'

Amelia pulled Mabel's mantilla over her eyes.

'No,' Con slurred, 'but I'm sure you will now, Edie.'

'Don't call me that. No one ever calls me that.'

Con chuckled. 'Ah no. That privilege was left to Al Monagle.'

Edith's baggy frame wobbled with indignation. 'There was a visitation in this house.'

'Is that right?' Con poured himself another slug of green liquid.

Amelia knelt beside the coffin, her head bent low. There was a funny smell about her dead grandmother. A kind of sweetish scent, half smothered by Yardley's Tweed. When the undertakers had deposited the body, two days ago now, it had smelled of nothing but disinfectant and wax. But after all the people had come and gone, breathing whiskey, pressing lipsticked mouths against her stiff cheek, Dolores had given her a blast of perfume. The bottle, she had mused, was probably as old as the crème de menthe.

'Indeed,' Edith replied. 'The Blessed Virgin, no less. She appeared in all her glory and majesty to this innocent child.'

Amelia felt Edith come up behind her, lay her clawed fingers on Mabel's musquash stole. Con laughed again. Amelia was irritated. He was the only one in the family to have ever got as far as a seminary and according to Great Aunt Edith, this gave him a position in the Catholic pecking order close to the Divine Throne. If he was going to pooh pooh her visitation, then she didn't have a chance of convincing her mother.

'D'you know, Edie, if I had a penny for every pubescent girl who thought she saw the Virgin Mary, I'd be a rich man.'

'You are a rich man, Con. All head-shrinks are.' Dolores staggered in from the kitchen, clutching the remains of last night's gin.

Con tapped the side of his nose. 'I'm rich because most of the silly cows that come to me don't realise that what they're seeing is a projection of their own sexual fantasies. You get up the duff without the inconvenience of a husband. "It was an angel, milord. Honest."'

Edith began to sob. Her fingernails dug into Amelia's neck. 'Oh, it's a good job Ma and Pa are no longer with us. It'd break their hearts to hear you talk like this, Con. To think what you could have been. A canon, by now, a bishop … One of the Holy Father's cardinals …'

'And instead I'm an atheistic psychiatrist who specialises in all things hysterical.'

'And you're a bloody soak. Where's all the crème de menthe?' Dolores asked.

'At least there's never been any danger of you, my dear niece, falling prey to such dangerous delusions.' Con lurched against the sideboard, setting off a domino effect with the arrayed funeral cards.

'What the hell's that supposed to mean?' Dolores demanded.

Con laughed. 'The whole of Liverpool knows what you and Ken get up to. What is it now? Car keys in the middle of the table or are you still vacuuming each other's back passages? Anyway, where is the illustrious Ken?'

Dolores snorted. 'On location. Filming. He told you at the wake.'

'Yes, I forgot he came to the send-off. He disappeared half way through,' Con said. 'Probably off to buy some Vaseline … and not just to get a mist effect on the lens …'

'Why are you all still here?' Marguerite breezed into the room. She reeked of bleach. 'The hearse will be here any minute. And you, Con, what are you drinking for? I thought you were taking Martha and Mary in the Jag.'

'Oh, Christ, yes. Forgot. Damn, they'll have to walk.'

Amelia began to giggle. Her grandmother's neighbours were both spinsters in their nineties. As far as she knew, neither of them had ever been able to walk without the aid of a stick.

But her mother was not inclined to join in with the joke. 'And Dolores, stop leaning on the table! I'll be putting the spread out in a minute. Do you think the egg sarnies will curl if I get them out now? And I've bought a stand pie and a bit of ham. Do you think it'll be enough? If all that lot from the Day Centre turn up, then we're done for. Mind you, I've got the cake left from Christmas and there's a Battenburg from Deirdre's. Oh, and the pickles …'

As she spoke, she wandered nervously around the mock Jacobean table, smoothing Grandma's best cloth, brushing away invisible specks of dust.

The doorbell rang and more elderly people pressed into the tiny parlour, uttering loud condolences and peering at the empty table in disappointment.

'Marguerite was always a last minute person,' one of them stage-whispered. 'Her mother would've got that tea out last night.'

Amelia's head throbbed and her knees ached. She was beginning to wonder if she might need Martha's spare stick. She thought about standing up, offering to help her mother with the food, but immediately knew that this would be a bad idea. The longer she remained in an attitude of prayer, the less likely she was to be questioned or kissed by any of her slack-lipped relatives.

In the coffin, Grandma appeared to have shrunk. Despite the healthy Max Factor glow to her face, the features had sunk back, so you could see the shape of her skull. Her hair was strange, too. It had been cut and blow-dried for her lying out and sprayed with so much of Dolores' Elnett hairspray that it could have been a judge's wig. She was wearing her best nightdress, the one with the cluster of rosebuds at the neck. The pale green nylon did even less for her appearance in death than it had in life. It clung to the bony collarbone and withered breasts like pond slime. Amelia thought someone should put a sheet over her, to make her look as though she was in bed, instead of like a grotesque baby doll in a wooden box. But the Goddess wouldn't mind. If She forgave cruelty and ignorance, then She would certainly overlook a green nightie.

'We'll have to call you a taxi, Con,' Marguerite was saying. 'You can't drive in that state and Martha and Mary need chaperoning.'

Con belched. 'I want to go in one of the cars. I'm her brother, for Christ's sake. I should go in —'

'You're not fit,' Edith clacked through ill-fitting teeth. 'You do right, Marguerite. You tell him.'

At that moment, the hearse arrived. Amelia felt its darkness sweep up the road, casting a shadow that would make each of Calvary Crescent's aged inhabitants shiver. Marguerite gave a little cry of alarm and dashed into the kitchen.

There were two funeral cars, booked over ten years earlier when Grandma had won on the Grand National (so Marguerite announced in her capacity as mien host-cum-referee). They were for family only, but most of the Day Centre mourners' ears were not what they had been and they were already piling into the vehicles before the coffin had been eased out of the front door. Amelia stayed behind with her mother, flattened against the wall in the crush. Caught in the back-draft stink of cabbage and pee, she wondered whether she ought to mention the imminent arrival of the Saviour of All Mankind. What if He were born in the church? Or worse. What if He made an appearance at the crematorium? She consoled herself. Catherine Mulhearn from Form 2b, whose mother everyone thought far too old for childbearing, had given birth to Catherine's baby brother, Simon, not long ago. Amelia had taken great interest. It had been months before he was ready to be born. Marguerite said it was like St Elizabeth and John the Baptist: 'disgusting at her age'.

'Good Lord, Amelia, what on earth are you wearing?' For the first time that day, Marguerite looked down at her. 'What's that net thing on your head? And that old fur. It reeks of mothballs. On a day like this too! You look like Bud Flanagan!'

Amelia was already regretting the musquash stole. It was hot and itchy against her skin. She also suspected that the mothballs hadn't worked very well, as occasionally, a winged creature flew out from the garment and made for the window. She sighed. Whatever she was wearing couldn't possibly look as peculiar as the black suit and ruffled blouse her mother had put on. She hardly ever saw Marguerite without a pinny and rubber gloves, and this new, sophisticated image was unsettling, as though someone had stolen her real mother and replaced her with a Joan Collins lookalike.

'Well, I suppose it's too late now,' she hissed at Amelia. 'We're in the first car. Now get a move on or we'll never get to the church. Oh dear, now, should I put the drinks out … Oh, and I meant to get the cups and saucers ready …'

They stepped out into the front garden and blinked in the September sunshine. Every front door in Calvary Crescent had been thrown open and neighbours in various stages of decay stood mournfully watching the hearse. Grandma's tea roses were in a second unseasonal flush, heavy and blowzy, perfuming the air with their headily sweet scent. Marguerite turned to lock the door, tutting as she fumbled with her mother's keys; the hearse revved up and moved serenely up the road, followed by the two funeral cars, Great Uncle Con's Jag, which was being driven by one of the carers from the Day Centre, and Number Forty-Seven's Indian motorbike. In slow-motion Amelia watched the funeral cortège that her mother had spent the past five days arranging, disappear from view. Marguerite looked up as the Indian blasted round the corner. She gave a little whimper then sat down on the step and began to cry.

Amelia peered over the gate at Mr Lawless from opposite. He was a retired magician of over eighty but still possessed an immaculately polished Ford Zephyr in the palest powder blue. He was buffing the fender now, while his wife enjoyed the funeral display.

'They've gone without us!' she shouted. 'Can you give us a lift?'

Mrs Lawless handed her cup and saucer to her husband and opened her gate. 'Why aren't you in the car?' she bellowed at Marguerite.

Amelia's mother sobbed all the more.

'They took all the seats,' Amelia wheezed. The stole was heavy as well as hot. 'They've gone without us.'

Mrs Lawless's smile couldn't have been any wider or her face would have broken in two. 'Come on, Arthur,' she said, prodding her husband in one of his ample buttocks. 'Get that car of yours going. We're off to a funeral.'

Due to Mr Lawless's love of speed and his superior knowledge of the roads around St. Jude's, they arrived at the church minutes before the hearse and Marguerite had time to fiddle with her hair and wipe the mascara from underneath her eyes before greeting the Donegal branch of the family.

'Now, whatever you do, don't sit on Pat's knee, he's a nasty bit of work and I should know. And don't ask Maura about her nose, the Big C, it was. And … Take that net off your head, Amelia. Don't make a show of me today, of all days,' she hissed as they climbed out of the car. 'And stand up straight. Half of this lot have never even seen you and now you turn up looking like a charity case.'

The church was packed. In widowhood, Amelia's grandmother had been what her grandfather called a 'vestry door nudger', one of the selfless women who garnered priestly approbation by sacrificing their Saturday mornings to bedeck the altar with tiger lilies and gypsophilia. She was well known and respected in the parish, though those old enough to remember Edith's Donegal summers with Father Monagle, were suspicious of the sister's intentions towards the skinny and uncharismatic Father Murphy.

As she and her mother followed the coffin down the aisle, Amelia was seized by a sudden desire to giggle. Some of their relations were already weeping, others were holding hankies at the ready, willing the tears to begin. If only they knew, she thought. If they could have seen the blaze of grace with which the Goddess had taken her grandmother's soul, they wouldn't be crying but rejoicing. As it was, she concluded, sliding into the front pew beside her mother, their belief in an outdated god whose main purpose was to punish those who strayed from his path meant that every death was treated as a tragedy. She would have to have a word with Father Murphy after Mass soon. Give him some advice on the true nature of Grandma's release and on the Good News to come.

The church doors were closed and the ribbon of hazy sunlight that had illuminated their path down the aisle disappeared, plunging the church into relative gloom. The first hymn began, cranked out on the organ by a boy of Amelia's age, a fat lump whose father ran the local scout troop. His rendition of 'The Lord is my Shepherd' sounded like a traction engine at full throttle. The relatives stopped looking round and picked up their Mass books, thoughtfully marked at the Funeral Rites page, and joined in with the psalm. On the last note, the congregation fell silent, stared up at the pulpit, where Father Murphy was fiddling with his grubby cassock.

'My dear sisters and brothers,' he began. 'We are here to celebrate the life of ...' he stared down at his notes, squinted. 'Susan? ... Sarah.'

There was a bang at the back of the church. The door was flung open again and light flooded the altar. Father Murphy looked up, looked down, then up again. He held his bony hands up to his eyes. Everyone was transfixed. Footsteps sounded down the aisle, a light but clicking gait, a ballerina wearing hobnailed boots. Amelia turned around, shaded her eyes against the intense light and saw, silhouetted within it, the strangest creature she had ever seen. It was tall and thin, with wisps and tufts of hair forming a bluish aura around its head. Things that looked suspiciously like the pelts of rabbits or foxes hung from its waist and moved sinuously as it walked. As the creature drew nearer, she could see that it was a young man who had made up his eyes with Kohl so that he looked like an Egyptian god. He was wearing a tattered tee shirt with the words 'Fuck the Pope' emblazoned across it in black. Amelia's heart began to thump rapidly. Was it …? It couldn't be. The young man stopped when he reached the end of their pew.

'John! You …' screeched Marguerite and fell into a dead faint on the kneeler.

CHAPTER 5

'Don't be daft, Ma, it's me. Julian,' the apparition said, squeezing into the narrow pew beside Amelia and her mother. As an afterthought, he grabbed Amelia's arm. 'Hiya, Sis.'

Marguerite blinked. 'Oh, Julian. With all that makeup on, I thought … I thought you were … you were …'

'Dad? Come on Ma, that's hardly likely to happen is it?' He grinned mirthlessly as Marguerite's eyelids began once more to close in another swoon of recognition.

Amelia knew it was the way of the Goddess to direct Her followers as She saw fit and that Julian, her only brother, was as much at the mercy of Her whim as anyone else. She watched him gently lift their mother from the kneeler and lie her head, in a theatrically Pieta-like pose, across his raggedy lap and silently thanked the Goddess for answering one of her most fervent prayers.

'How ya doin'?' he whispered when the service was once more under way. 'Cool?'

'Okay,' she replied cautiously. Julian had been gone almost eighteen months. She barely remembered whether she could trust him or not.

'Then we'll wait till Ma pulls herself together and get the fuck out of this place.' With difficulty, he pulled a packet of tobacco from his jeans pocket under Marguerite's head and began the process of what Amelia later learned to call 'skinning up'.

'It's Grandma's funeral,' Amelia said. 'We can't just walk out.'

'You wanna bet?'

Amelia bristled. It was all very well for her long-lost brother to turn up out of the blue looking like some god of the underworld, but his lack of respect for the dead was too much. All the same, the service was even more boring than usual. Father Murphy had no sense of occasion and the few lines he'd come up with to commemorate her grandmother's life were scarcely worth an audience. As if sensing her disappointment the priest gave her a despairing look and concluded his bleak little eulogy with a heartfelt appreciation of Sarah (or 'Seeera', as he said it) and her selfless flower arranging. Marguerite came round again when the organ began to creak out 'Immaculate Mary'. She blinked, gazed up into Julian's face. The priest sighed and glanced surreptitiously at his watch.

'Why have you come back now, on today of all days?' Marguerite accused, using her elbows to jerk herself upright. 'After —'

Julian clamped his hand over his mother's mouth. 'It's cool, Ma. Don't need the prodigal son routine.'

'But —'

Julian grinned and grabbed hold of Amelia's hand. 'You stayin' or what?' he hissed.

'Or what.' Amelia could be a prude when she wanted, but she had never been able to resist her brother. Not even, aged four, when he first dared her to brave the cockloft alone. And now, his rueful smile convinced her that wherever he was going was bound to be more fascinating than anything Father Murphy could come up with. She waited until her mother's head bent once more towards the Funeral Rites page, then pulled at his sleeve and nodded. Seconds later the two of them were running up the aisle and out of the church, guiltily entering the sunlit churchyard like primary school truants.

At the end of the drive the undertakers were waiting to take Grandma's mortal remains to the crematorium. One of them was smoking a cigarette, which he stubbed out hastily when he saw Amelia and her brother. He removed his sunglasses and gave them a self-conscious polish with the hem of his jacket. Another less solicitous pall bearer had removed his tie and unbuttoned his shirt and was sprawled across the bonnet of the hearse like one of the half-naked newspaper girls Marguerite ripped out before Amelia had a chance to look. He stayed put.

'Over here,' Julian said and tugged at her hand. Together, they leapt over broken graves, stumbled across tussocks of grass without pausing to look and remember, as Amelia often did, those long dead, buried beneath their feet. They stopped at a particularly magnificent tomb, an obelisk with the pyramid missing, perched atop a grey building the size of a small room. The tomb bore no inscription or indication of who might be buried within, but it was ostentatiously important. At some time it had been surrounded by a wrought iron fence, to be entered by a little gate; but that was long gone. It was overgrown and weedy, covered in empty beer cans and the sooty remains of a tramp's fire.

'Here,' Julian said, crouching down. 'We'll have a smoke and then wait in the vestry.'

He offered a hand-rolled cigarette to his sister who only hesitated a few seconds before accepting it. The Goddess, after all, had decreed that she must smoke.

'So, Sis,' he said. 'How you doin'?'

She shrugged, took a puff of acrid tobacco. 'Okay.'

'You been missing your big brother then?'

She frowned up at the obelisk. 'Not really. I got your room.'

He grinned. 'So much for sentiment.'

'And your bike.' Amelia turned to him, noticing the way the harsh sunlight exaggerated the pimples under his thickly made-up skin. 'And some wonderful things have been happening.' She began to cough and carried on so long that she was almost sick.

Julian stubbed out his cigarette on the vault and stood up. 'You'll have to give me my room back,' he announced. 'I'm here to stay. Listen, Sis, things got pretty heavy for me down south. I don't want Ma knowing about it, but I was banged up for six months. Only got out three days ago.'

'You never used to call her Ma. You used to say Mum, like me.'

'Yeah, well you'll find a lot's changed in the time I've been away.'

'And why are you wearing eye shadow?'

'It's Alternative.'

'What?'

'Alternative. As in The Cult and the —'

'I know what Alternative is.' Amelia, her cough subsiding, risked another cautious puff. 'Linda Marshall's brother was Alternative. He got beaten up by a load of Black Sabbath fans down the bus station in town. He's a Trendy now. Wears white socks and streaks his hair with his mum's kit.'

'Look, I don't care about Linda Marshall's brother. He can listen to the Nolan Sisters if he wants.'

'No one listens to the Nolans except nuns. They think they're ace.'

'Listen, Sis, I'm not in the mood —'

'For dancing … romancing …'

'Shut up. Have you got any money?'

Amelia nodded. Grandma had donated some quite substantial sums over the last few weeks of her life. It was all safely stored in the attic beneath the hem of the Goddess's altar cloth. This, however, was earmarked for another, less secular purpose.

'I have but I'm going to need it for the child's anointing.'

Julian, who had never really taken much notice of anything she said, spun around, dropping the penknife he'd been using to scratch DEAD OR ALIVE into the wall of the obelisk.

'What child?'

Amelia stroked her stomach fondly. 'The Messiah. You may as well be the first to know. After all, you'll be His uncle.'

'You can't be.' He grabbed her by the shoulders and she smiled into his bloodshot eyes, savouring the moment.

'I am pregnant with the Saviour of All Mankind.'

'Friggin' hell!' He let her go, walked back to the obelisk and kicked it with his steel-capped boot. 'You can't be. No way, never ...'

'Shush!' The church organ struck up the sombre but recognisable tune Amelia knew was played to accompany the coffin down the aisle. She gagged. The smell of dog-dirt in the grass was beginning to make her feel ill, that and the cigarette. She wasn't surprised. She'd heard about morning sickness from Catherine Mulhearn's mother.

'The Goddess,' she said. 'It is Her will.'

'... Stop joking, Sis. It's not possible. Pat. It was his, wasn't it? The bastard, I'll —'

'What do you want the money for?' Amelia asked as she began to stride back towards the church. 'I might be able to lend you some, as long as you give it back.'

'How much?' Julian blocked her path. Amelia could see that beneath the make-up he was different. He looked thinner, more savage. There was a greedy desperation in his kohl-ringed eyes.

She thought. 'Dunno. About a hundred?'

'A hundred?' He shook his head. 'Where's a kid like you getting that kind of money from?'

'Grandma gave it to me. And some was provided by the Goddess.'

Julian grinned. 'Well, that's some Goddess. And as for the dough the old cow gave you, then it's as much mine as yours. I was her favourite.'

'She wrote you out of her will,' Amelia informed him as they reached the church door. 'Mum has strict instructions not to give you a penny.'

'And you had strict instructions not to be running off in the middle of your Grandmother's funeral,' hissed Marguerite who was waiting near the baptismal font in the vestibule. She grabbed Amelia's arm and swung around to confront Julian. 'So, what brings my son and heir back on today of all days?'

Julian smiled and brushed his lips against his mother's cheek, leaving a smear of black. 'You know me, Ma. Like a bad penny.'

Later, after they had attended another far shorter service at the crematorium, watched Grandma's coffin glide jerkily through draylon curtains to the tinnily recorded strains of Mozart's Requiem; when Con had physically prevented Dolores from hurling herself on the conveyor belt after it, they shared another cigarette behind the chapel of rest and listened to Father Murphy singing The Wild Rover to himself in the portaloo which was right next door. And later still after they had spent some time standing around, greeting elderly friends and relatives, reading the messages stuck in the grass, meant for other people's ashes, the cortège set off for the funeral breakfast. Amelia climbed on the back of Julian's shining black Honda 125 and, despite her mother's

49

protestations, rode through the suburbs of South Liverpool, her yellow hair streaming behind her. As they passed St Gerard Magella's Church and rounded the corner into Gethsemane Drive to catch their first glimpse of Calvary Crescent, she felt a twinge of unaccustomed foreboding.

They arrived home before everyone else. Only Wally and Vera Baptiste, drawing up at their gate opposite in their Jaffa Orange bubble car, saw the Honda slide into the drive of Number Eighteen. Amelia went through the gate at the side of the house and around the back. She clambered up on the old coal bunker and managed to unhook the louvre window of the outhouse window. This small scullery room, (usually referred to as 'the doghouse' by the family, as it was the space in which adults, children and dogs in disgrace were sent to cool off) was attached to the kitchen and the adjoining door had long ago been removed. It was easy for Amelia to slip through the window, onto the twin tub and nip through the kitchen and into the hall.

The house was silent, save for a soft sighing sound, a deep pulse that she knew was the Goddess Irena's breath on the wind. On the table in the front parlour, a solitary bluebottle made a silent meal of the already turning stand pie. Amelia plucked the jar of Vicks she'd used to anoint her dying grandmother from the pocket of Aunt Mabel's rusty black dress and brought it smashing down into the pie. The bluebottle buzzed cheerfully up to the window. Amelia contemplated the ruined meat and egg and undid the Vicks jar. She took a deep, revitalizing draught before walking into the hall and opening the door for Julian.

'Where's the cash then, Sis?' Julian demanded once he was inside. 'It's urgent. An urgent case.'

'What do you want it for?' Amelia asked. 'The Goddess wouldn't like it to be put to immoral purposes.'

'Like what?'

She thought, remembering Aunt Edith's suspicions. 'The demon drink.'

Julian laughed and shook his head. 'No, nothing like that. Just need some running money for the next few days, till I get myself fixed up with a job. That's all.'

She cocked her head, nodded, understanding by the slight change in the Goddess's breathing, that She approved. 'So a hundred's all right, is it?'

'How much have you got, for Christ's sake?'

They were on the landing and she angled the hook into the handle of the cockloft door. A bright light poured onto the worn carpet. Amelia's head began to pound. The ladders came down easily, as though they had been freshly oiled. She put her foot on the first rung; excitement surged within her. It was happening again. Julian was obliterated by the light, as was the opening in the ceiling. All that she was aware of was the feel of the much-used wood beneath her hands, her breath coming in short gasps, the muscles in her legs and bottom flexing as she ascended the steps.

Everything was as she had left it before the funeral. Aunt Mabel's mourning box was near the entrance to the cockloft, furs and black lace spilling out over the beams. She could see the tilted mirror of the dressing table, reflecting Great Uncle Jack's stuffed parrot in the rafters, the skylight window swathed in its curtain of cobwebs. But all this seemed faded, misty, compared to the vision of the Goddess herself, who was shimmering, sparkling, against the wardrobe, her neon colours a swirl of pink and yellow and blue. Amelia surged through the cockloft door and prostrated herself.

'You okay up there?' Julian shouted from somewhere far away.

She tried to reply but found that the Goddess had sealed her lips. She tried to move but her limbs were frozen. She could only gaze in awe.

The Goddess was even more beautiful than she had been at Grandma's death. There was the same cloud of blonde curls, the curved enigmatic smile and translucent skin. Although she was wearing the dress, she was also floating above and beyond it, as though suspended in mid air. Amelia could make out her perfect little feet, the pearly toenails superimposed over the tattered organza. She held her hands out towards Amelia as though in supplication.

Child, she said. Fear not for thou hast found favour. Your womb hast conceived of a child and She shall be the Saviour of All Mankind.

She? Amelia thought. Surely a Saviour is a man.

The Goddess shook her lovely head. Not in this case, child.

Amelia smiled. Apart from Julian, who she hadn't yet decided on, boys were generally pretty awful. Perhaps a female Saviour was long overdue.

And henceforth, you shall be known as the Blessed Amelia of Calvary and though people may ridicule and scorn, you shall bear this child with courage and fortitude until her time is nigh.

The Goddess was fading now, fraying at the edges like the last television programme of the night.

Amelia tried to ask when the child's time would be nigh but the Goddess had vanished into a pinpoint of light, leaving the cockloft as it had been: dusty and dark and full of junk.

'Come back,' she muttered feebly, glad that the power of speech had been returned to her. 'Please …'

'Who the hell are you talking to up there?' Julian demanded. She could hear his footsteps on the ladder, but remembering his terror of heights, was sure he wouldn't make it past the third rung.

'The Goddess.'

'Have you found the money?'

Amelia squinted under the Goddess's dress. The black tin of cash was stashed behind the jar of limp and stinking chrysanthemums. She would have to replace them with some of Grandma's honesty. She crept forward, extracted the box, opened it and pulled out a handful of notes. Then, remembering the key on the chain around her neck, a key she didn't usually bother with as no one ventured into the cockloft except herself, she leaned forward and locked it. Before he left, Julian had stolen their mother's chequebook and forged over two hundred pounds worth of cheques before she found out. Vertigo or not, Amelia couldn't quite trust him to leave her money alone now he knew where it was kept.

'Here we are,' she said, climbing down the ladder.

'What were you doing up there?' Julian's face was white as a ghost.

'Talking with the Goddess about the baby. Apparently it's a girl saviour, this time. The boy saviours never work out too well. You know, Moses, Mohammed, Jesus ...'

Julian took the money, flicked his fingers through to count it. Most of the notes were tatty and crumpled. They had been concealed in Grandma's mattress for years.

'I thought I heard voices,' he said, throwing down a couple of massive notes that were over forty years out of date. 'Talking to yourself, Sis. It's the first sign, you know.' He put his hand on her shoulder. It made the stole even heavier. 'This business, with the baby and all — you'd best not tell Ma. Go to a doctor, a private one. You'll have to have an abortion. I'll sort it for you, once ...'

She pulled away from him in shock.

'Abortion is a mortal sin!'

'But ...' He was staring at the money, as though he couldn't wrest his gaze away. 'You can't ...'

'I can,' she said and walked past him, down the stairs into the front parlour, where the funeral guests were beginning to congregate around the smashed pie.

CHAPTER 6
27TH OCTOBER 1981

Catherine Mulhearn was sitting near the back of Amelia's class silhouetted against the long Georgian bay and hunched over a Latin primer. The rest of the class were queuing up for Sister Eileen's freshly fried doughnuts (a once a week treat) in the canteen. Catherine was too poor to afford them while Amelia's mother reckoned that teenage girls produced enough grease of their own without eating any more. It was a good job. The way Amelia was feeling, a fried anything, never mind a doughnut would be puked up on the classroom floor the second it entered her stomach. Even the smell was making her heave.

Amelia closed the lid of her desk with a bang and sneaked a glance at Catherine. She had been a best mate in First Year. Amelia had gone round to her house after school most evenings to cuddle the baby. Little Simon was the youngest of eight Mulhearn children all crammed into a three bedroomed council house with no bathroom and a mangle in the kitchen. Amelia thought the violet curtain dividing the girls from the boys in the big bedroom looked beautiful. When she asked Marguerite if she too could have such a curtain, Marguerite said Catherine's mum should get her dad seen to with a couple of bricks. 'I'd send him to the bloody vet's,' she said, every time Amelia mentioned them.

Amelia rarely mentioned them now because Catherine never bothered with her any more. She believed Amelia had stolen her tennis racquet, along with Liz McFee's and Sheila Jones's but it wasn't true. Amelia was rubbish at tennis and the last thing she wanted was a load of stolen Slazengers. But for a reason as unfathomable as it was miraculous, they had all ended up in her locker on the last day of the summer term. And when Mrs Gorgon, rummaging through the lockers during the holidays, discovered them hidden beneath a dank Aertex shirt, there had been all hell to pay. It had spelled the end of her friendship with Catherine and a coolness from many other class members. Not to mention a whole term of Wednesday detentions to endure up until Christmas. Fortunately, Marguerite worked late on Wednesdays and Edith never noticed. Sheila and Liz's racquets had now been returned and the several that remained unclaimed had been sneaked home in Amelia's duffle bag as an offering to the Goddess.

'Hello,' Amelia said, standing awkwardly near her desk. 'That Sextus and Titus are funny, aren't they?' She nodded at the text book.

Catherine looked up. Against the bright sunlit sky outside, it was hard to make out her expression. 'What do you want?'

Amelia took her compass and idly scratched the lid of Elaine Dingle's desk. 'Oh, nothing.'

'My mum said you're weird. And your family.'

Amelia sighed, thinking of the vet's and the brick punishment. 'Does she?'

'She said your Uncle Pat's a pervert and your Aunt Edith went out with a priest.'

'Oh, that would have been Father Monagle. He had teeth like a horse.' Amelia pulled back her lips, baring her gums, eliciting an involuntary snigger from Catherine. She didn't feel qualified to answer the accusation about Uncle Pat.

'So. You not going for a doughnut?' Catherine bent once more over Sextus and Titus who were gazing adoringly at a line-drawn dancing girl.

'No.' Amelia stroked her belly, fought her rising nausea and considered confiding in Catherine. She realised this was a silly idea. Catherine thought she was a thief and a liar. Catherine, like Liz and Sheila and the others, hated her. Amelia frowned, desperate. There was no one else she could ask. No one else who might give her an honest answer. She took a deep breath.

'I was wondering, well I wanted to ask how your mum was.'

Catherine looked up, her eyes narrowed. 'Why?'

'Oh, you know, having the baby and everything.'

'That was ages ago. She's fine.'

'And …' Amelia's face grew hot. She wanted to run out, to turn around and run right out of the door of Class 2a, but if she did that then she would never, ever find out. 'Well, I was thinking. Well, how did your mum have the baby?'

'What?' Catherine smirked.

'I mean …' Amelia's hand rose up to help her describe a fear she didn't know how to name. 'Not how it got there. I mean, I know that. God … No. I mean how it got out.'

Catherine's face stretched into a wide grin that was quite visible even in shadow. 'You don't know anything, do you? Babies get born out of your stomach. You get your belly button cut open with a knife and the baby pops out, crying. I heard it.'

'Heard it?'

Catherine was smug. 'Mum had Simon in bed upstairs. The midwife said it was the perfect birth but he didn't half make a noise.'

'But …' Amelia hopped from one leg to the other. 'The hole, the cut from the knife. It must have been very big to let a whole baby out … And Simon was big, wasn't he?'

'Ten pounds two ounces.'

'So what did she do with the cut? Did it bleed loads?'

Catherine turned and glanced out of the window. 'Oh, I don't know. A plaster or a bandage or … No, stitches. Seventy-two. Mum says she's like a patchwork quilt. Anyway,' she kept her head turned to the window, away from Amelia, 'Mum says she saw your Julian in the Co-op.'

Amelia sat down at Caroline Smith's desk. She didn't like the sound of the cut at all but at least she knew now the true nature of the burden placed upon her.

'Yes. Julian's back.' Seventy-two stitches. 'Is she really … you know, patchwork?'

'For God's sake! How would I know? Mum said your Julian was banged up; he's a bad lot.'

Amelia tried to digest the horrific thought of seventy-two stitches. It made her feel sicker than ever. That and the polish smell that was all over the school and the frying … She would offer her fears to the Goddess. She began to sweat, a dizziness came over her. To steady herself she silently tried to compose a 'cup runneth over' type prayer but Catherine was watching her intently.

'So?' Catherine said.

'What?' Seventy-two stitches? Where did they go, across her stomach or down to her front bottom? And what kind of stitches? Were they big hemming-the-curtain ones or little invisible-mending stitches like Sister Moira taught them in needlework? How much would it hurt?

'Your Julian, in prison. Is it true?'

Amelia stifled the nausea, concentrated. She was surprised the news about Julian had travelled so quickly, especially as her own mother didn't know about his spell of 'porridge' as he referred to it. No, best not to think of porridge, grey, lumpy, vile stuff. Sweat tricked down her back. She would talk about Julian.

'Yes. He was … banged up.'

Catherine abandoned all pretence of reading Latin, closed the book with a thump and crammed it into her desk. A faint aroma of pencil sharpeners and rubbers floated into the air.

'Tell me, what for?'

Amelia thought hard. Julian had never mentioned the reason for his sojourn, but it was so nice to have Catherine talking to her again. And Julian, since she'd given him the money and said there was no more, had hardly spoken to her at all. Con, who was the only one who ever dared to criticise

Julian to his face, had tried to talk to him in the dining room one evening when Coronation Street was on. It was the time when Stan Ogden had secretly put up his window-round for sale and Hilda, not knowing, had put in a bid. There had been an awful lot of shouting, from the screen and Con, but Amelia only remembered Con saying her brother was dicing with death. This would do.

'He was accused of murder,' she said in what she hoped was a nonchalant tone.

'What?' Catherine nearly shot out of her chair. Her pale, freckled skin glowed pinkly in excitement. 'Murder? Who?'

'Oh …' Amelia didn't want to cast her brother in too poor a light as it might put Catherine off her even more. But neither did she intend to glamorise him. 'It was a mistake. He had to go to prison but he never did anything and they released him when they found the real murderer.'

Catherine looked disappointed.

'So, is he going out with anyone?'

Amelia could see where this was heading and she didn't like it one bit. An odd phenomenon was occurring with increasing regularity in her class. Quite a few of the girls, girls who said they hated boys, thought them stinky and boring and stupid, had begun to ask after Julian, even before his return from the wilderness. No one had ever shown the least interest in him before. She decided to make him unavailable to all of them.

'Yes, he's got this gorgeous girlfriend called Paula who's into Bauhaus and the Dead Kennedys and stuff like that?'

'Who?' Catherine demanded. She stood up scraping her chair against the polished wooden floor.

The door of the classroom flung open. Dr Young, the ancient history-teacher whose head, Amelia thought, was the colour of lemon curd, burst in humming to himself.

Amelia leant on her desk in what she believed was a cool manner. 'Oh, Bauhaus and them,' she whispered. 'You know, Bela Lugosi's Dead …'

'Is he?' demanded Dr Young. 'What a shame. A particularly fine actor. Now, am I to take it that you girls are so keen on the Age of Enlightenment that you have come to class early?'

Catherine glanced at Amelia. Her lips were twitching. She was perhaps remembering the lemon curd thing which had been such a laugh in First Year.

'No, Sir,' they said in unison.

'And you are not desirous of Sister Eileen's excellent snacks?'

'No, Sir.'

'Then you can give out these sheets while I finish marking.' He slapped a pile of printed pages over Sextus and Titus. The moment was over. Amelia sighed. Seventy-two stitches. She hoped that when the time came, the Goddess was as neat as Sister Moira.

Chapter 7
17th November 1981

Sarah O'Dowd's will was to be read at the flyblown office of
Winsome and Sons over Miss Inch's hosiery shop on Bold
Street. Everyone but Julian had been summoned. Miss Inch's
was a female retreat of polished wood and curvaceous
manikins. The poky interior through which those seeking legal
representation were obliged to walk, was congested with
fabulous objects stiffened with bone and fastened with hook-
and-eye. It smelled of violets, sweat, face powder and thick
Yardley's lipstick. Amelia giggled as Con grumpily negotiated
the racks of hose. Flesh-coloured or black, flowing silk or
rigid structures of impenetrable elastine, these garments
entranced Amelia, signified the mysteries of womanhood into
which she, with the guidance of the Goddess, would soon
enter.

'Christ, that's all I need!' Marguerite, just ahead, hissed.

Con, in his eagerness to reach the solicitor had become
caught up in an armoured foundation garment on display near
the back stairs.

'You keep hold of his waistband, Amelia, or his trousers
will be round his ankles. The shame of it.' Marguerite wrestled
with her uncle's braces. Dolores hooted with gin-sodden
laughter. Con was stuck fast. Amelia found herself
rummaging inside Con's white doctor coat for the waistband
of his pants, located somewhere beneath his armpits. She was

nearly sick. He reeked of cigarettes and Denim aftershave. His skin was clammy to the touch. The three of them stood there for a minute or two, locked in mute crisis, until Edith sought the assistance of the amply upholstered Miss Inch, who had to remove the underwiring from a size forty cup to liberate him.

'Bet it's not the first time you've had a set-to with a double D, is it, eh, Con?' Dolores squawked.

'Just get up to Winsome's,' Con muttered, wrenching his trousers from Amelia's dutiful clutch. 'Typical of our bloody Sarah to trust her estate to some knicker seller.'

Edith coughed. 'At least she had an estate to leave,' she muttered. 'Didn't blow it all at the bookies every payday.'

Winsome had a malevolent glint in his pale eye and his hair was spiked up into two custard-coloured horns. He gave Amelia the creeps, presiding over his cluttered desk like an aged demon administering the laws of Hades. The dearth of chairs in his office meant that she had to stand for over an hour while he made his way through her grandmother's final wishes. She balanced on one leg for as long as she could and tried to make sense of his breathless and suggestively over familiar pronouncements.

Amelia, 'the lovely young lady', been left her grandmother's substantial collection of Spode (most of it lying in pieces in the attic), a rusty holy water font and an opal dress ring said to convey bad luck on any who wore it. (The unmarried) Con and Edith were jointly bequeathed the two dozen fancy horse brasses pinned up over the mantelpiece in the parlour. Dolores (the actress – ahem – of the family) was left a silver-backed dressing table set, including a hairbrush full of white hair. Julian was mentioned in passing as the 'hereby disinherited son of my oldest daughter'. Amelia's leg ached and she worried about varicose veins. Catherine Mulhearn's mother had recently been booked into the women's hospital to have hers stripped.

'There is a property,' Winsome announced after he had finished detailing the minutiae of Grandma's possessions.

'I know,' Edith clacked. 'We live in it.'

Winsome grinned. There wasn't a tooth in his head.

'The house on Calvary Crescent did not belong to Sarah, I'm afraid,' he said, looking as though he might devour her with those gummy jaws.

Marguerite coughed.

'Well who the hell's is it, then?' Dolores shrieked. She had been drinking all morning.

Winsome dabbed his red-veined nose with a tissue. 'It belongs to your landlord, a Mr O'Herd, I believe, son-in-law of the original owners, the Moorhouses? It was taken on a long-term lease back in 1934, when it was built. Your family have rented it since.'

'Mother never said anything about it being rented,' Marguerite said, quietly. 'And she'd been ill for over six months before she … I have been dealing with all her correspondence — the bills and everything.'

'Mr O'Herd, I am sure, will be contacting you shortly. We have informed him of your mother's death.'

Con, who had taken the morning off work from his nearby consultation rooms on Hope Street, rose unsteadily.

'And so,' he demanded. 'This house. The one in the will. She owned that?'

Winsome's smile broadened. The expanse of gum was disconcerting. 'It isn't actually a house,' he said slowly.

Con placed his hands on the desk and leaned forward. In his psychiatrist's white coat, with the cluster of shiny pens in his top pocket, he resembled a history book Himmler about to sanction a particularly vile human experiment. Behind him, Amelia hopped a little distance from the curved walnut chair he had commandeered, and towards the door; she counted to ten under her breath and then swapped legs. Her mother frowned and shook her head. Amelia returned to her side.

'So what is it?' Con shouted, making Winsome jump. 'Come on, man. We haven't got all bloody day.'

'A convent,' Winsome said. He pushed a large piece of thick yellowed paper covered with faded copperplate script towards Con. 'It's up in the Derrynasaggart Mountains, County Cork. Been in your family for over a hundred years. Madeline Bouet, the founder, came over from Burgundy in eighteen-forty-six. The history is all here. Holy Head they call it. She was given the money by Emily Smithson, one of your forebears. Emily's husband was quite a magnate in his day. It was said that he stocked four towns with Benin beauties down in South Carolina … Family history is quite fascinating, isn't it?'

Marguerite was shaking. 'Are you saying that the house we thought we owned was actually rented for forty-three years, while all the time Mother knew this convent place in Ireland was ours?'

'Did she make any money out of the Madeline Bouet lot?' Con asked.

The women tutted in unison. Amelia tutted too, but too late and it sounded more like someone sucking a sweet. Marguerite pinched her arm.

Winsome shook his head. 'There was an agreement made many years ago, between one of your great greats and the nuns. The sisters pray for your eternal souls, etcetera and they get to live in the place buckshee. Sarah even paid for the repairs. Leaking roof in fifty-two. New wall in sixty-eight. And last year, see, she recarpeted the house. That's as well as paying the staff.'

'Staff?' Marguerite demanded.

Winsome nodded. 'Oh, aye. Gardener, cook, housekeeper. That's to say nothing of the nuns' regular trips to Rome and the other necessities.'

'Necessities?'

Amelia looked anxiously at her mother. She sounded as though she was going to cry but there was no stopping Winsome, now that he was in full flow.

'In the last five years, she's paid for two visits to Lourdes, four en suite bathrooms, a new Landrover ... The list goes on. She left me to deal with it ...'

'But our Sarah hadn't two bob to rub together,' Con interrupted. 'How did she pay for it all? And tell me why, if this is a family legacy, was I never informed? I'm her brother.'

Winsome smiled beatifically. 'It is inherited through the matrilineal line. Your sister was the oldest girl. A condition of her inheritance from your Aunt Caitlin was that she must never disclose the details to anyone. This is where I fit in. I have been looking after the estate for over fifty years. Sarah, I am relieved to say, never made absolute secrecy a condition of the inheritance and with a family to bring up, she never had the time to deal with the nitty gritty matters, accounts and so forth ...'

'All that money,' Marguerite exclaimed. 'I've been supporting her for years, scraping a living for me and the kids when all the time ...'

'Your mother was very devout,' Winsome said as though this was enough.

'No she wasn't. I was the devout one,' Edith exclaimed. 'I would have taken Holy Orders myself if I hadn't —'

'How much money is there?' Con demanded. 'She must have been paying somehow.'

Winsome took out a sheaf of bank statements and examined them closely.

'Do you want me to say?' he asked Marguerite. 'After all, it's yours now.'

Marguerite nodded. She looked exhausted.

He shoved the latest statement towards her. 'Here. Over eight hundred thousand at the close of business on the thirty-first of October.'

Marguerite's face drained of all colour. Amelia, remembering the performance at the funeral when Julian turned up, made her way to her mother's side. Her heart thumped painfully. She wasn't quite sure what Winsome's pronouncement meant but she knew that all of this was the Goddess's doing.

'Well, I think it's a scream,' Dolores said. 'To end up with a convent on our hands. Good old Mum. Fancy keeping that to herself all this time. At least it puts an end to our problems, Marge. We'll sell the place and divvy up the returns.'

'I think …' Marguerite clasped Amelia's hand in her own. The palm was cold and slightly damp. Amelia wanted to remove hers but suspected it would be a treachery. 'I mean, I understand from what Mr Winsome has said … That the convent belongs to me?'

Winsome nodded.

'And the money. I mean the eight hundred thousand?'

Amelia's hand was losing all sensation. Again, Winsome agreed. He pushed forward a form, headed at the top with his own firm's name. In silence, Marguerite removed it from the desk.

'I've taken the liberty of drawing up this document,' he said. 'Just a formality, you understand. As the new owner, you will continue to need the services of a solicitor —'

'We'll sell the damned place,' Dolores muttered. 'You sort it out, Winsome. We'll make it worth your while.'

Con snorted. Despite the large yellowed No Smoking sign on Winsome's desk, he took out a Capstan and lit it. 'Always hated men, the women in our family. Bloody lesbians the lot of 'em. What I could have done with a convent of my own …'

Marguerite rose. She picked up Winsome's document and the deeds to the convent and shoved them in her battered leather handbag. She grabbed Amelia's hand and turned to leave.

'Thank you, Mr Winsome,' she said. 'I'll telephone when I've come to a decision.'

'If you could sign the form now …' Winsome's little eyes narrowed. 'We can talk about the nitty gritty later … at a more appropriate time. Your mother was most accommodating …'

'I am not my mother. Come on, Amelia, we've got to get you to school,' Marguerite said faintly. She pushed her way between Con and Edith, who for once looked uncannily alike: beady eyed and frantic.

Amelia took one look back at the room. The figures standing about the desk were so static, so formal, she was reminded of the portrait in Sister Anne Margaret's office at school: 'When did you last see your father?' The only thing missing was a child.

CHAPTER 8

Out on Bold Street the lunchtime rush was starting; students sauntered down from the art college, musicians from the Philharmonic. There was a hint of rain on the breeze, that soft, late autumn rain that lends a sheen to the dreariest of city views and clogs dead leaves in the gutters. Amelia turned to her mother, then looked away, up at the elegant spire of bombed out St Luke's. Marguerite's expression flickered between pain and ecstasy. Her eyes darted wildly, her mouth at once solemn and then stretched into a wide grin. It was a private expression; one, Amelia concluded, no daughter should have to witness upon a mother's face.

'Let's have lunch in Reeces,' Marguerite said. 'I'll treat us both. A nice piece of breaded fish and a rum baba for afters. How does that sound?'

Amelia nodded gleefully. 'I've never had a rum baba.'

'That's for me. You can have a doughnut, my lady. I'm not having another Dolores on my hands.' Marguerite tucked her hand through Amelia's arm and the two of them walked away from the corsetieres like a couple of bosom pals on a day out.

After Reeces' there was a taxi, called from the shop, no less. Amelia had only once been in a black cab and that was when her grandfather had died. Some second-cousin had been a driver and it saved on funeral cars. Now, she arrayed herself on the back seat, feeling like a queen. There was so much more room without a coffin.

'Sefton Park,' her mother announced. Amelia pulled a face. She'd hoped to escape school for the rest of day, especially as Sister Anne Margaret had still got a bee in her bonnet over the missing tennis rackets.

'Do I have to?' she whined.

Marguerite smiled. 'Have to what?'

'You know, school. I've missed more than half the day and it's double PE this afternoon and I don't think gym is good for me in my condition.'

'What condition? We've only been to hear the will read. Honestly, you are a most peculiar child, Amelia. No, we're not going to school, we're going to the park, to the glasshouse. I used to go there all the time when I was young. It's a good place for thinking.'

Amelia sat back as the taxi sped along Princes Avenue, past the slim townhouses that graced a once-fashionable Edwardian boulevard. The houses had all been converted into flats, graffiti decorated every wall and most of the bus stops had been smashed up or burned down. Marguerite was staring out of the window as though she had never been this way before, like a tourist on a day trip to some exotic and faraway place. And although Amelia had never actually been on holiday, unless you counted the short stay at Edith's at Edge Lane when there was all that fuss over Julian, she began to enjoy the game. She took the cue from her mother and gazed at the littered front gardens, the excrement-covered pavements, the broken-down lampposts, committing each detail to memory for a time when she might relate the events of the day to others.

They turned right at the lights near Amelia's school. She felt a slight sense of unease when she saw Sister Bridget from the sick bay, skip across the road in front of them, without paying heed to the traffic. She ran into the arms of the school chaplain, waiting to give her succour of some sort. Amelia ducked down. She liked Sister Bridget, even if the nun had rubbed horse liniment into her hockey-bruised thighs last month and taken most of the skin off. She hoped she was all right.

'Here, anywhere here,' Marguerite announced, tapping the driver on the shoulder, when they'd made it through the lights.

Amelia slumped. Double PE was on the menu after all. She knew how easy it would be to force herself to throw up, right there in the back of the taxi. But after the driver had been paid, with the addition of a handsome tip, her mother showed no inclination to turn back towards the school. Instead, she clutched at Amelia's hand and marched her to the edge of the park.

'When I was a bit older than you, I'd spend most of my summer holidays walking round here,' she said, sighing. 'I'd walk up from your Grandma's with my books on Shelley and Byron, and find a bench in the glass house.'

Amelia stared fixedly ahead, wondering if this required a reply. They were still only seconds away from school and a foot wrong now could mean an afternoon on the netball court.

'There was a boy … I forget his name now. That's if I ever knew it. He used to walk his dog here. An Irish setter it was. Beautiful. Same time every day. I'd wait for him … follow him round the boating lake …'

Amelia hazarded a glance up at her mother. Ever since Grandma's death, Marguerite had been undergoing a transformation. She'd had her hair done; cut short and layered and any grey had disappeared into a solid reddy-brown colour. Her clothes were different too. She'd taken to wearing what Grandma had disapprovingly referred to as 'slacks' and thrown out the reinforced roll-on that used to hold up her stockings. Amelia missed the roll-on. She'd enjoyed scrunching up little pieces of paper to replace the lost buttons on the suspenders. It had been her job to shove them down the stocking tops and force them through the fastening, so they looked like small, flesh coloured warts on her mother's otherwise smooth thighs. There was Marguerite's new lipstick too. Babylon Fire it was called. No more Fuchsia Silk, the family colour, worn by Grandma, Edith and Dolores alike. Amelia could do nothing about these changes but trust in the will of the Goddess.

They'd reached the glasshouse now and the rain had stopped. Sun burst through the black clouds making the windows gleam. One of the doors was open and the pungent scent of warm compost and orchid drifted across the wrought iron buttresses. Amelia thought it a most seductive and repulsive scent, a mixture of cherry-lip sweets and rotten wood; warm and syrupy and full of deathly portent. She hesitated before following her mother inside.

'Come on,' Marguerite said. 'You'll like it in here. There are all sorts. Monkeys, a toucan and everything.'

'Can I wait outside?' Amelia said. 'I'll sit on one of the benches and wait. I don't think … In my condition. The heat and everything.'

But her mother had already gone in and Amelia was forced to follow her determined stride. She decided to stay near the door, in case the smell and the monkeys got too much for her.

Inside, dusty rubber plants shared sandy soil with alien-looking cacti. A few palm trees had grown so tall they'd reached the domed roof and threatened to burst out through the glass in an effort to touch the sky. Orange and lemon trees were hung with withered green fruit. Everything was spiked and threatening and the thick air rang with screeches and chatters.

'Mum?' There was no sign of Marguerite. The two benches on either side of the entrance were empty though a dinted Tennent's Pilsner can, sporting a scantily clad young woman, showed that one had been recently occupied.

Amelia ran along the brick path, ignoring the enamelled signposts giving the names of plants in both Latin and English. Two monkeys swarmed down the trunk of one of the palms, spotted her and stopped. She looked away, detesting the malevolence in their muscular grey bodies and their bright and beady eyes. Overhead, a black bird with a violently yellow beak squawked in a mixture of Latin and English: 'Salve, salve. Hello hello. You bastard.'

'Mum? Mummy?'

Amelia had now circumnavigated the whole glasshouse and failed to locate Marguerite. Unless she was deliberately hiding, she was forced to conclude that her mother had been spirited away, perhaps by the demonic forces inhabiting the monkeys. Her heart thumped; the air grew more stifling by the second. The sun went in, plunging the place into darkness. Creatures scuttled in the moist earth. From the trees came a hissing, whispering sound: a pulse of evil plotting.

'Mum?'

'For pity's sake, Amelia, what are you doing down there, running round like a scalded hen?' Marguerite's voice sounded from above. She laughed, her mirth tinkling like musical notes. 'It's great up here. Haven't done this for years.'

Amelia looked up. In the centre of the glasshouse was a wrought iron spiral staircase climbing right up to a small platform where her mother was sitting. Her legs dangled into the abyss of false jungle. The toe of one of her Dr Scholl's touched a half-formed coconut on a bristlingly spiky tree. In the gloom, her hair had developed an auburn halo against the black clouds outside.

'Come on,' Marguerite urged. 'You feel like you're in the sky up here.'

Amelia closed her eyes and plunged into the undergrowth. She knew that scorpions and snakes and more of those horrible monkeys were waiting to pounce on her but she had to get to her mother. She reached the staircase, clung onto the white-painted iron, took a deep breath of foul air and gazed up at her mother.

'Under the shade of a coolibah tree,' Marguerite sang, happily. 'You know they're eucalyptus, don't you? From Australia. To think, we're the other side of the world.'

Obediently, Amelia stretched out her hand and plucked a leaf from the tree her mother indicated. The feel of the fresh, slightly crispy leaf reassured her. As she crushed it in her palm, a sweet scent obliterated the stench of the warm compost. She smiled to herself, invigorated, and ducked her head; she brushed her cheek against the smooth bark and put her right foot upon one intricately-patterned step. The undergrowth rustled as though a breeze was blowing through it. A circle of darkness came towards her, a rushing tunnel of black surrounded by fragments of colour, so bright they hurt her eyes. She clutched at the handrail.

Goddess, she couldn't say the word, only think it, will it. She was there, among the palms and the monkeys and reek of putrefaction, her crystalline skin and clear blue gaze beaming out towards Amelia, her Chosen One. Her Virgin Mother.

'I've decided.' From somewhere up above, Marguerite's voice. 'We're going to Ireland. You and me. Let's see exactly what Mum left us ... Do you know, love? I'm forty, next month. Forty. I've never been to Ireland. I've never been anywhere.'

The Goddess was fading. Amelia closed her eyes, hung on to the glorious image of her, but already the smell of the glasshouse was taking over. A monkey chittered down a rubber plant, laid a brazen claw on her bare calf. She flicked it away, looked up and began to ascend the spiral staircase.

'Before Christmas, we'll go. And when we've been to Ireland, I think we might go to France. I've always wanted to 'do' Europe. I blame all that E.M Forster we learned at school. And what an education for you, sweetheart. Sod sitting in a bloody classroom all day looking at algebra and English primers, we could go to the cradle of civilization, to …'

'Mum?' Amelia, now at the apex of the staircase, looked down. No Goddess, just obscenely calling monkeys and birds. They knew, they knew even if her mother didn't. 'Mum, I need to tell you a secret.'

Marguerite, pulled from her reverie, jerked upright from where she had been sitting and swung her legs over the cavern of the glasshouse.

'Oh, there you are. Better be getting back, Darling. Are you all right?' She stood up and briefly peered at Amelia. Appearing satisfied with what she saw, she patted her head and twisted past so that she could begin to descend the steps. 'As I said, we'll begin with Ireland, just you and me. Your brother burned his bridges … although, when I think of him as a baby, he was so helpless. Whereas you were strong as an ox … Miss Independent, we used to call you …'

'Mum?' Amelia grabbed her mother's hand. 'Please … I need help.'

'Come on, keep tight hold.' Marguerite pulled Amelia in close. 'I used to be the same. It's okay when you're going up, it's looking down that's the problem. But you have to face your fear. One step then the next. All right? God, the big four-oh coming up. Well, that's what I'm doing, sweetheart, facing my fear, looking down the years at my own bloody death and I tell you what …'

'What, Mum?' Amelia's legs trembled, her head pounded. Why had the Goddess come to her here, in this terrible place? Was it to reassure, to support, or …

Amelia closed her eyes as she reached the last stair on the terrifying spiral and stepped onto firm ground. Or was it to check up on her? Perhaps when she saw Amelia enter the glasshouse she suspected she had gone over to the other side, the side of the evil chattering monkeys. Did Irena believe that she would place the precious child she was carrying in jeopardy? This thought filled her with foreboding. What if her Goddess no longer trusted her?

'You'll not find me pegging out in the same house I was born in, sister. Oh, no,' Marguerite concluded. 'I'll be in San Tropez with a bronzed Adonis on my arm, or sitting in the Ritz, sipping champers … My God, Amelia, you look as though you've seen a ghost.'

Not a ghost, thought Amelia as they left the horror of the glasshouse, but a warning.

CHAPTER 9
19TH NOVEMBER 1981

A faint whiff of bonfires had invaded the doghouse. Julian was at the far end of the back garden near the shed, sprawled on Grandma's sodden deckchair and singing along to the Dead Kennedys' tape he had forced Amelia to listen to the day before. His thin voice rose over the neighbourhood with the smoke from his ever-present roll-up, demanding to be drugged and drugged. It was embarrassing. Amelia perched on the stool near the oven and allowed Irena's peace to wash over her. Although she hadn't seen Her since the glasshouse incident, She was always near, in the crackle of light she sometimes sensed at the periphery of her vision, in the soft, stroking sensation running along her arms; in the child growing within. Silently, she muttered a short prayer that involved stars over the sea. The front door slammed and Edith screamed.

Amelia opened her eyes.

Edith was wrenching at the fridge door. 'Butter. I need to put some butter on …' she whimpered, holding out her seared left arm. She grabbed half a pound of Lurpak, peeled the paper off and pressed it to the burn. The hob was still on full. Black smoke billowed from the frying pan.

'My God, look at the state of this place,' Marguerite yelled, bursting into the kitchen late from work. She had still not managed to hand in her notice.

'Hi, Mum.' Amelia held her nose. The smell was awful.

Marguerite gave her daughter's shoulder a reassuring squeeze. 'It's bloody freezing out there. I've been working my fingers to the bone to keep the lot of you and I come home to find a funeral pyre in my kitchen! What the hell are you making?'

'Beef Risotto,' Edith said resentfully. 'Packet rubbish.' A gloop of butter slid from arm to lino. Marguerite ignored it and pulled an envelope from her mac pocket.

'I've been into town, to Thomas Cook. I've got the tickets!'

Edith sighed. 'Well don't mind me. I'm just trying to make your poor children a bite to eat.' She threw rice into the conflagration in the pan. A watery blister appeared on her forearm; it wobbled disconcertingly in time to the clacking of her teeth.

'What children?' Marguerite said in a devil-may-care kind of voice. 'Surely you don't mean that hulking pair who are quite capable of shoving some toast under the grill.'

'Your own flesh and blood, though maybe now you've a convent to look after, you've no time.'

Marguerite gave Edith a cursory kiss on the cheek. 'I'm going over there next week. Just got to clear it with work. Look, here's my passport! You and me, Amelia, love. We'll have a fine old time.' She winked at her daughter.

Amelia glared gloomily at the cigarette-burned lino. She didn't want to go to the Derrynasaggart Mountains. She didn't want to go to Ireland at all, not when the Goddess was here, in Liverpool, not when the Saviour of All Mankind was, at this very moment, curled within her womb. On the hob, the rice exuded a noxious odour.

'I could have been a nun,' Edith began bitterly. 'If only I'd known ...'

'Well, there's no time like the present,' Marguerite said, opening the cutlery drawer. 'If you want to be a nun, Edith, then no one's stopping you. If you like, you can come over with Amelia and me. Say your vows, shave your head or whatever it is they do.'

'The time is past,' Edith groaned. The rice had now stuck to the pan creating more thick smoke. She stabbed at the risotto viciously with a melted plastic spatula and added the freeze-dried meat. 'They say this is convenience food. If I'd shot the cow myself it couldn't be more inconvenient. Since when have we eaten this foreign rubbish, anyway?'

'Since I found flour, five years old and full of weevils, and a jar of Branston pickle growing penicillin in the cupboard. That's to say nothing of the forty-five tins of Ambrosia creamed rice. Anyway, I bought a box of those faggots they're going on about on the telly. I don't think they're foreign,' Marguerite replied.

Edith hurled the spatula to the lino where it stuck. She clutched at her chest. 'And you think I'd be eating faggots at a time like this. With my sister not in her grave six months and finding that she's been keeping the convent from me a lifetime ...' As she spoke, her teeth eased between her lips until she was wearing them on the outside of her mouth.

Marguerite winked at Amelia and bent to retrieve the spatula. She grabbed hold of the ruined pan and hurled it into the swing bin. Amelia, obeying her mother's silent entreaty, gently took Edith's hand and led her into the parlour which, since the removal of her grandmother's corpse, had become more of a sitting room, though the suite, made from some stiff red cotton fabric was neither comfortable nor appealing to the eye.

'It's all right,' Amelia whispered. 'Honest. I'll pray for you. There's no need for you to eat foreign rubbish. I bet Mum'll get fish and chips.'

Two glistening tears negotiated the gulleys of Edith's cheeks. 'You're a good girl,' she said, squeezing Amelia's hands so tightly that they went numb. 'You, love, are all that keeps me from following our Sarah to an early grave. You seeing the Virgin like that, well it's given me faith. Faith in God. Faith in the future … And faith that our Sarah didn't die in vain.'

Amelia helped her elderly aunt to the chair nearest the gas fire and crouched down. Her stomach growled. The Saviour was starving and so was she. Fish and chips would be brilliant but she hoped she wouldn't be sent out for them as she felt a sudden need to commune with the Goddess, to ask her advice about the Irish trip. There was no way Amelia wanted to leave home before the baby came, but then again, Ireland was known for the devoutness of its citizens. Maybe there, the Goddess would find an acceptance she never could while hidden away in a Liverpool cockloft.

Her stomach gave a sudden lurch and she clutched at it worriedly. There had been no more blood or sickness. In fact, for the last week or so she had felt almost back to normal. Perhaps the time had come and she was going to give birth in the parlour in front of Edith and her teeth. But then she relaxed, remembering Catherine Mulhearn's mum. Her belly had bounced and leapt as though it were full of frogs for months before the Knife. Amelia touched the growing mound in wonder. It gave an impatient hiccough. Tears of joy sprang to her eyes. The Saviour of the World was communicating with her.

'What are you standing like one of Woolworths for?' Marguerite demanded, thrusting a five pound note at Amelia. 'You look like a half-wit. Now, here's money for the chippy. After Edith's burnt offerings I couldn't face cooking. Run along now. It shuts at five-thirty tonight.'

'Can't Julian go?' said Amelia, seeing her brother skulk along the hall. 'He's been lying in the back garden all afternoon and I …'

'I couldn't trust him not to spend the money on himself,' Marguerite snorted. 'But you're right, love. It's dark out there. Julian! You walk with your sister to the chippy. It'll do you good.'

Julian's emaciated form appeared in the doorway. He fixed Amelia with one of his most vindictive looks, the looks that in the distant past had preceded a vicious fight. Then slowly, deliberately, he raised two fingers at Marguerite.

'Wash your mouth out with soap and water!' Edith said.

Amelia sighed and stuffed the money down the waistband of her jeans, aware that Julian's kohl ringed eyes had followed its progress. Since his dramatic return, he seemed to have faded and become indistinct, like a charcoal drawing, blurred and rubbed out. Every day he got up, left the house, often not reappearing until the early hours of the next morning. Sometimes she didn't see him for days on end.

'Okay, Ma,' Julian said. 'Have it your way. I'll protect little Sis from all the rapists and muggers we get round here.'

'Don't talk nonsense,' Marguerite snorted, opening the drawer in the sideboard where the sauces and pickles were kept. Amelia could tell, from the firm appearance of her back that she had forgotten about them already.

It was a dank, misty evening, smelling of earth and dog dirt and the exhaust fumes that hung over the estate in wet weather. Amelia and Julian left by the back gate, crossed the waste ground behind the house and cut through the sycamore-lined council estate to the main road. Alone, Amelia would never have negotiated the estate. Marguerite insisted that it was a 'rough' place and discouraged friendships with children who lived there. To Amelia, it had become an exotic and forbidden world. She wondered what was meant by 'rough' and concluded that the roughness must occur mostly behind closed doors, or at least at the dead of night. You could hardly tell when Olive Mount gave way to the Vintner Grove. The lawns were equally tidy, the front doors freshly painted. Just because the estate dwellers could not choose the

84

colour of their door but were forced to make do with a functional railway carriage maroon, didn't mean, surely, that their homes ran any less smoothly than those belonging to the inhabitants of Calvary Crescent who encrusted their mock Tudor semis with pebbledash, garden lanterns and plastic window frames.

Julian was silent but for his hacking cough and the annoying slurping noise he made on his cigarette. Amelia didn't care. The Saviour had growled a second time. She stared at her brother's heavy workmen's boots as he clomped along the road, and worried about the circumstances of the birth. As far as she knew, there was not a single local stable and she'd never seen a shepherd or a king. A cattery had opened up on the main road and there was the Winnicot Poodle Salon over the chemist's in Woolton village, but oxen and asses were in pitifully short supply. They reached St Gerard Magella's, the 'roughies' Catholic Church on the edge of the estate, according to Marguerite. She reckoned that only 'poor people' went there, and you were likely to pick up lice or ringworm if you joined the congregation. Amelia stared at the faithful lining up now for evening Mass, watched over by a white-glossed Christ on his slightly askew crucifix. She had never seen any sign of poverty. In fact the lace mantillas were more intricate than those in her own superior parish and many of the women had beautiful gold sovereigns on their fingers. She sighed. Some of her mother's ideas were decidedly peculiar.

Past the church to the row of shops where Grandma had bought almost everything before the new Tesco opened up on the main road. There was Hallelujah Mildred's Boutique, (Mildred had joined a new Christian sect who praised the lord and collected money in the high street with tambourines and triangles), the pet shop owned by the flame-haired Taggart sisters, Finbar's Tuck Shop, Cousins' Bakery (still known as Charlie's though he had sold up and left some twenty years earlier), the butcher's and greengrocer's and finally, Harry Wong's chip shop. This little row (or parade as Grandma had grandly referred to it) backed onto a maze of mean terraced streets. If the council estate was considered by Marguerite to be too 'rough' for someone of Amelia's gentility, then Mafeking Drive and its Boer War neighbours was a no-man's land of thieves and villains. Yet however hard Amelia studied those who emerged from the sea of red brick, she had yet to spot anyone who looked like a criminal. She stopped and peered into the gloom and watched an old woman on two sticks emerge backwards from one of the dwellings.

Julian gripped her shoulder, digging his fingers in so that she had to squirm to get away.

'You got the money?' he demanded.

Amelia stumbled on the broken pavement. 'What money?'

Her brother tutted and looked skywards. 'The fish-shop-money, stupid.'

The five pound note crackled against Amelia's hip. She looked up at him, trying not to let her gaze fall on an inflamed pimple on his upper lip that glistened in the yellow street light.

'You know that I have.'

'Well, let me have it.'

Amelia stepped backwards. Julian looked desperate, ill. Sweat ran in thin rivulets from his hairline, giving a faintly blue-black cast to his pancaked complexion. His pupils were enormous making his eyes seem wholly black, like a dog or a cow.

'Mum said I was to keep hold of it and pay.'

'Fuck what Ma said.' In a second he had her in an arm lock, his elbow around her throat and his other hand slid down to the waistband of her tracksuit pants. As she struggled to push him away, she spotted a young woman leaving the chip shop, balancing a packet of chips on the handle of an old-fashioned coach-built pram. She pointed and he followed the direction of her finger. He was distracted long enough for her to wrench his hand out of her trousers. Julian's arm jerked upwards, he groped out to stop himself falling and his hand landed on her swollen and rather sore right breast. He gave a sharp cry and pulled away.

'Jesus Christ, your tits are growing. The sprog'll be showing soon and everyone'll know my little sis has been fu …'

She spun away from him, almost falling over. 'Any harm you inflict upon me, you inflict upon the Saviour of all Mankind,' she announced as the woman with the pram came steadily nearer. She was grabbing handfuls of chips and stuffing them into her mouth as though she hadn't eaten for days.

'You stupid, stupid cow. Christ! The money,' Julian said. 'I need it.'

'You're always wanting money. I've given you all I've got spare,' Amelia reminded him. 'What on earth are you doing with it all?'

He wiped his brow. The sleeve of his jacket rolled back to reveal long pencil lines trailing from the inside of his elbow almost to his wrist. The lines were punctuated by small black holes. She wondered if it was a form of Stigmata. Some medieval saints had walked about for years with great holes through their hands and feet, though they were usually pouring with blood. Mrs Gorgon at school was always going on about Padre Pio and his open wounds. She hoped, for Julian's sake, that he would be spared such a gruesome miracle.

'If you don't give it to me, I'll tell Ma about the sprog. I'll tell her everything and you'll be put in that home for delinquent girls on Woolton Road. You shouldn't be pregnant, not at your age, you can't be! It's illegal,' he shouted.

'Is that right, Jules?' The woman parked the pram between Amelia and her brother. 'I wish I'd known at the time.'

Julian looked up, shocked. 'Paula,' he said weakly.

Amelia stared at the welcome interruption with a twinge of recognition. The girl was about the same age as Julian, thin and scrawny with dirty bleach-blonde hair pulled away from her face with a fraying elastic band. Her lips and chin were covered in cold sores and she smelled strongly of sweat and baby powder.

'I heard you were back,' she said, bending over the pram and pulling away the grubby cotton blanket. A baby slumbered beneath. Julian groaned and lurched forward, gripped the edge of the pram. Amelia, fascinated by the child, put out a hand to steady him. 'She's almost a year old,' Paula continued. 'I called her Patti. After Patti Smith.'

Julian gave a whimper and turned away. The child awoke, focussed her blue eyes on him, and set up a loud wailing.

'What's the matter? Don't you even want to look?' Paula demanded. 'She's yours.'

'Patti is my niece?' Amelia exclaimed happily. Everything was fitting into place. Hadn't John the Baptist been a cousin of Jesus? Patti had been sent to pave the way for the Messiah. She remembered that Paula had been to the house on several occasions, though Julian had treated her rather rudely.

'Fuck off, Sis,' Julian hissed. 'How d'you know it's mine?' he turned on Paula. 'At the time …'

'She's yours,' Paula said wearily. There were tears in her dull black eyes. 'I didn't realise. Not for ages. With the smack and all … She cried for a week after she was born. This thin awful cry, not like any of the other babies on the ward. They took her away.'

'You stupid cow. You said you were on the Pill.'

Amelia frowned and shook her head. No wonder the poor child cried and got taken away if she was smacked.

'I must have forgotten to take it … In those days I was so wasted.' Paula stretched out one thin arm and touched Julian's shoulder. He flinched and pulled away.

'Well you can keep your kid. It's got nothing to do with me.'

'You look awful,' Paula said to Julian and gently leaned into the pram to comfort the child. The light from Harry Wong's oriental window display glinted on sparse yellow curls, exactly the same colour as Amelia's.

'Can I hold her?' Amelia asked, anxious to feel the plump little body. 'If she is my niece?'

Paula dumped the baby into her outstretched arms. 'She's only crying because she's teething,' she explained, wiping the child's face with a filthy handkerchief. 'There's been no smack for nine months now. They put me on the methadone programme. I've been clean for six weeks.'

'Good for you.' Julian sounded bitter. He kicked a nearby wall, refused to look at Paula or the baby.

Patti stared up at Amelia and gave her a toothy smile. She smelled rank: of wee and sour milk. Her nappy against Amelia's palm was damp, but the proud aunt fell immediately in love. She knew that she was looking into the face of a new prophet, the one who was born to prepare the way for the Saviour.

'Don't you feel anything?' Paula demanded. 'Your own daughter, for fuck's sake, and you deny her!'

Amelia thought of St Peter and the cock crowing and held Patti close.

'Put the kid back,' Julian said. 'We've got to go the chippy.'

'I'm not asking you for money or anything,' Paula replied. 'If you'd just own up, it'd be a start. I wouldn't expect anything else from you. Not in your state. Anyhow, the Social are paying up.'

'We're going.' Julian tried to grab the baby away from Amelia but she held on tight. 'And you're not to say a word of this to anyone, you hear?'

Reluctantly, Amelia handed Patti back to her mother, though it was difficult as the baby had snuggled into her new aunt's shoulder. 'She's beautiful,' she said. 'I would love to see more of her.'

'Your little sister's got more feeling in her little finger than you've got in your whole body,' Paula accused. 'I'm sorry I ever knew you, Jules. Honest, I am.'

'You're not the only one,' Julian said.

Amelia's gaze took in the scuffed pram, the baby's grimy clothes, the mother's drawn face and felt a stab of pity. As mother of the New Messiah she suspected that she ought to be known for her acts of saintliness so, on impulse, she grabbed the five-pound note from the waistband of her trousers and pushed it into Paula's hand. The girl looked down at it as though it had fallen from the sky.

'What's this for?' she asked.

'For you. For the baby.'

'Thank you.' Tears rolled down Paula's face, streaking her cheeks with black mascara. 'I won't forget this, kid. Honest I won't. Come and see her whenever you like. I live on Passion Close. Number Three. Anytime. Just call.'

'That's just brilliant!' Julian shouted as Paula walked away. 'What the hell are we going to say happened to the money?'

Amelia smiled. 'The Goddess will provide.'

'Provide what? Fish and bloody chips for nothing?'

At that moment, the bulky figure of Mr Lawless could be seen lumbering into view, intent on his nightly fish and chip supper.

'I'm sure She'll think of something,' Amelia replied, rummaging in her pocket.

Julian rubbed his eyes with the heels of his hands.

'And if she doesn't?'

Amelia tilted her head, looked up to the orange glow of the streetlight with its halo of bright mist. Triumphantly, she held up a ten pence piece. 'Then you will.'

CHAPTER 10
20TH NOVEMBER 1981

Amelia woke early. There was a pain in her back and her mouth felt furry and metallic. Through the net curtains, the sun illuminated her Holly Hobby nightie case hanging on the back of the door, giving Holly's down-turned face a penitent air. A shard of light had lodged into the breast of the statue of Our Lady. The statue had been inscribed in biro by Great Aunt Edith: 'For Amelia and your life with The Virgin' on the occasion of her First Holy Communion. Sitting at the edge of the bed, Amelia felt around for her slippers with her feet and found herself wondering: was her Goddess one and the same as Edith's Virgin; could the Mother of Christ, that distraught woman who had wept at the foot of the cross, be the same as the magnificent creature who had appeared to her in the cockloft and the glasshouse? Impossible. Mary was a vague figure with her blue robes and half-closed eyes. Her feet, on Amelia's statue, were not even on the ground, but astride the moon and a snake. Stars glittered on the mound of heaven in between. Mary was in Heaven now. Her job had been done over two thousand years ago. Irena's had yet to begin.

She put on her slippers and padded to the bathroom. The grandmother clock in the hall struck six, jarring the sleeping house with its awkward chime. Her bladder was bursting and she only just reached the loo in time. She prodded at her stomach and said the prayer Edith taught her when she was tiny:

'Oh, my Goddess, support me in that hour in the strong arms of Thy Sacraments, and by the fresh fragrance of Thy consolations. Let the absolving words be said over me, and the holy oil sign and seal me, and Thy own Body be my food, and Thy Blood my sprinkling; and let my sweet Goddess breathe on me that in Her, and through Her, I may receive the gift of perseverance, and die, as I desire to live, in Thy faith, in Thy … in Thy service, and in Thy love. Amen.'

Amelia was obliged to alter a few of the words and some of them were difficult to replace, but the prayer was suitable for the moment. In the last few days she had come to accept that she might die bringing the Saviour into being. She knew that her purpose lay in offering Her hope to the world and that once this task was over, Irena might want to take her to heaven for herself. A sense of righteous trust fell over her shoulders like a holy mantle. She flushed the toilet and made her way downstairs.

A loud clack and a tut in the front parlour gave away Edith's presence. The old woman, Amelia knew, had not slept well since Grandma had died, but she still remained in bed until after nine on most days. Amelia pushed open the door to find the gas fire on full and the room hazy with cigarette smoke.

'What are you doing up at this time, child?' Edith demanded, springing away from the table.

'I couldn't sleep,' Amelia said. 'I was thirsty.' She nearly said, 'and the Saviour was grumbling,' but she stopped herself. No one but Julian knew of the child to be.

Edith put a copy of the Catholic Herald over some unsuccessfully concealed papers.

'Well, let's make us both a cup of tea,' she said. 'We're a pair of insouciants ... I never sleep past four and, like a nun at matins, I have spent the last two hours in private contemplation of the Holy Mysteries. I didn't want to wake your dear mother so I came down here.'

Amelia knew this wasn't true, but she didn't say so. The ashtray bulging with butts was hardly the result of any prayerful communion with the Lord. Instead, she waited until Edith was in the kitchen, before removing the Herald.

Underneath, shoved untidily into a brown foolscap envelope addressed to her mother, was a letter and a few photographs. She heard Edith filling the kettle, coughing into the sink. She listened to her taking the cups down from the cupboard, the sigh as she settled herself onto the stool beside the cooker, waiting for the water to boil, before she carefully emptied the envelope.

The letter was headed 'The Convent of the Holy Head, Derrynasaggart.' The handwriting was thick and black. It looked as though it had been written in indelible marker.

My dear Marguerite, it began. I write to introduce myself and our tiny community, here in the mountains of Cork. By the time you receive this simple missive, you will know that our lives are now in your hands. Your Mother, God Bless her, was most kind and magnanimous in her dealings with us, as was the kindly Mr Winsome and his father before him, God be praised, who has kept our meagre interests close to his heart. We are a poor order, asking little but a roof and enough food to keep us alive for our prayers and devotions to the Holy Head. Your dear departed mother, however, insisted on making our lives more comfortable by providing …

Edith coughed. 'You want marmalade on your toast, love?'

'No thanks'

More chinking of crockery, spoons stirring, the strike of a match as yet another cigarette was ignited. Amelia was safe for now.

… us with the little extra we needed to make our home safe and available to the poor who are in daily need of our ministrations. In gratitude and humility we have and will always keep your mother's soul and the souls of you and all your wonderful family in our thoughts and prayers.

Although it brings me great pain to bring this matter to your attention, aware as I am of your recent troubles, I write not only to welcome you as Patron of the Convent of the Holy Head, but to tell you that our Order is in grave danger, so desperate are the financial straits in which we find ourselves. This would not be such a tragedy for those of us sisters still with our health and strength, but there are amongst us several older sisters who were taken into the convent in the days of the 1914-18 war. These sisters, long separated from family and friends would be forced onto the streets where they would, without a doubt, be —

'What are you looking at, Amelia?' Edith demanded, rattling into the room with cups of tea and hot buttered toast. 'That's private. Not for your eyes.'

'It's addressed to Mum,' Amelia pointed out.

'Your mother and I have no secrets.' Edith put down the tray and began to gather the contents of the envelope together.

'Well, I'll ask her if I can look at it, too, then.' Amelia gave a simpering smile. 'I think I heard her moving about upstairs.'

'There's no need for that,' Edith snapped. 'I've made us both some breakfast. What do you want to know?'

Amelia shrugged and took a slice of toast. Marguerite would never eat Edith's toast. She said it was unhygienic. She said that she spread the butter with her claw-like fingernails that were daubed in chipped fuchsia nail polish. The butter did sit in little raised peaks as though Edith had been patting it into place, but Amelia didn't care. Edith's nails couldn't be dirtier than the knives that missed the washing up and ended up back in the drawer encrusted with egg.

'Well, all right,' Edith said. 'To be honest, it's good to have someone to share my troubles with. Especially you, Amelia. You were always my —'

'It's from that convent Mum inherited. Looks like they want more money.'

'Well, have you seen the pictures of the place? It ought to be condemned.' Edith reached into the envelope. Greasy blobs of butter covered the address. She pulled out several black and white photographs, all small, no more than five centimetres square. 'See? And that cowshed needs to go. Those poor sisters. Braving the weather up there, praying for our eternal souls and living in such squalor.'

Amelia studied the pictures. They were out of focus and spotted with mildew.

'They look very old, don't they?'

Edith's teeth protruded. 'They've probably only got a box brownie. Nuns take a vow of poverty you know. They're not like Dolores and her fancy Polaroid. But will you just look at that convent.' She pulled out another picture, depicting a tumbledown domed building that reminded Amelia of the slides Sister Anne Margaret had shown the school of her trip to The Holy Land last Easter. 'That paint is all peeling and the place is shored up with scaffolding to hold it up. Those poor sisters …'

'I didn't know they had palm trees in Ireland,' Amelia remarked but Edith was shuffling through the pictures and now held up a photograph of the convent's interior.

'And that terrible cell. The ceiling is falling in and there's barely room to swing a cat. And I bet it's damp. You shouldn't keep elderly nuns in those conditions. They'll get hypermania. Marguerite will have to give them more money.'

Amelia put the photos down onto the table and sighed. 'It's only a week till Mum's going over there. She'll be able to see for herself.'

'I know.' Edith slowly replaced the photographs and the letter. 'I wish it were me … I know it's a sin to convert your

98

neighbour's ox, but I still feel the convent should have been left to me.'

'So do I,' Amelia agreed. 'You wouldn't make me go over there, would you? I keep telling Mum I'll be quite okay here. I won't play truant from school or anything … And anyway …' she placed a hand over her stomach, '… it could actually be dangerous.'

Edith was only half listening. She gazed at the window, her rheumy eyes full of longing.

'Al and I went there once. Up into the mountains. We stayed near a little shrine. I remember it was autumn and oh what beautiful weather we had. The moors were on fire with red and gold. And to think our Marguerite owns a convent in those very hills. Al and I rented a little cottage. It belonged to a farm and —'

'Why don't you go with Mum?' Amelia asked. 'Mum's already said you can and you could have my ticket, no problem. I'll be fine here …'

'What was that, dear?' Edith jolted herself from her reverie and finally remembered that her great-niece was in the room.

'The trip, to the convent. You could take my place!'

Edith picked up her cup and warmed her hands on it. Her teeth lurched forward and reached the tea inside before her lips. With her hair bound so tightly in curlers beneath her hairnet, her usually crinkled skin was stretched and girlishly smooth; she didn't look like herself. Amelia couldn't help but think of her grandmother, laid out and plastered in waxy foundation.

'Why, don't you want to go?' Edith asked in astonishment. 'The convent will be yours one day.'

'I don't care,' Amelia said, excited now the idea had occurred to her. 'I'd much rather you went to the convent. Maybe you could do what Mum said. You could join the nuns, like you've always wanted. You could —'

'No.' Edith laid one of her veiny, liver-spotted hands on the table. 'I'm too old for such a journey. It would probably kill me.'

'But I'm with child!'

Amelia hadn't intended to confess this to Edith. In fact she had consciously put off the moment when she would have to confront any of the adults with her condition. She knew that even if they believed her, they would ruin it for her by inventing one of the cruel adult things she could neither foresee nor defy, designed to tarnish her absolute joy. But she did not intend to go on a wild goose chase to a convent in the middle of Southern Ireland either, especially not with her new primped and dyed and over made-up mother, the chief destroyer of dreams.

'What?' Edith was startled. Her mouth hung slackly open and her upper dentures came adrift and closed over the lower set leaving an expanse of raw-looking gum.

Amelia stood up and pulled open her dressing gown; she took hold of one of Edith's hands and laid it upon her stomach.

'I am pregnant with the New Messiah,' she announced.

Edith clawed her stomach then pulled her hand away.

'Pregnant! What have you been doing, child? You're barely out of nappies yourself.'

'Well I am. I have been touched by The Great Goddess. And she has chosen me to bear the future Saviour of the World. She will be a girl-child.' Amelia knelt down and put her head on Edith's lap. The old woman lit another cigarette.

'Pregnant!' she said. She sucked on the cigarette. Amelia could hear it rattling through her clogged lungs. 'Dear God. Holy Mother of God, this family is cursed.' She sucked again.

'Be happy for me,' Amelia murmured into her lap. It smelled faintly of pee and stale Rive Gauche.

'Happy!' Edith coughed and brought up a lump of phlegm in her hand that she wiped on the tablecloth. She sat for a few moments, hardly moving, smoking her cigarette and staring straight ahead. Her body gave a strange jerk and she sprang from her chair, knocking Amelia to the floor.

'Did this ... did this happen during The Visitation?' she demanded.

Amelia thought hard. Had it happened then? It seemed so long ago now, she could barely remember it. The blood had come on the morning of her grandmother's funeral, a few days after the Goddess appeared in the attic. She had not seen Irena again until she returned to the cockloft with Julian. By then she had already known she was with child.

'It must have been,' she cried excitedly. 'She must have filled my womb with the —'

'Then it wasn't the Virgin at all, but an angel: Gabriel.' To Edith the situation was crystal clear. 'He's the one who did the annunciation for Mary. There's nothing to suppose ...'

'It was the Goddess.'

'Goddess, angel, it's all the same. The fact of the matter is that you are with child through the power of God.'

'It was the Goddess,' Amelia insisted.

'And you're sure you've known no man?' Edith was over excited. She grabbed Amelia by the shoulders and stared into her eyes. 'Child, I don't know if your mother ever told you the facts of life ...'

Amelia rolled her eyes. 'Mum said Grandma gave her a pamphlet about the Virgin Mary and St Joseph and the Holy Ghost. She said she'd never do that to me.'

'I take it ...' Edith looked furtive. She glanced at the door and took another cigarette from her packet of Rothmans. 'Your monthlies have ceased?'

'Ages ago!' Amelia retorted. Didn't Edith listen to anything? She had stopped her monthly visits to the elocution teacher over a year ago when she finished primary school. Madame La Guerre was probably still engaged in her lifelong battle against the Liverpool accent or, as she put it, 'sounding less than the thing', her 'Haow Naow Braown Caow' was still chiming over the rooftops of Woolton, but Amelia, thank the Goddess, was now spared.

'Then, God in all His infinite glory and majesty be praised.' Edith's knees cracked as she knelt on the hearth rug. The long tube of ash on her cigarette toppled and fell down the sleeve of her housecoat.

'So you see I can't go on the trip,' Amelia insisted. 'It wouldn't be right.'

Edith was absorbed in the potted version of the Latin Mass that came rasping and rattling through her teeth. A large black hole was appearing on the nylon hearthrug where her cigarette had dropped. A low winter sun pierced the grubby net curtains and shone into Amelia's eyes. Her great aunt finished her prayers, looked up at her, gave a little shriek and prostrated herself over the smouldering mat.

'My God, what the hell's going on in here?' Marguerite announced, from the doorway. 'Something's burning, for Christ's sake.' She saw Edith and ran forward. She was wearing a satin negligee, her newly mahoganied locks kirby-gripped into an elaborate pattern of kiss curls. Even in this state of undress, she had seen fit to slash some scarlet across her lips.

'The child ...' Edith gasped. 'The child. She is the chosen one, without stain of sin, without ...'

'Amelia, give me a hand. I think she may have had a stroke.' Her mother's voice was so authoritative that Amelia obeyed and helped pull Edith onto one of the stiff easy chairs. 'I warned her. Sixty Rothmans a day is too much at her age. I told her she ought to slow down a bit ... Edith! Edith, can you hear me?'

She slapped the old woman's face and Edith, shocked out of her mumbled prayer, slapped her back.

'What did you do that for?' she demanded, groping in her pocket for her cigarettes.

'I thought you were ill,' Marguerite whispered. There was a large red imprint of Edith's fingers on her cheek. She turned to the table. 'And what the hell is my private letter doing down here? I left it locked in the kitchen drawer. God, Edith, if you wanted a look, you should have asked.'

'Your child is to be the virgin mother of the new messiah.' Edith pointed at Amelia who was still bathed in early sun. 'And I, praise be to the Holy Trinity and Prince Andrew himself, am the one in whom she chose to confide.'

Marguerite snatched up her letter and wiped the toast crumbs from it in disgust. 'You have no right to go poking around in my private affairs.'

'Pray with me now,' Edith said, rising to grasp Marguerite's hand. 'For surely this is the most glorious day in the history of humankind since the announcement …'

'What announcement? I won't forget this, Edith, I really won't. It's too much … And what are you doing there with your stomach sticking out?' Marguerite turned on Amelia. 'Go and get dressed. You've got school in an hour.'

'You can't send her to school,' Edith shouted. 'Not when she's …'

'If I were you, Edith, I would keep my mouth shut this morning. I'm in no mood for this nonsense. Get up those stairs, Amelia, or so help me, I'll …'

Amelia bounded out of the parlour and up to her bedroom. While she attempted to button up her slightly tight school skirt, she heard someone hammering on the front door. Her mother and aunt were arguing so ferociously in the parlour that they were oblivious. When the knocking came a third time, Amelia slipped down and opened it.

'Bastard. Fucking bastard.' Dolores was on the step in a state of disarray. Her blonde hair was tousled and her lips bled fuchsia up to her nostrils. Mascara had streaked her cheeks and she wore an old blue coat that had evidently been thrown in a hurry over a see-through nylon nightie, the like of which Amelia had never seen outside a Carry On film. At the gate, a black cab was revving the engine. He beeped impatiently.

'No money,' Dolores said, pushing past Amelia. 'You'll have to pay him.'

Amelia ran upstairs and took some notes from her secret stash under the floorboards. Only yesterday she had caught Julian attempting the cockloft ladders and she had to think of more cunning ways to conceal her cash. Dolores must have been on a very long journey, as the fare came to over seventeen pounds but Amelia paid him hurriedly.

'If I were you, I'd get a new frock,' the cabbie said cheerfully pocketing the money. 'Or leave off the buns.'

'I am not an elephant,' Amelia said haughtily and clanged the gate so loudly she disturbed Mrs Lawless over the road, who nearly lost her duster out of the window she was pretending to clean.

Chapter 11
21st November

Dolores moved in. She had left Ken after being forced to appear in one of his wildlife films.

'I didn't mind the others, they had consenting adults,' she wept to Marguerite many times over the next few days. 'But animals! Ugh. A bloody great donkey. And the thing kept braying all the time. Its breath stank of rotten cabbage.'

Amelia thought Dolores was being histrionical. Hadn't Jesus arrived in Jerusalem on a donkey? And she had never heard of Johnny Morris complaining about cabbage breath. But then, she thought, sighing, he was a Professional.

Edith presented Dolores with a silver St Francis locket containing a curl of ginger hair inside, origin unknown.

'There,' she said. 'Wear this and you'll be kinder to the animals.'

Without consultation, Amelia was evicted from her bedroom and forced into her grandmother's old room to share a bed with her mother. Dolores was to luxuriate in Amelia's room while Edith took over Marguerite's. Julian remained in the damp and rarely used shed at the end of the back garden, to where he had been relegated after the business with Mr Lawless and the chip shop money, which Marguerite was convinced had been squandered on something to make Julian 'high'. Amelia kept her counsel. She was pretty sure that the truth of what happened to the money would upset her mother far more. Occasionally, spirals of smoke would seep from the shed window, writhing around the tinkling honesty in the rose bed. The packet of cinder toffee Edith had bought, and then regretted after gluing her dentures together, was missing from the kitchen cupboard.

Edith, silenced by the drama of Dolores and Ken, fell to incomprehensible mutterings about visitations and virgin births, but no one seemed to notice. Amelia, making herself scarce, kept a worried eye on her great aunt.

It was two days before the dreaded trip to Ireland. With the morning and Dolores' arrival over with, after a hurried lunch of tinned mincemeat on toast (a recipe Edith had once seen Fanny Craddock perform) and strong tea, Marguerite announced that she was going into town to buy some new clothes. She had her eye on some jeans, she said and Amelia shuddered. The thought of her mother scaling an Irish mountain in denim was too revolting to contemplate.

'And you, young lady,' she said, appearing to notice her daughter for the first time in days, 'you can come with me. That dress is getting a bit tight.'

Amelia glanced at Edith, convinced that the old woman was going to tell everyone her secret; sooner or later someone would believe her ramblings. But her aunt merely nodded and whispered a Hail Mary.

It was Saturday.

'Town', her mother said, cheerfully, 'will probably be hell.' She ordered a taxi, forgoing the usual preamble of the Number Eighty bus.

'What about me?' Dolores wailed as they waited in the hall. 'I've left everything back home. I can't spend the rest of my life looking like Linda Lovelace. Can I come? You've enough money to fork out for a get-up for me.'

Linda Lovelace, whoever she was, couldn't look as bad as her aunt, Amelia decided. The poor woman, by her own admission, had not slept in days and survived on nothing but cheap sherry and cigarettes. She still wore the frilled nightdress, made modest by one of her mother's checked housecoats, but her face was ravaged, her blonde hair plastered to her head, no longer the elaborately coiffed confection of recent years.

Amelia lingered near the stairs, discreetly fastening the waistband of one of Aunt Mabel's floor-length fishtail skirts. Her best dress, after Marguerite's comments, had been consigned to the mourning box in the attic. She would not be needing it for some time. Fortunately, the long dead Mabel, though diminutive in stature, had made up for it in girth. Edith, the only one old enough to remember Mabel's idiosyncrasies, once recalled that her aunt had eaten an entire wedding cake at one sitting. The cake, Mabel's own, was made for a marriage that never happened, as her beloved was found dead in a Belgian trench, days before the nuptials were to take place. Rats had eaten away half of his face, so the story went, and he was only identified by his uniform. It was a sad fact that whenever Amelia plundered the mourning box, this image would come to her, unbidden, along with the smell of naphthalene and mould.

'Then go home and fetch your clothes,' Marguerite said calmly. 'I'm sure Ken won't be up to any farmyard antics at this time on a Saturday morning.'

Dolores' breath blasted across Amelia's face. 'I'm never going back there. Never. I shall go to confession later, instead. Father Murphy and I had a long chat yesterday ... Oh Margie. I only need a few bits. A black dress, some tights. A new mantilla.'

Marguerite sniffed contemptuously as the black taxi beeped outside. Without looking at her sister, she grabbed Amelia's hand and they left for town.

The trip was a big mistake. The Christmas rush had already started and Lord Street was packed with shoppers, despite the fine haze of rain. Hideous gnomes and sinister Santas gazed from shop windows foaming with cotton wool snow. And the din! The Human League's angst ridden ditty about a waitress's rise to fame burst from the doors of Woolies, while a more sedate, Winter Wonderland polluted the air outside Smith's. Slade and Mud vying for attention in Argos, added to the eclectic mix.

The usual 'lift' music was playing in George Henry Lee's, where Marguerite bought stockings in a racy near-black tone. In Chelsea Girl (to Bette Davis Eyes) she tried on a pair of indigo stretch jeans that clung to her buttocks and thighs like polythene. These she topped with a magenta and black striped top that left one shoulder almost bare.

'Mum, you can't wear that,' Amelia said, aghast. 'You look like … like Debbie Harry or Annie Lennox. Apart from the wrinkles.'

'Debbie Harry is only a few years younger than me,' Marguerite retorted and stalked back into the changing rooms.

In Bus Stop (to the strains of an Indian sitar) she bought a cotton skirt, pleated all over, a long diaphanous scarf and a gypsy top. At Top Shop, without accompaniment, she considered a sea-green ra-ra skirt shot through with silver and black, but forgot it in her joy at finding a pair of black cargo pants that ballooned out from her waist like the trousers on a whirling dervish. They did, Amelia conceded, conceal her ample buttocks, but provided scant disguise for the shortness of her legs.

Eventually, after three arduous hours, the purchase of eight carrier bags of clothes and a make-up set that wouldn't have looked out of place in a dressing room at the Empire Theatre, Marguerite remembered her daughter.

'You,' she said, rounding on Amelia in the British Home Stores' cafe, where they were tucking into steak and kidney pie. 'You need a few clothes, too. You're getting puppy fat. I'm not having my flesh and blood walking round bursting out of her frock. People will talk, and those poor nuns won't like to have our obvious affluence thrust in their faces.'

Amelia glanced down at her stomach. The meal had swollen her up, and her breasts, formally referred to as 'two fried eggs' by Con, were straining out of her trainer bra. She wondered, almost hoped, that her mother might notice; might, if she was in one of her particularly perceptive moods, guess at the forthcoming happy event, but a glance at Marguerite's face removed any doubt. Her mother, one hand up to tease her already messy hair into a messier position, was smiling, entranced by her own self reflected in the polished chrome hot meals counter.

'I would like a new sm … a frock and some shoes, these ones are pinching. Oh, and a new mantilla,' Amelia stated calmly, feeling the child within belch in appreciation of the pie.

Marguerite almost choked on her lukewarm tea. 'A mantilla! You, as well? What is happening to my family? Everyone is turning into a religious nut. I thought Edith was the worst, but no! Now my very own daughter is …' She held up her hands in mock supplication. 'Jesus, Lord, maybe the convent is the place for the lot of you.'

Amelia nodded in what she hoped was a sympathetic but superior fashion, clasped her hands in prayer and offered a few silent words to the Goddess.

'Mind,' Marguerite stuck her leg out from under the table and looked at her own feet, 'I don't know about you but I am exhausted. Shall we leave your stuff for another day?'

Amelia experienced a small tingle of alarm. She needed some clothes, and soon. Most of her old things were too tight and even Mabel's supply would run out sooner or later.

'It's okay, Mum. Why don't you give me the money and stay here? I won't be long.'

Marguerite looked into Amelia's eyes and smiled softly.

'Oh, you are growing up, aren't you, sweetheart? Well, I suppose you're thirteen now. You don't want your old mum choosing your clothes any more. Here,' she opened her purse and took out a twenty pound note. Amelia nearly fainted. 'There you are, love. You go buy some things you like.'

Amelia grabbed the money and made her way past the serving counter as quickly as she could before her mother changed her mind. One of the dour and greasy women serving shepherd's pie and chips, stared down at her stomach and shook her head. Amelia bolted from the store.

Smocks, it turned out, were in short supply in any of the usual shops, so Amelia nipped into Lewis's and bought a blue and white checked shirt and a pair of black trousers with a waistband that stretched up to forty-six inches. Then she visited Boots where she chose a pale pink bib for the Saviour. The selection of baby's bottles and breast pumps she regarded with interest, but decided to ignore for now. She plumped for an enormous maternity bra with cups that unhooked. She wasn't sure how large her bosom was going to be, but judging from the way it was expanding now, and the size of Mrs Mulhearn's, she played safe and chose one of the biggest on the rack. The Saturday girl on the till, only a little older than Amelia, examined it with some amusement before packing it away in a carrier bag.

'You could wear those as a couple of swimming caps,' she said, grinning.

Amelia blushed furiously. 'I could not!'

'Or netball goals … on a pole, like.'

Amelia snatched the bag from her and left without waiting for her complimentary packet of breast pads.

Marguerite was finishing a rum baba and a second coffee, when Amelia arrived back at the British Home Stores, damp with rain and pink with annoyance.

'Let's see what you've got, then, Darling,' she said, prodding at Amelia's bag. 'I hope it's not unsuitable. Gosh, my mother would never have let me choose for myself at thirteen.'

'Oh, nothing much,' Amelia said. She pulled out a trouser leg. 'See. Some black pants and this shirt, see …'

'I didn't know the lumberjack look was in,' Marguerite said. 'And what else have you got …?' She pulled the maternity bra onto the table where the cups sat upright, like two gigantic meringues. 'Blimey. Darling this is huge … And it's a nursing bra. You need to get measured. You don't just pick up the first one you see … You probably need the next size training bra. Put it in the bag. We'll take it back, but not today, Amelia. Right now, I want to go home.'

Amelia sat, clutching at the bra strap, staring at the words on the ticket: Bustenhalter. This was her moment. She could tell her mother the truth. She imagined herself saying it: 'Mum, I'm having a baby. Mum, the New Messiah …' She imagined her mother's face. Activity in the busy canteen slowed. The clatter of knives and forks, of cups being banged on tables, of chairs being scraped back, receded and all she could hear was the blood pounding in her own head. No. She couldn't speak. She couldn't tell, not today. Soon, she reassured herself, as the world again became noisy and demanding. Soon she would have to tell her mother.

'Thank God for that,' Marguerite said as they ploughed past harassed mothers and squalling babies in prams to leave the shop. 'That side of my life is over. Young babies are so difficult.'

'What do you mean?' Amelia demanded, shocked.

'Oh, all the crying and the nappy changes and everything. It's a full time job. You don't even get a mo to put your lipstick on half the time. No, if I had my life again, I think I'd opt for spinsterhood and barrenness.'

'Mum!' Amelia, breathless at keeping up with her mother's bullish charge, blinked back tears. 'You mean you wish you'd never had me and our Julian? You wish you'd never married?'

'I wish I'd never clapped eyes on your damned father,' she said, pulling Amelia through the Lord Street crowds. 'He —'

'Mum!'

Marguerite spun round and her face softened. She dropped her carrier bags and patted Amelia's shoulder, then bent and kissed her cheek. She smelled of Yardley's Blue Grass and frying and other people's cigarettes.

'Sorry, sweetheart. I didn't mean … Well, you know I love you, don't you? It's just that in my day, there was no choice but to get married and have children. Unless you were lucky enough to be caught up in the so-called swinging sixties. It was all that religion, I suppose. The nuns, the idea that everyone ends up with a handsome prince … Only it doesn't work out like that. But never think I regret having you, or Julian, though he has lead me a merry dance and still does. You are the most precious people in the world to me.' She stooped and retrieved her bags. 'It's just that having children young, as I did, I feel I missed out on such a lot. I was clever at school, you know …'

Amelia nodded. She set off for the A to Z bus stops.

Her mother followed, sighing deeply. 'I was never given any encouragement or anything to aspire to. It was either marriage or the veil. Anything else was seen as downright sinful …'

Fortunately the Number Eighty bus was drawing up to the stop or Amelia might have had to endure the tale of her mother's juvenile poetry being published in the Liverpool Echo.

The bus was hot and grimy. The windows opaque with condensation. Several of the seats had been slashed and the few passengers looked depressed, grey from shopping and negotiating crowds. Marguerite paid and at Amelia's insistence, followed her up the stairs to the top deck, where they managed to bag a front window seat.

'It's just that I don't want you to end up the same way, pet,' Marguerite said, stroking Amelia's hand. 'I don't want you saddled with kids when you're barely old enough to understand what's going on.'

A man was smoking a pipe on the other front seat; the heavy fumes hit Amelia's weak stomach and she felt sick.

'Can we go downstairs, Mum?' she asked. 'It's just that …'

'You miss out on so much, having children young. I could have gone to university, got a degree, become educated. I could have travelled the world … But instead?'

'Mum?' Amelia gripped her throat. She'd thought this phase was over.

'I met your father. God, I wish I'd listened to sense. Even your grandmother knew enough to …'

'Mum!' It was too late. The pie, half-digested chips and peas, now a greyish, greenish sludge came spewing from her mouth, over her mother's carrier bags. She saw a chunk of pinkish brown kidney shoot into the jeans bag, a misshapen pea lodge on the pipe smoker's lace-up brogue.

'Good God, Amelia. What the hell did you do that for?' Marguerite demanded, brushing down her coat, which fortunately had received only the lightest of spatters. 'Were your eyes greedier than your tummy?'

The New Messiah burped triumphantly inside Amelia's womb and she lurched forward. The bus stopped and passengers began to clamber up from the stairwell. Most were smoking cigarettes and those who weren't still exuded the bittersweet smell of smoky pubs. Amelia retched again. Then knowing she could stand it no longer, she rose in one fluid movement.

'Mum, I've got to get off the bus.'

'Thanks a lot.' Marguerite shook out her Bus Stop carrier. 'And leave me with the puke.'

'I'm sorry, Mum. I couldn't help it. It's the bus … and people smoking. I think I ate too much.'

'Well that's the last time I treat you to a lunch out.' She sighed. 'Okay. I can see that little friend of yours, the Mulhearn girl at the bus stop down there, God help her. If that bloody father of hers was mine, I'd get him seen to with a couple of —'

Amelia was down the stairs before her mother could say 'bricks'.

CHAPTER 12

A deep gloom hung over eighteen Calvary Crescent when Amelia finally arrived back from town. She was cold and miserable and her feet hurt more than ever. Some sort of family meeting was going on. Con was sitting at the table opposite Julian, his white Himmler coat replaced by his off-duty uniform of ginger sports jacket and green bow tie; Marguerite perched at the head of the table looking irritated. Her sick-spattered coat was piled in a heap on top of her shopping bags. Amelia almost fell over them in the doorway. A family meeting could only ever mean one thing: a family row.

Julian pulled a bottle of R White's lemonade from Con.

'Well, Edith's not here so we'll just have to decide without her,' he said, swigging deeply. He caught Amelia's eye and his own slid away, guiltily.

'Thank the good Lord for that, the woman's away with the fairies,' Con boomed. 'It must be the loss of oestrogen; she's lost so much she's almost a man. Look at her beard!'

Marguerite tutted. 'That's enough, Con.' She slammed her hand down on the table. 'She's an old lady now, you don't have to be so nasty, not while you're under my roof.'

Amelia, seeing that hostilities were already under way, tried to back out of the room but it was too late, she had been spotted. Her mother smiled wearily and beckoned her in.

'Just it's … it's not, is it though?' Con said, blowing smoke into her face.

'Not what?'

'Your house. Not yours, not mine. It wasn't even Sarah's.'

Amelia began to unbutton her school gabardine; the fuzz of raindrops on the nap was beginning to evaporate in the hot-house atmosphere of the front parlour and it exuded the noxious odour of damp dog. As usual the gas fire was on full.

'No.' Marguerite sounded bored. 'Anyway, Con, just what is this all about? I thought you never wanted to clap eyes on me again. Last time we met, you accused me of some filthy things.'

'And I stick by 'em. You're all lesbians. You, Sarah, Edith, the lot of you. I only hope Amelia doesn't go the same way.'

'Con! I am sick to the back teeth of this rubbish.'

Amelia again attempted to ease her way from the parlour but Con swung back on his chair as she tried to squeeze past. She shied away, staggered and fell against the barley-twist sideboard.

'Come here, love,' he said, reaching out to grab the sleeve of her dress. His breath reeked of alcohol. 'You're all right at the moment. They haven't corrupted you yet, but they will. Them and the nuns and the …'

'Enough!' Marguerite clapped her hands. 'Just tell me what you want to discuss. And Julian, as you're here, I wouldn't mind hearing what happened to the fish and chip money the other night and why Mr Lawless accused you of trying to replace his double fish supper with a radioactive orange saveloy?'

Julian, who was not only indulging in one of Con's Capstans but had a foul-smelling roll-up on the go as well, coughed and squinted up at his mother.

'Old Lawless lost it when he realised I'd swapped the dinners on the counter. Got really mad and started on about being in the Magic Circle. Ending up dropping the saveloy on the floor trying to show me how to make it appear and disappear. You'd have thought I'd lifted his wallet.'

Amelia winced; Julian had no idea how to cover his tracks.

'For God's sake,' Marguerite held her hands up in despair. 'Fancy trying to steal a dinner from a magician whose whole act was about sleight of hand. No wonder he was angry! Though you still haven't mentioned where the money went …'

Amelia felt her cheeks burning. Should she say anything about Paula? She looked over to Julian who narrowed his eyes, daring her to give him away. Amelia shrugged, the moment passed; Marguerite tapped on the table and cleared her throat.

'Anyway … if this is a family meeting then we really should have Dolores here. Where is she – not run back to Ken, I hope?'

Con sniggered and grabbed the bottle of clear liquid from the table. 'Old Macdonald, you mean? I heard about the stable scene.'

'Me and Con have been talking about your inheritance, Mum,' Julian spluttered, wafting smoke away. 'And I think … we both think that it's not on, you inheriting the lot. There's Con, her loving brother, and me —'

'The less said about you the better,' Marguerite said.

'Well, we're not happy.'

Marguerite laughed.

'And there's poor Edith,' Con said.

'I'll look after Edith, you know I will,' Marguerite said.

Con sniffed loudly and dramatically, rubbed his eyes.

'Don't think you're going to get away with this. You've stitched us up. I'm not having it, you hear me? A load of hysterical women stealing my birthright … There you are, gallivanting off to Ireland with Amelia …'

Amelia groaned.

'… without so much as a by your leave when the rest of us are scratching around to eke a living.'

Marguerite rolled her eyes. Her face suffused with fury. She rose, kicking back her chair to face Con.

'Will you stop your carrying on and think of someone other than yourself for a change? It never was your birthright. There you are, money pouring out of your ears from all those deluded woman who think you can help them, and you've no wife to be spending it. You've a fine mansion up at Calderstones Park and all you can do is complain about me inheriting some tumbledown convent and a few quid. I never thought I'd say this Con, not to one of my elders, but I think you're a spoiled and selfish man, and if all you can do is sit there smoking and drinking my mother's poteen, then I'd rather you cleared off back to Allerton and left the rest of us in peace. Amelia and I have to pack.'

'Mum.' Amelia tugged at her mother's sleeve, hoping that maybe this was the time she could get out of the trip. 'I don't want —'

'I need the money same as you do,' Con yelled. His eyes popped alarmingly. 'Don't you realise —'

'The gee gees, Ma. We've all got our little peccadilloes.' Julian sat back, looking smug. Another wave of heat drifted over Amelia's flushed face. She sat down quickly in one of the stiff armchairs, wishing she had donned her new maternity trousers. They might fit better than Mabel's skirt.

'What do you mean?' Marguerite demanded.

'I've run up a few debts here and there,' Con admitted. His voice sounded strangled and odd.

'Debts! How can —'

Dolores burst into the room, half dragging, half carrying a half-dead-looking Edith, whose mantilla had slipped over her face. Dolores was wearing one of Edith's coats over her dead mother's housecoat. Far too small in every way, the combination gave her a startling décolletage. She was wild-eyed and hysterical and, as Marguerite commented later, looked like someone who had escaped from Rainhill Mental Hospital. She dragged out a dining chair and dumped Edith onto it, pulled a packet of Lambert and Butler from her pocket, rammed two in her mouth and lit both of them. Edith mumbled incoherently. A thin line of spittle oozed from the crease at the corner of her mouth to her chin. Even to Amelia's untutored eye, she looked seriously ill.

'I can't bear any more!' Dolores shrieked, sucking furiously at her cigarettes. 'I only wanted to confess to that lovely Father Murphy, when this stupid woman threw herself onto the altar, carrying on like there was no tomorrow. I'd hardly got "bless me father, for I have sinned" out when she started. I had to leave the confessional! Well, poor Father, he was red as a beetroot. An old woman like that, showing off her all-in-one. And then the statue. God, I won't be able to hold my head up in public at this rate … she … she …'

Marguerite knelt at Edith's side and loosened her Lourdes scarf. Amelia too, knelt and peered at her aunt in consternation.

'Edith!' Marguerite said, patting her cheeks. 'Are you all right? Tell me what happened.'

'Weeping, she was,' Edith croaked. 'Weeping and bleeding … The day of the Lord is coming. Salivation is at hand.' As though only now noticing her presence, she clutched at Amelia's arm and pumped it up and down with surprising ferocity.

'Is she ill, Mum?' Amelia asked, beginning to panic. What would she do if Edith died? She would not have an ally left in the world.

'Ill, my backside,' said Con, looming. 'I told you. It's her bloody hormones. She's —'

'Shut up, Con,' said Marguerite. 'Dolores, what happened?'

Dolores stubbed her two cigarettes out in the ashtray. The tablecloth was covered in ash and spilled lemonade, or whatever had been in the bottle.

'She's not ill, just crazy. Lost her bloody wits, she has. Bring back Al Monagle, that's what I say. At least he kept her in check.'

'The Virgin,' Edith muttered. 'I saw her. Bleeding and weeping from her hands.'

'Not this nonsense again.' Marguerite rose and began to retrieve her dropped clothes. 'Thank God we're off to Ireland the day after tomorrow. This atmosphere is not healthy for anyone. Look, Edith. There is no Virgin. No bleeding hands, no bloody weeping. I know you're missing your sister, but this is getting ridiculous —'

'She brought Amelia's First Holy Communion Madonna to confession,' Dolores said with a sigh. 'It was smeared with tomato sauce or paint. Father Murphy didn't know where to put himself and there was me telling him all about the things Ken made me do —'

'He probably wanted a good ham shank,' said Con.

'Quiet, Con.' Marguerite helped Edith to her feet. 'Amelia, make your aunts a cup of tea and get upstairs. It's time we started to pack. I wish I'd booked an earlier sailing.'

'But, Mum, I don't want —'

Marguerite, in no mood to listen to dissent, shoved her out of the room.

'Tea,' she commanded.

Amelia opened the kitchen window. A revolting concoction was bubbling away in a pan on the stove and the room had steamed up. She lifted the lid to be assaulted by the warm, bloody smell of boiling offal. She ran to the sink and vomited until her insides were raw and the last of the steak and kidney pie had been purged. She filled the kettle and sank onto Edith's seat near the stove. Tears of rage and frustration gathered in her eyes. It wasn't fair. There was Edith, poor devout Edith, who knew that Amelia was carrying the Saviour, treated as though she was mad. And Amelia having to go on some stupid trip with her mother and her stupid new clothes. And Con being rude and cruel and Dolores carrying on and her mother acting like nothing mattered except herself. And the Goddess was listening to it all, watching …

What if She changed her mind? What if She decided that Amelia's family was just too awful and took the Saviour back? Then Amelia would be responsible for keeping the souls of men in bondage, and anything could happen: the Day of Judgement when men were divided into sheep and goats. She frowned. She wasn't quite sure why men had to be made into livestock but she would be glad to be left as a girl on the Final Day.

The baby growled and she hugged her arms around her stomach. 'Don't worry,' she crooned. 'Dear Saviour, I shall deliver you into this world safely. I won't let all these people corrupt you …'

The heat began to mount on her skin. Her fingers and toes itched. The room began to swim. The smell of liver was unbearable. Her head pounded. She smelled blood, warm and metallic, it thudded in her ears, flooded the room. The grubby lino became red, splattered. She felt as though she couldn't breathe, the blood was lapping above her head, choking, drowning. Amelia opened her eyes, tried to see beyond the relentless tide of red, to push it back and away with her hands, but it poured over her, bursting through the kitchen, knocking the pan off the stove and splashing her arms with boiling gravy.

'No!' she screamed. 'Stop! Stop!'

The blood parted. A brilliant light threw it back against the walls. Amelia could see the lino again, made clean and new. Cool fingers touched her skin, caressing her face and arms.

Do not be afraid, child.

The Goddess, more lovely than ever, rose before her, stroked her hair and body with the lightest of touches.

You are seeing the world as it would be without the Saviour. Only Her holy blood can cleanse mankind. She will be born to you at Pentecost and her name will be —

Amelia never heard the Saviour's name. Dolores clattered into the kitchen and yanked her arm nearly out of its socket.

'What are you doing?' she demanded. 'The tea's all over the place and you're lying there like one of Woolworths'.'

Amelia looked up. For some reason she was sprawled on the floor. The lino was covered in liver and gravy and above her, the gas ring burned futilely, heating nothing but the air. The light of the Goddess evaporated along with the blood. The Saviour spun. Amelia burst into tears.

'Oh, you poor kid.' Dolores knelt and cradled Amelia's head in her arms. Her aunt smelled of perfume, cigarettes and incense. 'This house is full of evil, wickedness. You shouldn't have to see it all. That Con and his filthy ways and your brother in league with him. Never mind Edith's delusions. Poor you. I bet you don't know what the world's coming to.' She patted her on the head absent-mindedly and leaned against the cooker. She allowed her hand to rest upon Amelia's stomach.

'You know,' she continued, 'this won't last forever. Your mother will sell the convent, get us all somewhere decent to live. We're all in mourning, me especially, and I don't mean for your Grandma. I was sad when she went, of course I was, but she was a very old lady and to be honest it was a bit of a relief …' She wiped an invisible tear from her eye. 'No. I mourn, stupidly I suppose, for the condition of matrimony. Condition makes it sound like an illness, doesn't it? Perhaps that is just what it is. Ken had me bound to him as strongly as any disease, these last fifteen years …' Her blood red fingernails dug into the fabric of Great Aunt Mabel's fishtail, felt the smooth dome of Amelia's stomach. She pulled away, shaking her head.

'Christ, kid, you're getting puppy fat. The last time I knew a stomach like that was when Ken's brother got into the jacuzzi with me, and he's a ten-pints-a-night man.'

The tears rolled down Amelia's cheeks. She knew that the time had come to tell people the truth, about the Goddess, the baby, about the wonderful events that were beginning to unfold. She prayed to Irena that her news would not be greeted with derision.

Dolores stood up and glanced down into the sink, reeling back when she saw its contents.

'And you've been sick … My God.' She crouched down, allowing her palm to run across Amelia's stomach. She drew in her breath, put her hand under her niece's chin and pulled her face close.

'That's not puppy fat though, is it?' she demanded, slowly pulling up Amelia's overstretched school jumper. 'You're up the spout, preggers, up shit bloody creek without a paddle. Lord above! I must say, I never expected it of you. I didn't even know you'd had a boyfriend.'

'No, I —'

'Listen kid, I've been around the block more times than you've had hot dinners. I think I know when someone's got a bun in the oven.' Dolores gripped the oven door handle and heaved herself up. 'Does your mother know?'

Amelia shook her head, crossed her fingers and sent up a silent plea to Irena.

'We'll have to tell her. This'll put the kibosh on her little trip. God-all-bloody-mighty. She'll go crazy.'

'Please!' Amelia staggered to her feet in desperation, knowing that this might be her one and only chance to convince anyone other than Edith of the Truth. She grabbed her aunt's hand.

'Remember the night Grandma died, the vision, the Goddess I saw, remember? You said you saw the light too and so did Aunt Edith and I know Grandma did … Well Aunt Edith was right; it was a Visitation. She came to give me the

Saviour to bear. Like the Angel Gabriel did with the Virgin Mary. I didn't know, at the time, but I've seen Her since. She appeared to me just now, that's why the liver's on the floor ...' Amelia stopped, exhausted by the torrent of words and the ever present feeling of sickness. She had to make Dolores understand.

She had to get Dolores to stop the Irish trip.

She didn't dare think about what her mother would say once she heard the news.

Dolores stalked over to the bread bin and retrieved a bottle of gin. She unscrewed the cap and took a deep slug, closed her eyes and leaned against the grime-encrusted cupboard doors.

'So this is why Edith's gone off her rocker,' she said, sighing and groping round in Grandma's old checked housecoat, which was straining at the bust. 'Jesus, what a time to run out of cigs.'

Amelia smiled involuntarily. Again the Goddess was at work. Mrs Mulhearn had once said that cigarettes were bad for unborn babies. Amelia was infused with the knowledge that everything would be all right. That was the message the Goddess had come to deliver. She must just keep the Faith.

'But what about Mum?' she demanded. 'What about the trip? I don't want to go. The baby is to be born at Pentecost. There are preparations to make —'

'It's not too late for an abortion, then?'

'You can't abort the Saviour of all Mankind!'

'Father Murphy said there would be a sign from God that I had done the right thing, leaving Ken. He said that God would speak to me in his own way. I only had to be open and receptive ...' Dolores picked at the Gordons' label on the gin bottle. 'Can it be? Surely not. You! For one thing, Mary was born without stain of sin. Were you?'

Amelia shrugged. This was one piece of theology she had not considered. 'Dunno.'

'Well you can't have been. Someone would have noticed by now, those nuns at school ... Edith. If you had never sinned, then we'd all know about it. I don't know. You'd have a halo.'

'I haven't got a halo but Edith has noticed,' Amelia confessed. 'She knows all about it. She believes I've been visited by the Angel Gabriel or someone ...' She began to cry. 'Or the Blessed Virgin. But it's —'

'Right!' Dolores took a final swig of gin, replaced the cap and hurled it back into the bread bin. 'We must speak to Father Murphy, decide what must be done. We can't have you going round believing you're the mother of Christ, especially if it's not true. On the other hand we can't have the whole of Liverpool going on about your morals, if it is.'

Amelia stood up, tried to escape her aunt's desperate grip, but Dolores tugged her back. They collided with Edith as she lurched from the parlour in need of the toilet. Amelia's stomach came up against Edith's sunken bosom as the old woman fell. Edith grabbed at Mabel's fishtail skirt to stop herself ending up on the floor, looked up, and gasped: 'Holy

Mother of God, all the saints and Prince Charles, I have never seen such a thing. A young girl, my own flesh —'

'Quiet, you stupid old woman,' Dolores hissed. 'Amelia doesn't want everyone to know.'

'The Lord speaks in mysterious ways,' Edith said, 'His wonders to —'

'Just shut your mouth.' Dolores slapped Edith across her slack jowls. 'I'm sorry, but I have to do this for your own good. I'm off to see Father Murphy. He'll point us in the right direction.'

Amelia, aware of the trickle of warm pee splashing on Edith's shoes, the stench of alcohol and stale cigarettes, twisted from the grasp of both aunts and flattened herself against the anaglypta.

'Look, I don't want to see Father Murphy or anyone. He wouldn't know what to do, anyway. The Goddess …' She thought quickly. 'The Virgin requests only that you protect me from harm, that you heed my wishes, that you …' She blushed and crossed her fingers, hoping that the Goddess wouldn't mind the white lie too much. After all, it was in her interests that she remain in Liverpool as long as possible. And she closed her eyes, praying fervently, that her mother didn't find out about any of it.

'You mean,' said Edith, stepping back. 'You mean there could be a place for me in the story of the New Saviour?'

Amelia shrugged. 'I suppose so.'

'And me?' Dolores asked. 'Perhaps this is what my life has been leading up to. This point. All that awful stuff with Ken, there is no wonder it turned my stomach and I'm about to file for divorce. It isn't a sin to cast off your husband but the ultimate sacrifice. Jesus was a fisher of men and you, you Amelia are a fisher of women …' She looked a little puzzled after this declaration, and afterwards admitted that the theory behind it was somewhat shaky, but it seemed apt enough at the time.

Edith nodded vehemently. The door to the parlour began to open and Dolores immediately clapped her hand over the old woman's mouth. Marguerite gave the three of them an old-fashioned look before stalking off upstairs.

CHAPTER 13
22ND NOVEMBER 1981

It was to be a long journey. The itinerary was sellotaped to the fridge for all to study. In two days, the Leominster would leave the port of Liverpool for Dublin. Marguerite had already booked a taxi to take herself and Amelia down to the passenger ferry terminal at Victoria dock for eight-thirty on the morning in question. The ferry would take a good eight hours to cross the Irish Sea, and was to be followed by a train journey from Dublin to Cork. Another taxi would take them to the town of Macroom where the Holy Head farm cart was to collect the pilgrims for the arduous trip up into the mountains to the convent. There was not a moment to lose, Edith and Dolores agreed over a shared Rothmans; Amelia had to get out of this ridiculous and potentially dangerous trip.

'You could pretend to be ill?' Dolores suggested. 'Edith and I would cover for you. It'd be a crying shame if the Saviour got associated with some moth-eaten old convent in Ireland when he or she or whoever could do their first miracles at our house. You know what nuns are like, they take all the credit.'

'Yes,' Edith nodded enthusiastically, not noticing the slur on the clergy. 'And it would be succour to the heart of a dying woman to know her own niece is the vessel through which the Lord has chosen to perform his Holy miracles …'

'What dying woman?' Dolores demanded. She was slightly drunk having just polished off the bread bin gin. 'There's no one dying round here. Mum died last ...'

Amelia, huddled in the back room with her aunts, sighed and rocked lightly backwards and forwards in the way she had developed when she was a small child. Then, it had been to comfort herself; now she was comforting the child within her. A grey light leaked through the window. It was raining heavily. The air, inside and out, was scented almost unbearably with rotting leaves and damp earth. Exhaustion threatened to overwhelm her. The effort of keeping her pregnancy away from her mother was increasingly difficult. It was bad enough having to get changed in the bathroom and feeling sick all the time. At least she could avoid her most of the day. Spending a fortnight together could spell disaster.

'We could tell her,' she said, more to herself than to either of her aunts. Perhaps this was what Irena wanted. Perhaps her mother would be a support, a disciple, rather than an enemy.

Dolores shuddered theatrically. 'Don't be stupid! The Truth is quite out of the question, at least before the trip.' She paused for a moment in her ceaseless smoking and pacing, crossing herself before the sticky, nicotine-coated Infant of Prague. 'Our Margie would go spare. She hates religion so much that sometimes I wonder if she's a Roman Catholic at all, or someone Mum, God rest her soul, would have called a Bush Baptist.'

'What's one of those?' Amelia asked, conjuring visions of John in the wilderness, sporting loincloth and beard.

Dolores wafted her smoke in the general direction of the window. 'Oh, you know. One of them breakaway Methodists who think Christianity is all about Socialism. Dad used to force the poor buggers off the pavement and into the gutter on Sunday mornings. Mind, he got himself into trouble for it. He spat and shouted so loudly at the Orangemen during their annual parade through South Liverpool, he got banged up overnight in the local nick to stop him starting a riot. Our Margie once accused him of helping fund the IRA. I never heard what he answered but she was grounded for ages ...' She sighed, crossed herself and straightened her rosary. 'Anyhow, Al Monagle was a republican sympathiser, wasn't he Edith, and Dad thought the world of him. He must be spinning in his grave to hear what Margie thinks of the Church.'

Edith sucked in her cheeks and looked as though she was about to speak. Instead, she caught Amelia's eye and blessed herself.

Whatever excuse they invented to save Amelia from the trip to Ireland, one whiff of a religious vision or a divine messenger would guarantee her seat on the next boat out of Liverpool.

'We'll have to wangle it that you can't take the time off school,' Dolores said with sudden conviction. 'That's the best we have to work on so far. What if your headmistress, Sister-what's-her-face, phoned our Margie and said that Amelia wasn't allowed to go away as she'll miss too much school. Your mum sent you in with a letter, didn't she? Well, what if it

135

didn't go down too well? She could make out that her entire future is in the balance. You have some exams coming up soon, haven't you?'

Amelia shrugged. 'Only end of term ones. Not like I'm doing O-levels yet, or anything.'

Dolores shook her head violently. 'Doesn't matter. Missing school is serious, very serious. We can make Sister Bun-face sound really angry; really pull Marguerite's guilt strings. I can see —'

Edith nodded so vigorously that the loose skin on her neck took a few moments to settle. 'Sister Anne Margaret will back me up,' she said. 'We were old school friends. She was a good friend of Father Monagle as well.'

'I bet she was,' Dolores said, raising her over-plucked eyebrows at Amelia. 'He was a popular man with ladies and small boys.'

The next hour went far more smoothly than Amelia could ever have hoped. Dolores sneaked out to the phone-box on Gethsemane Road. Marguerite, crammed into her new jeans and sparkly off-the-shoulder top, was repacking her suitcase when the telephone went. She teetered downstairs to pick up the receiver, leaving the bedroom awash with underwear and unguents. Her hair, freshly dyed, glowed dull tangerine in the light of the setting sun and her lipstick, today a dark maroon, gave her a vampish air.

'Let's get ...' The strains of Olivia Newton John getting Physical thumped down the stairs. Edith and Amelia hid behind the dining room door. Amelia clutched at the nappy pin she used to keep Mabel's skirt from falling down. The pin jabbed into her palm. She was so anxious, she scarcely felt it pierce her skin.

'Speak up. I can't hear a word you're saying. Sister ...? Really?' Marguerite bellowed into the receiver, as she teased her hair with blood-red fingernails. 'That's too bad. I don't know what poor Amelia will say when she hears this. But ... I suppose her education is more important than anything.'

Amelia and Edith crossed themselves behind the dining room door. Neither noticed the self-inflicted wound on Amelia's hand. Marguerite, however, was alerted to their presence by the loud rattling of teeth and rosary beads.

'Why the hell are you two skulking about like a couple of deaths heads?' she demanded, having plonked down the receiver with a loud sigh. 'And will you put those damned medals and crucifixes down for a minute. What are you trying to exorcise?'

Edith stuffed her St. Christopher down her top. Amelia guiltily held her rosary behind her back. Unfortunately the scapula of St John the Evangelist, a souvenir from Knock in 1936, was more difficult to conceal due to its thick green ribbon. Amelia had pinned it to the front of her school jumper to hide the cigarette burn, but her mother snatched it off as she squeezed past.

'What is this nonsense?' she demanded. 'I forbid you to go giving Amelia any more of this rubbish, Edith. This is the 1980s, not the dark ages. Talking of which, I'd better phone our family order. I'm afraid you won't be coming with me to Ireland.'

Later, Dolores confessed that she'd paid off a couple of teenagers who were hammering on the door of the phone box. She'd had to muffle the receiver with her scarf to minimise the noise. Her Stanley Baxteresque impression of Amelia's headmistress would hardly go down too well with all that swearing in the background. Despite these difficulties, the ruse was a resounding success. Amelia affected an air of tragedy, but took care not to appear too upset in case her mother had a change of heart and decided to ignore the school.

'So sorry, Darling,' Marguerite went on, 'it would have been a lovely holiday for you. The mountains, the boat trip over, but never mind, we'll go another day. Sister Anne Margaret was most insistent, aggressive almost. Mind you, I've got to say, I never knew she had such a gruff voice, almost as though she smokes ... But your education must come first ... Anyway, I'll try and get hold of the nuns at the Holy Head convent to let them know I'll be travelling alone ... I'm surprised, really, they have a phone at all. From what the Mother Superior says, their lives are very frugal.'

Con swung his massive body down the stairs, accompanied by the sound of the toilet flushing too loudly.

'Overflow's blocked again,' he announced. 'Phone the nuns indeed. Wonder any of the poor sods learned to use the dial, stuck up in the mountains with no man to service them.'

'My God, Con, you always have to reduce everything down to sex,' Marguerite shouted. She stalked into the back room and applied an extra layer of lipstick, looking in the mirror over the mantelpiece. The mirror itself was so thick with nicotine, she had to scrub a hole big enough for a reflection of her face with a J cloth. She shuddered at the resulting smear of brownish yellow.

'Sex is all there is in the end,' Con replied, sucking on his Capstan. 'Makes the world go round for those of us who are getting any. And for those who aren't …' he stared pointedly at Edith, 'the world stopped years ago.'

Edith lifted one sagging bosom to a more comfortable position and crossed herself. The last rays of sun hit the faded print of Our Lady of Perpetual Succour, making the prematurely aged Infant Christ gleam.

'You, Con, would never have been rejected from the priesthood if you had kept your surges under control. You wouldn't be stuck in Liverpool now, but in the Holy Father's palaces in Rome.'

Con chose to ignore this, settled down in his favourite chair, scratched his crotch and gazed lustfully at the attractive young woman demonstrating the latest Vauxhall Viva as a potential prize on Sale of the Century.

'According to my last letter, the Holy Head nuns are preparing for my visit with prayer and fasting.' Marguerite giggled. 'I only hope there are some left alive when I actually get there. Some of them sound positively prehistoric!'

'Where's the candle?' sniggered Con. 'Or the soap?'

Marguerite spent the rest of the day packing, trying on clothes and applying make-up in thicker and thicker layers. The new, cloying perfume she had bought at George Henry Lee's department store was squirted generously around the house, making the rest of the family sneeze and Amelia feel nauseous. Her cases were packed and repacked, her tickets for the journey checked and rechecked. Amelia was off the hook.

During the long night before the trip, the Goddess appeared, hovering over the chest of drawers in the room Amelia now shared with her mother. Inside her stomach, the Saviour rumbled with dread. In the bed alongside her, Marguerite snored gently, unaware of the great events unfolding in her own bedroom.

You conduct yourself well, the Goddess decreed. You have gathered disciples around you. The child will be born in this house, where She was conceived and She will be named —

Again, Amelia could not catch the name as Marguerite's alarm clock declared the morning with a thunderous ring.

Chapter 14
9.30am. 25th November

Belle Ville was an old school, over one hundred and forty years old if the stories of The Blessed Marie Duchamp and her acolytes were to be believed. On entering first year, each new girl was furnished with a slim paperback volume entitled Duchamp's Demoiselles, that had originally been published about twenty years earlier. It related, in sickly prose, the history and tenets of the convent order. Black and white photographs of young nuns dashing about on the netball pitch or leaning over a pupil's shoulder, all solicitous smiles and patronising pats on the back, adorned each prayerful chapter.

Amelia's copy was open on the 'Maintaining Friendships with Boys' page. A picture of a demure if old-fashioned-looking former Belle Ville pupil graced the instructions, which, as far as Amelia could make out, were all about sitting on books rather than boy's knees, even at the cinema, and keeping a convenient fence, gate or hedge between yourself and your boyfriend should you indulge in any kissing at the end of the night.

She glanced at the page as she sat down, trying to concentrate on something other than feeling sick. She had already chucked up in the toilets twice that morning, much to the disgust of Sheila Murphy who'd been smoking out of the tiny window. Why on earth were such precautions necessary between girls and boys and why did some of the girls in her class think it was all such a huge joke?

It was Wednesday morning. Marguerite was safely ensconced at the convent of the Holy Head. The rain had finally stopped and the sun bounced off the old pan-tiled roof of the school canteen and into Form 2a where Mrs Gorgon was taking the register, mentioning as she did so, the tally of Order Marks each girl had to attain before she was sent into detention for the week. Mrs Gorgon, a not very good French teacher, adored giving people detentions. It was, as Amelia's friend Martha said pompously, her 'raison d'être'. Mrs Gorgon was a large woman of uncertain age, bad teeth and earlobes stretched by the pendulous earrings she favoured. She was ostentatiously religious, clutching rosary beads and saying her prayers louder than anyone else in school Mass.

Everyone detested her, especially Miss Farrow, the gym teacher, whose jodhpur thighs were a source of constant fascination and dread for her pupils. Mrs Gorgon taunted Miss Farrow whenever the opportunity arose. Once she had complained about her shorts, which were too short, at assembly in front of all the school. And on Speech Day the year before, she'd commented on her tights, which were too red, over the microphone in the Philharmonic. On both occasions, the hapless Miss Farrow had been reduced to tears, gaining her the sympathy and devotion of all Belle Ville girls possessed of a shred of sentiment.

Today, Mrs Gorgon was even more furious than usual. She took her place at the lectern in front of the blackboard, rapped her pen on the desk top and glared around the classroom like a Gestapo officer looking for someone to shoot.

'Adams. Catherine,' she began, opening the register. 'Black. Tracy.'

A rubber shot across the room, bounced off the back of Amelia's head and hit the window. Mrs Gorgon looked up.

'Who did that?'

A note was being passed behind Amelia. She could hear the rustle of paper, the ensuing gasp as it was read by each pupil in turn.

'Amelia?' Mrs Gorgon's gimlet eyes were upon her. Her rusty black gown swung up behind her head like the wings on a giant crow. 'What did you throw?'

Amelia glanced around at her classmates and attempted a careless grin. No one met her eye.

'Nothing, Miss.'

'Stand up.' Mrs Gorgon was on her feet, stalking down from her podium to land at Amelia's side. 'Come along girl, I haven't got all day.'

Amelia rose, embarrassedly conscious of Aunt Mabel's fishtail skirt, most certainly not an item of school uniform, digging into her stomach, her school shirt, bursting at the buttons as it tried to accommodate her newly-expanded breasts.

'I will ask you again.' Mrs Gorgon fixed her with a penetrating glare. 'Did you throw something? And there is no use in lying girl. I saw you.'

The blood pounded in Amelia's head. She closed her eyes. She hated Mrs Gorgon, hated her more than anyone else at that moment. Silently she prayed to the Goddess for assistance. No one spoke or moved. Even the note, whatever it was, had stopped passing between the girls. The classroom stank of rubbers and ink, unwashed hair and sweat and that peculiar, metallic, girl-smell. Mrs Gorgon, in contrast, smelled old, of decay and disappointment. Her breath was stale, her cheeks sagged down below the line of her chin. She didn't speak, but her hand rose, clutching the wooden stick she used to indicate her French holiday destinations.

'Show me your palm, girl,' she demanded. 'Hold out your hand, you lying shrew of a child.'

'But, Miss …' Amelia was shaking but not with fear. 'I didn't throw …'

There was a snigger from the back of the class, a crunch of paper. Amelia reluctantly bared her palm. The stick lifted higher. Her heart throbbed painfully. She felt a swipe of air pass her face as the stick came down, the combined indrawn breath of thirty pupils. Amelia braced herself for the inevitable pain.

'My God.' Mrs Gorgon, when Amelia looked, had turned quite white. Her jowls shook, her eyes were opened wide in terror and awe.

'Miss?'

The teacher crossed herself. Her clawed hands were shaking.

'How long …?' The stick dropped to the floor, clattered against the legs of Amelia's desk. She took Amelia's upturned hand in her own, caressed it tenderly. Amelia looked down. In the centre of her hand, in the triangle between the lifeline and the heart line and the headline, a small gash poured with blood.

'Stigmata!' Mrs Gorgon cried.

'Miss?'

'Your hand, it bears the mark of Christ …'

Amelia shook her head. The nappy pin. A Mexican wave of whispering flowed across the classroom. Mrs Gorgon, seeming to regain some of her former composure, touched the bloody hand, crossed herself. A piece of paper fluttered onto Amelia's desk. Time slowed, became thick, viscous as mud. Amelia tried to focus on her teacher's face, to hear the words she was saying but they seemed to be emanating from far away, far beyond the room. The air was heavy, too dense to breathe. Sweat broke out on her hairline, her upper lip. If she concentrated, she could make out Mrs Gorgon's lips moving, muttering. She saw the teacher stoop to retrieve the note from her desk. A shadow passed over the classroom. The Goddess Irena floated past the map of 'Le Sud' on her way to the window.

A cracking sound brought Amelia back to reality. Rapping her stick sharply upon the desk, Mrs Gorgon said 'Wake up, girl. Is this true?'

Amelia stared at the note. It was torn from an exercise book, the blue ink lines slightly fuzzy as though water had been spilled upon them. The writing, in blue-black Quink, jumped across the page. She screwed up her eyes, willing the Goddess to help her, to whisk her away from the teacher and the classroom, from the life to which she no longer belonged.

'Are you pregnant?'

The class emitted a communal gasp. Amelia glanced down at her expanding breasts and smiled. The floor gave way beneath her. The last thing she remembered was the Goddess's pearly toes hovering inches away from her face and Mrs Gorgon's breath, foul against her cheek.

CHAPTER 15
7.30PM. 25TH NOVEMBER

'Well I think it's hilarious,' Con announced. In the yellow light of the single bulb, his face had taken on a waxy cast. 'Our Amelia up the bloody duff and not one of you prepared to admit that only a man could have got her that way.'

'I'm sorry, love,' Edith gasped at Amelia. 'I didn't mean to tell him. It just came out … You'd left some sick on the toilet seat this morning and he'd already put two and two together.'

Amelia, banished from school, the subject of much tittle tattle, not to say downright bitchery from her so-called mates, couldn't have cared less whether Con knew or not. It was her mother finding out that she dreaded.

'Oh, shut up feeling guilty, Edith,' Dolores said. 'There's more to it than that, anyway.' She was holding an unlit cigarette. Since the revelation of the forthcoming miraculous birth, she had given up smoking the things, just held them, occasionally raising one to her lips and sucking as though her life depended upon it.

'It's not just a normal pregnancy. The girl is some sort of a saint. You should have been here the night Mum died, Con. There was a heavenly light and an odour of sanctimoniousness and the thing is, what with the Pope coming here, to Liverpool on Pentecost Sunday, well I think he should be informed.'

Amelia helped herself to another Viscount biscuit. They were the mint ones, her favourite. Her mother had only been gone two days and already the usual decorum of meals had gone out of the window. Tea tonight had consisted of a Findus crispy pancake, still frozen in the middle, and a bottle of Jameson's Whiskey for any who wanted it. Even Edith had availed herself, though Amelia abstained; the smell of whiskey made her want to puke at the best of times and in her current condition, she suspected that alcohol should be avoided. The Viscounts were the most successful part of the meal. She had eaten three as no one else in the family seemed tempted by the delicious combination of peppermint and shortbread and milk chocolate. In fact, she realised now, since her mother had boarded the boat to Dublin, no one had done anything much except drink and smoke.

Even Julian had abandoned the shed to join in. 'Well I think it's all a load of bollocks,' he said. He was thinner in the face than he'd been when he arrived back from prison and his hair was slick with grease. 'If Our Amelia has been impregnated by the Holy Spirit or whoever the hell you think her paramour is, then the best thing we can do is ignore it all. The last time it happened, poor old Mary was stuck in a stable with an ox and ass. We don't want that happening to Amelia …'

Con slammed his hand on the table in appreciation. 'Very good, Jules, very good. If you'd just leave off chasing the old Golden Dragon, you could be quite bright.'

'I told you, Uncle Con, I'm clean.'

'Yeah, and Amelia's the mother of the New Messiah.'

Surreptitiously, Amelia pulled another Viscount from the plate. They were all so busy arguing that she could have eaten the whole packet by now and no one would have noticed.

'The way I see it,' Con intoned gloomily, 'whether Amelia is preggers by the Holy Ghost or some scally on the estate doesn't make much difference. No one's going to swallow the former and they'll think the latter whether we like it or not. The only two options I can see are, A: she has the baby, bold as brass and we bring it up as part of the family as she's far too young to do the honours herself, B: we put her in a home for unmarried women, she has the baby secretly and we put it up for adoption, C: we get it vacuumed out of her.'

Amelia stopped opening her fourth Viscount to listen. She had no idea what Con was talking about but, as usual, his conversation was inducing in Edith a look of horrified disapproval. Clack, her teeth chomped together involuntarily over a half-smoked fag and fuchsia lipstick oozed slowly up the lines around her mouth.

Amelia thought of her mother in her new jeans, skipping light-heartedly to the taxi which took her to the ferry terminal. It was as though she intended to forget completely about the family, as though she didn't care whether they lived or died in her absence. A sadness settled on Amelia. Although Marguerite got on her nerves, nagging and carrying on, she was her mother, the only one she had. As she gazed around the faces of her family now, she worried that without Marguerite, the family was in danger of tearing itself to bits.

'Your soul will go straight to hell when you die, Con,' Dolores said, forgetting her own suggestion a couple of days earlier. 'Abortion is a mortal sin. It's tantamount to murder. You ask Father Murphy, there's a display about it at the back of the church. Uggh! Some of those poor foetuses!'

'And making some young kid have a child of her own, making her go through a whole pregnancy, get ostracised by her friends, pilloried by the school. Forcing her body to distort so young, that's all right is it? You honestly think that is less sinful than getting shot of the unborn baby?' Without waiting for an answer, Con said 'And it's not too late. Twenty-four weeks you can go up to. From what you said, Edith, that would make her only about eleven, twelve weeks. Not even three months. I know a couple of discreet gynae doctors who owe me a favour or two …'

Dolores sucked on her unlit cigarette; Edith puffed at her lit one. Amelia crunched her fourth Viscount. The Saviour murmured inside her. She understood then what Con was suggesting.

'What about what I think?' she said. 'I mean about the Saviour.'

All faces turned to her.

'You?' Julian sneered. 'What do you know about what's good for you? You're just a kid. Get rid of it, the sooner the better.'

Amelia sighed and willed the Goddess to infuse her with patience. 'What do you mean, "just a kid"?'

'I mean you were stupid enough to get up the spout in the first place. I doubt you'd have brains enough to know what to do with the baby when it arrived.' Julian casually helped himself to one of Con's Capstans and lit it. The room was already smoky as hell, or how Amelia imagined hell to be. The faces of her family were faint beyond the fog. 'Children are hard work you know. You ask Mum.'

'I could ask Paula,' she said. She was planning to visit her niece soon.

Julian blushed furiously. For once he looked almost healthy. 'Fuck off!'

'Don't swear,' Edith said, crossing herself. 'Not in front of the mother of the New ...'

'New what?' Julian demanded. 'This is all lunacy. You know Amelia, sweet little holier-than-thou-Amelia had been robbing Gran for months before she died. You should see the stash she's got up in the cockloft ... And she's —'

Amelia threw her half eaten Viscount at her brother. He ducked and the melted chocolate hit Edith on the shoulder and stuck there, looking like a bizarre epaulette. Julian and Amelia both saw it and started to laugh.

'Gran gave me that money,' Amelia said.

Con snorted. 'Sarah never gave anything away except Mass cards and colds. The woman was tight as a bear's arse.'

'And how would you know how tight a bear's arse is, Con?' Dolores said. 'Been drinking with Ken again?'

'Ha bloody ha.' Con poured himself another generous whiskey. 'Sarah was mean, that's all. Whatever that money Julian's talking about is, then I doubt it came from Sarah.'

Amelia's attention wandered. Yet another row was in full flow. She remembered the letter in her school bag, written by the headmistress, Sister Anne Margaret in lieu of a phonecall. It had been thrust in her face as she stood to attention beside Mrs Gorgon. Her school bag was on the floor at her feet; as everyone bickered, she slid the crisp manilla envelope from between the pages of Lord of the Flies and began to ease it open. She placed the letter onto her knee, carefully unfolded it and began to read.

Dear Mrs O'Dowd,

I write to inform you of a very serious incident regarding your daughter Amelia. Today, in Amelia's locker, several items, recently reported stolen by other pupils, were discovered, as well as a packet of cigarettes, a lighter (forbidden at school), a bottle of consecrated altar wine and three blackboard dusters. When Amelia was questioned she insisted that the thefts had been perpetrated by her imaginary friend (or convenient alibi) the Goddess Irena. This is not, as I am sure you will remember, the first incident of this nature in which Amelia has been involved.

Of more concern to us here at Belle Ville, however, is your daughter's claim that she is several weeks pregnant. This too, she blames upon her 'Goddess', even asserting that the child she carries is the 'Saviour', a claim which is not only untrue, but blasphemous.

I'm sure you will appreciate that your daughter's behaviour puts us in a very difficult position. As a Catholic school upholding the sanctity of marriage and the chastity of the body, we cannot have unmarried mothers attending lessons in our classes, nor can we tolerate lying, theft and blasphemy from any of our pupils. Until such time as Amelia's pregnancy is confirmed, the baby and her behaviour repented, or the pregnancy is refuted, I must suspend her from school. If you wish to call in and discuss this matter, then I will be happy to speak to you.

God rest the soul of your dear departed mother,

Sister Anne Margaret.

It had been Sheila Murphy's fault. She'd been in the toilets when Amelia chucked her guts up that morning. She must have been watching and realised what was going on, hence the note. Sheila already had a grudge to bear — her tennis racquet had been one of the missing ones until it was found in Amelia's locker.

And when Sister Anne and Goggles Gorgon ganged up on Amelia demanding to know if the note was true, what was she supposed to do; lie about the Saviour of All Mankind?

Amelia shuddered. Suspended from school. Her mother would have a blue fit if she found out. She crumpled up the paper and vowed to offer it to the Goddess later. She would know that Amelia had never been blasphemous in her life and that the accusations of theft were completely unjustified. The Goddess had furnished her with the things found in her locker, the Goddess and no one else. Why the tennis racquets, though? She pondered this for a moment. What possible use would the Goddess have for all those racquets, to say nothing of the dusters and wine and cigarettes she had found recently. Trust in Her, she admonished herself. She has a higher purpose ...

The scene in the headmistress's office had been grim. Sister Anne Margaret was weeping, very upset about it all, though it was difficult for Goggles Gorgon to suppress her grin of triumph. Amelia's suspension was a cut above the usual run of order marks and detentions. It was only a shame that no one had been at home when she had phoned to inform the O'Dowd family of their youngest member's misdemeanours. A suspension was probably the pinnacle of her career.

She blushed, remembering her final walk through the school gates. Although she spent the afternoon in the headmistress's office and hadn't spoken to another soul, her suspension and the reasons for it had travelled like wildfire. Her classmates were waiting for her at the gates, some jeering, some asking questions, all curious as to the father of her unborn child. No one had offered any support, not even those she had once considered friends: Martha Hallmark, Catherine Mulhearn and Mary Mullen. They only stared at her stomach in mute fascination.

'I hate you all,' Amelia shouted as she ran the gauntlet of their questions. 'Leave me alone!' She sprinted to the bus stop and managed to board the early bus before anyone else caught up.

There may be, she considered, some benefits to being suspended from school. For a start, she had never liked the place. Too many rules and regulations, too much time taken up in boring lessons she knew she would never make use of in later life. Did the Mother of the New Saviour really need to read Jane Austin, know how many wives Henry the Eighth beheaded, the manner in which sheep farmers in Australia go about their daily routine? She doubted it. What she needed to do now was to prepare for her new role by spending time in quiet contemplation. She thought of the attic, wished she could sneak up there for a while, but since her grandmother's death, the house always seemed so full of people. Con had taken up residence at the dining room table while Dolores lurked around the place, wearing her mantilla and jet rosary looking more like a young version of Edith every day. The only time she left the house was to visit Father Murphy who was taking what Con described as an 'unnatural' interest in her marital troubles.

And there was the problem of Julian, sneaking about watching her every move, wanting money for his dubious practices. She told him quite forcefully that there was no more, that she needed the cash for her baby, but she could sense his desperation mounting daily. Sweat beaded his upper lip, his black-lined eyes were bloodshot and when he held out his hand it shook. His moods swung from utter depression and lethargy to a happy, almost hysterical energy. At other times, he would be spiteful and aggressive. He could change in seconds.

'Sis,' he said, tapping the table with his fingers like a maniac, his foot beneath the table repeatedly bashing on Amelia's chair. 'Sis is having you all on. Just because she's only a kid doesn't mean she hasn't got the bits that work …'

'We are born as sexual beings,' said Con, licking his lips. 'Though I'm still in shock. I never thought Amelia or her mother had a sexual appetite. I could have sorted 'em out if I'd known.'

'What were you going to do, Con, put bromide in their tea? Is that what you do to all your patients?' asked Dolores.

'You've a nasty mind, Dolores,' Con said. 'You might be done up like some vestry door nudger, hanging around that priest — who, I'd bet money, is a bloody homo — but we all know what your real calling is.'

'Jesus, Mary, Joseph,' Edith clacked. 'I have never heard such words, and in front of Amelia too. You'll be sent to Hell, the pair of you.'

'I bet it's a damned sight more interesting than this place,' Con retorted. 'And fairer. I doubt if Old Nick'd put up with a lot of hysterical women.'

Julian guffawed. His eyes were wild and dancing, his lips dry. Amelia was afraid for him and wondered if lack of money had made him ill. Her mother often said that money worries had ruined her health. Maybe it was doing the same to Julian.

'Shut up, the lot of you,' Julian said when he finished laughing. 'Let's decide what's to be done. Our Amelia is up the duff and it needs sorting. Sis.' He grabbed her by the shoulder. His fingers dug in, hurting her. 'You're going to have to prove this Mother of God story. No one believes it.'

Amelia closed her eyes. Her family was exhausting. When she opened them, the Goddess was standing behind Julian, showering him in Her heavenly light and shaking her head in the manner of a disappointed parent.

'Goddess ...' Amelia tried to speak but the words would not come out. 'Please ... Goddess ...' She could feel her mouth opening and closing like a goldfish. She gripped the table, the texture of the cloth was rough against her fingers, she repeatedly squeezed at it, ran her hand over the embroidery her grandmother had completed in 1941 in the Anderson shelter that had been in the back garden. There was a smell coming from Julian, a sweet, almost exotic aroma. She drank it in. The Goddess placed her hands on Julian's shoulders. He had closed his eyes. His face was paler than ever.

'Can't you feel it?' Amelia mouthed. 'Or see Her wondrous light? Julian?'

Julian's breath sounded louder, ratcheting through his lungs like air through an old bellows. His head lolled back, his eyes rolled. His skin was pale and glistened with sweat.

'Jesus!' Con was on his feet immediately. 'Something will have to be done about this lad. What the hell is he on?' He moved around the edge of the table until he was standing behind Julian. The Goddess's divine form was half in, half out of Con's stout body. Amelia screamed.

'Quiet,' Dolores said, staring transfixed at Julian. 'What's wrong with him? Is he ill, Con?'

Unaware of the Goddess's uncomfortable proximity, Con tore at Julian's clothes, pulled the neck of his tee shirt, undid the button on his already baggy jeans.

'Open the window, Amelia,' he ordered in such a voice that she wouldn't have dared disobey. 'And, Dee. Get your arse in the kitchen and fetch a glass of water.'

Dolores staggered to her feet, tossed her head. 'You've a damned cheek,' she said before stalking out.

Amelia opened the window and turned to stare back at her brother. Con had him prone on the carpet. He looked like a dead saint, or Jesus, having just been removed from the cross. Her heart beat louder. This was the work of the Goddess.

'You'll have to help me,' Con said. 'Amelia, hold his head. I think his heart's stopped.'

'His heart?' Surely the Goddess wouldn't be so cruel as to cut down her brother in the prime of his life.

'Yup. Heroin. Bloody shitty little idiot. They're all at it. The disaffected youth of our country. I blame Harold Wilson. Look what he did to the docks. Your grandfather must be turning in his grave.'

Although Amelia barely understood what Con was going on about, it was flattering to be called a heroine, when he was usually so rude to her, especially as her help was being sought to save her brother's life.

'Thanks,' she said.

'Get his head. If he throws up, turn his neck to the side. You'll have to be on the ball or he could choke.'

'What's the matter with him?' demanded Dolores, returning to the room with a glass of water and a bottle of Jameson's.

'He'll be dead meat if we don't move it,' Con said. He took the water from Dolores and threw it over Julian's head. Julian groaned. His face creased up for a moment, he let out a huge explosion of breath and his body sagged.

'Shit!' Con pressed two fingers to Julian's neck, then pushed Amelia out of the way and set about pumping his nephew's chest and blowing into his mouth.

'Jesus, Mary, Joseph!' Edith wrung her hands helplessly. 'He's dead! Julian's dead!'

Amelia's mouth went dry. Her hands sweated gently under Julian's thick head of hair. She couldn't imagine her brother dead. He was too young. She silently offered a prayer. Our Irena, who art in this room, hallowed be thy —

Julian let out a gasp, followed by a choking, gagging noise. His body shuddered, convulsed. Amelia could feel the life flowing back into his limbs.

'Here we go, lad,' Con said. 'You're up and running again.'

Julian sat up, almost knocking Amelia over. With the righteously ceremonial air of one who has just cheated death, he puked over the remaining Viscounts.

PART TWO
THE LUMINOUS MYSTERIES

CHAPTER 16
30TH NOVEMBER 1981

Edith used a red biro to cross off the day on the kitchen calendar. 'Twenty-six weeks before Pope John Paul II arrives at Speke Airport,' she sombrely announced over breakfast. 'Say an Our Father or two for his safe passage.'

An hour later, Sister Anne Margaret hobbled down the path to Number Eighteen Calvary Crescent. Amelia happened to be looking out of her bedroom window at the time, wondering what she was supposed to be doing now she was banned from school. The air was thick with the smell of rotting leaves. It being pension day at the post office, Mr and Mrs Lawless were strolling along the pavement, arm in arm, his enormous rump sashaying to some internal rhythm. The Labrador puppy over the road was scampering under the gate of Number Twenty-Seven, the home of the Unmarried Mother, whose child was said to be retarded. Vera and Wally Baptiste were loading oranges into their bubble car. The sky was misty and full of promise.

Except for Sister Anne Margaret.

Amelia closed her eyes. The letter was one thing, easily hidden, destroyed even. The headmistress in person was quite another. So far no one in the family had noticed that Amelia had not trundled up to the bus stop as usual, or if they had, they didn't think it important enough to mention. But once the news of her suspension was out, she knew that her new status as mother of the New Saviour could be ruined by stupid tales of petty theft and smoking. She would never convince Edith that her word was truer than a nun's. She put her hands together, squeezed her eyes tight shut. The Goddess would tell her what to do.

She did.

Sister Anne Margaret slowed her pace. She looked up at the window, directly at Amelia. Amelia ducked down, crawled across the floor to the landing. She eased the ladders from the cockloft, for once oblivious to their creaks and coughs. This was an emergency. Aunt Mabel's mourning box was just inside the trapdoor, frothing over with black lace and navy blue serge. Amelia climbed the ladders, reached inside the box and pulled.

The moment she heard Sister Anne Margaret lift the knocker, Amelia flung open the front door and greeted the elderly nun as a fellow sister of the cloth.

'Can I help you?' Amelia, sweating in blue wool, demanded.

Sister Anne Margaret frowned. 'Have I come to the right house? I'm looking for the parents of Amelia O'Dowd ... She is one of my pupils ... At Belle Ville.'

Amelia nodded behind Aunt Mabel's pebble lenses. 'Entre,' she said in what she hoped was a convincing French accent. Mabel had joined a Marseilles order of nuns for a few months after her fiancé died. Her devotion lasted as long as it took the gardener to compromise her reputation, though she did manage to take a vow of chastity beforehand. Her habit was hardly worn and, as it was from her younger and slimmer days, fitted Amelia as though it had been made for her.

Sister Anne Margaret squinted into the house and waved her arm vaguely in front of her. Without her glasses she was unable to see beyond her own nose and almost missed her footing as she barged past Amelia into the hall. Fortunately Edith and Dolores were at church, Con was at his consulting rooms and Julian was in the shed, still recovering from his trauma the previous night. For once Amelia had the house almost to herself.

'Vud you be liking some tea?' she asked, pointing to the settee in the parlour. 'Please sit and I vill bring some.'

Sister Anne Margaret took a seat and smiled myopically somewhere in the direction of Amelia's right ear.

'I didn't realise that the Little Sisters of Verité were still going,' she said. 'And I didn't know that Amelia O'Dowd had connections … My Aunt, you know, was in your order, originally, though she crossed to the Carmelites in 1919. The order was sadly depleted by the Spanish flu epidemic … She only died a few years ago. Perhaps you knew her? Sister Gregory. She lived at your convent in Marseilles for many years.'

Amelia shook her head.

'Our order is enclosed,' she explained, desperately trying to remember the RE lesson Sister Gabrielle at school had given about the Little Sisters of the Poor. 'I never vreally got to know any other of ze nuns.' She sniffed as her accent slid across Europe.

Sister Anne Margaret looked puzzled for a moment, then pulled up one of the dining room chairs. She placed her briefcase on the table between them and frowned. Amelia shuddered. This looked serious.

'Tea?' she asked.

The nun nodded. 'That would be lovely though, Sister, I am afraid that my call is not a social one.'

Amelia hurried into the kitchen, almost tripping on Edith's fluffy slippers, left in the middle of the lino. She made the tea, filling the cup only half way and topping it up with Con's diabolical brew. Most who ventured through the front door of eighteen Calvary Crescent ended up on the poteen at some point. Her headmistress's introduction to it would be sooner rather than later. She slung a few rich tea biscuits, age and origin unknown, onto a plate and took them through to the dining room.

'I'm afraid that Amelia and her mother are out of the country at the moment,' she said, slopping the tea into its saucer as she handed it to Sister Anne. 'They've inherited a convent, their own order. Amelia may join. She has the Vocation, you know.'

This last was a desperate bid to get the nun on her side. They were always going on at school about how nuns were an endangered species these days, how the whole idea of sisterhood would die out if some of today's schoolgirls didn't take the veil. A few weeks ago, an advert had appeared on the notice-board outside the gym, a soft focus picture of a couple of nuns in an arbour. Why not be a nun? it demanded. Someone had crossed out 'nun' and graffitied 'astronaut' in Tippex. The poster was quickly removed and replaced with a picture of Pope Jean Paul II. Scribbling on him would be tantamount to treason.

'Is that so?' Sister Anne took a swig of tea and an immediate flush coloured her cheeks. 'Well I must say, Sister …?'

'Sister … Scholastica. Call me Scolly.' This was the name of Amelia's favourite saint, though she immediately worried that it didn't sound French enough.

'Scholastica, lovely.' Sister Anne took another gulp. 'Most unusual. And you are related to her in some way …?'

'Oh, je suis Amelia's long lost aunt.' Amelia sat down opposite her teacher, glad of the cushion used by Edith to protect bony hindquarters, to give herself height. Through the thick glasses, her teacher looked enormous.

'Well, I suppose I must talk to you, though under normal circumstances, I would speak to the mother.' Sister Anne gulped again, hiccupped. 'Or Edith, dear Edith. Such a shame she could never combat her natural drives. Between you and me, there was quite a scandal when she took up with Father M.'

'Edith's not here. Fire away.' Amelia put a rich tea to her lips. Too late she noticed the white fur on its underside but didn't want to draw attention to it. A long lost nun aunt was hardly likely to be given mouldy biscuits, even by Aunt Edith.

Sister Anne Margaret opened her briefcase and extracted some papers. They looked terribly official.

'Amelia, as you know, has attended Belle Ville for over a year and we have never had a problem with her before. In fact, as pupils go, she was probably as near to ideal as you could get. No trouble at all, though she did let herself down in the exams last year.'

Amelia flushed up. She had no idea how well thought of she was. She sensed, however, the 'but' that was on its way.

'But recently, her behaviour has become increasingly erratic. Erratic to a point of criminality. In fact …' The nun sighed and dropped her teacup with a crash back down on the saucer. 'I am afraid that she has developed a distinctly unpleasant streak.'

She pointed to one of the pieces of paper, a form of some sort, which had been scrawled upon in navy blue ink.

Amelia recognised the handwriting immediately.

'Mrs Gorgon never liked Amelia,' she said. 'Had it in for her from Day One. All that going on about order marks and things. Awful.'

Sister Anne Margaret looked up quickly, shook her head and drained her cup.

'You are close, you and Amelia?' she asked, smiling. 'It must be a comfort for her to have you to talk to. I understand her parents are … Always a difficult scenario. Children need both mother and father, but I'm afraid in this day and age when —'

'Yes, Amelia's father died many years ago. It was tragic. Such a handsome man.'

'I was under the impression —' Sister Anne consulted her notes again, picked them up and studied them until they were only inches away from her nose. Amelia almost offered her a loan of the glasses which were beginning to give her a headache.

'Well, never mind, the past is past. My concern is the child herself. You must be aware of her current predicament?'

Amelia nodded half-heartedly.

'We sisters of Belle Ville got our heads together about it.' She tilted her cup, saw there was no more tea, sighed and pulled a letter from her sheaf of papers. 'We are not entirely lacking in compassion. For all we know she could have been raped, anything. It isn't fair to blame Amelia. She is too young to understand what is going on. So …' Sister Anne crossed herself and offered the paper to Amelia. 'We thought that a stay in the Convent of the Immaculate Infant might be the answer.'

She handed a small pamphlet to Amelia. The cover bore an illustration of a young boy. His hands and feet were pouring with blood and his head bore the marks of Jesus' crown of thorns. Above the picture were the words, 'Immaculate Infant Home for Unmarried Mothers', alongside a blurred black and white photo of a young girl who looked as though she was about to burst into tears. Beneath this was an address somewhere near Widnes.

'Woolly-back land,' Amelia said, opening the pamphlet. 'You want me … I mean her to go there?'

The badly-reproduced photographs inside showed thin teenaged girls with scraped-back hair and scrubbed faces. They all held very young babies and were surrounded by grimly smiling nuns. The text mentioned adoption and the rights of the unborn child, the protection of young mothers and the enormous debt they owed to society.

'Woolly …?' The nun looked confused for a moment then took the pamphlet gently from Amelia's hands. 'You are probably unfamiliar with the area, having lived abroad for so long. The place is Widnes, near the Ward Blenkinsop Factory. There is nothing woolly about it.'

Amelia rose. The room was growing hotter. A cold snap was forecast and she wished it would hurry up and start. She breathed deeply. She was doing okay. Sister Anne Margaret had no idea. As far as she was concerned, Amelia was an elderly sister, a woman who had devoted her life to Jesus while the girl in question was her long lost niece. She beamed at the nun.

'I'm afraid we've already made arrangements,' she said. 'Amelia is staying at the Convent of the Holy Head in Ireland. The nuns there will take care of her. She will have the baby. It will be the Saviour of all Mankind.'

'Really?' Sister Anne blinked owlishly through the wire-rimmed specs she had eventually extracted from the folds of

her habit. 'The saviour of all mankind. But surely that was ...'
She looked vague as she struggled to recall the name of Jesus.
'I thought that had already been. I mean Amelia is a lovely girl
but ...' She rose with arthritic dignity. She was over six inches
taller than Amelia. 'Amelia O'Dowd has been stealing. Father
Andrew's altar wine has gone missing and his cigarettes;
several tennis racquets, a Parker pen and more. All were found
in her locker. This is a serious offence. But of course, if she is
with the Sisters of the Holy Head, then she will be safe.
Maybe you had better —'

At that moment a terrible screech split the still suburban
street. An unearthly squealing began; the sound of a creature
neither feathered nor furred.

'Lord God Almighty, what can it be?' Sister Anne Margaret
said, rushing over to the window. Amelia's heart thudded. Just
like when her grandmother died, she sensed a soul wanting to
rise up to heaven, the Goddess nearby waiting to guide the
way. She glanced at Sister Anne Margaret, threw down the
ridiculous glasses and ran out of the house.

The street was empty, save for Dolores tottering round the
corner, and Mr Lawless's car, parked untidily half up on the
pavement. And Mr Lawless himself, who was kneeling in the
road, looking under the car. There was a dent in the right
wing.

'What happened?' Amelia demanded, forgetting her habit
and the fact that she was supposed to be French. 'I heard a car
—'

Mr Lawless's head emerged tortoise-like from beneath the car. Tears were trickling down his flushed cheeks.

I've killed him,' he said, sobbing. 'I've killed him and there was nothing I could do to stop it. Look, there.' He pointed under the tyre and Amelia saw the crushed wheel of a pushchair. She remembered seeing the Unmarried Mother walking down the road, pushing her son earlier that morning. Marguerite reckoned that she was cruel to the child. There were always bruises on his arms. Amelia wondered if she had pushed him under the Ford Zephyr as it raced down the crescent. She prepared herself for the worst.

'You'll have to move the car, Mr Lawless,' she said quietly. 'We'll never get him out otherwise.'

'I can't bear to,' the old man sobbed. 'I have done a terrible thing.'

Sister Anne Margaret bustled out of the house at this point. Her face was the colour of pink blancmange. 'Sister Scholastica, I have been waiting. You ran out. I really believe that Amelia is far more important than ...'

'There has been a terrible accident,' Amelia announced in her own voice. 'A child has been murdered.'

'Murder!' moaned Mr Lawless. He rolled over onto his side and lay helplessly on the edge of the pavement, weeping into the gutter.

'An accident?' Sister Anne peered under the car. A yelp sounded nearby, some whining. The sun shone weakly in a powder-blue sky, giving a temperate warmth to the winter morning. The scent of death and decay was abroad. Amelia felt sick again.

'The little boy over the road. His mother has always wanted to kill him,' she began, convinced of foul play.

Mr Lawless sobbed uncontrollably.

'Then we must move the car, phone the police,' Sister Anne Margaret said, though her voice was trembling.

There was no sign of the boy except his broken pushchair squashed under the front wheel.

'And this poor man must be taken indoors. He has had an awful shock. Here.' From the folds of her habit, she drew out a bottle of some noxious smelling liquid. She pulled out the cork and waved it under Mr Lawless's nose. He coughed, spluttered, and spat on the ground.

'Death and destruction,' he muttered darkly. 'This is what my life has come to.'

Amelia looked towards the house of the Unmarried Mother. The curtains were twitching. She thought about the terrible crime that had been committed. Should she, in her position as Mother of the Saviour of the World, forgive the poor woman? Should she condemn her to everlasting torment? The front door opened. A thin clawed hand crept around the edge.

Sister Anne Margaret saw it and dashed up the path, shouting, 'Have you a telephone? The police, an ambulance must be called.'

The Unmarried Mother opened the door fully. She was dressed in a pink housecoat; her blonde hair had been dragged into curlers.

'Ya wha?' Her mouth, holding a cigarette butt, went slack.

The nun pointed to Mr Lawless on the pavement, the carnage beneath the car. In slow motion, the woman walked down the path, her high-heeled fluffy slippers trip-trapping as she went. She tossed her head and a tendril of yellow escaped one of the rollers.

'What the bleedin' hell's goin' on, here?' she demanded. She spotted her child's pushchair, the crumpled wheels, the ripped seat. She opened her mouth. The cigarette fell but no sound. The nun, realising who she was, rushed to her aid and as the Unmarried Mother fell backwards in a dead faint, the headmistress of Belle Ville was there to catch her.

Amelia became aware of a whimpering, squawking noise beneath the car. Hardly daring to look, she bent down. A hot little hand grabbed her own and a voice: 'Mama, Mama.' Amelia was dizzy with hope.

She opened her eyes. Mr Lawless was clutching at her shoulder. The boy, the Retarded Son of the Unmarried Mother, was crawling out from beneath the fender of the Ford Zephyr without a scratch on him.

'I've never seen anything like it,' whispered Mr Lawless, absent-mindedly scratching his bum. 'The boy was dead. I could have sworn it on the Bible and now here he is, large as life and twice as ugly.'

The boy hugged Amelia who had never actually seen him at close quarters. He was drooling a little and one eye looked askance, but apart from that he seemed a normal toddler.

'Well, I don't know,' Amelia began. 'Perhaps he just —'

'A miracle!' Dolores was at her side, her spiritual batteries recharged by her three hour talk with Father Murphy. 'You say the boy has been brought back from the dead?'

Mr Lawless, still stunned, nodded.

'Then the Holy Father must be informed. This girl is to be known throughout the world.' Dolores dropped to her knees. Amelia, hot and itchy in the ancient habit, scratched her head and the veil fell off.

'Amelia?' Sister Anne Margaret demanded. 'Was it you all the time?'

'She has just performed a miracle,' Dolores breathed. 'All hail the power of the unborn saviour.'

Looking confused and not altogether too pleased at this announcement, Sister Anne Margaret looked at her watch, took the smelling salts from her habit and wafted them under her own nose.

CHAPTER 17

It was wonderful that young Dominic had risen from the dead beneath Mr Lawless's gleaming Ford and toddled off to receive more bruises from his mother. Amelia wept with gratitude, sank to her knees on the gritty tarmac and praised the Goddess to the heavens.

But there had been another casualty in the accident, one whose humble canine status had caused him to be overlooked in the fuss. Not for long. Once Dominic's body was pronounced intact, without a mark to indicate how close death had been, the source of the blood pooling in the gutter was located. Portly, the golden Labrador puppy from Number Twenty-One was still trapped beneath Mr Lawless's careless tyres. A delicate operation was mounted. Mr Lawless, overcome by fresh weeping, was required to move his Zephyr. The Baptistes, the dog's owners, were sent for. The worst was feared.

A slightly dishevelled Sister Anne, assumed authority with the barked, 'Silence!' she used in Belle Ville assembly each morning. A scraggy heap of pulsating fur was delivered into the wintry sunlight by her own hand. Mrs Baptiste gently eased him onto a makeshift stretcher, made from the travel rug Mrs Lawless wore over her legs on long journeys. The small crowd sighed collectively. He was such a different specimen from the bouncy little dog Amelia and other unoccupied, unemployed or nosey neighbours had watched pee against every lamp-post each morning.

As Amelia solemnly followed Portly's expiring form into Number Eighteen, panic rose in her breast. Why was the dog being taken to her house? Was she supposed to take charge, save him, perform another miracle? She tried to recall other animals being pulled from the brink of certain death by religious devotion. St Francis of Assisi, patron saint of all animals, spoke to the birds and even the odd wolf, but pet dogs? But she knew, looking at Portly's distraught owners that she had to try. If she, Amelia O'Dowd, the instrument of the Goddess, really was responsible for preserving a little boy's life, then the dog felled in the same horrific accident must be given the same chance.

'There is,' wheezed Sister Anne, helping plonk the unconscious and unexpectedly heavy dog onto the dining room carpet, 'just a possibility that Dominic was never dead at all. Maybe he was alive and kicking as he is now. It was Portly who got caught under the wheels ...'

'Nonsense,' shrieked Dolores. 'I saw the whole thing. It was a miracle.' She nudged Portly with her toe. 'Put a newspaper under him. Our Marg will go ballistic if she comes home and finds the place awash with dog's blood.'

'True.' The colour was returning to Mr Lawless's pallid cheeks. The whiff of sal volatile, provided by Amelia's headmistress had done him the world of good. 'The boy was dead as a dodo. I think the puppy's life was swapped for his ...'

Amelia thought about this but decided it couldn't be the case. The poor pup had as much a right to survive Mr

Lawless's hazardous driving as anyone else. Surely the Goddess wouldn't be so cruel to an innocent animal.

'You must save him,' insisted Vera Baptiste through a soggy paper hanky. 'You saved the boy, now …' Another fit of weeping overtook her and she retired into her husband's arms.

Amelia closed her eyes. There was a chance, she thought, that Irena was somewhere near, that maybe She could help her. After all, it was only a small extra miracle she was asking for, not like stopping some worldwide disaster or anything. But no matter how hard she tried to summon her mysterious powers, the pup remained resolutely at death's door. Amelia knelt beside the dog, placed her hand upon its fragile skull and felt its hold on life gently fluttering from her grasp.

'What the hell and buggery is going on here?' Con, returning from work for a midday snack and nap, broke the awed silence. He threw his briefcase to the floor and unscrewed the lid of the poteen bottle which had been left on the table. 'And who's been at the booze?'

Sister Anne Margaret blushed. 'It has been quite a traumatic morning,' she whispered. 'Your granddaughter, or niece, or, should I say, Sister Scholastica …?' she directed her narrow-eyed gaze at Amelia. 'Well, anyway, Amelia has apparently been performing miracles. Please be quiet and you might see another.'

'Poppycock and bollocks!' Con announced. He was in a good mood. 'I've spent my day peering into the minds of three deluded women, heard things you wouldn't come up

175

with in your wildest imaginings. I'm not about to hear our Amelia taken for some sort of —'

'Amelia has brought a boy back to life,' Dolores said, sounding miffed. 'You should have come back earlier. You've missed all the fun.'

'And what the hell is that dog doing on my parlour floor?'

'It's not your floor, Con,' Dolores reminded.

'The dog?'

Vera and Wally Baptiste eased from behind the dining room door where they had been trapped since Con's exuberant arrival. They were both crying. Courtesy of the Jaffa marketing department, she was sporting her Nell Gwynn uniform, all heaving bosom over the frilled neckline. Wally wore the garb of a medieval peasant. Outside, their bubble car was bursting with oranges.

'We only took our eyes off Portly for a second,' she explained, dabbing at her eyes. 'And what with the miracle Amelia worked on the boy, who is, after all backward, when there's nothing wrong with the dog, then …' Mrs Baptiste resplendent with her plump if rather veiny bosoms, realised she had gone too far. She gazed upon the dying puppy and gave way to a fresh wave of tears.

Amelia looked around at the adults. Edith, teeth protruding, had returned. She was standing near the picture of Our Lady of Perpetual Succour, muttering to herself. Con was sitting on a dining room chair, his back resolutely to the puppy, swigging poteen out of the bottle. The Baptistes were caressing the bloody fur of their dog while Dolores spun around the room, her black mantilla only half covering her head. It was all very well, some of them thinking she, Amelia, had brought the boy back to life. And of course they were keen for her to show off her resurrection technique again, but she knew she had to conserve her strength for the months ahead. None of the adults, except perhaps poor Edith who was too old to help, realised the magnitude of what would occur very soon. She closed her eyes, knew the spirit of the holy child within. Never had she felt so alone and never had she needed solitude so badly. She rose, and ignoring Mrs Baptiste's entreaties to save her 'poor baby doggy', wandered into the kitchen.

The sun blazed through the yellowed nets. The kettle whistled on the hob. In the doorway of the doghouse, Julian's ragged frame was silhouetted by sunlight. He was singing a song under his breath that made her tremble. 'I'm gonna fuckin' kill myself, I'm gonna fuckin' kill you too ...'

She hadn't seen him since his near death experience; she hadn't wanted to. Most days she wished he had never returned. Julian had been her brother, but it seemed so long ago. She remembered fragments of the past, a time when they were together, fighting or playing or just reading. It had been Julian who taught her to read her first book, Mr Quiet, whose life in Loudland was so intolerable. She smiled. With the row emanating from the parlour, the whining of the pup, she understood his despair. It had been Julian who first taught her to ride a two-wheeler, a skill she had never quite mastered, Julian who sat with her and read Twinkle stories when she had measles, Julian who took her to the swimming baths in Woolton Village, held her as she thrashed about in the water. The Julian she remembered was so different to the secretive, resentful, desperate person he was today.

'What do you want?' he demanded. 'Stop staring like I was some kind of ghost. What's up with you?'

'Nothing.' Amelia switched the gas off under the whistling kettle. That was one noise at least, from which she was spared. 'How are you today?'

'Fucking shit.'

Amelia swallowed, tried to ignore the foul words. 'You were so ill, I thought you were dying.'

'I need some more money, that's all.'

'Why?'

Julian ignored her question and moved into the kitchen. He was very pale. His clothes were spattered with sick and his black hair was limp and greasy, with pale brown roots showing near his scalp.

'You stink,' Amelia said.

'So?'

'Maybe you've got cancer.' There was a girl at school, an older girl who had the tiniest feet Amelia had ever seen, so small that she looked about to topple over. She had smelled of fried onions. Amelia remembered standing next to her once during assembly, wondering if she had bubble and squeak every night. Her name had been Elizabeth Harris. Aged sixteen, she got some kind of bone cancer and died. The whole school was invited by Sister Anne Margaret to mourn, but as they stood listening to the eulogies of her classmates, Amelia could only remember the fried onions and pray they had bubble and squeak in heaven.

'Ta very much. Cancer, stupid cow. Why the hell would you think I had cancer?'

Julian advanced into the room looking wild and ill. Every sinew of his body seemed to quiver with unspent energy.

'That money,' he said. 'The money from the attic. I need it, Sis, desperado. It could save me life.'

Sister Anne Margaret stumbled into the room. She seemed in almost as poor a condition as Julian. Her glasses were crooked and her veil was all astray, exposing tufty clumps of grey hair. Amelia stared, fascinated. She had never seen a nun without her headdress and had thought they were completely bald. Confronted with those unwieldy lumps of hair, she decided that taking the veil wasn't for her after all.

'Is it true what they're saying about you, Amelia?' Sister Anne Margaret demanded, smothering a little giggle. 'Is it true that you had a Visitation?'

Amelia nodded. Now was the time. Her Good News would be known by all. 'I am to be the Mother of the New Saviour,' she said, sticking out her stomach. 'That's probably why I can bring people back from the dead.'

'This ...' the nun giggled, her plump face ran with rivulets of sweat, 'is a very serious claim. It will ...' she doubled up, burst into a torrent of laughter. The poor woman looked quite mad. '... it will have to be investigated. We need to get word to ...' It was no good. Sister Anne, bending forwards so her nose almost touched her knees, was laughing so much that she couldn't speak.

'This is bloody crap,' Julian said. 'Never heard such crap in me life. Where's the money, Sis?'

'You can't have the money,' she whispered. 'It's for me and the baby.'

'You're not going to need a few piddling quid once this loada religious nuts spread the good news. They'll have the Pope over before you know it.'

Amelia felt tears starting in her eyes. Julian, even in his worst moments, never used to speak to her like this.

'You don't believe me, do you?' she said. 'You think I'm making it all up.'

'Of course he doesn't, Darling,' Dolores said, swanning into the room. The three sets of rosary beads around her neck chinked and tinkled as she moved. 'Father Murphy said that time will tell. He said that many claims like yours have been made over the centuries, but without a miracle or two, then nothing can be sub … substantiated. Well, we have our miracle. I think bringing a child back from the dead is enough to convince the most sceptical —'

'What child?' Julian demanded.

'Dominic, the little boy over the road,' Amelia said.

At that moment, Portly gave an ear-piercing yelp. Mrs Baptiste's caterwaul was almost as loud. Dolores rushed into the parlour.

'Amelia,' she shouted. 'Amelia, come quickly!'

CHAPTER 18

Granddad's knife collection had never been as extensive as he would have liked. Despite the receipt of monthly mail order catalogues and trips to various stately homes to covet Samurai swords, karud daggers, medieval halberds and Scottish claymores, he had ended up with a couple of bayonets, a broadsword, and a pearl-handled paper knife. All the same, he had lovingly made and varnished a wooden board onto which each of these precious possessions was mounted, their name and provenance engraved in brass beneath.

When Amelia entered the parlour, the first thing she noticed was that the board was askew, two knives were dangling; two were missing. The next thing she saw, peering beyond Dolores' scraggy arm, was Mrs Baptiste holding the broadsword aloft as though she was performing a sacrifice in one of those old bible films about Moses or David or someone.

'Vera, Vera, stop!' Mr Baptiste was shouting. 'There has to be an easier way than this!'

'Eight miscarriages. Two stillbirths. And now, Portly!' Mrs Baptiste wailed and plunged the blade into the quivering puppy. 'I have so much love to give. So much ...'

The room fell silent. The puppy gave a last sigh and became still. Edith's teeth fell out.

'Look at its penis,' Dolores hissed. 'Fancy getting a hard-on at a time like this.'

All eyes swivelled to Mr Baptiste's groin, but Amelia's remained firmly on the dog, from whose underbelly, a thin telescope of pinky-purple flesh had emerged.

'My God,' said Con. 'This place is going to the dogs.'

The smell of warm blood permeated the room. Amelia's throat filled with bile. She gripped the Vicks jar, wondering if it was okay to anoint an animal or whether it would be considered sacrilegious. At the same moment, she realised that there were no rules for this situation; it had never happened before. When Jesus was born, there had been no rules either, only the old ones, the ones adhered to by the Pharisees and rabbis and He soon dispensed with them. Boldly, she extracted the Vicks from the pocket of Aunt Mabel's habit. She unscrewed the lid, dipped in her finger and approached the table. Like Moses and the Red Sea, the adults moved away, allowing her to reach the puppy.

She wasn't prepared for the sight of the poor dead creature. Its eyes were open, black like polished marbles, its tongue lolled from the side of its mouth. Blood still pumped from the savage wound in its side. The smell was almost unbearable.

'In the name of our Blessed Goddess, I anoint thee, Portly.' Amelia pronounced. 'May your soul rise up to heaven with the saints and the angels and live at the right hand of the Goddess for ever and ever, Amen.'

She knew the Goddess was coming, could smell her delicious perfume of rose and eucalyptus. Irena was coming to take the soul of the dead Portly. Amelia threw herself to the floor as a magnificent light flowed through the room.

'Move out of the way,' Con said from somewhere in the distance. 'Give the kid some air.'

'Is it a Visitation?' asked Edith. The light changed. 'Look at the child's face.'

'Loosen her clothing.' Con was down at Amelia's side, she felt his sweaty fingers fumbling with her clothes as though her skin had become inches thicker and touch was a sense removed.

The Goddess was above, spreading her love, her light. Her kiss was as light as a cobweb, though it stung like a burn on Amelia's cheek. Inside her, the child gurgled, recognising the one from whom it had emanated.

'Goddess.' Amelia could not move her lips. The Goddess, communed with her in a different way. There was a word for it, Amelia tried to remember, but words slipped away.

Thank you, child, for the sacrifice of this dog's life, Irena said. His eternal life begins now. You have done well.

'I never ...' It was important for the Goddess to know, that Amelia herself hadn't murdered the dog. That had been the work of Mr Lawless and Mrs Baptiste.

Child, the instrument is of as little import as the victim. You have dedicated the life of this dog to me. In gratitude, I will spare your brother. Give him the money, child, you will not need it. Manna from heaven will sustain you.

Then she was gone.

Amelia was in Con's arms when the light dispersed. He was staring at her face, a stethoscope on her chest.

'You all right now, love?' he said, removing the stethoscope and releasing her. 'How do you feel? Got a headache, I expect.'

Amelia nodded. The dull throb that accompanied any visit from the Goddess was already beginning.

'Sit up.' Con, for the first time ever, sounded genuinely concerned. His hand gently cradled her back as he helped her to a sitting position. She didn't remember lying on the ground, wondered how she had got there, but the Goddess moved in mysterious ways.

'What's happening?' Mr Baptiste was leaning over Con's shoulders. Amelia, who had never really looked at him before, found him utterly repulsive. There were thick black hairs sprouting from his nostrils, a large, ready-to-be-squeezed pimple on his chin. His face had the sweaty, sinewy texture of beef in the butcher's window.

'Get lost, will you,' Con commanded. 'Look what you've done to the lass. And take your dead dog with you.'

Mrs Baptiste's tear-crumpled features appeared beside her husband's. 'You could have saved Portly,' she accused. 'If you fetched that boy back from the dead, then you could have —'

'Come along, dear,' Mr Baptiste said, shoving his wife. 'Er … Do you have a bin bag?'

Amelia closed her eyes. It was comfortable lying in Con's substantial arms and if she ignored the smell of alcohol on his breath, she could have drifted off to sleep.

'Is she ill?' Sister Anne Margaret asked timidly.

'Just piss off, will you!' Con spat. 'There's always one of your lot butting their nose in when something like this happens. Where the hell are you from, anyway?'

Amelia was compelled to reply. 'She's my headmistress. Came to see Mum.'

The nun was still a little the worse for wear, though chastened by Amelia's sudden fall. 'I'm sorry, I didn't want to impose. Only ... well there have been a few problems lately and now with the miracle ...'

'What miracle?'

'With the boy ... And Amelia's pregnancy. Maybe we should tell someone. A priest, someone.'

'This nonsense again.' Con gently lowered Amelia to the floor and stood up. His knees gave a loud creak. 'Just leave the kid alone. It's bad enough being an adolescent as it is. All those hormones flying around, all those urges. She doesn't need a dried up old bat like you poking her nose in.'

'I really wasn't ...'

'Just get out!' Con shoved the nun towards the door. She pointed feebly towards her black briefcase, now spattered with blood.

'Out!' he repeated and she was gone.

Chapter 19
3rd December 1981

Marguerite's voice down the phone line sounded querulous, young. 'Amelia?'

Amelia stared at the receiver. 'Mum!' She flushed to think that she had almost forgotten about her mother, up in the mountains in the Convent of the Holy Head. So much had happened.

'Amelia, are you all right? Are they looking after you properly? I know Edith does her best, but really, she is getting on and I wouldn't trust Dolores any further than I could throw her. Is she there, by the way, Dolores?'

'No, Mum. She's with Father Murphy at the church again.'

'Why aren't you at school?'

Amelia crossed her fingers behind her back. How could she tell her mother that she had been expelled due to theft and pregnancy? All the same, she longed to feel Marguerite's arms round her, to know that everything would be all right.

Her voice trembled. 'I didn't feel so good this morning, Mum. Anyway, it's revision time. Christmas exams, they don't really care.'

Marguerite needed a moment to digest this information. 'So, who's there looking after you?'

'Er … well Aunt Edith's with Dolores. There's Julian.'

'Julian. He hasn't disappeared then?'

Again, Amelia crossed her fingers. Julian had not been seen for two days, ever since she had given him her last two hundred pounds. Con reckoned he had gone on 'a bender' whatever that was.

'Well, thank goodness for small mercies, I suppose. Anyway, as long as you are all right. And don't you want to know how I'm getting on? Oh, love, I wish you were here with me. The views are magnificent ... Darling, I met this man. A lovely man. He lives down the road from the convent, away from the rat race, he says. A disc jockey, he is, on a Dublin radio station; he's quite famous over here. And he's a writer. Says he wants to be the next Joyce. Oh, and I've been to Dublin, Darling. He took me round all those places I'm reading about in Ulysses at the moment. His name is Patrick ... Pádraig in his own language. Last night he ... Well.' Marguerite was silent then, though her breathing was unnaturally heavy.

'Mum?' The waistband on Aunt Mabel's summer frock was unbearably itchy. Amelia had found two pins in it when she put it on. Mabel was rather remiss when it came to finishing the garments she wore. Unfortunately, the maternity trousers in which she had invested her mother's money, were still so big they would require a pair of Con's braces to keep them up and she had yet to ask him.

'Darling, are you sure everything is okay there?'

'Yes, Mum. We had kippers for tea last night. They were lovely.'

'Good. Patrick took me to a lovely little café. Right here in the mountains, you'd never think it would you? I mean it all seems so rural, so quaint.'

'No, Mum.'

'We had real Irish soda bread and this sort of stew made from offal, and corned beef with cabbage. I could hardly walk when we left. Though I had to walk … It's a bloody long way back to the convent …' Marguerite wittered on.

Amelia sat on the floor, wound the telephone wire around her fingers. Her stomach was rounding. She could imagine the baby twirling and fluttering below her ribcage; the thought made her gasp sometimes. Her clothes were beginning to feel uncomfortable and she had begun to wear the outsize checked shirt she had bought on the shopping trip with Marguerite. Her breasts felt heavy and swollen, though they were nowhere big enough to completely fill the enormous Boots bra. What would her mother say if she saw her now? In the short time she had been in Ireland, Amelia's shape was beginning to change. Soon there would no hope of concealing her condition.

'Amelia? Amelia, are you listening to me? What a child, always with her head in the clouds …' Someone else had entered the room. Marguerite had adopted her showing-off, slightly embarrassed tone.

'Yes, Mum. What's your convent like?'

Marguerite sighed. 'It's not what I was expecting.'

'Is it a real mess? It looked awful on those photos.' It was a relief to drop the subject of herself; Ireland and the convent were a much safer bet.

'God, no! It's like a first class hotel. All mod cons and the nuns are fat as houses. They eat smoked salmon, have hampers flown in from Fortnum and Mason's. They hadn't received my letter so were a bit shocked when I turned up ...'

The pips started go on the phone.

'Oh, hell, I've run out of money. Amelia ... Amelia Darling, look I'm going to stay a bit longer. Be good. Give my love to ...' The line went dead.

Amelia replaced the receiver, feeling the tension ease. Sweat poured down her face. She had got away with it. Her mother was so taken up with her own life that she wasn't really bothered what was going on in Liverpool. All the same, it had been good to hear her voice. Amelia's lower lip began to tremble. She forced her mother out of sight, out of mind and tried to concentrate on other matters. A copy of the Catholic Herald on the telephone table was splashed with a full colour picture of the Pope. He looked like an earnest baby with his pink cheeks and a concentrated frown. A smaller picture of the Catholic Cathedral was printed beside him. "Five months to go!" the paper joyously announced. "What will the Holy Father make of Paddy's Wigwam?"

'Who was that on the phone?' Con had not gone to his consulting rooms that morning. He had sat alone in the parlour all night, drinking poteen, smoking. Thinking, he said, though Dolores said he looked like no philosopher she had ever known.

'Mum. She's fine. She said she was going to stay a bit longer …' The pain of separation from her mother stabbed Amelia in the chest. Tears welled unbidden.

Con nodded. Despite his mammoth drinking binge, he seemed more sober than usual. 'You doing all right, lass?'

'Yup.' Amelia wiped away the tears, unhappily aware that Con was staring at her stomach.

'I think you and I need to have a chat,' he said. 'You should be seen by a doctor.'

'I'm fine.' Amelia did her best to look cheerful but the image of her mother and this new man kept interrupting her thoughts. 'I was going to get a prayer card out of the attic —'

'You don't need to go up there. Edith's got a box full. There's nothing in the attic but a load of old junk. Come in here. Now lie down on the couch. You need to be checked over.'

Con's hands, when he laid them on her stomach, were cool and surprisingly soft. Surprising because everything about him seemed tough and leathery and soaked in drink. He pulled up her dress and prodded the mound of her abdomen, palpating slightly with the heel of his hand, frowning and nodding. As his hands performed their professional examination, she shut her eyes tight, remembering. A long time ago, the night of her grandmother's wake. She remembered smooth hands following the contours of her body, a sharp pain between her legs. No way never … In the morning, it had all seemed like a dream.

After he finished, he pulled down her dress and scratched his head. His face was unnaturally flushed. 'Well. There can be no doubt about your condition, love. The baby's coming along nicely, though you … The question is how you got in this state. And I've been wondering … Listen, Amelia, these visitations you've been having. I want you to go through it with me: beginning to end.'

Amelia blinked. Her encounters with the Goddess were so intense, so personal, and Con had been so scathing about them, she was reluctant to speak.

'What do you want to know?' she murmured, sullenly.

The doorbell went. Saved, she thought, as Con left the room. Thanks to the Goddess, no doubt. The baby belched. She swung her legs back over the edge of the sofa and sat demurely awaiting his return.

'Not in this fucking house,' Con was yelling, 'not here.'

She stood up, crept towards the door, curious. A child's head butted into her knees.

Dominic, fully recovered from his ordeal beneath Mr Lawless's Zephyr, toddled into the room, shrieking with laughter, wearing only a grubby-looking nappy. His back and arms were yellow and green with old bruises.

'Get out of this house!' Con bellowed in the hall. 'You've no right, there's nothing to see.'

Trying to keep one eye on Dominic, Amelia peered around the door. Con, in one of his violent tempers, the ones Edith said would give him a heart attack or land him in jail, was holding a small wizened man by the collar and shaking him hard.

'Listen, you busy-bodying little bastard. You leave us alone or if God is my witness, I'll …'

'Mr O'Dowd,' said Dominic's mother in a conciliatory tone. 'There was a miracle here. Everyone says so. Several people saw it out of their windows and your sister saw it and my little lad wouldn't be alive now if it weren't for your Amelia …' She was wearing her best summer dress, a chiffon green and yellow thing, gathered under the bust. With her hair up, lipstick on, she looked almost pretty. She walked into the parlour, saw Amelia and pointed accusingly. 'Look, there she is, there. Amelia O'Dowd, the girl who saved me son!'

The little man in Uncle Con's clutches shook himself free and bolted into the room.

'You're Amelia O'Dowd?' he demanded. His moustache was peppered with rough shag tobacco.

She nodded. Dominic was about to grab hold of one of the huge Chinese vases that resided either side of the mantelpiece like bad-taste bookends. They were red and gold and black, a little chipped and faded with constant washing, but, according to Edith, worth 'a bomb'. He lunged for the least cracked one. In one swift movement, Amelia caught the boy by his arm. He squealed in frustration.

'I would appreciate it if you could spare me five minutes of your time to answer a few questions.' The little man, ducking Con's lunging hands, was sweating profusely.

Dominic set up a wailing. The vase teetered, fell down and smashed into pieces in the hearth. The scapula of St Bernadette dug into the soft skin on Amelia's neck. She let go of the boy for a second. He made for the matching vase, pushed and knocked that one down too.

'The heirlooms!' Amelia gasped. 'Aunt Edith will go mad.'

'People are saying that you performed a miracle on Monday,' the little man said. He held a small notebook and scribbled furiously. 'Amelia, can you tell me what you did?'

Amelia crouched down, began to retrieve the shards of broken vase. They were the only things that poor Edith had ever owned, a legacy from her godmother, a woman who had been on the stage at the turn of the century. She said they were worth thousands, that one day she would sell them and give the money to the order she joined. Amelia remembered clearly how every time she had approached them as a child, her arm had been slapped and the story of their great value repeated. Now, in less than a minute, they were gone.

'Amelia,' the man repeated.

'Don't talk to him,' ordered Con. He saw the vases, turned and pushed Dominic's mother. 'Jesus, you seen what that daft lad of yours has done?'

'I suppose you're wishing, now, Mr O'Dowd, that Amelia had not saved the boy,' the little man said, sniggering in a way Amelia found most annoying.

'Too right,' Con said. 'That stupid damned dog was a better bet than him.'

'So, you are admitting now that Amelia did indeed save the boy,' the man said. His eyes gleamed black. A twitch had developed on his right cheek. A smell of damp and old tobacco rose from him every time he moved.

'Oh, sod off, will you,' Con shouted, pushing the man out of the way to get to the vases. 'You lot are the scum of the earth.'

'May I quote you, Mr O'Dowd?' the man enquired politely. 'I see that your consulting rooms are on Hope Street, that you have a number of prestigious clients on your lists … Your reputation, may I suggest, Mr O'Dowd, precedes you.'

'Bugger off!'

Dominic's mother, put out by Con's rough handling of her son, flounced into the parlour and grabbed him. Her nails were long, painted a dark maroon colour; they dug into the boy's arm.

'Come on, love,' she said, stalking out of the room. 'We're getting out of here. This is no place for a kiddy. I was only trying to help.'

'I'm sorry, madam,' the little man said, adjusting his collar. 'You shouldn't have been subjected to such an ordeal.'

'What about Edith's damned vases?' Con demanded.

'I'm sure we can cover the costs of those if you can provide us with some evidence as to the nature of the miracle.' The man's voice was oily, wheezy. He licked his lips as he spoke.

'Jesus!' Con reared up one more. He seized the man under the elbows, picked him a good foot off the floor and stalked out of the room with him. The front door closed with a bang.

Amelia slowly retrieved the fragments of the vases. One had smashed into fifteen separate bits, the other was worse. Tiny splinters of porcelain had been thrown across the room. It would be impossible to mend.

'See! No good can come of all this,' said Con from the hall. 'Madness, that's what it is. Hysterical bloody women. Bloody madness.'

'Who was that man?' Amelia wanted to know. She heard a key in the front door.

'Bloody scum of a reporter, that's who,' said Con. 'They come sniffing like rats up a drainpipe if they get so much as a whiff of a so-called miracle. Pathetic it is, that's what.'

'Why would a reporter be interested in us?' Julian said, strolling into the room as though he had left it minutes, rather than two days, before. 'It's not because our Amelia's up the duff, is it?'

'Bloody miracles, virgin births that aren't going to happen.' Con pulled the Herald out of his back pocket. 'The Pope's going to be here in May. The more religious lunacy they can drum up, the better. They don't care that real lives are at stake to say nothing of my business. If anyone in my profession gets wind of this nonsense, I could be out of a job. As if things aren't bad enough!'

Julian took a dining room seat, still rusty with Portly's blood. He looked better than he had for some time, wearing a

195

new set of clothes, a spotless Sex Pistols tee shirt and white jeans. Thoughtfully, he rolled a cigarette. 'A reporter, eh? I suppose a miracle is dynamite to a reporter.'

'And just where have you been?' Con demanded. 'You nearly die on us, then you piss off for days and come back large as life wanting to know everyone's business.'

Julian shrugged, smiled the new secretive smile that struck terror in Amelia's heart.

'That's for me to know and you to find out.'

Con glared into Julian's eyes. 'You're off your head, lad,' he accused. 'Off your bloody head. I can tell by your eyes. Where did you get the money, for God's sake. Your mother's done her best to keep you clean. She even had to lock up the housekeeping money, to stop you sticking it in your veins. How do you think that makes her feel, heh? Knowing her only son is out there blowing his brains out on a load of crap. It's a waste of time, son. You'll never do a damned thing with your life.'

'The money was mine by rights, Con,' Julian said sulkily. 'Grandma might have given it all to Amelia but at one time it would have been me.'

'Yeah and why did she turn?' Con demanded, his voice tight with sarcasm. 'Why? Could it have been when you pawned her wedding ring and Churchill crowns? Could it have been when you nicked your granddad's medals and flogged them to a dealer? Or maybe it was that time you came back so out of your brains, you hit your own mother in front of her.'

Amelia went to the sideboard, took out a tube of UHU. One of the vases might patch up, she thought. The other was probably finished, but if she could save one, maybe Edith would not be too distraught. She balanced the pieces of vase together on the sideboard, ran the glue along the edges of the porcelain. It was harder than she anticipated. The pieces didn't glue together immediately. She would have to do a couple at a time, then, like a jigsaw, put it all together at the end. The smell of the glue was good, sharp and tangy, giving her a pleasant, light-headed feeling.

She switched off from the still raging argument and imagined her life in a few months. The New Saviour would be lying in her lap, clad in frothing pink. She had seen a baby down Gethsemane Drive, wearing frills from her neck down to her lacy booties. Marguerite said the child looked 'common', but to Amelia, she was the loveliest baby in the world. The New Saviour would be just as beautiful, she decided. She might even get her ears pierced, despite what her mother said about only roughies mutilating their children. Amelia's thoughts turned to the birth, where they strayed more and more often these days. She wondered if some Magi would turn up to worship, bringing with them precious gifts. Would a star in the sky indicate Her presence and would there be shepherds and announcing angels? Would Her Nativity be like the one of old?

She glued a third piece to the vase and found that her fingers had stuck fast to the flourishing tail of an exotic painted bird. Prising her hand away, she left a piece of skin still clinging.

'Maybe going to the press isn't such a bad idea,' Julian was saying, as Amelia sucked her bleeding digit. 'They pay. Lots of people pay. This could be the answer you're looking for, Con. You were conned out of your inheritance, maybe this is a way to reclaim it.'

'I couldn't.' Con brought a small silver bottle from the pocket of his trousers. He unscrewed the cap, wiped his brow with the back of his hand and took a swig. 'It's not real. None of it is real, I can assure you. I've been a shrink more years than you've had fixes. I am a professional, a scientist. I can't be involved in any hocus pocus. My reputation would be severely compromised. Once my rivals found out, they'd have my guts for garters. I'd be struck off.' He looked bad, with sweat oozing from his red face, his eyes bloodshot and watery.

The parlour behind its thick nets was cool, thanks to a sudden December drop in outside temperature and the gas fire being mysteriously turned off for the first time in over a year. Con loosened his shirt, coughed. For a moment, he held on to the back of a chair, steadying himself. He seemed very old. His skin was waxy, purplish in colour, the black veins on his nose stood out like iron filings. Amelia experienced a spasm of fear. The Goddess, she was close, hovering. Was she waiting for Con's eternal soul?

CHAPTER 20
9TH DECEMBER 1981

Passion Close was the most disreputable street in the neighbourhood. Many of the lawns went unmowed for entire summers and gardens were littered with broken bicycles and chip wrappers. Some of the houses had been converted into flats where, according to Marguerite, 'undesirables' lived. Undesirables were worse than roughies, apparently. They were people rejected by the worst of neighbourhoods. Not even in those high rise flats of Netherley, or the less salubrious districts of Kirkby and Fazakerly were they welcome, though Amelia would have loved to live in Fazakerly. It sounded so foreign and exotic.

She didn't understand her mother's reasoning, her casual condemnation of entire districts. She suspected that if Marguerite were to venture into some of these places she might find herself in a balmy land of palm trees and beaches, rather than the confines of Calvary Crescent where she was the only adult under fifty. She suspected that her mother was afraid of the places, of the people, the exotic names, maybe of the land itself.

Although it was only around the corner, Marguerite gave Passion Close a wide berth as though the heady intoxication of its name might rub off on her. Amelia didn't understand fully what passion meant, except in the context of Jesus' last week on earth and that was bad enough, starting out with palm leaves and ending up on a cross. Maybe Marguerite thought that she might find herself nailed to the bus stop. Or suspected that once she ventured into such provocatively named territory, she herself might become passionate in the manner of an old film star grabbed around the waist and kissed hard upon the lips. Well, Amelia wasn't scared of such things. There were no crucifixions in Liverpool in 1981 and if someone were to kiss her passionately, she might just kiss him back. If she liked him.

She came to a halt outside Number Three. The houses had been getting steadily worse as she passed from one-hundred-and-eighty down to fifty. They looked almost derelict from twenty-five on. All the same, she thought, it was time she paid her niece, the new prophet, a visit. Julian might not care about the fruit of his loins, but she certainly did. She paused. What a loin was she had no idea, except that they made very good chops.

Snow had fallen overnight, thawed, then frozen over. The leaden clouds overhead suggested more to come. There were dangerous patches of black ice on the pavement and suspicious-looking lumps that could have been frozen dog turds or tin cans. The papers were saying it was the coldest December for over a hundred years. Amelia shivered. Thickly wrapped in an army greatcoat she'd found in the attic, a yellow oilskin sou'wester and her too-tight, last-year's wellies, she was well prepared for the Arctic temperatures, though the cold still penetrated. But she liked the snow. For one thing it gave everywhere a fresh, clean appearance, even Passion Close where rusting prams and supermarket trolleys were imbued with a sculptural elegance. Despite it being term time, people had taken the day off. Children, faces red and hands blue, scrabbled for snowballs and built stunted snowmen in unusually clear gardens whose usual rubble was interred beneath virgin snow; a few boys were playing an enthusiastic game of football in the street. The thud of the ball as it hit a row of garages was deadened by a landscape now fulsome with a voluptuous whiteness. Outside Number Five, a group of old women had gathered to gossip. Made giddy by the weather, they edged their forearms under their heavy busts when a particularly juicy piece of scandal was related; Les Dawson in quadruple. They stared when Amelia breezed up the path. She protectively held her growing stomach under the thick serge of the greatcoat. They tutted loudly and went on with their conversation.

Paula was gazing out of the window of her ground floor flat, her face wan, her thin fingers curled around a grey net curtain. Amelia waved hesitantly as she negotiated two concealed motorbike tyres. Paula rubbed away condensation, distorting her expression behind the glass to one of blurred grief. She raised a hand in greeting. Amelia wished she hadn't come.

Nothing could have prepared her for the conditions in which her niece was being brought up. Marguerite, feeling hard done to, had claimed that Eighteen Calvary Crescent was a 'midden', and on really bad days, a 'shithole', but her house was a palace compared to Paula's flat. The architecture, which was standard between-the-wars, serviceable council stock, would have been all right if properly cared for. The front door opened onto a wide central staircase with two flats on each floor, accessed by front doors on either side. There were only three floors, all devoid of carpet and frippery. Everything was concrete, hard and indestructible, except the eight gas and electricity meters, which had all been broken into at some time or another and were nothing but twisted metal. Amelia wondered how she paid her bills. There was a smell of damp and decay and human urine.

'Wharra you doin' 'ere?' Paula demanded as Amelia closed the front door behind her, shutting out all light. In her cold hand she clutched a bunch of dried honesty, plundered from the front garden at home. She had brought two tiny suits (found, oddly, in Mabel's mourning box) for the baby, which she hoped were the right size.

'I've come to see Patti,' Amelia said hesitantly, blundering into the darkness of the hall. The speech she had rehearsed in her mind, the speech informing Paula of the importance of her daughter's birth, seemed incongruous. She didn't want to mention the New Saviour in this filthy place, as though She could be tarnished by association.

Paula threw open her own door and a band of faded wintry light brightened their path.

'You can come in if you want but I've nothin' to give yer. No tea, just half a can of Special Brew and you're not getting your mitts on that. And the heating's bust, so unless you've brought a couple of logs or some coal to throw on the fire, you'd better keep your coat on. Like it, by the way, the coat. Very Joy Division.'

Paula was a different person from the one Amelia had met only weeks ago. Frail and apologetic, in the presence of Julian, now she was a painted demon with re-dyed brassy blonde hair, a powdered chalk-white face against which her teeth glowed an unpleasant shade of yellow. With her kohl-ringed eyes, she resembled a puffy, miserable skull.

Amelia followed her into the sparsely furnished flat. A filthy sofa with horsehair bulging out of the seams, sat in the middle of the living room. A foldaway table and a baby's cot were the only other items of furniture. The kitchenette was grimy, plates piled up. The only heat was provided by the two gas rings on the filthy cooker hob. They were on full but to no avail. It was colder than outside.

'Nor exactly what you're used to, is it?' Paula demanded. 'But it's all I can afford.'

Amelia approached the cot. The baby was squealing, wrapped in a grey blanket. She stank of fresh wee. Amelia thought of swaddling clothes, of mangers and oxen. The sheets were dirty, covered in excrement. It was all Amelia could do to stop herself throwing up.

'She needs changing!' she accused, before she could stop herself. 'It's awful. Poor Patti, and in this cold too.'

'You do it then, if you're so bothered.' Paula indicated a pile of freshly-laundered nappies near the door. There were also tiny baby clothes drying on an airer. The flat itself was not too dirty, only the baby and the cot.

Gingerly, Amelia extracted her niece from the cot. She was wet and crying but when she saw Amelia, her eyes brightened. Amelia dangled her away from her own body, hands tight around the stout little waist. Patti kicked enthusiastically.

'Hello,' said Amelia, smiling. Feeling favoured, she forgot the smell. 'I'm your auntie.'

'Shame your brother doesn't think to stop by.' Paula lit a cigarette and switched on the black and white portable television. An old war film thundered gunshots into the quiet room. 'Never heard a thing from him since I saw you last.'

'He's been ill,' Amelia defended. She was ashamed of Julian's behaviour. 'He nearly died the other night.'

'Look.' Paula stood up, held her arm at an angle from her body, the cigarette still smoking in her hand. 'I don't know why you've come and thanks for the dried flowers and all, but I don't think —'

'Can we try the clothes on Patti?' Amelia suggested. 'I wasn't sure if the size was right. You never do with stuff you get from the cockloft —'

'If you want, though I doubt Patti gives a damn. Doesn't care about anything, she doesn't. Whatever I do, it's never enough.'

'That's what Mum used to say about our Julian.' Carefully, Amelia laid the little girl on the floor. Her legs kicked wildly. She rolled over onto her front and began to crawl. She reached the sofa and Paula, then heaved herself to her feet.

'She can walk?' Amelia asked. She had no idea when babies did these things.

'Last month.' There was a twinge of pride in Paula's flat nasal voice. 'But she gets into all sorts of trouble so it's better to leave her in the cot.'

Amelia looked around. There were overflowing ashtrays on the floor, matches, a lighter. Despite the sub zero temperature outside, the window was open.

'Paula?' Amelia said, hoping she wouldn't take offence. 'Do you mind if I close a window? It's a bit chilly in here.'

Paula shrugged and stared vacantly at the television. Amelia stuck her head out of the sash window, gulped fresh outside air, then held her breath, keeping it in her lungs for as long as she could as she pulled the sash down. In the bathroom she found some baby lotion and an almost-clean towel. She took one of the new nappies and set about trying to catch her niece but Patti toddled away like a small drunk. Amelia loved the plump little limbs, the cherubic smile, the golden curls so like her own. And all the time she wondered if she could help poor Paula. Patti looked neglected. Amelia thought of everything Marguerite had said about Dominic over the road, how his mother beat and ignored him, but Dominic even as a young baby had never looked as dirty as this, nor smelled as bad.

When Patti was as clean as possible, given the squirming and the grubby towel, Amelia took Mabel's little knitted sailor suit and dropped it over the child's head. She looked better, brighter, properly cared for, if a little old-fashioned. It was warm too, just right for the weather. Through it all, Paula stared at the film on television as though it was the most riveting thing she had ever seen.

'What do you think?' Amelia said when she had finished.

Paula took a long drag of her roll-up, looked over at Patti who was scaling the fold-up table with glee. Her face softened. For a moment she looked about to cry, and then the hard mask slipped down again. 'Okay.'

'Maybe you should bring her over … to Calvary Crescent. I mean, I don't think Julian wants anyone to know about Patti, but who cares? We're her family, after all.'

For the first time, Paula turned to face Amelia. Before now, she had done no more than given her a cursory glance. Now she looked her up and down as though she were an item for sale. A look of repugnance replaced her usual hard sneer.

'You're preggers, aren't you? I heard you and Jules that night by the chippy.' She pointed with her cigarette at Amelia's stomach, safely concealed within the greatcoat. 'Who did that to you? Not Jules? God, you're only a kid.'

Amelia picked up Patti and sat on the sofa beside Paula.

'That's sort of what I've come to tell you about,' she confided.

'My God, he's worse than I thought. His own sister!'

'Patti is the New Prophet. Like John the Baptist only a girl, 'cos the New Saviour will be a girl too. The Goddess doesn't think it worked out very well before just having men …'

'I'll kill him. I will, I'll kill him. Jesus!' She covered her face with her hands and began to sob. 'I was clean months till last night. Months. If I hadn't met Stan the Man down the chippy, I never would have bothered but it was such a temptation.'

'That's right! Jesus was tempted, John the Baptist was tempted. Lead us not into temptation …' Amelia stopped, puzzled. She could not think who on earth Stan the Man could be, or what he was tempting Paula with, unless of course … She thought about Jesus in the desert. She'd been reading the bible a lot recently, but not those passages where the devil came down to tempt Him. The devil was Satan, only one letter removed from Stan.

'The problem was,' Paula scooped up little Patti and kissed her head, 'it was so damned good. Just left me wanting more, like the old days. I wish I'd never run into your brother. I wish I was dead.'

Patti, heedless of her mother's anguish, wriggled from her grasp and slithered to the floor. Holding onto the sofa, she stood up, toddled over to Amelia and began to clamber back up onto her knee. Outside, the snow fell in a blizzard, whirling through an ashen sky, obliterating the houses over the road. Silence fell, exhaustion overcame Amelia. She wanted to sleep. She wanted Paula and the child and all their problems to be out of her life. For the first time since her grandmother's death, she wanted to be free again, a normal girl at school, messing about with her two friends, the two friends who had deserted her. She wanted her body back and the visions to go away. She missed her mother.

'Who do you love the most?' she asked, the words bursting out of her. 'Stan or Patti?'

'What?' Paula frowned. She stubbed out her cigarette in the ashtray, brushed her knees. 'What a friggin' question. Of course I love Patti. Stan's only a scummy dealer.'

'Patti is a prophet,' Amelia intoned. 'You must take special care of her and when my baby comes, she must be there … Well maybe in a few years. John the Baptist didn't turn up for ages.'

'Look.' Paula rose. Her eyes were wild. 'I don't know why you've come here, or what the hell you're talking about. I want to be left alone. I'll look after Patti.'

Amelia heaved herself up from the sofa. There was nothing more she could say. She wished she could take the child away, back to Calvary Crescent which, despite its faults was a lot better than Passion Close, but Paula was pacing the floor, barring her way to the door.

'But what can I do? Mam's not speaking to me. Me dad's down in Stoke with a barmaid off the Royal Iris. My next door neighbour's a prozzie, the kids down the street will rob you soon as looking, I'm on the dole without two pennies to rub together …'

'I'll speak to Julian,' Amelia promised. 'He'll have to help you. Patti's his daughter.'

'Your brother is a worthless lump of shit.'

'Even so …' Amelia blew a kiss to Patti and made for the door. She tried not to inhale the foul smells of the passageway. Her baby was groaning as though she too sensed the hopelessness of the place.

'You hear me?' Paula bellowed. 'A worthless shithead! I loved him once. I was an idiot. He's ruined my life!'

Amelia stumbled out of the building, slithered down the path. The snow was falling so thickly she could barely see ahead; it stuck to her lips and eyelashes, drifted down the back of her neck, exposed by the gaping collar of the greatcoat. She began to cry, lurching sobs propelled her body forwards, her feet slithering, sliding, faster and faster. Where was the Goddess? Her Prophet was in mortal danger. How could she allow such an important child to live in dire poverty? Standing at the gate of Eighteen Calvary Crescent at last, she looked to the skies for an answer but the snow stung her eyes and she was forced to gaze again at her feet. The big toe on her right foot throbbed painfully. Her wellies were really far too small.

CHAPTER 21

She was so busy staring at her boots and heading for the front door that Amelia didn't notice the group of people lurking in the small front garden. There were about twelve in all, oblivious to the snowstorm, huddled together behind the pampas grass on the whited-out lawn near Grandma's skeletal rose bushes. It was four o'clock, almost tea time and a strong smell of bacon was drifting from the house.

'It's her. It has to be,' a middle-aged woman bellowed as Amelia walked down the front path. 'Ah, the little saint. I didn't think she'd be so ... so shabby. You wouldn't think it, would you, in someone holy, that they'd let themselves go. Mind you, it might just be that funny coat.'

The others turned, saw Amelia and began muttering prayers; some sank to their knees. A stout elderly man fainted. A weird hush descended. Amelia smiled nervously, unsure whether she should speak to them or make a run for the house.

'Can I touch you?' A young woman in a beret that was far too small for the inclement day, rushed forward, her hands outstretched.

'If you want,' Amelia said. 'Only I'm starving and I think Aunt Edith's got the tea on ...'

'You're the one who saved the boy?' another woman demanded. She was very old and pink in the face.

Amelia nodded, hastily.

An elderly couple who were on their knees by the overgrown, though bald, laveteria began a querulous Hail Mary. Several others joined in.

'My son has leukaemia,' the bereted woman said. 'If you could just touch him, lay your hands on him, then he would be cured.'

Amelia frowned. The sister of one of the young mothers Edith knew in church had died of leukaemia and that was after they'd done a play and a jumble sale to send her to Lourdes.

'I don't think …' she began but was stopped by Con, charging out of the house, panting, red, and very fierce. This time he had been spared by the Goddess. He hissed at the crowd, grabbed Amelia by the arm and pulled her inside.

'Who are all those people?' she asked, as he slammed the door. 'They weren't there this morning.'

'No.' Con stalked through into the parlour, picked up a copy of the Liverpool Echo that lay on the table, and thrust it under her nose. 'That's because the weasely little bastard hadn't printed this then.'

Amelia looked at the article. 'Snow joke for local buses.' There was an interesting story about a Number Fifty skidding into the A to Zs below.

'Not that one, you daft bat. Look!' Con's pudgy finger prodded a blurred picture of a girl in a Belle Ville uniform. 'Local girl: the New Bernadette?'

'What's that got to do with us?' she asked, but the truth was slowly dawning. She read through the piece. Mostly the reporter had quoted Mrs Baptiste and Carol Brand, the unmarried mother of Dominic. Miss Brand had exclaimed over the 'miracle that allowed her son to live', the 'heavenly light', the way her dead child had been 'dragged from the brink of death'. Even the sacrifice of the puppy was mentioned.

'News was bound to get out, Con,' Edith clacked from her chair near the fire. 'You can't have the child going round bringing people back from the dead without anyone making a fuss. And then there's the other news … Of course, no one except us and Father Murphy knows yet, but once that …'

'It's like Chinese whispers,' Con exclaimed. 'It'll get worse and worse, the truth will be distorted out of all recognition. What the hell have I done to deserve this? My sister is a religious lunatic, my niece has buggered off to some bunch of frustrated nuns in Ireland, Dolores spends all her time hanging round the parish priest, my great nephew, Julian, is doped up to his eyeballs and Amelia … well, where do I begin?'

Amelia plonked herself down on the opposite chair to Edith. She closed her eyes. This was all getting too much. Edith had the gas fire on full. At first it was pleasantly warm and thawing but after a while her legs, beneath Mabel's thick woollen skirt, began to feel very hot. She didn't move. The baby settled for the first time since Passion Close and a peace descended on her, soft and innocent as the snow. However many people were outside the house, no matter what Miss Brand said to any reporters, Amelia was carrying a miraculous truth, a truth that would soon be known throughout the world.

'The thing is,' Edith insisted, 'you can't stop people —'

Con sighed. Amelia sensed him move heavily around the room, towards the window. He drew the heavy draylon curtains against the darkening afternoon.

'I was sixty-three last January,' he said. 'I should be retiring in just over a year, with a decent pension, some credit to my name. The way things are going, I shall be defrocked and exposed as some seedy fraud. I can't keep up this ridiculous charade. This business with Amelia has gone too far. These visions … Fits … And as for curing dead children, well, I wasn't there, but I'd bet the shirt on my back that there's some other explanation. The Catholic Church doesn't like this kind of rubbish any more. Bloody stigmata and Lazarus. It's 1981, not the Middle Ages.'

The front door slammed. A pink and giggling Dolores rushed into the room.

'Have you seen what's going on out there?' she said. 'Jesus, Ken will be round any minute with his bloody camera. Sod pigs and donkeys. That lot are from no zoo I've ever seen.'

A man's voice: 'Dolores, if I may console you … You're overwrought. You've been through such a trying time. It is better not to overreact.'

Amelia's eyes snapped open. This was the first time Father Murphy had visited the house since he drank too much sherry at Grandma's funeral.

'Ooh, Father,' Dolores simpered. 'You do take such good care of me.'

'I tend all my flock,' Father Murphy said. 'But to those in especial need, I offer special attention.'

'You'll never save her soul,' Con retorted. 'Dolores was damned back in seventy-four when she married that pervert.'

Edith's teeth made an excruciating grinding sound. 'Father Murphy, so good to see you. Here, take my chair. I've just made a pot of tea and then I'll get us a morsel to eat. You will stay, won't you? Only a humble repast, I'm afraid, but Our Lord Jesus shared with us his flesh and blood in the form of water and wine … and bread.'

'Bread is the staff of life,' Father Murphy replied, mechanically. The snow on his black priest's coat had melted and he was beginning to steam. 'It is very kind of you to invite me.'

There was a slight struggle as he attempted to pass Edith on the way to her chair. Both tried to squeeze between Con and the sideboard but Con was standing foursquare, glaring with contempt at the priest.

'Er … Do excuse me,' Father Murphy addressed the floor.

'Listen, pal,' Con began. His voice shook with warning. 'I don't know what you're doing in this house, sniffing round my niece like a randy dog. We don't want your sort here.'

'Oh, and what sort is that?' Edith cowered and the priest managed to negotiate Con's bulk to reach the chair.

'Crows, scavengers, clergy.' Con glared down on the quivering Father Murphy. 'You know, I've travelled. When I was young, I nearly went in for the priesthood. That was until a trip to the Holy Land. I lost my faith in 1948. Standing at the Wailing Wall, watching the Jews and the Christians and the Muslims pass by, I was struck by the absolute absurdity of it. All wars come from religious belief. Get rid of religion and you get rid of war. Easy.'

'Now, Con, don't start,' Edith muttered.

'Oh you would take the crow's side, wouldn't you, eh? You and your paddy boyo, pretending it was all hearts and shamrocks when really the IRA were blasting the —'

'How dare you,' Edith clacked, pummelling her brother's substantial stomach. 'When your own family were denied the right to rule their own country by King Billy and the Orangemen. And then with the potato famine and the cruel Protestant landlords who would have let them all starve. They had to come to Liverpool …'

Con snorted. 'DeValera was responsible for all this self-pitying bollocks. Next thing we'll have nuns playing bodhrans round the table.'

Silence descended as always after one of these heated exchanges. Both parties withdrew to muster further ammunition. Father Murphy, relatively new to the parish, and Con's proclivaties, looked visibly relieved and settled down in his armchair. This was enough to galvanize Con into fresh paroxysms of rage.

'The whole place needs drowning. And every black-frocked bloody cleric with it.'

Edith's eyes filled with tears; she looked beseechingly at Father Murphy. 'You see, Father, what I have to countenance. My own brother tried to drown the Archbishop of Liverpool in the Mersey, you might have seen it. February 1965, I'll never forget it. It made the front page of the Liverpool Echo. Another time, he punched the Mother Superior who had come to him for therapeutic advice,' She lit another cigarette; her last was still burning in the ashtray. 'Thank the Lord, she had a tasty left hook herself, and gave as good as she got. The two had to be separated by Con's cleaner. The shame of it.'

'She bloody deserved it, damned dyke,' Con mumbled. Father Murphy blushed furiously.

'The tragedy is,' Edith complained, 'Con would have made a good clergyman himself. If only, when he was in the seminary, he'd been able to keep his eyes, and his hands, off the girls from the Physical Education College next door. If only,' she complained, 'he'd not become a Communist and started to believe all that "opium of the people" nonsense.'

She gave a tragic smile. 'A cup of tea, Father,' she muttered, handing the priest a china cup smeared with fuchsia lipstick. 'Just as you like it. Milky with a half spoon of sugar. I'll get the food on in a minute.'

Con looked as though he was about to rally to the argument again but thought better of it and instead slammed from the room.

Father Murphy took the cup, turned the lipstick side away from him, sipped and grimaced. 'Have you showed this the tea?' he asked. 'It's nothing but hot water and milk.'

'Only the second use of the teabag, Father,' Edith said huffily. 'We are fasting now before his Holy Majesty comes to visit.'

'There is no need to fast for the next five months, I assure you. Pope John wouldn't expect us to be going without. We should be celebrating his visit not …'

'He's not here yet, Father,' Edith reminded. 'Once his Holiness kisses the tarmac, then the macaroons will come out of the freezer.' She shuffled out into the kitchen, wearing her most pious expression.

'So, child.' Father Murphy turned to Amelia. 'I hear that you are in the family way?'

Amelia nodded. She knew that she ought to explain more to the priest, tell him of Irena's message, but a draining lethargy prevented her.

'You have been to a doctor?'

She frowned, shook her head.

'It is just that the claims you have been making, the conception of the child and so on … Well, all must be verified before the Church can consider …' He took another sip of tea and grimaced. 'It's a shame poor Edith couldn't give up the cigarettes,' he said, winking at Amelia, 'rather than the teabags. She makes the worse tea out of all my ladies. Now, where were we?'

'My Uncle Con examined me. He is a doctor,' Amelia remembered.

'And what did he say?'

217

Amelia shrugged. Con was not the best person to ask about anything at the moment. It seemed that any reference to Virgin Births sent him into apoplectic fury and after his last outburst, Amelia had decided not to mention it to him again.

'He is struggling with his Faith,' Dolores rescued her. 'Poor Con. He is a deluded and vicious man. His chosen profession says it all. No real man, no man with any kind of morality would consider his job.'

Father Murphy looked puzzled. 'But he's a doctor?'

'Hmm.' Dolores crouched on the floor at the priest's knee, and touched his arm as though she would have liked to rip his steaming coat away and feel the skin beneath. 'If you want to call it that. He was thrown out of a seminary, you know.'

'Not all of us have a real vocation for the priesthood. For many, God's purpose lies in the secular world.'

'You have managed to sacrifice the secular side of life, Father,' Dolores remarked, gazing adoringly.

'Egg sandwiches!' Edith arrived balancing a tray, her chipped scarlet nails smothered in lumps of egg white.

'Sometimes ...' Father Murphy fidgeted with his cassock, 'I too wrestle with temptation.'

'You won't go far wrong wrestling with one of my sandwiches.' Edith thrust the plate under his nose. 'Here, these will put any carnal thoughts right from your mind.'

'I don't know ...' He took a sandwich, and stared longingly at Edith's St Francis locket dangling between Dolores' plump bosoms. He forced his eyes away, glancing down at the sandwich. Salad cream oozed into his cuff. 'But back to the matter in hand. This child, and the baby she carries, do you have any idea who the father could be?'

'That, Father, is a matter of prayer and faith,' said Edith, taking a seat at the table. 'It seems that the Angel Gabriel came down and blessed her, as he did another virgin two thousand years ago.'

'I'm not sure.' Father Murphy shifted uncomfortably.

Dolores nibbled delicately at a sandwich, the filling dripping down her chin.

'For the Church to accept such an idea, there would have to be authentication. I apologise if I am embarrassing anyone, but we would have to be unequivocally assured of the child's virginity. That would mean verification by a recognised practitioner in the field. And we would have to interrogate Amelia, make sure there is no confabulation. The matter of the miracle, raising the boy from the dead and so on, this too would have to be studied. You see, over the years there have been many such claims. Young girls in Amelia's position are often afraid of the consequences of their actions. They will lie, cheat, steal to make their condition seem anything other than it is … Believe me, I have seen such things with my own eyes.'

'Father!' Dolores rose, her bloodshot eyes brimming with tears. 'How could you suggest such a thing when I myself was witness to the most wonderful miracle?'

Amelia, chomping earnestly on a sandwich, realised that Father Murphy was right. For anyone to believe that the child inside her was the New Saviour, she would have to prove the existence of a Goddess who no one had seen but herself. The Baptistes, the people outside, even Edith and Dolores, none of them could convince the Church of the truth. Only Amelia and the New Saviour could do that.

Chapter 22
10th December 1981

It was lovely and quiet in the kitchen, a blessed relief, which was why Amelia sought it out at such a late hour. It had been days since she had experienced the solitude needed for the contemplation of holy mysteries. Even now she was not truly alone. Julian lurked in the doghouse behind the twin tub, looking odd. He reminded her of the looming man in the background of Aunt Edith's faded reproduction of The Girlhood of Mary Virgin. This ancient picture hung above Edith's bed. Its twin, Ecce Ancilla Domini, by the same artist, Dante Gabriel Rossetti, had graced the wall opposite, until Edith took it down when Con said Mary looked like 'a lady of the night', cowering before the Angel Gabriel.

Julian, like the man tangled in beautifully painted vine, appeared faint and indistinct in the darkness of the doghouse. His left arm flexed at an awkward angle. One end of Marguerite's Hermes scarf was tied around his bicep while the other end was in his mouth, gripped between his big yellow teeth. His face was a mask of concentration, with his eyes half closed and his mouth gnashing the scarf. He looked in pain.

'Julian?' She was glad to find him there, despite her need to pray. Most nights he either went out or sat at the dining room table drinking with Con. She desperately needed to speak to him, especially after the disastrous afternoon with Paula and Patti

'Piss off.' His voice was little more than a sigh. He finished what he was doing and let the scarf fall from his mouth.

Amelia leaned against the cooker. A pan of pork stew sat cooling on the hob, the fat congealing on top in white greasy blobs. The snow that continued unabated outside did nothing to assuage the inner heat prickling her skin. Con had not returned after storming off yesterday and, overnight, a group of over two hundred people had crammed themselves into the front garden to sing hymns and scatter prayers like seed upon the muddy white lawn. No one in the house had managed a wink of sleep with the noise.

A holy water font had been lugged from some shrine or other and Our Lady of Lourdes now beamed fluorescently from the naked lavatera. People were splashing wounds and filling bottles from the garden tap, plucking dried poppy heads and teasels from the wintry garden. As the day had worn on, more and more arrived; the quiet cul-de-sac was changed. Cars queued around the corner and horns beeped in frustration. An altercation sprang up between a couple of drivers, and fists were thrown across snowbound bonnets. In the end the police were called and one of the protagonists led away in handcuffs. In the distance, an ice-cream van struck up 'Immaculate Mary' in ding-dong chimes, and a hot dog stall was doing a roaring trade on the junction between Gethsemane Drive and Olive Mount.

Amelia opened the biscuit tin, surprised to find an unopened packet of fig rolls and three chocolate digestives.

Ever since Dolores had given up smoking, the biscuit tin had been raided regularly. She helped herself and closed the lid.

'What were you doing, then?' she demanded, glaring at Julian standing gormlessly in the same position. 'You look like one of Lewis's.'

'Nothing to do with you, Sis.'

'You look a real gawp.'

Julian spat on the floor and grinned recklessly. Marguerite's scarf was still tied around his arm. There was craziness and danger in his walk.

'Listen, Sis. There's nothing wrong, nothing. I'm going to get through, Sis, honest. I need some money, that's all, then I'm going to apply to Art College, like I always said. But first …' He took her by the shoulders, swung her around. 'I need to paint, like I used to, remember?'

He pointed to a stack of boards and canvases in the corner of the doghouse. Some were age spotted and mildewed. All were paintings of himself in various styles and colours. Some, Amelia thought, were quite good. Others, like the ones of him as a leering skull, were gruesome.

'… And get myself a portfolio together, you know? Then I can apply and get a grant and then —'

'Well do it,' Amelia said. Julian was frightening her, standing so menacingly in the doorway between the kitchen and the doghouse. He was too close, too loud and jumpy. His eyes, staring into her own, were quite quite mad.

'I will,' he said, swinging her around some more. 'I can do anything. I'll get into Art College and paint and paint and make my name and you and Mum can sod off with your convent and all your money 'cos I won't need it, see? I'll make my own.'

'And what about Paula and little Patti?' Amelia said quietly.

'What about them?'

'Paula has got nothing, no money or anything and she lives in this awful flat on Passion Close. And she has been tempted by someone called Stan the Man. It's terrible, Julian, honest. Patti needed her nappy changed and everything. I think Paula loves her but because of this awful Stan who I think is really Satan …'

Julian laughed. A horrible sound, raucous and sneering.

'You've no idea what you're talking about, Sis,' he said. 'So Little-Miss-Perfect isn't so very perfect after all. I bloody knew it!'

'She said she was tempted because of you. Oh, Julian, Patti is a prophet. She will go ahead and broadcast the news of the Saviour's birth to the world.'

'Look, Sis, I don't know what you're on but it's a better fuckin' cut than mine —'

'Don't swear. You know what Mum thinks of that word.'

'She thinks it's common just like all the other decent Anglo Saxon words in the dictionary. Mum doesn't know a friggin' thing about anything and as for that stupid bitch, Paula —'

'She has given birth to your child!' Amelia shouted. 'You should have married her; you should be looking after her like Zachariah looked after Elizabeth.'

224

'Julian?' Edith was standing in the doorway of the kitchen, a cigarette dangling from her mouth. There was no way of knowing how much she had heard.

'Aunt Edith,' Julian said, smiling insanely. 'I was just talking to Sis about —'

'You have a child?' Edith looked sad. The greenish fluorescent light of the kitchen cast lilac shadows in the hollows of her cheeks. 'You, Julian, after all the upset you have caused your poor mother and your grandmother who was put in an early grave ...' She paused, sucked in her teeth, took another drag on her cigarette. 'You have a child?'

Julian tried to edge past his elderly aunt, out of the door. He laughed again, as though it had all been a joke, a stupid misunderstanding.

'Amelia is very imaginative,' he said. 'She comes up with some daft tales.'

Edith, quick as anything, put out her hand and refused to allow him past.

'I know you think I'm a stupid old woman,' she said. 'But I won't have this, I'm telling you. I won't. Amelia, as the mother of the New Messiah, isn't going to be making up tales about you having a child. Not at a time like this with all those people queuing up in the garden.'

'Why are they queuing?' Julian demanded. 'It's like the first day of the Christmas Sales out there.'

'People have heard of the Miracle.' Edith banged the door with the flat of her hand, in frustration. 'And it's only you and Con who live under the same roof as the dear sainted child, who won't believe. Tell me about your child. Where is it? Who is the mother?'

Amelia stared through the condensation out of the kitchen window. In the sulphurous glow of the street lights, she could see the snow still falling and felt sorry for all those queuing. A few hardy souls had scaled the bolted gate into the back garden. A face appeared on the other side of the glass. Amelia pulled the curtains together before she could catch his eye.

'There is no child,' Julian said.

Amelia glared at him. To think he could deny his own flesh and blood. She was reminded of St Peter and the cock crowing.

'Julian,' she said softly. 'You'll have to tell. The baby could be in danger. What with the temptation of Paula and all.'

'Huh. Temptation of Paula. She told me she was clean. Bitch.'

'Julian!' Edith moved across the room, towards Julian in the doghouse. Her loose body shuddered with anger. 'Tell me the truth or as God is my witness, I'll —'

'What? You'll hit me?' Julian held his arms up in mock surrender.

'Have you sired a child or not?'

Amelia prodded Julian's arm. It was so thin she touched bone. He nodded reluctantly.

'Okay. I never knew till a few weeks ago.' His eyes, though still glittering, dulled slightly. 'I never wanted a kid.'

'You have a child!' Edith began to cry. Big tears spilled down her face. 'Another child in the family and we never knew. I always wanted a baby, my own baby. Always —'

'I thought you wanted to go into the convent,' Julian said. 'You can't have both.'

'No. And there was the problem.' Edith looked old, more like her dead sister. Her skin has assumed a greyish hue and was more lined than ever. Her mouth was tight with pain.

'Look, the mother of the kid is, well, not fit to be one,' Julian muttered. 'Stupid cow. Can't fu —'

'How old is the child? Where does he live?'

'She,' Amelia corrected. 'Patti lives in Passion Close with her mum, Paula. You remember Paula. You liked her when she went out with Julian. You remember, the one with the white hair.'

'Paula?' Edith looked puzzled for a moment. 'Not Paula Roberts, Jack's daughter ... No, must be granddaughter. Yes, nice girl. Image of Jack.'

'Okay.' Julian looked irritated. 'She's the mother. But I don't want anything to do with it. She had it without telling me and now what am I supposed to do, with her a smackhead and living round the corner in some scummy flat. It was never as though we were going to get married for fuck's sake.'

'Julian, what have you done?' Edith selected a wooden spoon and prodded at the pan of pork, breaking the lumps of fat into manageable chunks. 'You have a daughter in the world and you're ignoring her, not even telling your family about her. I am so ... Disappointed in you.'

Amelia flinched at the D word. She and Julian had joked years ago that it didn't matter how much of a telling-off you got, so long as they didn't use the D word which would reduce you to a quivering mass of shame.

'So am I,' said Amelia. 'I think we should bring Patti here until Paula has recovered from her Temptation.'

'What?' Julian was outraged. 'Bring her here? I don't want sight or sound of it, you hear me? I don't want anything to do with it. And as for Paula, well she'll never get clean, you hear? Never.' He turned back into the doghouse, opened the back door and admitted a blast of snow-flecked cold. The door banged against the twin-tub. The peg bag clattered to the floor. 'I'm not standing around to listen to any more of this —'

Julian disappeared. A small man with oriental features, pushed his way into the kitchen, followed by a Great Dane and three elderly women.

'Save him,' one of the women commanded. She had one hand on the dog's lead, the other clutching the twin-tub. 'The vet says he's got to be put down.'

'She doesn't do dogs,' Edith said, 'And what are you doing in our kitchen?'

'My wife, she said you will cure her of the growth,' the oriental man announced. 'Her breasts they are all eaten away, she say. She say she will die and our children be without their mother. She say I must find another wife but I cannot. I want only her.'

'Deary me,' said Edith. 'How sad. But you really shouldn't be in our kitchen, you know. It's private property.'

'What about Humphrey?' one of the women said. 'Please, if you could just try …'

The women and the man crowded round Amelia pressed up against the oven. The casserole exuded a dead animal stench.

'This is madness,' Julian said, lurching back into the kitchen like Frankenstein's monster, covered in snow. 'Get out, all of you. What the hell —'

'We will pay.' One of the women thrust a handful of notes under Julian's nose. 'Anything, if you will just help Humphrey.'

Julian grabbed the money, stared at it in disbelief. 'Amelia,' he ordered. 'Have a look at this dog, will you. I think maybe it's about time your Goddess started living up to her reputation.'

The women moved away from Amelia, allowing her to escape the smell of rotten pork. The dog was lying on the cool lino, a look of utter exhaustion in his limpid eyes.

'What's the matter with him?' she asked.

'We don't know,' one of the women replied. 'The vet says that he could do surgery to find out. It pains him to walk the shortest distance. He's out of breath. My sisters and I had to carry him here.'

Amelia looked from the enormous dog to the three tiny women and wondered how on earth they managed. 'I don't know if I can help,' she said, aware of Julian sidling out of the back door, clutching the money. 'And I couldn't take your money …' Julian was gone.

'Please.' The smallest of the women begged in a voice so high it was nearly on the dogs-only register. 'Please try. Humphrey is all we have. The man of the house since Daddy died.'

Amelia crouched down on her haunches. The oriental man was at her shoulder, breathing gingery fumes down her neck. She stroked the dog's head, remembering the puppy from over the road. Youthful Portly had died in spite of her ministrations. This dog didn't stand a chance. It looked ancient with its mournful eyebrows flecked with grey, and eyes that were bloodshot and pale. His heaving ribs, clearly visible beneath a dull coat showed he was having terrible difficulty breathing. She placed her hands where she thought his heart might be and closed her eyes. She thought of Irena, of her new baby growing within her. She tried to summon up the power that had cured Dominic, but the smell of pork, dying dog and ginger put her off. The Chinese man breathed heavily in her ear. She was completely useless.

The air stirred. A draught of cold whipped around her neck, then a dampness, as though she were walking in early morning grass covered with dew. Her face was stroked, tickled by a moth's wing, cobwebby lightness of touch. It was a welcome relief. A hand was upon her shoulder, a loving hand, telling her to trust in whatever happened. Her heart slowed. Warm fur stirred beneath her touch, warm breath against her skin. Movement, life, vigour. The dog was on his feet. She heard retching. The dog was vomiting. Nausea rose in her own gullet. What if she had done more harm than good? Someone began to clap, a short, staccato sound, others joined in until the kitchen was full of rapturous applause. Amelia felt cold, slightly woozy. She opened her eyes and the dog was running about the kitchen, lively as a puppy. On the floor was a slimy Tesco carrier bag.

'It is a miracle,' one of the sisters said, reaching out to touch Amelia's arm. 'You have saved him. How would we have known he had eaten the bag as well as the shopping?' She knelt, her sisters knelt. The Oriental man crossed himself.

Edith lit another cigarette and clutched her rosary. 'I've seen it with my own eyes, now. Father Murphy can eat his hat. You are a living saint. Not, of course, that I ever doubted it. Amelia, dear girl, people will be shouting your name from the rooftops for years to come.'

Chapter 23
12th December 1981

Con didn't return to the house for two days. On the night of the Humphrey Miracle, Dolores reported seeing him outside The Three Legs as she walked home, supported by Father Murphy, whose footwear was more suited to the weather than her own. She said Con was lying in the snow, shouting about the Pope and she was so ashamed, she had hurried on right past him as though he was nothing to do with her. On returning to the fold, he was in good spirits, and there wasn't the usual reek of alcohol about him. His pink face had been scrubbed till it gleamed and he was wearing his best suit that was only slightly shiny about the elbows and thighs.

'I see your fan club is growing, Amelia, my girl,' he boomed, bursting into the parlour where Amelia was sitting in her dressing gown, munching on a bowl of Coco Pops.

She nodded, glad to see him. Con might do an awful lot of complaining, but he kept Julian in order and ever since her brother's collapse, she worried that if it happened again, herself, Dolores and Edith wouldn't have a clue what to do.

'There were two hundred and eight people there yesterday. Dolores counted. Billy Butler from Radio City phoned up and asked if he could do an interview.'

Con frowned, but it hardly ruffled his cheerful expression.

'Not yet, dear niece. Not yet. We don't want all the loonies from Rainhill turning up and making this into any more of a circus.'

'You shouldn't call them "loonies",' said Dolores who had spent three months in the hospital the year before. Looking at her, Amelia wondered if she was due another visit. Dolores had transformed overnight. She was clad from head to toe in black with lots of black eyeliner smeared around her eyes and she had whitened her cheeks with stage makeup. Amelia suspected she was turning into a New Romantic, which was awful enough in her school-friends. In a thirty-six year old woman, it was a complete disgrace. Amelia hated Steve Strange and Adam Ant.

'Any tea to be had round here, today?' Con asked, patting Amelia on the head in a way he had never done before. 'Got a thirst on me like ten good men and true. Get the kettle on, Dolores. I want to talk to Our Amelia.'

'Tea? Bit tame for you, isn't it, Con?' Dolores said. 'You're usually on your second bottle by this time.'

'Oh, just get the tea, will you? This is important.'

The snow gave the morning a peculiar, unearthly quality, a luminous muffled silence. Con plonked his bulk into the chair beside Amelia. She munched her Coco Pops with their delicious chocolaty milk. It was like a milkshake only better.

'I want to talk straight to you,' Con said, picking up Amelia's piece of toast and jam and tucking in. 'You're my niece, I've known you since you were knee high to a grasshopper but I think you're old enough now to get what I'm talking about.'

Amelia nodded. Her cheeks were scarlet. She hated it when adults spoke in this way, pretending she was equal to them when all the time they were giving her a telling off.

'I've been talking to that two-bob priest down there and he's very worried.'

Amelia held the bowl up to her lips and allowed the last of the chocolate milk to slide down her throat. She would have to ask for another piece of toast.

'He thinks that all this … virgin birth business is out of control. All these people etcetera.' He waved his arm vaguely in the direction of the window. 'If it's still going on when the Pope gets here in May, then we're in trouble.'

Amelia shrugged, an action she knew annoyed Con.

'I don't know why they're all here,' she said. 'It's not my fault. They want me to do miracles.' She blushed.

Since her success with Humphrey, she had attempted to cure an old woman of some wasting disease, a cat of flu, and a small boy of some awful facial disfigurement. None of these attempts had produced anything like the results she had hoped for, but the hopeful, far from being disappointed, had gone away happy that "the Will of God" had been done. Edith put a plank against the back door to stop anyone else getting into the house but that morning, a young journalist had managed to climb down the chimney and been given short shrift by Dolores in her black negligee. She phoned the police and an officer was stationed outside the front door as though the prime minister lived there.

'I know, love.' Con finished Amelia's toast, wiped his greasy lips with the back of his hand and patted her arm. 'And I hear you have indeed performed some miracles.'

Amelia nodded, conscious of Con, staring at her swollen breasts inside her thin nightdress. 'There was the boy over the road and the dog, Humphrey ...'

Con smiled. 'You're a clever girl. I've always thought it.'

Amelia frowned. Con usually said she was as thick as two planks, just like Edith.

'But the thing is ... If you intend to go on with this charade, then you could be in big trouble.'

'What charade?'

Con looked annoyed, no longer friendly. 'Father Murphy called me yesterday. He warned me that if you carry on saying you're the Mother of God, the Catholic Mafia will have you put away. You'll end up in Rainhill like Dolores — or somewhere worse.'

'Why?' Amelia rose with difficulty. 'I've done nothing wrong.'

'Of course you haven't. You weren't to know. A little joke that went too far ...'

'It's not a joke!' Tears pricked Amelia's eyes. Con never believed her. Not even when she was seven and saw burglars in the garden next door. He had sent her back to bed and Martha Morgan's fake Fabergé egg had been stolen from the windowsill.

'Oh, Jesus!' Con rose, tried to calm Amelia by placing a hand on her shoulder. 'Look, I don't want you upset, lass. It's just that saying you're having the daughter of God when you're a virgin ... and then these so-called miracles. Well, you're drawing attention to yourself. And without some kind of proof, then I'm afraid you'll be ... You can't listen to that lot of hysterics!' He flung his arm wide, knocking the light-shade making it swing violently. 'Amelia, love ...'

Edith stalked in, carrying a tray of tea. Last night she had dropped her teeth down the toilet and flushed before she realised, leaving the bottom half of her face folded into a bunch of wrinkled flesh, making her nose overly large and her neck a continuation of her baggy cheeks.

'The post has arrived,' she announced, sucking at her gums. 'And here is the tea, Con. Never ask Dolores. She puts new tea in every pot.'

There was a great pile of letters, all with a Liverpool postmark, except one, from Ireland, addressed in Marguerite's neat hand. Every one was marked for Amelia's urgent attention. She trembled with excitement. She loved receiving letters and hardly ever did. This was a new and unexpected pleasure. She seized the first one and ripped it open. Money, five pound notes, spilled out onto the table. With it came a letter from a desperate mother, begging Amelia to cure her baby who had been born with spina bifida. Con seized the letter, spread out the notes on the table. One hundred and fifty pounds. Amelia opened another envelope, again stuffed with money, this time asking her to cure a husband whose mind had gone. Con and Amelia worked through the rest of the mail. All were sad tales of illness and despair, many had enclosed money. By the time Amelia got round to opening her mother's, there was over four hundred pounds in a neat pile on her table mat.

'Well, well, well,' Con said, lighting a Capstan. 'You've got a right little cottage industry going here. Miracles for money. And in the twentieth century too, the new scientific age …'

'Science can't answer everything,' Edith said, slowly. 'Only God can do that.'

'But I'm not God.' Amelia gazed down at the money. It couldn't be right that these people thought that it would buy her help. She knew that she couldn't help most of them, would not even try. Although the Goddess was powerful, she couldn't be expected to spend her whole time preventing death.

'You can't take that money,' Edith said. 'Blood money. Desperation money. Our Lord Jesus never got paid for his services. You'll have to send it back.'

Amelia nodded, mesmerised by the pile of letters, the taller pile of cash and cheques.

'I'll help you,' Edith said. 'I'll buy a packet of envelopes and a Basildon Bond pad. We'll tell them —'

'Not so fast,' Con placed his hand over Amelia's. 'Just think. How much is it going to cost? Envelopes, writing paper, stamps. It'll cost a fortune and you're giving a fortune back. I can't cure all the people who walk into my consulting rooms. Even they know that, but they're willing to pay for hope.

That's what this money is, not blood money. It is paying for a little slice of hope and who are we to take that away?'

'People can still have hope,' Edith replied. 'You don't have to pay for it. Once they know the New Saviour is about to be born, then that should be enough. It was the same in Jesus' time.'

'People today do not believe that anything of any worth comes for free. Without payment, they think they are being fobbed off, patronised. They will sink back into despair before you know it. Amelia, we need to think carefully before we act.'

Amelia sighed. What with the windows tight shut against the snow and the gas fire on full and the growing baby, her body was heating up. Outside, someone played a guitar, while the rosary was being prayed through a loud speaker. The speaker's unfortunate stutter, meant that every Hail Mary took twice as long as it should. Rosary beads clacked, children wailed. In a few days, Eighteen Calvary Crescent had become a prison. If she so much as opened a door, she was mobbed by desperate people. And now there was the money.

'My cup floweth over,' Amelia said, thinking of Jesus in the garden in Gethsemane.

'Oh, for crying out loud,' Con said. 'Stop being so bloody dramatic. You set yourself up as this born again Virgin Mary. This is the consequence.'

'She didn't "set herself up",' Edith said. 'When God chooses us for his special purpose, then we cannot refuse.'

Amelia tore open the last letter in the pile, the letter from her mother. It was hand-written upon headed notepaper, expensive stuff bearing the insignia of the Convent of the Holy Head. An embossed seal showing a Turin-shroud-type mournful Christ took up nearly half the page.

Dear Amelia,

How are you? I thought you would have written by now. You have the address after all and I have heard nothing from you or anyone else in the family since my last phone call. I hope you are doing well in your exams. The sisters here have said prayers for you.

You will be glad to know that I'll be home very soon. Suffice to say that the convent was not at all as I expected. I also have some wonderful news for you. Please write and tell me how you are doing. I would also appreciate a letter from one of your aunts. I will be back soon.

Look after yourself,

Mum xxxxxxx

Amelia placed the letter face down on the table and sipped her milky tea. Her mother would be home soon. She shuddered. Would the baby be born by then? She wouldn't be able to disguise her expanding stomach, that was for sure, and then there would be all those people queuing up outside to explain. Marguerite would have one of her Blue Fits. Amelia was too tired to imagine what might happen. She knew that her mother would find a way to put a stop to it all, like she ruined her success as Eurydice in the school play by telling her that the "peas had got above the sticks" and she should concentrate on doing her lessons rather than "wafting around in a piece of net".

Now, Dolores was back and Con and Edith were coming to blows. Edith scrabbled for the letters and money. Con lunged for the notes that were wafting down from her skinny arms towards the gas fire that was turned up so high it was going into meltdown.

'You stupid old cow,' Con bellowed, rescuing the money as quickly as it was falling. 'We can't afford to throw all this away. You've got to think of the future, not that I'll have one once news of this bloody farce leaks out. A shrink whose niece gets up the duff by the Angel Gabriel is hardly going to get work from people in mental distress. I'll look a proper charlatan.'

'You don't need Amelia to do that,' Edith retorted. 'Most of Liverpool knows what you're like.'

'Yeah. We all read the Echo last year,' Dolores joined in. 'That poor woman, Gladys Cliff, committed suicide when she was on the train to Chester, going home from seeing you and there was that other thing that was never proved — the woman who reckoned you and her had a fling. The kid's got a nose just like yours. And, for the record, I agree with Edith over the cash. It should be returned.'

'Mum's coming home soon,' Amelia announced. Why did she, as the youngest, have to take on her mother's role as the only adult in her family, especially when they fell to bickering? 'We'll have to have it all sorted out before then.'

Silence fell in the room, broken only by a rendition of kum by ya sung outside to the strumming of a tuneless guitar.

Dolores sighed loudly. 'This never would have happened if Marguerite had been around.'

The telephone rang. Everyone stared at each other, convinced it was Marguerite, that she had caught wind of the good news and wanted to know what was going on.

'I'll answer it,' Dolores said. 'I'm supposed to be in charge here. Now that Ken and I ... Well, I see myself as Amelia's protector in the absence of her mother.' She tottered into the hall, her face grim.

'Don't worry, love,' Edith said, patting Amelia's head. 'The Blessed Virgin didn't have it easy but she got through in the end.'

Dolores was gone for less than a minute, but when she returned, she looked more worried than ever.

'It was a woman called Paula. A friend of Julian's apparently. She says she's left a parcel for us down the hozzi. It belongs to us apparently.'

CHAPTER 24

The arrival of the squalling Patti in the arms of a policewoman brought a welcome diversion. Paula had left the baby in the Royal Liverpool Hospital, a note as to where she should be delivered pinned to her romper suit. The child was wrapped in a grubby green blanket, her face red and furious below the yellow hair. As soon as Edith saw her, she began to gush and coo, her dicky knee gave way and she dropped to the floor, bashing her thigh on the corner of the hearth. In the excitement, no one noticed except Amelia.

The thing about a baby in the house, Amelia realised, was that it stopped everyone from arguing. There was so much to do, what with finding somewhere for the child to sleep (the huge top drawer was taken out of the barley twist sideboard), mashing up carrot and potato for her tea, changing her napkin (Paula had provided a bag of clean terry nappies), and generally entertaining the poor little thing who, prophet or no, looked completely perplexed by her new environment. While all this was going on, Amelia attempted to explain Julian's part in Patti's existence to Con but found herself struggling when trying to work out how he came to be a father. So wrong, and so arbitrary.

'Paula was his girlfriend,' she said. 'They must have got married before the baby was born.'

'How do you work that one out?' Con demanded, shaking his head. 'I think I need a drink. Here I go falling off the bloody wagon as soon as I've climbed on. It's this crazy family, it's enough to drive anyone to Gin Alley.'

'Not me,' said Dolores, sorting through some ancient baby clothes Amelia had brought down from the cockloft. 'I've given up. Do you think these smell too musty?' She shoved an ornate christening gown under Con's nose.

'That was mine,' he said, fingering the disintegrating lace. 'It's over sixty years old. You can't put the kid in that.'

'Well, Amelia's wearing one of Mabel's tea frocks and that goes back to before the war so I can't see what the problem is.'

'I can.' Con opened the drinks cabinet, sadly depleted since Grandma's death. He extracted a bottle of Angostura bitters and a miniature of navy rum, held the bottles up to the snow-bright window. They were empty, their contents long ago congealed to a sticky deposit on the sides of the glass. He left them on the windowsill next to the Cornish piskie perched on a pebble; a souvenir from Newquay.

The baby made a difference to the people outside. All loud singing and praying ceased and a hush descended, as though everyone was waiting for an announcement from the Papal window in Rome. The silence was not restful, rather it was a palpable, breathing silence full of expectation and longing.

'Patti,' Amelia informed her family, 'is the prophet, a bit like John the Baptist only a girl. She'll be the one to announce the Saviour when it's time.'

'This place is a bloody lunatic asylum,' Con said. 'Dolores, have you got any gin?'

'You can have any that's left. I've all but taken the pledge.'

Con shuffled off into the kitchen, shaking his head.

'Where is the mother, anyway?' Dolores had really taken to Patti, sitting with her on her knee, crooning and smiling down at the little trusting face.

'She lives up the road. Passion Close,' Amelia said.

'But why has she sent the baby here?'

Amelia told her about the depressing visit. 'I think she's worried about the Temptation,' she finished. 'Maybe she thinks the baby will be better off with us.'

'I hope she's right,' Dolores looked down on Patti. 'It's funny, she's so like you. Sometimes I wish I'd had children but Ken would've made a lousy father. I never meet the right people until it's too late ... Father Murphy thinks I was wasted on Ken.'

Amelia was hardly listening. Her mother said that Dolores was a "law unto herself". Apparently, even when they were young, Marguerite had to take her in hand. There was the time Dolores came home in tears from school, after being told that the black baby she had purchased with two old pence from a visiting missionary priest would, after all, remain in Africa with his mother. She had been so convinced that her charitable donation would result in the child being delivered to her school, that she cried tears of rage and frustration all evening. Marguerite had to calm her by putting the picture of the baby on their bedroom wall, over the St Francis calendar Aunt Alice bought them every year. Amelia smiled, remembering her mother's contempt as she related the tale.

Remembering felt good, better than the present. The baby inside her was growing fast and the Goddess was turning up all the time, her last materialisation being less than an hour earlier, when she had appeared in a blaze of light up in the cockloft. Amelia had dropped all the mould and moth blighted baby clothes in awe. Did this mean that her time of confinement was close at hand? Would it be over by the time her mother disembarked the ferry? And what would Marguerite do when she found out that she had become a grandmother twice over during the three weeks she had been away?

A vision of her freshly dyed hair, the new skin-tight jeans and the ra-ra skirt deposed any doting grey-haired grandma fantasy Amelia briefly entertained. There would almost certainly be a Blue Fit.

She left Patti and Dolores, rapt in each other's company, and plodded into the kitchen. She was no longer walking like a thirteen year old, but someone well into middle age, weighty of jowl and thick of ankle. Con and Julian were sharing the last of Dolores' gin and counting the "hope" money Amelia had been sent through the post. Their eyes had grown smaller and they both wore the same expression of calculating greed as they contemplated the piles of one, five, ten and twenty pound notes. Amelia, not wanting to speak to either of them, ducked behind the door, and prayed to Irena that they would clear out of the kitchen so she could investigate the biscuit tin.

'Marge owns a convent and half a million,' Con complained. 'And Edith wants to give this cash back.'

'Well she can't.' Julian grabbed a handful of notes.

'I wouldn't bet on it.' Con sighed and sipped at the gin. 'It's not ours to keep, that's the problem. By rights it belongs to Amelia but if we let her have it, that means going public with the whole virgin birth thing and my reputation just wouldn't stand it.'

'How much do you earn?' Julian demanded. 'Go on, during the average month, what do you bring home?'

Con shrugged. 'I don't know. About a thousand, I suppose, after tax.'

Julian brandished the money. 'There's over a thousand here. Amelia earned that in less than a week. You don't need your sodding business. If we play this right, we could be millionaires in no time at all. Mum can keep her convent.'

'We'd never get away with it.'

Julian grinned. 'Looks like I've a kid to bring up. I want to go to college, get myself an education. I want to be someone. You can't do that without money.'

'The amount of money you've been shooting into your arm would probably buy you a modest penthouse. Anyway, what the hell would Marguerite say if she knew we'd peddled the kid to the public?'

Julian shrugged. He pocketed a few notes, drank more gin. His movements were jerky and uncoordinated. He looked thinner than ever, his skin deathly white against the murky yellow and black of the kitchen tiles.

'What we need,' Con said, thoughtfully, 'is someone to take up the cause for us. If it's us spreading the word, then it looks dodgy. We get some bona fide religious dignitary to talk about it, then we might convince the powers that be.'

'That's right.' Julian jumped up. 'The Pope's coming to Liverpool next year sometime. Edith's always banging on about it. Why don't we write to him?'

'Don't be daft, lad,' Con said shaking his head. 'To get the Pope to endorse a miracle is about as hard as getting Dolores to admit she's a whore. No, we need more grist to our mill, we need a miracle of our own.'

The telephone rang shrilly, disturbing Con's reverie and sending Amelia into a blind panic. She staggered into the hall and seized the receiver, fully expecting her mother to be at the other end, saying she was at the ferry terminal in Liverpool waiting for a cab. Instead, found herself talking to a woman with a strong Irish accent, who introduced herself as the Mother Superior of the Convent of the Holy Head.

'Does Marguerite O'Dowd live there?' Her tone was ingratiating and annoyed.

'Mum?' Amelia said. 'She's in Ireland, at your convent.'

'Ah, you must be the girl, Amelia,' the nun replied, greasily. 'I have heard so much about you. May the Lord walk with you.'

'Why are you asking for Mum?'

'Can I speak to an adult?' the nun said. 'This is a matter for a grown up.'

'But where is my Mum?'

'Who is it?' Dolores called from the parlour.

Amelia held the phone handset on her shoulder. 'The Convent where Mum's staying. They want to know if she's here.'

At once, Con was at her side, wresting the receiver from her grip.

'Hello, hello,' he said. 'I'm so glad you called …' He shooed Amelia out of the hall into the parlour and closed the door behind her.

Amelia sat with Dolores who was cradling Patti. A strong feeling of impending doom washed over her.

'Why would that nun be asking if Mum was here?' she asked.

'I don't know, love,' Dolores said. 'Ah, look at her, don't you think she's cute?'

Amelia nodded, smiled briefly at baby Patti. 'But what about Mum? What if she's disappeared? She's in Ireland and there's the IRA and everything. What if she's been bombed?'

Dolores rocked Patti who was drifting off to sleep.

'I'm sure I don't know, but this little creature has settled in well, don't you think? It's almost as though she recognises me as family.'

Amelia gave up. She thought of her mother's last letter. Marguerite had mentioned some important news. Maybe she was in danger. She had said nothing about leaving the convent … A terrible thought occurred to Amelia. What if, annoyed that no one had written from home, she had decided to return from Ireland early to catch her out on whatever it was her mother suspected her of doing?

Amelia caught sight of her own startled face in the spotted mirror on the sideboard. She looked hot and flushed, her yellow hair clashing with the slight orange tinge to her skin. Her face had become fatter, her cheeks more rounded; she was developing a double chin. She thought about her friends, who were starting to go out with boys. Although she didn't miss school one little bit, she missed Martha and Catherine and the others, remembered with fondness their idle chat about the Blue Coat schoolboys on the bus home, their plans for new hairstyles and clothes. She wondered if she would ever have a boyfriend, now that she had been chosen by Irena. There was a boy who lived on Gethsemane Drive, who used to stare at her intently when she walked up to the shop for her mother. They had never spoken, but Amelia liked the look of him. She used to think about him sometimes but never for too long. The nuns at school had warned them all about the dangers of boys, of letting them anywhere near without a convenient hedge or a gate to keep them at bay. Sins of thought were just as potent as those acted out.

'Marguerite's done a bunk,' Con said, bursting through the door. 'The nuns haven't a clue where she's gone. Thought she was here. Can you imagine! She's run off from her own bloody convent!'

Amelia's heart tightened with worry. So it was true. Marguerite had either been kidnapped by the IRA or was at this moment on her way home. She didn't want either of these things to happen, but right now, faced with explaining the pregnancy, she preferred the IRA option, and after all, Edith had been so sorry for that poor Bobby Sands whose name was spray-painted all over the M62 motorway bridge near Huyton.

'Maybe she's sightseeing,' Dolores suggested. 'There are some lovely places over there and she doesn't get away often.'

'Ah, I used to love going to the Old Country with Father Monagle,' Edith announced, sucking loudly on her toothless gums. 'We had our favourite places. Little out-of-the-way farms, small hotels in the towns. Those were the days.'

'You'd think Al Monagle was still alive and well and living round the corner,' Dolores said, cheerfully. 'Not in his grave twenty years. Now then, look at this little one.' She gazed down with absolute fondness. 'I fink it's time you went to beddy weddy,' she said, kissing the curly head. 'Up the wooden hill to Bedfordshire …'

If Marguerite came through the door now, Amelia thought, what would happen? Would she shout and rail? Would she believe her story? Would the Goddess protect her?

'Anyway, the upshot is,' Con said, 'I've invited Sister Polycarp over. She wants to take a reckie of the place the Pope's going to visit. Sounds a fine woman, she does, if a little bossy. Don't think she got on too well with Marguerite, but then not a lot of people do.'

'Sister Polycarp?' Edith adopted the pious expression that accompanied any mention of the clergy.

'Mother Superior of the Convent of the Holy Head.' Con sat down at the table and smiled secretively. Amelia, seeing him, dreaded what this could mean.

Chapter 25
13th December

The crowd were praying and singing as fiercely as ever. The brief reprieve caused by the arrival of Patti was over by Sunday. With the approach of Christmas, the hymns had adopted a nativity theme; The Angel Gabriel To Mary Came, was a big favourite, with In The Bleak Midwinter coming a close second, the latter being sung with more than a hint of irony. The snow had returned with increased vigour, obliterating the usual landscape of Calvary Crescent and the many worshippers, whose icy forms loomed like gravestones in the front garden and beyond. Many had signed up to a rota of duty so that only the hardiest would have to stand outside for a long time.

It was not all rosary beads and muttering. There was some good natured bantering in between religious observances. A book was running on the probability of a White Christmas (currently 3 to 4 against), the hot dog stall had been joined by a holy medal stand, doing swift business with some hastily knocked up 'Virgin of the Garden' statuettes and Human League sweatshirts suitable for 'arctic conditions'. The local Brownies handed out blankets fashioned from knitted squares in all the colours of the rainbow.

All this was made irrelevant by the Goddess Irena as she shimmered over the scene, her magnificent form blossoming over the parameters of the fence, billowing out so that she was almost in next-door's frozen compost heap.

'Goddess,' Amelia prayed from her grandmother's bedroom window. 'Where is Mum?'

The phone rang in the hall.

The Goddess smiled. Her eyes were liquid silver, gleaming and unearthly, her hair the colour of white gold, blending into the blizzard. Irena shook her head, looked upon Her disciple with pity. *She is safe. Do not worry.*

'But what if she comes home before the baby. What if …'

Again Irena tossed her gleaming locks. *Do not concern yourself. You have many trials to face before the time is nigh. The first is almost upon you but do not be afraid, do not let it steer you from your course.*

'What trial? Where?'

The Goddess raised her hand in farewell. Amelia stared intently as the form dissolved into snow, wishing she was as excited, as overawed as she had been that far off day in the cockloft when, after such a long wait, She had first appeared.

Irena had changed. Now, instead of vanishing in a blaze of heavenly light, there was a dark patch where she had been, a slowly rotating black hole. The garden began to swirl, as though being sucked inwards, a kaleidoscope of black and white forms, natural and man-made, whizzing into a dark whirlpool. Amelia gripped the windowsill. She was dizzy, out of control. Irena was gone; the garden and the bedroom disappeared. All that was left was a terrifying hole, sucking her ever inwards. She tried to move away from the window, but couldn't keep her balance. Her knees giving way, her body falling, falling, into the dark …

'Get off the floor, Amelia,' Con said. 'You're going to have to look after your brother's baby for a while, I've a consultation at ten and God knows, I need to keep hold of the patients I've still got. No idea where Julian's off to. Down Toxteth, scoring, no doubt.' He wrenched at her arm but she couldn't move. 'And there's another problem. The bishop … the bloody Archbishop of Liverpool's secretary has just phoned up and demanded that we go down and see him. You are causing a hell of a fuss, Amelia. I hope you're proud of yourself.'

Amelia thought her head was about to explode. She tried to sit up, but her body was too heavy. For some reason she was crammed between the huge carved Egyptian bed and the dressing table.

'Amelia?' Con edged round the side of the bed.

'I can't …' She reached for the edge of the dressing table as it swam from view.

'Amelia, what's the matter?' Con was lifting her head, looking into her face. He took a torch from his pocket and shone it into each eye.

'Can you see that?' He swung the beam this way and that. Amelia's eyes began to water. He straightened her shoulders so that she was lying flat on her back on the floor, staring up at the ceiling. There was a damp stain in the plaster, in the shape of a praying child. Con shook his head as though trying to rid his ear of an annoying fly.

'This isn't the first time you've had one of these dizzy spells, is it?' he asked. 'Have you fallen before?'

'Is the baby all right?' she asked, panicking.

'Never mind the baby. Patti's asleep. I am more concerned with these falls of yours.'

She sat up and blinked. 'I must have tripped over,' she said, wondering how she had arrived on the floor. 'I saw the Goddess outside the window and —'

Con replaced the torch. 'I think ... Oh God, this is all I need,' he said, despairingly. 'Your Goddess is an aura, love. You need a neurologist, never mind an archbishop ... Oh, hell, I said I'd go now ... Look, forget I said anything. There is too much at stake here.'

Anaura. This had a pleasingly religious ring. It was the first time he had acknowledged that Irena existed. If her head hadn't been pounding so much, Amelia would have leaped in joy.

Con was not in the mood to talk about his sudden conversion. He stood up, patted down his white doctor's coat, and went to the window. Amelia's eyelids were so heavy. She had hardly slept the night before, imagining terrible scenarios for Marguerite's disappearance. By the morning, Amelia had convinced herself that Marguerite was lying in a gutter somewhere, shot dead by a criminal.

She climbed onto her grandmother's bed. The candlewick bedspread and lumpy mattress made the most inviting, the most comfortable bed in the world. She closed her eyes. She was at peace, her mother was safe, Irena had told her so. So long as she ignored the whirling blackness, she could convince herself that all was well.

The room was in darkness when Amelia awoke. The carols were still going on outside, but not nearly so loudly, and she suspected that people had left their posts as night fell, gone home to their families and tea on the table. Only that morning, Con had gloomily intoned that they would all go for good once they realised there was a little chance of another miracle as the first had been a travesty. And the weather had taken a turn for the worst. Dolores reminded him of Lourdes which, as far as she knew, had been miracle-free for donkey's years. The conversation deteriorated into the usual row.

The noise outside might have dimmed but there sounded to be quite a crowd downstairs from what Amelia could gather. A lot of people were talking all at once, in the parlour directly below her grandmother's room. She sat up, thinking at first that her mother might have returned but quickly decided that there was no way Marguerite would have let her slob about in bed for a whole day unless she was ill. Had Con brought in some people from outside? Maybe he sympathised with them out there in the night air and invited them in for a drink and a biscuit. She frowned. No, that was more Edith's style. But she wouldn't dare invite any of the devotees Con referred to as 'loonies', into the front parlour unless he had gone home early.

She swung her legs over the side of the bed. The baby gave a little purr and Amelia pictured her, tiny and perfect, pirouetting inside. She shivered and groped on the floor for her slippers.

As she hesitated at the top of the stairs, she could hear voices, female and Irish, she didn't recognise. She made her way down. Each breath was an effort and her heart thudded painfully. She remembered Catherine Mulhearn's mother in the days before her confinement, complaining that her baby was pushing up into the space her lungs usually filled, taking up all the air. This was how Amelia felt, though her stomach was relatively small. Her progress was slow and silent.

The parlour was full. The six dining room chairs were taken up by Edith, Dolores and four nuns in old-fashioned winged wimples. Father Murphy was sitting on one of the easy chairs and Mr Lawless was on the other. Con stood with his back to the window while Julian perched on the kitchen stool, swaying slightly. His eyes were swivelling in opposite directions as though someone had hit him on the head. At first no one noticed Amelia, they were all so busy with their own affairs.

'Gwendolyn can't take much more,' Mr Lawless was saying in his whispery voice. 'She's on sleeping tablets, now. More and more every night. I'm afraid she'll do herself a mischief. Can't you do anything?'

'It must be hard for you,' Father Murphy said, looking not the least bit interested.

'I hope it's not too hard for you,' Dolores said, leaning back in her chair to grip the priest's knee. 'You're a tower of strength.'

One of the nuns was taller than the others. She wore a pair of horn-rimmed glasses. Her face was the colour and shape of the rich tea biscuits piled on one of Grandma's best plates. She helped herself to another one, while munching thoughtfully on her last.

'Only plain until His Holiness comes,' Edith explained handing them around the table. 'Usually we have chocolate digestives when there's clergy.'

The other nuns each took a biscuit and nibbled silently. The taller one noticed Amelia and fixed her with a mournful stare.

'You must be the girl,' she barked in a harsh Northern Irish accent. 'Come here, let me look at you.'

Amelia attempted to edge around the chairs, but what with the nuns and the girth of her neighbour, she became wedged between Edith and Mr Lawless.

'I'm sorry,' she said as Edith heaved herself up.

Mr Lawless remained where he was, looking disgruntled.

'I've only just got settled,' he complained. 'And you've caused me enough discomfort in recent days.'

'I'm sorry,' she said.

'No need to be. Get in the light, child,' the nun commanded. 'I need to have a look at you.'

The nun rose from her chair. It shocked Amelia how tall she was. Taller than Con, or anyone in the room She was well over six feet and with a bosom that hung like a grassy promontory over a cliff face. Her glasses were the size of small goldfish bowls and magnified her eyes to a ridiculous degree. She prodded Amelia's stomach and sighed loudly.

'You never told me on the phone that she was pregnant,' she accused. 'About three months, you say? Surely you can see that I can't take her on in this condition.'

'It's the New Saviour,' Amelia explained.

'Whoever it is, dear,' the nun said, 'there is only one way to get in that state and that is to copulate with a male of the species. Now either you are a liar or you're a fool, girl. Either way, you're no good to me.'

'This is Sister Polycarp,' Con announced. 'Good Mother of the Convent of the Holy Head, Derrynasaggart Mountains.'

'Where's Mum?' Amelia demanded. 'You were looking for her.'

The nun gave Con a filthy look. 'Your mother left us on Wednesday. She didn't give a forwarding address.'

'Well, where is she?'

Sister Polycarp looked embarrassed for a moment, then covered it over with a disapproving stare.

'How am I supposed to know? She was in her cell when I left her on Wednesday morning to say matins. Her belongings and her personage were gone before breakfast at six-thirty. No goodbyes, nothing.'

'That's not like her,' Amelia said. Her mother was known for her meticulous planning. She would never take off without informing half the world of her destination. But she had been acting rather oddly since Grandma died. There was the hair colour, the lipstick, the weird clothes. And the surprise she had for Amelia, promised in her last letter.

'I assure you, she was quite well,' Sister Polycarp said with a sickly smile, revealing vampirish canines. 'More than well. The Lord himself can only know what she was getting up to in that room with Pádraig.'

Con sniggered.

'Anyway,' the nun continued. 'This is all beside the point. I thought you had a girl for us, Mr O'Dowd. Ready to take the veil you said and now I find myself looking at a schoolchild with a bellyful of baby.'

'You mean Amelia's to become a nun,' Edith exclaimed. 'Oh, the Lord works in mysterious ways, Sister. I would have taken the veil myself, you know. Given myself as a bride of Christ but I was —'

'Sister Polycarp, how many novices did you have at your convent, the last time you counted?' Con asked.

The nun, still standing, looked up at the ceiling. There was a big crack running diagonally from corner to corner, a reminder of the bomb that fell on Gethsemane Drive in 1940.

'Not a single girl has come to us in more than thirty years,' another nun piped up. She was small and bent, wizened as a tree root.

'Thank you, Swithbert,' Sister Polycarp snapped. 'Yes, it's true. We've had some difficulty recruiting sisters in the last few years, but we never give up hope. There is life in me yet to hand on the mantle to the young.'

'And if no young come forward?' Con was standing close to the tall nun, looking at her enormous bust with scorn.

'Then our Order will be finished.'

A moment of silence ensued, as everyone in the room digested this uncomfortable fact along with the dry rich tea biscuits. One of the nuns, smaller than Swithbert and just as ancient, began to sob. Swithbert helped herself to another biscuit and bit it delicately, like a rabbit nibbling a carrot. She didn't seem the least put out that her Order was on the brink of extinction.

'This is all fine and dandy,' Mr Lawless piped up. 'Only people are camping in my front garden. My winter pansies are completely ruined and I can't tell you what havoc they've wreaked with the brassicas. Leaves all over the shop. I was going to build a rock garden next Spring. Mrs L likes a rock garden; thought it might cheer her up. Heard about them on Gardener's World. I've all the gubbins.'

Everyone ignored him.

'You must remember that this family have kept you going for years,' Con said. 'It is no coincidence that we thought of you when this unfortunate accident happened.'

'Payback time,' said Sister Swithbert, cheerfully. 'It was bound to come, Poll.'

'Don't call me Poll.' Sister Polycarp pushed her chair back so that it went flying, the backrest landing on Mr Lawless's fat arm. He screeched in pain.

'I will not be blackmailed,' she said. 'If we take on this girl, there will be questions.'

Con brushed aside the net curtains, opening them to the night. Half a dozen faces pressed against the glass.

'Already half of Liverpool is hailing her as the new Bernadette,' he explained. 'The sooner she joins your convent the better. The fuss will die down. In this situation, it's the best solution for everyone.'

The weeping nun gave a little barking cry and raised herself up. At full height she could barely see over the table.

'Sit down, Annunciata,' Polycarp said. 'We'll take you to the latrine in a minute.'

The tiny nun fell back into her chair and resumed her weeping.

Amelia, who had remained standing throughout this entire discourse, thought she ought to speak. They were, after all, discussing her as though she were one of the cows she had seen at a market being sold to the highest bidder. The only trouble was, she wasn't quite sure what to say. It was very hot and smelly in the room, and there was the smoke belching from Edith and Con's cigarettes to contend with, to say nothing of the stench rising from Father Murphy's cassock that was so near the fire it was beginning to scorch. She wondered what the Goddess must think about all these religious people arguing over her. She tried not to remember the black whirlpool that had accompanied Her last visit.

'None of you are thinking straight,' Father Murphy said, rescuing her. 'You haven't asked the child what it is she wants.'

Every head in the room turned to him. This was the last thing they had considered.

'And hiding pregnant girls in convents is, surely, a thing of the past,' he concluded, less confidently.

'Not in Ireland,' Sister Swithbert replied. 'Except parents never pick our convent. It's too out of the way. No one has heard of it since 1952 when there was the —'

'Enough!' Sister Polycarp spluttered. 'This conversation is going in circles. We have been travelling for forty-eight hours, we have missed evening prayers and rich tea biscuits are not quite what I had in mind for supper.'

Edith sprang to attention. 'Let me make you some soup,' she said. 'I've had the bones boiling from the Sunday roast. There's lovely stock and I can always add some potato and carrot.'

'Thank you,' Polycarp sounded disappointed. 'But we passed a fish and chip shop on the way here. Perhaps one of you would be good enough to fetch us some.'

Everyone looked at Amelia who was feeling rather peckish herself. Getting out of the house, was not going to be an easy matter for her as she was likely to be mobbed by the faithful. In the end Father Murphy, being the youngest and fittest of the group, agreed to go with Dolores. Julian refused by affecting a coma. Mr Lawless perked up when he ordered his usual double fish and chips and a pickled egg.

The room emptied. Edith scuttled into the kitchen to warm plates and make a pot of tea. Con closeted himself in the doghouse with Sister Polycarp. Swithbert and her unnamed companion levered Annunciata upstairs to the bathroom. Amelia, as though she had never existed, was left alone with Mr Lawless. She inched round to the easy chair opposite and plonked herself down.

They sat for some time, dolefully listening to Edith clattering in the kitchen and the singing outside. Away In A Manger had given way to The Lord Of The Dance, a hymn Amelia particularly hated. There was something demonic in the notion of the Lord leaping around heaven and earth. Mr Lawless didn't seem to be enjoying it, either. His breathing sounded like a rattling engine, running out of petrol.

'Awfully hot in here,' he said at length.

Amelia nodded. She liked Mr Lawless and was sorry for the way he was bossed so cruelly by his wife. Often, he would be innocently hoeing the front garden or cleaning his car when Mrs Lawless would emerge screeching from the house, demanding he did some other menial task, or redid the one he was about to her satisfaction. His life, Amelia thought, was a series of insignificant triumphs over her tyrannical rule. Once she had caught him making bunny rabbit ears behind his wife's head. Another time, she saw him deliberately leave his trowel right beside the step where he knew she would trip over it. On both these occasions, Amelia had silently applauded his minor rebellions.

'Aunt Edith feels the cold,' she explained.

Mr Lawless nodded. 'Those people.' He gesticulated in the air so that she had no way of knowing if he was referring to those inside or outside the house. 'Awful fuss, I think. My wife says she's having a nervous breakdown. Taken to her bed.' He didn't sound too worried about Mrs Lawless's mental health.

In contrast, he was almost joyous in his pronouncement. 'Any idea how long this circus is likely to carry on?'

Amelia shrugged.

'And you're in the family way, I hear.' He nodded towards her stomach. 'Often wished we'd had nippers ourselves but the wife wouldn't hear about it while there was still time. "Make a mess," she said. "They'd ruin the carpets". I think there's more to life than a clean carpet though, don't you?'

Amelia nodded.

'To be perfectly honest with you,' he rubbed a plump finger up and down the right side of his nose, 'I think children are the best things since sliced bread, so good on you. You might be starting a little young but it'll leave you plenty of time to enjoy them.'

Amelia smiled. It was a relief talking to him. He treated her like a human being instead of a child. It reminded her of previous chats they had enjoyed, he leaning over his car, she hanging on the gate in the way they both knew Mrs Lawless hated. Those days seemed so far away.

Their companionable silence was broken by a loud wailing. Baby Patti had woken in the back room. Amelia rose. Until that afternoon when she had fallen asleep, Patti's care had been shared between herself and Dolores. She had been fed and changed and winded and played with until the little girl was quite worn out. Edith thought it was good for her to have experience of motherhood. Dolores would have taken on the entire role herself, but Father Murphy's presence made this difficult. He was helping her through her marriage breakup as well as saving her soul, she explained with a devout lowering of her eyes. 'A tall order for any man.'

'I'll have to go and help,' Amelia said. 'The baby …'

Mr Lawless nodded. There was real sadness in his eyes. 'Off you go, lass, and don't you mind what they're all saying. Things have a way of working out for the best.'

Amelia left the room, suspecting that things had not worked out that way for Mr Lawless.

CHAPTER 26
14TH DECEMBER 1981

Sister Polycarp accompanied Con to the emergency meeting with the Archbishop of Liverpool at an undisclosed hour on Monday morning. When Amelia arose bleary-eyed after a night visited by the spectres of Marguerite (bloody and headless), Mr Lawless (fat and pleading) and the Goddess (icily beautiful but more frightening than ever before), they were gone already and it was up to Edith, pious in jet rosary and torn mantilla to convey the news.

'The Archbishop,' the old woman announced joyfully over her overdone egg. 'It's a miracle in itself he'd ask to see Con, considering his reputation. Even more of a wonder the way my brother's in cahoots with the Order of the Holy Head. You've performed some miracles Amelia, but leading Our Con to seek advice from Sister Polycarp and the Archbishop himself is the work of a living saint.'

Amelia smiled weakly. She couldn't face the array of hot-buttered soldiers, the egg still spattered in hen poo. She drank stewed tea in silence and prayed to the Goddess for her mother to return. Whatever the consequences.

Con was back at eleven, his sports jacket dusted with powdery snow. Sister Polycarp had joined her sisters in exploring the neighbourhood, though Con speculated that it was more likely she'd called in at Madge's Caff on Cana Close for a full English. She'd moaned all morning that she was starving, even to the Archbishop.

'Damned embarrassing,' he concluded with an indulgent grin. 'Supposed to be there on spiritual matters and she was just thinking of her stomach.'

Edith, her yellow Marigolds ruining the effect of the mantilla, took her brother's hand and asked, 'And his Grace, how was he? What's he like?'

'A nonentity.' Con lit a Capstan and coughed. 'Old Lawless has got more about him. Now, Polly's not the only one needing to be fed. I've not eaten a thing since those dried-up chips last night. What's for elevenses?'

'I should have known,' Edith shouted. 'You ignorant pig. Fancy letting you into His Grace's Holy Palace … There are crumpets under the grill.'

'Well, I wouldn't like to waltz around wearing that Archbishop's hat all day,' Dolores said, breezing in with Father Murphy. They had left together the previous night on account of the shortage of sleeping accommodation at Eighteen Calvary Crescent. He had offered her the spare bed in the presbytery. Only Amelia wondered why they hadn't taken some of the nuns with them.

'And there's no way he can ever be taken seriously wearing a frock,' Dolores continued, warming to the subject. 'Put off anyone, that get-up would. You reckon that it is high time the clergy got to wear civvies in Mass, don't you, Matt …?' Father Murphy flushed as she pawed him. 'Mind you, when you look at Ken, there's a market for all tastes.'

'I hardly think the Archbishop is going to have a menagerie in his quarters. Or a video camera,' Con retorted.

'You can never account for taste, Con,' Dolores giggled. 'Ken's friend, Stanley, once knew a man who was in love with his Gloucester Old Spot. Wanted to get married and everything. Priest in his local parish wouldn't hear of it. Ended up converting to some happy clappy lot who agreed to play the organ in his sty.'

'Less of this blasphemy,' Edith said, wiping her fingers on the tablecloth. 'Con, you weren't summoned to the Holy Palace to talk about livestock. What did His Grace have to say about Amelia?'

Con cleared some phlegm from his chest, took a roll-up from the tin he used when he'd run out of Capstans.

'Well, nothing really. I think he thought I was ready for the loony bin. I mean it's 1981. Virgin mothers and religious visionaries are hardly high on his list of priorities. Good whiskey though.'

Amelia shifted uncomfortably on the chair in which she had spent the night. Poor Sister Annunciata had been so exhausted by climbing the stairs that she was settled in Amelia's bed and had not yet emerged. The other nuns had slept three-abreast in the Egyptian double. Under the watchful eye of Sister Polycarp, Amelia had been incarcerated in the front room, the hem of her nightie smoking in the heat of the gas fire. She had slept, eventually, when the fire was turned off in the early hours.

'Did he believe you?' she asked.

Con smoked. 'To be perfectly honest, His Grace is so scared of a public outcry when the Pope turns up, that he thinks you should bugger off out of Liverpool. He liked the idea of the Holy Head nuns until I told him they were planning on hanging round till the Pope hits the Speke tarmac.'

'What do you mean, public outcry?' Edith's concave face folded in on itself in indignation. Her gums made the wet, flapping noise that reminded Amelia of horses' lips.

'Look at them.' Con drew back the nicotine-stained nets to reveal the dozens of people queuing in the slushy snow down Calvary Crescent. There was no way of telling how many there were, only that they were multiplying, and that age, class, wealth were, for once, forgotten. Saturday's Echo had depicted a former Miss Liverpool outside the front gate, posed beside a couple of tramps and a seedy turf accountant who knew Con by name. There were teachers and dockers, drunks and Methodists, nuns and gardeners, all in line, all hoping for the healing touch of Amelia's hand. Failing this, a glimpse of her would do; they would have a souvenir to take back to friends and family, some hint of her magic.

'Stupid bastards,' Con concluded matter-of-factly, then burst into a coughing fit so bad, he was forced to stub out his cigarette.

'I don't want to go to the Convent of the Holy Head,' Amelia said. 'I want to know where Mum is.'

'So do I,' Edith said, shouting over Con's hacking. 'It's not right the nuns being here and her being there. It's not as though she ever had the calling.'

'So the Archbishop was no help?' Dolores said when Con had quite recovered.

'I wouldn't say that,' Con relit his cigarette. 'He's a lot on his plate, poor lad. You can't expect him to believe some cock-and-bull tale. His main worry is that lot out there. Apparently, word has already reached the Vatican. They don't take kindly to this kind of thing.'

At that moment, the front door burst open and Polycarp's voice shrilled through the house. 'Annunciata, what in the Lord's name are you doing up there?'

Amelia, desperate for a pee, rushed into the hall, looked up to see poor Sister Annunciata, balanced half way down the stairs on two sticks like a pathetic spider caught in its own web. She was wearing her habit inside-out. Her wimple was all awry, her left arm had not been inserted into a sleeve but poked out of the neck of her gown. The sleeve itself dangled uselessly like a withered limb. She looked faintly exotic; the toga-wearing patron of a Turkish bath as she squinted down at Amelia and the nuns. They stared back, then surged forward as one as she began to topple head first down the narrow stairwell. Seeing that the elderly nun was safely caught, Amelia sneaked behind them to the loo.

The toilet of Number Eighteen was a tiny room, separate to the bathroom, tiled in yellow and black. It was a claustrophobic little space, given to unpleasant odours in the summer and Siberian cold in the winter. It was not a room in which anyone but Con and his copy of the Sunday People was inclined to linger. The sheer number of people in the house meant the toilet was even more pungent than usual, what with the tiny window sealed with layers of gloss and dead insects. Amelia felt the accustomed rush of nausea as she closed the door. She gripped the seat and gulped fetid air. Outside, she heard the nuns scrabble past, muffling the deep sobs of Sister Annunciata.

A hammering started up on the lavatory door. Amelia, unsure whether she could stop chucking up long enough to relieve her bladder, gave a muffled cry.

'Let me in, Sis,' Julian hissed. 'I haven't got much time.'

She wearily sat down on the toilet and peed quickly. 'What d'you want?'

'Open up, Sis. Need to speak to you, pronto.'

Amelia pulled up Aunt Mabel's padded knickers. Apparently in later life she had lost control of her bladder. Although the knickers fitted fairly well, Amelia was glad she hadn't to avail herself of their original function. She gripped the bolt on the door. The handle was turning furiously. Her brother had always been impatient.

'Hang on,' she said, still grappling with her incontinence wear. A surge of nausea overcame her and she turned back to the toilet.

He jiggled the handle again. This time, loosening the lock was enough for the door to swing open. He gagged.

'God almighty, what the hell are you doing? It smells like a sewer in here.'

Amelia, head in the toilet bowl, hands clutching the seat emitted a terrible groan. Her stomach was churning around like an electric mixer.

'We need to talk,' he said, shutting the door. 'God, it stinks! Anyway, you've made another three hundred smackeroonies today. Who knows what it will be tomorrow. But we need to keep the momentum up. We need another miracle.'

Amelia retched a final time. Nothing emerged. She wiped her mouth on a piece of toilet paper and attempted to stand up. Julian was taking up all the space and her body was wedged beneath the loo. She tried to force him back as she rose but she was too weak. Miserably she stared into the toilet, watched a piece of loo roll floating round, swirling in the faint breeze from the sewers. The Goddess was rising from the toilet. Her brilliant hair gleamed polished gold, her eyes were of the purest cornflower blue. Amelia held the side of her head. She wasn't sure she wanted Irena to turn up when she was so ill and Julian was moaning about the smell and lack of miracles. But she could not refuse Her glorious appearance. She hung her head, swallowed her nausea, waited for the Goddess's advice.

Amelia, your time of confinement is nearing. You must withdraw from the temptations, the sights and smells of the world. Withdraw within until it is the time for your child to be born.

'Where's Mum?' Amelia demanded in her head, feeling orphaned, alone and unloved by all but Irena.

Irena smiled enigmatically. Nearby, she said.

'And what about the convent? Must I go there in order to fulfil my Vocation?'

The Goddess smiled. All will become clear in the fullness of time.

Julian flushed the chain. Irena disappeared. Heartbroken, Amelia watched her fade away, to be consumed by a blackness that whirled up from the depths of the lavatory to fill the room and swoop about Amelia's head pulling her into its dark heart. She gasped for air, tried to escape, but it would not let go. She was sucked down, down into unconsciousness.

Amelia lay in her old bedroom, the one she had before her grandmother died, before Dolores moved in. She blinked a few times, trying to remember. It was as though nothing had happened, nothing of the last weeks and months. Was Grandma in the next room? Was the Goddess a dream? She lay, her eyes closed, wondering if she would prefer it like this.

A small whimper sounded nearby, above the insistent hum of outside prayer. Reality flooded back. At first she thought it must be Patti, awake and demanding food, but Patti was not in the room. Another sound, a cry. Amelia sat up and peered into the darkness. Nothing. She swung her legs over the side. Her foot touched wooden slats. The warm air stirred. She felt the breath of another touch her cheek. Carefully, she rose and groped around the room. A bed, or rather the cot belonging

274

to Cousin Ronald, by all accounts a very small man, a midget, had been taken down from the top of the Anubis wardrobe in Grandma's room and placed at the foot of Amelia's bed. Inside lay the unmistakeable form of Sister Annunciata. Amelia held her breath.Why was there a nun in her bedroom? Especially that nun, so ancient and weeping. In the silence of the room, the sound of her grief was unbearable.

'Sister!'

The weeping ceased, she sniffed loudly. There followed a tremulous sense of anticipation. Even the baby, poised within Amelia's womb growled with the suspense.

'I can't get to sleep with your crying like that. What is the matter?'

The nun sighed heavily. Outside, the Our Father was finishing; a rosary had begun to gather steam.

'They took my child too,' she whispered when the faithful reached "fruit of thy womb" in their first Hail Mary. 'Took me in, just like you. Made me scrub floors, tend the older nuns. Even in those days, the convent was full of geriatrics, only then of course there were others, girls like myself, banished from our families for the sins we committed.'

'Sins?' Amelia felt sleepy. Sister Annunciata had a soft, whispering burr, her words poured like honey into the cold night air.

'Sins. Going with boys, with young men, out of wedlock. Conceiving of children we would never mother.'

Amelia frowned into the darkness. "Going with boys" was one of those phrases beloved of Edith. There was a hint of the unsavoury about it, she was disgusted and underhand in her slightly lowered tone.

'I loved a boy name of Donal. We would meet in the hayloft on my uncle's farm, where he worked. It was summer. I was helping my aunt in the kitchen. It was so warm, I only wore a cotton dress, nothing underneath. When he stuck his thing inside of me, there was no protection and I fell pregnant straight away, though I knew nothing of what had happened to me. I was fourteen years of age, a child. He was all of twenty-seven with a wife and four children already. My courses stopped. My stomach swelled. My aunt bundled me into the cart and let the farrier from the village deliver me to the convent. I was absorbed into their life. I never returned to my family.'

'So you had a baby when you were fourteen?' said Amelia, puzzled. All the stuff about Donal and his wife and his "thing" frightened her.

'Fourteen. My beautiful boy was born and sent to the abbey. They only wanted girl babies at the convent. They kept me though, against my will. If there had been chains it could not have been any worse. I was kept as a skivvy to the nuns throughout my youth. Cooking and cleaning and washing up after those filthy old sisters. In those days, before your grandma took over the running, the place was not fit even for the pigs. My hands and feet were red raw. My knees bled night after night. There was no heating. All of us suffered chilblains, cold-sores. Sisters died of the cold, they did, though no one was ever informed. There was a girl who came in with me, a young girl, beautiful. She too was delivered of a boy though he died on his first day. She was left in a cold room, the depths of winter. There was snow laying on the mountain track. No cart could come up with supplies and the older nuns ate all the food. She developed a fever and passed away screaming with the pain. I was holding her head at the time.'

Amelia stretched. The baby gave a low rumble in response to the story and there was no way she was going to get any sleep now. What with the prayers outside and the faint echo of Patti howling somewhere nearby, it was noisier than the A to Z bus stops in town of a Saturday afternoon. And she was hungry. Food had been in increasingly short supply since Edith started fasting for the Pope and Amelia was often left hungry. Judging from the dark outside, she had missed out on the whole day. She thought hard, trying to remember what had happened after she saw Irena in the toilet bowl. Julian had been there and then ... nothing. Her memory had torn. Holes and fragments remained where there should be solid fact. She shivered, saw her breath billow into the chilly bedroom.

'Would you like some toast?' she asked. Amelia would have liked someone to make her hot buttered toast and bring it up on a tray with a glass of milk and a sheet of kitchen roll. She missed her mother so much it hurt.

Sister Annunicata rose from the cot like a banshee from a sea mist. Her head without the wimple was tiny and bald as a baby bird, her eyes large and luminous. Even her white nightgown gave her an odd, other-worldly appearance. For a moment, Amelia thought the old woman had died and this was her ghost.

The nun, clinging to Amelia's mattress, asked 'Have you any marmalade?'

Amelia had to use her own bulk to ease the infirm nun down the stairs. The morning light shone through the stained glass on the landing with a faint aubergine glimmer. An eerie silence had followed the last batch of rosaries and when Amelia peeped through the oval of glass in the front door, she saw many sleeping forms draped over the hoary gardens of Calvary crescent. Even the surplus-to-requirement ice-cream man was slumbering behind the wheel of his Mr Softee van. Grateful for the silence, she helped Annunciata into the kitchen and offered her a glass of milk. The nun gulped greedily, her great eyes never leaving Amelia's face.

'Do not go to the Convent of the Holy Head,' the cadaverous mouth warned as it closed over a thick slice of buttered toast. 'Or you will never see your child again.'

For Amelia, this was the most sensible piece of advice she had heard in a long time.

PART THREE
THE SORROWFUL MYSTERIES

CHAPTER 27
15TH DECEMBER 1981

It was easy to avoid the nuns next day. A consortium of monks and lay brothers had arrived from somewhere near Widnes during the night and, as dawn rose, their brown-clad forms bustled round the sleeping pilgrims with flasks of tea and bags of broken biscuits. The brothers attracted the nuns who swarmed to help them, tripping over crutches, knocking into wheelchairs and trampling the already flattened honesty bush. No one cared about the state of her grandmother's garden, Amelia thought. Overnight, without anyone's by or leave, a stone structure had appeared in the spot where Granddad once planted a magnolia tree that had withered to a stump within weeks. Grandma never had the heart to throw it out so there it had remained for years, dry and black, among Grandma's own magnificent blooms.

Until this morning.

Now, a grotto of concrete and pebble-dash loomed outside the bay window of Number Eighteen. It was crammed with iced chrysanthemums of dubious origin and a lime green statue of Our Lady of Lourdes. This was fast becoming the focal point of the neighbourhood. By eight, an orderly queue had formed, stretching out of the tiny garden and round the corner into Calvary Crescent. One of the brothers was liberally dousing each pilgrim with water, splattered from a golden dispenser on a stick. Those who had queued for hours were happy enough with this, and turned away dripping, hope lighting their eyes.

Amelia watched from her grandmother's window, glad of the privacy afforded by the grubby net curtains. Sister Annunciata was sleeping again, tucked into Old Ronald's cot, and baby Patti, after her night's howling was safely snoring in a barley twist drawer. Both were in Amelia's care since Edith and Dolores had more important things to do.

Both women exuded an air of girlish mystery as they shoved through the crowds towards the bus stop. Amelia noticed that they had become disconcertingly alike. Dolores's stooped black-draped form was so like Edith's that they could have been mistaken, except Edith would never wear a top quite so see-through.

With both her charges asleep, the house devoid of nuns and family, Amelia was lonely and increasingly scared. Nothing had been done about the disappearance of Marguerite, and what would happen when the baby came? Already her body was changing but what would it feel like in the days before the birth? Really, she had no idea what was involved in the whole business. She knew from Catherine that there was a lot of blood and gore and seventy-two stitches. Also that there would be a lot of screaming, Mrs Mulhearn had woken the whole street, and that she wouldn't be able to sit down afterwards, or if she did, it would be on a child's swimming ring. It all sounded appalling and she wasn't too confident that Edith and Dolores could help much as neither of them had any experience of childbirth.

There was also the paradox of the Goddess, whose appearances were more frequent, more fabulous but more terrifying. The black tunnel and everything spinning made the world so dizzying, Amelia was beginning to dread Irena's arrivals. It was upsetting that her Goddess, the one being in whom she had trusted to get her through the Saviour's birth, was no longer particularly welcome. Now, Amelia would rather she stayed away.

Absent-mindedly, she picked up a photograph of her mother, taken when she was about Amelia's age, eyes screwed, squinting against the sun, and pressed it to her breast. She knew that if her mother was home, then everything would be taken care of. There was no way Marguerite would have all those nuns staying, even if they did come from the Convent of the Holy Head. And as for the people in the garden, Amelia suspected that her mother would have phoned the police by now, as she had last August when Number Sixteen's eightieth birthday party overflowed the parameters of his fence and spilled into Number Eighteen's back garden. The dwellers of sixteen were 'roughies', Marguerite said at the time, sniffing at their Co-op sherry decanter. 'They should keep to their own midden'.

She tucked the photograph into the capacious pocket of Mabel's "leisure" habit and left Annunciata snoring. The ancient nun's story had shaken her. She had no intention of being bundled off to a convent, her baby taken away. Her vocation was here, in Liverpool, with her family.

Almost without thinking, she pulled down the ladders to the cockloft and began to ascend the steps. Up there among the possessions of the dead and disappointed, she found solace. It was days since she had ventured up there, weeks since she had paid Irena the courtesy of a few flowers, a simple prayer. Perhaps Irena's new materialisations were simply a result of Her displeasure. After all, no Goddess would take kindly to being ignored. She cast around for some floral tribute to lay as an offering and decided upon the faded silk poppies that had been rammed into a dusty case on the landing windowsill for as long as anyone could remember.

As Amelia's head rose above the level of the ceiling, she noticed first that the air beneath the rafters was stifling. There was a funny smell, sweetish, vaguely ominous, and a buzzing noise. Despite the snow-bright filtering through the roof window, the attic was in darkness. All this, Amelia only half took in. Her eyes were fixed upon the Goddess's robe. It seemed transformed in way she could not quite understand. Amelia flicked on the light switch and blinked.

The blackness that enveloped her was not the fairground ride of recent visions. This was loud, insistent, riotous. A droning noise filled the dusty air, things brushed and flew against her cheek, crawled on the skin of her arms, tiny wings beating. The room pulsated with insects. She turned to escape back down the ladders and they swarmed about her, a force of their own, preventing her from moving. They crawled about her eyes, ears, nose. She felt that every cavity of her body would be filled before she was allowed to leave the attic.

'Goddess!' she screamed, searching frantically with her eyes for her wondrous form, 'Help me.'

No help. The Goddess was dark, shifting with the weight of a million bluebottles. In front of her, obscuring her, Amelia could see a new form, distinct from the familiar boxes and books of the attic. This swung slowly, to and fro like a pendulum; it heaved with flies.

She thought afterwards that she knew what she would find, that some sixth sense brought her there. But nothing could have prepared her for the horror that was hanging in her place of refuge. Scraping the flies from her eyes and mouth, she advanced forward, slowly, on hands and knees, crushing juicy bodies as she went, propelled by more than curiosity. The insistent buzz of the flies had entered her soul so that her bones and body throbbed. She feared for the baby, for she was sure that these winged creatures were tainted, corrupt and hellish.

But the desire to meet her first great trial was too great.

She crawled towards the hanging thing, eyes to the floor where chunks of ancient asbestos protruded from between hastily nailed-together boards. Her grandfather had never been much of a handyman.

'Arrgh! You will not have my child!' Sister Annunciata shouted from below. Her cry set off Patti who began to wail.

Amelia steeled herself, looked up and screamed.

Hanging from the rafter was the body of a young woman. Her features could not be seen, nor the colour of her hair or the clothes she was wearing. All were alive with bluebottles. As Amelia watched in morbid fascination, they were multiplying on the corpse, growing into a throbbing mass of thousands.

'Save me,' Sister Annunciata shouted faintly. 'Help.'

Amelia rose, difficult in such a confined space. The body was hanging with the light chord around its neck, the neck at a funny angle. Although dead, the insects gave it a lifelike appearance. The arms and legs swung lightly, as though in a breeze. The gaping mouth could have been about to speak as it thrummed with black bodies. She forced herself to touch the body, not only to identify it, but also with a ghastly desire to know how it felt. Her grandmother's pristine corpse had never given off this noxious scent; it never throbbed with insects. This body was corrupt, Amelia knew, and as her fingers reached up to touch the face, she also knew why: temptation.

She vomited, passed out; awoke to find the Goddess bending over her, lips curved into the half smile that was so familiar. Light had exuded from her every pore, eliminating the darkness and the vision of hell. Amelia had been so relieved, reassured. Maybe the hanging body was a vision sent to remind her that all flesh is corrupt. She had read as much in Aunt Edith's Fireside Aquinus. Maybe the body was a figment of her own overwrought imagination. No. The swirling black hole swallowed her again, down into its blessed oblivion. She fought the depths of darkness, knowing that this time she must return to confront the awful vision, not simply accept it. She lay on her back perilously close to the cockloft entrance, staring up at the rafters. She focused upon Paula's insect-covered face and knew she couldn't stay up there a moment longer. Amelia slithered down the ladders, landing with a thump in a shaft of coloured light and began to scream. 'Temptation. Temptation.'

Fortunately, Con had returned from a morning in his consulting rooms. Unfortunately, he had put away several pints of best and whisky chasers in the Bodega Club over lunch, so was not in the best of moods to deal with a tragedy.

'That's all I bloody need,' he roared.

The police arrived, flanked by an ambulance. Paula was taken away in a black zip-up bag, manoeuvred down the stairs by two huge men in mourning suits. Other people arrived and went up to the attic to test for fingerprints and other clues. All consoled Con, who everyone thought had found the body, that the verdict would be suicide.

'Poor bitch,' Con said later. 'Don't stand a chance once you're on that rubbish. Takes your life, it does.'

'What rubbish?' Amelia enquired, wishing that Con would take Patti off her hands for long enough for her to pee. And Sister Annunciata was still shouting upstairs.

Con muttered incomprehensibly about a heroine and lit a cigarette. 'Makes you feel as though you're on top of the bloody world, when really you're almost in your grave. Our Julian will be next.'

'Next for what?'

Con stared thoughtfully as a perfect smoke ring rose up to cover his face. 'I dunno, love. Delusions, I suppose. You're not the only one who glimpses immortality, you know.'

Chapter 28
16th December

When the nuns returned from their day among the faithful, they were in buoyant mood. Not only had they thoroughly enjoyed helping the Widnes Brothers dole out tea and biscuits, but they had collected a small fortune in donations to the Convent of the Holy Head.

'I think,' Sister Polycarp announced over their second fish supper in two days, 'we shall take Amelia, after all. It seems she has brought us great luck.'

'I won't go,' Amelia replied, folding her arms, trying to ban the memory of what she had seen in the attic, which couldn't be construed as good luck by any standards. 'Sister Annunciata told me what you did with her baby. There's no way I'm going there as well.'

Polycarp swelled and rose like proving bread. 'I shall speak to your uncle about this.'

The Detective Inspector, who was leaving, stole one of Amelia's chips and gave her a wink. 'Well I hope she gets more joy out of him than I did,' he whispered. 'Had a few over the eight from what I can see.'

Con was doing his best to appear sober, but the shock of Paula's death had left him with a most peculiar expression on his face. Earlier, he had told Amelia and the Detective that the suicide must be kept quiet as his professional reputation would suffer. Unfortunately, the swelling audience queuing up for the garden was quite enough to put paid to any idea that a death in Number Eighteen Calvary Crescent should go unnoticed.

'So far,' he said in a mechanical tone, 'the newspapers have stayed away but it's only a matter of time.' He sat in his customary chair at the table, staring straight ahead, his eyes glassy, his cheeks a ruddy pink and the remains of his hair fluffed into a white halo. Only when reaching out towards his bottle for another slug of whisky did he seem like his usual self.

Sister Polycarp and the other nuns had not been told about Paula's death. They simply accepted the presence of the police forensic department and Con's silent drinking and bustled about, preparing for evening prayers and chanting irritatingly in Gaelic.

Amelia finished her chips and wished she could rid her ears of the buzzing that plagued her. Her eyes were closing in exhaustion when a scream from Patti reminded her that she had other obligations. The poor motherless child would need some comfort. With Paula gone and Julian not caring whether she lived or died, Patti must be adopted into the family for good. Feeling bowed down by the weight of responsibility, she made for the back room where her niece was struggling with her over-tight blanket to escape the barley twist drawer. The baby was red in the face, shaking her fist furiously, like a bad tempered driver in rush-hour. She was also stinking the room out. Amelia knelt down beside her, gently lifting her. As soon as the sodden nappy was removed, the cries stopped and her little mouth began making the desperate sucking sounds she used to tell everyone she was hungry.

'Mamamamama,' she whimpered. 'Mama.'

Amelia wiped her. Patti's bottom was red raw, reeked of ammonia and covered in nappy rash. Amelia applied some talc and cream as she had seen Dolores do, then held her tight. She was such a warm weight in her arms, so vulnerable, so helpless. A great knot of fear bunched in Amelia's stomach. Babies were so dependent. How could she look after such a needy creature, especially one who would one day become the Saviour of the world? Why had such an onerous task been allotted to her?

She rummaged in the bag Dolores had left, found a jar of carrot and potato mash, opened it, and without thinking, began to spoon dollops of it into the child's mouth. Patti was so hungry, she didn't notice her dinner was cold. When she had finished, Amelia sat on the floor and allowed the child to toddle about. She stared out at the skeletal horse-chestnuts, the bright winter sky. For the first time, she prayed to be released from her vocation.

Time ticked by. The house was silent. With the nuns quietly chanting and Con still immobile in the parlour, Dolores and Edith out and the people outside engaged in hushed prayer, apart from Patti's cheerful babble, only the grandmother clock could be heard, slowly ticking away Amelia's confinement. She tried to picture what her baby might look like. Would she resemble Patti and inherit her yellow hair and red face, or would she look more like the Goddess, beautiful and ethereal as the Snow Queen, with her translucent skin and pale blue eyes? There were also practical matters to consider. With two babies in the house, some sort of nursery ought to be made, with cots and toys and mobiles that caught the light. And who would look after them? Amelia was sure she would be forced to return to school once her mother returned from obscurity. Amelia closed her eyes, squeezed out a few tears. Why her? She looked wildly around the room for the Goddess. Catherine Mulhearn's mother had given birth at home, with a midwife and her husband in attendance. She was a school-kid, unprepared for motherhood and the pain. Who would deliver the New Saviour safely into the world?

'Sis?'

She hadn't noticed Julian, his dark form hunched up in one of the battered old chairs. He must have been there all the time, staring at her intently with his strangely glittering eyes.

'What?' Patti tottered towards her. Amelia grabbed the child and held her tight.

'Con told me. About Paula.'

Two lines of black mascara ran down each cheek, like biro. She nodded and turned away, unable to bear his tragic expression.

'I can't believe she did it here. How did she get in? Why the cockloft?'

Amelia shrugged. The ways of the Goddess were becoming darker.

'I suppose she sneaked into the house. There are so many people around, nuns and that lot in the garden, and Aunts Edith and Dolores are in and out all the time. Would we have noticed?'

'She did it to get at me.' Julian sounded bitter. 'Bitch. So I could never forget her. My one bloody mistake.'

'You can't call this gorgeous baby a mistake,' Amelia said. 'Look at her. Your own child and you've never even held her.'

Julian stood shakily and approached the child who was sitting peacefully on Amelia's lap, playing with an empty Regal packet. The late evening sun slanted across the room, lighting up the nicotine-dulled gold on Our Lady of Perpetual Succour's halo. In this sunlit room, Julian was out of place, dressed in black, his face white and ghostly. He was the opposite of light, an absorbent being who fed on the light in others. She shivered.

'I'll hold her now,' he said, holding out rigid arms. 'If you think it's so important, then here, I'll hold her.'

Amelia pulled the child closer. The underside of Julian's arms were etched in dark lines, punctuated by small holes. She had once read a book where vampires walked abroad. They too had holes in their bodies where the teeth of their creators had bitten deep. Come to think of it, Julian reminded her of a vampire in other ways. He was rarely seen in the daytime and wore dark glasses as though his eyes couldn't manage the light. Ever since his unexpected arrival at their grandmother's funeral, he had been a shadowy, nocturnal figure, insubstantial in daylight as he was scary at night.

'What happened to your arms?' she demanded. 'They look awful. So do you.'

He half smiled, ran the index finger of his right hand up the underside of his left arm. '"It's my wife, it's my life,"' he sang. 'Lou Reed. You heard it?'

She shook her head. She hated it when he talked in riddles.

'I'm a mess, Sis. A disaster, a failure. I'm a junkie. Mum knows it, so does Con. And Dolores. I'm not even allowed in the doghouse any more. Why do you think they put me in the shed? I'm contaminated, a filthy impostor. No one wants me around.'

Patti had nodded off. Carefully, Amelia placed the contented child in the drawer and covered her over.

'That's not true,' she said.

'It damned well is. They don't want me anywhere near you. Dolores said yesterday. I'm not good for you. "A bad influence", she said.'

'She can't have meant it. You know what Dolores is like. She says things, stupid things sometimes. Mum said she was a bit odd.'

'I wish Dad was still around.'

Amelia could not have been more surprised if Julian had announced that he was going to join a Buddhist Monastery. Their father was never mentioned in Calvary Crescent. Marguerite had once told her that he had caused a blight on her life. She commanded that Amelia never ask about him and she never did. He had died when she was two and she couldn't remember anything. All the photographs had been destroyed, all but one, which Marguerite didn't realise had ended up in the attic in a suitcase of old underwear. The details were written on the back in his own spidery handwriting. It showed a young man, barely seventeen, standing on a stile in Abersoch, North Wales. He wore a pair of swimming trunks and a feather boa and squinted at the camera. She hid the picture in the box under the Goddess's dress and only looked at it occasionally. Without the photo, it was as though he had never existed.

'Dad?' she said. 'What's he got to do with it?'

'He wouldn't have condemned me like the rest. He would have understood, tried to help.'

'How do you know?' Amelia was scornful. 'You were only a kid when he died, too.'

'I was eight. That's old enough. He was brilliant, was Dad. Good fun, always had time to listen to your problems, not like Mum who's more interested in working and cleaning than anything else. She doesn't give a damn about me, or you, or anyone except herself. You wait, now she's got that money, we'll probably never see her again.'

'That's not true,' Amelia said. 'She'll come back. She only went to see the convent —'

'Where the hell is she, then?'

'I don't know.' Amelia wanted to cry. Julian had no right to say things about their mother like that. He had always been vicious, even when much younger. He enjoyed the power he had to hurt people. She had often wondered about their father, not so much when she was at home with the family, but when she visited friends and saw the way they lived. The nuclear way: Mum, Dad, two children. Even Mr Mulhearn was better than no dad at all despite the need for bricks.

Julian sighed. 'I always reckoned Mum bumped him off.'

'No!'

He grinned evilly. 'Well, I just remember he was there and then he wasn't. Overnight it happened. He read me a story, from The Moomins, kissed me goodnight. That was the last I ever saw of him.'

Amelia thought back, tried to remember what life had been like when their father was around. They had lived in a different house then, a couple of miles away. It was smaller but cosy. She could picture her bedroom, painted pink with a picture of Snow White on the wall. The chest of drawers was pale blue and covered in stickers of bears and cuddly toys. There was a smell of Johnson's powder in the air, a remnant of her babyhood. Who had painted the room? Who had stuck on those stickers, so lovingly? No matter how hard she tried, staring at the picture in the cockloft, she could not recall the real face of the man who was her father. She retained a hazy impression of a rough chin, the smell of tobacco, his voice singing Rock-a-bye-baby and these memories she stifled out of loyalty to her mother. Could it really be that her mother was somehow instrumental in his death? She didn't want to consider it.

'The other option is that Dad isn't dead at all.' Julian was very white, his hands, gripping the arm of the sofa, were shaking.

'What do you mean? Of course he's dead.'

'There was never a funeral. Not one I can remember. Oh, they all sat about, Mum, Gran and Dolores, crying and breast-beating as though there had been a death, but there was never an end to it: a burial or cremation. They just carried on as though he was never there in the first place.'

'You're talking rubbish,' Amelia said, leaning over the cot. Patti smiled up at her.

'Well, if you can't stand hearing the truth ...'

'And what about Patti?' Amelia demanded. 'You're so upset that Dad left in whatever way he did, how do you think she's going to feel when she's old enough to realise you never even held her?'

Julian shook his head. He rubbed his eyes with his fingers, smudging the mascara even more.

'I never wanted a kid. That's the difference. Mum and Dad must have wanted us. They married. They did it all properly.'

'But we never asked to be born. Just like Patti.'

Julian gave a sharp cry, rose and staggered over to Amelia. She thought he might hit her, or worse, the baby, and instinctively covered the child with her arms. He paused, hovered over her like a bird of prey waiting to pounce. Then he teetered. He caught the edge of a cushion as he went down, clutched at it as though he were drowning. He hit the floor, his body writhing. White spittle foamed at his mouth. His teeth clattered together. He twisted and contorted in a way that reminded her of Paula, hanging from the beam in the attic. She pulled the drawer away from Julian, over to the window. Patti said, 'Mama.'

'Julian, stop it,' she demanded. 'You're not funny.'

He tried to speak but the words came out garbled. He clutched his stomach and groaned. A thin stream of vomit spewed from his mouth, jet-propelled onto the velour curtains. Some of it spattered onto Patti's blanket. He lay and shuddered, his breath thick and rasping.

Amelia knew he was not joking. She thought back to his collapse in the parlour. He was seriously ill. She shouted out for Con, for help, remembered too late Con's paralysis. No help would be forthcoming. It was up to her.

She approached him in the way, only yesterday, she had approached the dead body of Paula. Was this all the work of the Goddess? If so, then she wasn't sure she wanted part of it any more. She had never asked for all this death and illness, all this pain. Where was her mother?

Julian was lying quite still, his breath rattling in his chest. He was on his back and there was sick in his mouth. Automatically, she knelt at his side. Her womb felt as though it could burst at any moment. She remembered Con turning Julian on his side the last time, bringing his arm under his face. She did this, wishing she could pray, wishing that Irena was the same Goddess who appeared to her on the day of her grandmother's death, but she knew that to summon her would bring the blackness again and She could do no good. But the light was appearing, glowing from ceiling to floor, a thin tunnel of unearthly brightness. She saw Her feet materialise in front of her, knew that if she looked upwards, Her heavenly form would be hovering above her head. She closed her eyes, laid her hands on Julian's arm and became aware of a power coursing through her.

'Sweet Lord in his heaven, what is happening here?'

Amelia heard Sister Polycarp, could sense her presence in the room, but could not see her. Everything was obliterated by sparkling shards of colour. Like confetti, tinsel, they came to her from the darkness, swirling madly. The air thickened, possessing the viscosity of water. She couldn't breath. The colours were being sucked into her lungs, filling her mind with glittering forms. And in the middle of it all, the Goddess looked down on her, smiling that curved smile of Hers that could no longer reassure. Amelia lifted her arms, attempted to ward the vision away, only to feel herself drawn more into Her heavenly sphere. She felt her body rise, up, up, so that she was glued to the ceiling, looking down at the scene below. She saw herself, lying beside Julian, her eyes open, her mouth curved into the Goddess's same smile. A sudden terror took hold. What if, like Julian, she was dying? Perhaps they would both go together. Maybe the new Saviour would never be born. She forced herself to descend, while the darkness surged about her. She sank, plummeted down, down, into a blackness that would never end.

CHAPTER 29
17TH DECEMBER

'The heroin has done for him,' Con intoned gloomily. 'It's my fault, I should have stopped him. He'll be brain damaged, I reckon, the amount of stuff he was on.'

'What on earth could you have done to stop the stupid little sod?' Dolores demanded. 'Any fool who gets into that stuff is finished as soon as they start. That friend of Kenneth's, what was his name now, Andy-became-Mandy, was mad on heroin. Went off on one, he did, screaming along the Dock Road like a banshee. They said he was selling his body in the end to pay for the stuff, though what was left of his poor bottie, I don't know. Some of them dockers are big lads.'

Amelia opened one eye. She was hot, so hot that sweat was trickling in rivulets between her breasts and her hair was plastered to her face. The cause of the heat was blazing onto her legs now, sending a thrill of rosy goosebumps up her right calf.

'Please …?' She sat up and swung her body away from the gas fire before she burst into flame.

'She's awakening now, poor lamb,' Edith announced, springing to Amelia's side. 'Are you all right, child? We should have known, leaving you there like that, with him. It was a terrible thing to do.'

'What happened?' Amelia remembered Julian falling, the flying, the Goddess, but nothing else. Huge gaps remained.

And questions. How had she managed to gravitate to the floor in the parlour? Why was the sun high in the sky when it had been going down?

'Your brother's had an accident, dear,' Edith said. Without her teeth and upside down, she seemed ancient as an Egyptian mummy. 'He's had to go to the hozzy. He'll be —'

'You said his brain was damaged.' Amelia knew what she had heard.

'The thing is, you tried to help him. You did help him, saved his life,' Con said, matter-of-factly. 'You remembered the recovery position, the lifesaving instructions I showed you. That's what matters. Julian is alive though he doesn't deserve to be. The question now is what to do about you.'

'Holy Mary, Mother of God and all the Saints,' Edith sank to the floor. She was wearing her threadbare tweed coat and leopard-print Stetson. 'The child has performed another miracle!'

'Not quite, Edie, don't be jumping to conclusions.' Con rose imperiously. 'There's enough trouble with those bloody nuns —' He jerked his thumb and lowered his voice. 'Finding Amelia like that. They think —'

As if on cue, the living room door burst open and an apologetic-looking young police officer walked into the parlour, closely followed by Sister Polycarp and Father Murphy.

'There she is, Father!' The nun, looking even more fierce than usual, thrust her index finger at Amelia who was half lying, half sitting, near the heat of the fire. 'They're calling her the new Bernadette. I call her possessed. The divil himself has got a hold of her soul. Get out your sacramental wine and bells, Father, it's going to be a long night exorcising —'

'Sorry ... I couldn't stop her. She said she was staying here,' the officer mumbled.

'That's all right,' Con said, affably. 'Only you don't mind sticking about a bit, do you? Might need to make a hasty exit myself and having one of Her Majesty's Officers at your disposal makes you feel safe.'

Dolores, standing solicitously beside Amelia, rushed to Father Murphy. The size of the room and the cumbersome furniture made all movement difficult. She stumbled over Con's varicose-veined legs, coming to land on all fours.

'Father, Father' she cried, lunging for his black-clad thighs. 'I'm here ...'

The priest looked down, shook his head, gave Amelia a pained expression and turned away as if to leave.

'Oh no, you don't, Father,' Polycarp yelled, gripping his sleeve. 'There are matters here worthy of your attention. The fate of all our souls may rest upon it.'

Amelia attempted to stand. She felt odd, light-headed and slightly giddy. Whatever had happened since the Goddess's last appearance was the cause of much commotion. Julian in hospital, Dolores on the floor, Sister Polycarp in a great state of consternation. And Con, usually the first to start shouting, had scarcely looked up. She sat down again. Everyone seemed to have forgotten about poor Paula and her missing mother.

'Sister,' Father Murphy began, 'I am most sorry you feel this way, but I really don't think that Alice has anything to do with anything. She is only —'

'Amelia. The child's name is Amelia. And typical she should have a heathen's name when all's said and done,' Sister Polycarp retorted.

'Good God, woman, don't lie there, gawping.' Con held out a hand to Dolores and helped her up. The young officer looked away as she struggled with her skirt.

'The thing is,' he explained patiently to any who would listen, 'what you — Sister Polycarp — saw in there was, well, unfortunate. Poor Julian has for some time been receiving treatment for —'

Sister Polycarp brushed his comments aside. 'I'm not concerned with the fate of the boy, but with his demon sister. For all we know she could be carrying the spawn of the devil.'

Dolores giggled. 'What, like that film, Rosemary's Baby? Ken did a version of that using —'

'If I'm not needed …' the policeman ventured. His face had assumed the texture and hue of melted wax; his eyes bulged. He edged nearer the door.

'Off you go,' Con said. 'Don't mind if I don't get up. Lost the use of me legs for the time being. And if you could shift any of that lot out there in the front garden then we'd be ever so grateful. Every time we open the door, there's mayhem and it's not exactly Wembley Stadium.'

'It is becoming a security problem,' the officer agreed. His shoulder was through the door. 'We are all aware of it at HQ.

Keeping an eye on the situation. Wouldn't want a riot to break out. Wouldn't want …' But he was gone.

Sister Polycarp forced her way into the room, pushing past the priest and Dolores, tripping over Con's legs and prompting a groan of agony. She managed to remain upright.

'That girl,' she announced, yanking a chunk of Amelia's hair so hard that Amelia thought it might come out, 'is a fake, a charlatan. She has never communed with the Virgin. She is in league with Satan! Oh, and to think I went to see the Archbishop. I have been duped!'

The room went black. A loud cracking noise rent the atmosphere. Outside, a wind blew up, a fierce and terrifying wind that howled down the chimney breast and forced the net curtains to billow into the room, knocking china ornaments to the floor. Polycarp wailed and dropped to her knees. Con smiled beatifically, raised his face to the storm. Dolores clutched at Father Murphy, bringing her knee up around his waist as though this could save her. Only Amelia herself remained seated, apprehensive but prepared for the call of the Goddess.

It didn't come. In fact nothing much happened for several minutes except more of the same. The storm continued. People outside shrieked. People inside remained still for a moment and then realising there would be no let up from the noise, began to make plans for the End of the World. Sister Polycarp dashed out of the room to find her sisters and together they sent up a chant, half Irish, half Latin: 'Sabhail a Chinn Naoimhe! Holy Head, save us, save us!' Dolores, having remained flamingo-like upon one leg for at least a minute, became a biped once more and flung herself at the priest, who returned her ministrations with much enthusiasm. Con's trance continued unabated.

'What is it?' Amelia asked when it was clear that the Goddess was not going to appear. No one answered, so she rose and went to the window. A mysterious force had blown the gardens front and back to bits, sending the faithful in all directions, crying in terror. To top it all, the sun had gone in, some cloud, perhaps a UFO, was making the earth darken. Amelia believed anything was possible. She stuck her head out of the window, peered up, saw the great whirring blades of a helicopter hacking the topmost branches of Number Twenty-Two's horse-chestnut. In the cabin, she could make out two figures. The pilot, a man wearing Second World War airman's jacket and Snoopy flying goggles. His passenger, a woman with glowing auburn hair.

'Mum!' yelled Amelia, straining out of the window. 'Con, Edith, Dolores, look, it's Mum!'

Con stirred, his pale eyes lit from within by some curious fire. 'It's my fault,' he said to himself. 'All my fault. This is my punishment from God.'

The helicopter spun around and lowered behind the house. The sky darkened further.

'God almighty, Mother of God. The Holy Head himself must be coming to save us!' The nuns, bunched in the hall, began screaming. Their increasingly bizarre prayers were offered up at random, the usual disciplined chant abandoned in the face of eternity.

'It's Mum!' Amelia shouted, looking around the room for someone to take notice of her. Dolores looked up briefly from beneath Father Murphy's heaving cassock, moaned, then disappeared again.

Con stared thoughtfully ahead, smiled and said, 'Perhaps now is the hour. My hour of reasoning. Perhaps now I shall know once and for all the nature of the game I am engaged in …'

'Uncle Con. Mum's back from Ireland.'

As quickly as the many obstacles en route would allow, Amelia made for the back door, stumbling over Dolores and the priest, jostling the nuns at prayer. She lurched through the kitchen where Edith had run away to prepare tea. Even the arrival of a huge helicopter in the neighbourhood had failed to distract her from the task in hand. A mountain of egg sandwiches, the eggs and salad cream mixed with her own varnished fingernails, was rising from a willow pattern platter.

Amelia reached the kitchen door and thrust it open as the rotor blades of the helicopter were whooshing to a standstill on the waste ground behind the garden. The privet was in shreds. She stumbled over prostrate forms in the icy garden, people making final confessions and pleading for mercy on their eternal souls, and squeezed through the fence and hedge. Marguerite or her glamorous doppelganger was descending the 'copter steps with the swagger of a film star.

'Mum,' Amelia cried, forgetting her own bizarre appearance and the state of the garden. 'What are you doing in that thing?'

Marguerite stepped onto terra firma, took one look at her daughter and went a ghastly white beneath the large sunglasses.

'Jesus,' she said, staring at Amelia's newly voluptuous figure, exposed by Mabel's indecently clinging leisure habit. 'What has been going on?'

CHAPTER 30

'Margie, Margie, calm down.' A man, a young man, much younger than Marguerite, hopped down from the pilot's seat. His hair was black and slicked back in the style of a 1940s American airman. He too wore dark glasses, his skin was burnished bronze, his jacket casually unzipped to the waist, despite the sub-zero temperature. Amelia thought he was the most beautiful man she had ever seen.

'Look at you!' Marguerite yelled at Amelia. 'Your stomach … You look … different.'

Amelia smiled beatifically. 'Yes, I am with child.' She raised her arms to the heavens and adopted what she hoped was a suitable pose for One Chosen by the Goddess.

The airman walked around to Marguerite's side and placed an arm protectively around her shoulders.

'You going to introduce us?' he asked in a faintly transatlantic drawl. 'This the young lady you've told me so much about?'

'Yes, yes, but I don't believe what I'm seeing.' Marguerite removed her sunglasses and Amelia saw that her face beneath them was almost as tanned as the pilot's. Her mother's hair, now she had smoothed it down from the after-effects of the landing, had changed too; it had been reshaped into a fashionable, spiky style. Even her clothes were new, not the ones she had bought during the trip to town, but really new. She wore culottes in a moss green, a matching, tight-fitting, waisted jacket, a bronze checked blouse. Her boots were polished brown leather and came high on her leg, almost to her thigh. The most startling thing about her, however, was the make-up. Except for powder and fuchsia lipstick, her mother had scarcely worn any before. Now, her eyes were made up like some New Romantic and her lips sported the deepest, shiniest red. Marguerite didn't look like Amelia's mother any more. She didn't look like anyone's mother. She looked like someone off the telly.

Unfortunately, though, her behaviour had not changed. She caught hold of her daughter's elbow with unnecessary violence. 'I think we need to have a chat, young lady.'

Amelia swallowed nervously, considered how to put off the inevitable row.

'Where have you been?' she asked in her most pathetic little girl voice, the one that worked on Edith. 'I thought you had been killed in the Troubles.' Despite the performance, the full swell of her fears rose up and her eyes overflowed. 'Oh, Mum … Mummy, I'm so glad to see you.'

'Oh, I've … We've …' Marguerite let go of Amelia and pulled the airman forward. 'We've been everywhere and nowhere …' For a moment their hands lingered in a mutual caress, then Marguerite pulled away. 'But who cares? It's all ruined now! I should never have gone. Now, get inside, Amelia, and stop putting on that stupid accent.'

There was quite a deputation lined up in the hall when Marguerite, the mysterious pilot, and Amelia ventured inside. The full set of nuns had arranged themselves against the banister in an attitude of astonished prayer. Con, at last roused from his shock-induced trance, was blocking the entrance to the parlour, while Dolores and Father Murphy, both looking somewhat the worse for wear, were ravenously attacking the egg sandwiches so thoughtfully prepared by Edith.

'Good God, why are that lot here?' Marguerite demanded, seeing the nuns and taking a step back. 'It was all I could do to escape the convent and now I come home to find them.'

Con looked apologetic and, Amelia thought, slightly mad. In her short absence, he had donned his white coat, the professional regalia he wore in his consulting rooms. Rather than restore an air of normality, it made him sinister in an unhinged, unpredictable way. His glasses hung from a twisted chain about his neck, one eye twitched, the other gazed fixedly at some spot in the middle distance. The remains of his silver hair stuck up and wafted like duckweed.

Marguerite lunged towards him. 'What has happened?' She sounded hysterical. She grabbed Dolores by the arm. Father Murphy, licking salad cream from his lips, backed away.

'I feel like I'm in some two bob Brian Rix farce. And you!' She rounded on Sister Polycarp. 'You should be bloody ashamed of yourself. Keeping me locked in my room as though it was a prison. All the smoked salmon canapés in the world couldn't hold me there. You are a disgrace!'

'Marguerite.' Con stepped forward and extended a hand to the pilot. 'You haven't introduced us.'

'Hi. Pádraig O'Sullivan at your service. Pleased to meet you.'

'Paddy. Yes. Charmed.' Con developed another facial tic. His mouth jerked open sideways, exposing a neat row of yellow teeth, before closing again with a snap.

'Pleased to meet you. You are Dr O'Dowd, the eminent Psychologist?' Pádraig could have been laughing but Amelia couldn't understand why. She was more concerned by Con's twitches and her mother's horrified expression. She knew full well that once these introductions were over the ructions would begin. Her mother would never take kindly to the prospect of grandmotherhood, or the shrine in the front garden or the mass of pilgrims. In fact, Amelia reflected gloomily, her mother's oft-threatened Blue Fit seemed unavoidable.

'Pádraig, I think I need a drink,' Marguerite said, staggering to the pilot's side. 'I'm sorry about this, I really am. I had no idea ... And all those people in the front garden ... Why?'

'No bother,' Pádraig said, putting a proprietorial arm around Marguerite's shoulders and kissing the top of her glowing auburn head. 'Jaysus, it makes a change from that shite little radio station ...'

'Come in and sit down, Marguerite.' Edith, sensing a starring role for her catering skills, recovered her wits first. She stepped towards her niece, extending her arms. Pádraig moved away, aghast. Edith reeked of tobacco; she was quite skeletal and her lips flapped loosely without the teeth to keep them in shape. With the black mantilla drooped down either side of her face, her eyes hollow with devotion, she looked, even to Amelia, like some harbinger of death, some fairytale crone set to prey upon healthy children.

'Mum, come and sit in the front parlour,' Amelia said, pushing herself forward and gripping the flesh on her mother's forearm. 'I'll explain everything. Honest. I know it seems, well … we've got some marvellous news …' her voice sounded flat and scared and unconvinced.

'Julian's in hospital,' Dolores said, clutching at Father Murphy's cassock. 'Overdose. Idiot. Oh, and his girlfriend topped herself in the cockloft.'

Marguerite teetered forward into the parlour. Beneath the make-up, her skin took on a greenish hue. She made it to one of the easy chairs before bursting into tears. Unfortunately, this served to galvanise the nuns into action. Moving as one body, they surged into the tiny, overheated room.

'Marguerite, Miss O'Dowd, please …? We hoped you would enjoy our hospitality at the little convent of the Holy Head. As you could see, our lives are modest and we ask nothing but —'

'Modest! You're living like millionaires,' the pilot said. 'I know you're running the dry-out clinic on the side … But caviar for supper, holidays to the south of France! You've even got a sauna. I've never known anything like it. So much for a vow of poverty, or was it the same one as the Pope's?'

The nuns gasped in unison.

'We take nothing we do not need. If you hadn't come snooping around our private quarters, then we would never have been forced to come here,' Polycarp retorted.

'Okay, maybe you think it was a poor trick for me to research some leads I'd had on your place, maybe you're right,' Pádraig said. 'But maybe the public have a right to know what the Holy Head Charity is all about — alkie footballer holidays and champagne Catholicism!'

'I've never had champagne in my life,' Swithbert muttered.

Polycarp, tutting loudly, shoved the sisters out of the parlour and a few minutes later, Amelia heard the front door slam.

She turned to her mother. The smart boots were in danger of melting beside the fire. The section of Marguerite's leg that she could see above them was bare, tanned a streaky golden brown and even though her eyes were closed and the accustomed furrow of worry still divided her eyebrows, she looked younger, healthier than Amelia had ever known her.

'Mum?' Amelia placed her hand over her mother's. Her unborn child, who had kept fairly quiet for the rest of the day, gave a flutter.

'What's happened, Amelia?' Marguerite groaned. 'I should never have gone and left you like this. I should have known. The first time in years I have been free of children, free of responsibility and now ... Oh, Amelia, who did this to you?' She opened her eyes, leaned forward and took her daughter's face in her hands. 'And have you been seen by a doctor, a midwife? Oh, I should have been here.'

Amelia could see tears on her mother's cheeks and shook herself away. She too was in danger of crying but worried that once she began, she wouldn't be able to stop. Time for that later, when the Saviour was safely born. Right now, Marguerite was owed some explanations and she couldn't leave it to Con, Edith or Dolores to do a decent job.

She stood up and took a deep breath. 'Mum, this might sound a bit, well, strange … But I am to be the mother of the New Messiah. I had a Vision, a Visitation as Edith puts it, from a Goddess. Her name is Irena and I first saw her in the cockloft on the day Grandma died —' It all came out in a gasping rush. Marguerite seemed unimpressed.

'A vision? What vision? Don't talk nonsense.'

Amelia stamped her foot. 'It's not nonsense, it's the honest-to-God-and-hope-to-die-truth. I swear on my child's life …'

Marguerite sighed, turned her face towards the greasy antimacassar over on the back of the chair. 'I will find out, never you fear, my girl … And whoever has done this to you will be taken to the police … But Darling, why are the nuns here? And all those people in the front garden?'

Tears of self-pity sprang into Amelia's eyes. 'The nuns wanted to take me back with them. They wanted me to give birth at the convent. But I wouldn't go. They'd have taken my baby away like they did with Sister Annunciata. They would've forced me to be a nun and then I'd end up like her, on sticks and still crying for my baby in ninety years.'

Marguerite gave a low chuckle but her face didn't betray any amusement. Outside, a new decade of rosaries was being chanted over the megaphone by a man with a lisp.

'And all that lot out the front!' She jerked her thumb towards the window.

Amelia sniffed and tried to stem her tears. 'I saved the boy over the road, brought him back to life and it was a miracle and now all these people want me to cure them and I've been thrown out of school for being an unmarried mother and everyone knows I nicked those tennis racquets but I don't know why ...' Amelia was sobbing without control. All the worries and fears she had pent up since Marguerite's departure came to the fore. The sheer effort of trying to explain everything, made her realise the enormity of her situation. But the tears were shed not only in fear, but relief. Marguerite, her mother, her mum was home. She would make everything right.

Marguerite distractedly stroked back Amelia's coarse yellow hair. 'And Julian is in hospital. It is all too awful to contemplate. There are malign influences working on this family.' She sat up straight in her chair. The make-up was running down from her eyes, streaking the sides of her nose a sooty black. Even her hair, so sleek and shiny when she stepped from the helicopter had arranged itself about her head in its old wiry, defeated style.

A rattle of teacups announced Edith who staggered into the room with a tray laden with sandwiches, mugs of tea and garibaldi biscuits.

'You'll be needing these,' she gasped, loading the tray onto the table already cluttered with dirty crockery. 'After your long journey. Ah, tell me all about Ireland, Marge. I've been thinking of you over there all the time. And praying for you. I was very surprised to hear you didn't stay in the convent.'

Marguerite rose slowly, as though she was an arthritic old woman. She brushed down her clothes. Edith appeared to shrink further into her sack of baggy skin. A Hail Mary came to a breathy halt outside the window. The speaker began to cough, then gasp. A communal rush made the curtains flutter inwards.

'I left Amelia in your care,' Marguerite accused. 'You were the only one I could trust. I thought you'd have more sense than to allow her to …'

'Is it not just the most wonderful news?' Edith replied, smiling gummily. 'To think that our Amelia is the next Virgin.'

'She is thirteen years of age, far too young to have a child. How could you let this happen?'

Edith was grinning stupidly as Marguerite's face began to contort with the pain of understanding.

'Only it hasn't just happened, has it?' She placed a warm hand on Amelia's stomach. 'This kid must be what, over three months gone for it to show at all, which means she was up the duff before I ever went to Ireland. How come I never noticed? Why didn't anyone tell me?'

Padraig shuffled his feet and cleared his throat. He seemed about to say something but thought better of it.

'No one knew,' Amelia said. 'Well, not till just before you went to the convent, anyway.'

'But who did you sleep with? Who did this to you? I thought you were so innocent, love. Not yet interested in boys … If it was your Great Uncle Pat, then I'll …'

Amelia, who had never actually met the legendary Pat, gazed upon her mother with new interest. She'd suspected that this must be the beginning of the oft-threatened Blue Fit but it was far less dramatic. Marguerite looked tired and disappointed. Only Julian could usually elicit this expression.

'Drink your tea,' Edith ordered. She handed her a china cup. 'I've sugared it well for you. And there are egg sandwiches, bis —'

'Sod the tea.' Marguerite pushed the cup from Edith's hand. It flew towards Amelia, the scalding liquid spattering her dress. 'Don't any of you understand how serious this is? How illegal? What about Con … and Dolores? Can't any of you see the danger Amelia is in? And getting those bloody nuns in is about the last straw. They're living the life of Riley over there, conning celebrities into thinking their place is a retreat from worldly stress. The only thing they're worried about is me pulling the plug on their cushy life.'

'Don't be upsetting yourself, Marguerite, me darlin',' Pádraig said, brushing her knee with a tanned and manicured hand. 'I'm sure there is a rational explanation for it all. Though, got to say, I thought it was only in Ireland that we had the visitations and apparitions and all that guff.'

At the mention of her name, her full name, not Margie, Mum or Mags, Marguerite tried to pull herself around. She slumped back down into the chair again and allowed Pádraig

315

to put an arm on her shoulder. She leaned slightly towards him, smiling, her whole body almost melting into his. Amelia felt a flicker of alarm. Her mother's face softened into an expression as bright and shiny as her new clothes. Even Amelia, her own daughter, pregnant with the New Messiah, the focus of all activities in Calvary Crescent, could not command her attention like Pádraig. The flicker became a surge. Something was wrong. Her mother should have carried on shouting, perhaps clouted Amelia around the head as had sometimes happened in the past when words deserted her. She should be making it all better, not leaning against some stranger with teeth like a Colgate advert.

He was grinning at Amelia an intimate, leery smile. Amelia glared back. She didn't like him one bit. Those teeth were too white, his hair was too slimy. And his voice was annoying too. It was Irish but had a hint of America about it, as though he were a British actor affecting a Californian drawl. Everything about him was phoney: his too-good-looks, his smarmy way of gazing right into her eyes as though she were the most important person in the world, and the way his clothes looked as if they'd come off a catalogue model. She looked down at her growing stomach and prayed for Irena to strike him down.

'You're a lot prettier than I expected,' he said. 'Pregnancy suits you.'

'What?' Marguerite jerked forward, pushed him away. 'Don't say that. She's too young to be having a child!'

'Hey, shush,' He pulled Marguerite against his broad shoulder. 'You can't turn back the clock. She's pregnant. She's lovely, blooming. You can't change that.' Amelia blushed, hating him more. He craned towards her, bending over Marguerite to do so. 'And you'll have a bonny wee babby, you wait and see. No worries.'

'No worries?' Marguerite demanded. 'I'm out of my bloody mind with worry.'

Amelia plonked herself in one of the hard-backed dining room chairs and helped herself to a stale garibaldi. Marguerite was back. The Goddess had answered that prayer at least.

Chapter 31
18th December

No Blue Fit. No nuns. All curtains and blinds closed against the faithful. In the watery gloom of the parlour, Amelia counted tennis racquets, the three original ones, plus others she had pilfered since. What were they for? Why had she taken them from school when they clearly belonged to other people: Angie Street, Liz Wilson, Michelle Jones, Janet Lee, Barbara McLean. The names, scrawled or scratched in biro or compass point, swam in her tears. Would these people, schoolgirls now, but perhaps future priestesses, be the Saviour's Disciples? This did not take away from the fact that Amelia had unwittingly stolen the racquets and concealed them in her locker, then brought them home, one by one, wrapped in her school cardie and bundled into her duffle bag. Since September, they had lain recumbent in the attic. Now, freed by police activity brought about by Paula's tragic suicide, they were piled up in the parlour. If Goggles Gorgon had not opened her locker that day, the pile would be even higher. Nearby, the Goddess hovered, barely visible in the feeble light afforded by the single forty watt bulb. She had been there all afternoon, silent but watchful, ever since Amelia had been left alone.

'Please, Irena, what did you want from the tennis racquets?'

Nothing.

'Please … Why can't I remember taking them? And Julian. Will he be okay?'

Everything seemed shabby and pointless. The gas fire had been switched off for the first time in days and there was a chill in the room. Marguerite had retired to Grandma's old bed, thrown the sheets being used by the nuns into the twin tub and replaced them with fresh lavender-scented linen from the airing cupboard. Pádraig joined her upstairs for a rest. It was as though the fuss of their arrival had never happened. The house was again taken up with Con, Edith and Dolores; the family, all watching Secret Army on television in the other room. The grandmother clock in the hall ticked on, meting out the quarter hours with its measured chime. Tea was drunk, cigarettes were smoked. The low hum of television and conversation drowned all but the most fervent prayer outside. Amelia could not move, her limbs were so heavy she was sunk into the chair. Her eyes were closing; even the Goddess could not keep her awake.

'Amelia!' It was Con, shaking her so hard that her teeth began to rattle.

'What?' Secret Army must be over.

'We've got to talk — all of us. Decide what to do. While your mother's upstairs.'

Amelia was still very tired but Con had changed. Gone were the grubby white coat, the cracked spectacles, the crazed expression, and in their place a new Con had emerged, clad comfortably in sports jacket and check shirt. A Con with neatly flattened hair, plastered to his skull with grease. A Con in control and unlikely to be troubled by helicopters or missing nieces, suicides and psychopathic nephews. The old but somehow modified Con.

'What is there to decide?' Edith demanded. She was ensconced at the table with a pot of tea and Dolores. Amelia wondered how long they had been there. 'The Pope will be here in a matter of months. We need to contact him as soon as we can, let him know about the Sainted child, Amelia. Now, I don't know if he is likely to do any canonisations on the living but I should think that if he was, then ... Mind, don't you have to be a Blessed first —'

'Shut up, Edie,' Con said wearily. 'Before you get carried away about the Pope and all, there is a lot to consider. The sisters of the Holy Head Convent seem to have turned against us. We need to think seriously before this gets any more out of hand. As it is, my reputation is ruined. I went into my office yesterday, just for a break, to find some sanity, when what should I find outside but a group of women, all desperate for children, for fertility. Some of them were over sixty. They wanted you, Amelia, they wanted you to cure them of their incurable gynaecological problems. Some of them wanted to recapture their youth, their fertile youth. I can't do that, after fifty years treating them for depression and alcoholism and no end of other problems, Amelia. Can you?'

Amelia stared at the tablecloth. It was fashioned from white lawn with creases starched into it. At each corner a lily had been embroidered in pink and white with tiny green leaves. The lily drooping now onto her thigh was smaller than the rest. It had been started in the wrong place with not enough room to finish it properly. The resulting bloom seemed withered, stunted, compared to the others. Her grandmother had spent hours and hours embroidering tea clothes and hankies and still she made mistakes. What was it for? Just as Con, by his own admission, had spent many years of his life perfecting his skills as a psychiatrist and yet he could not perform miracles on his patients. How could Amelia expect to cure the sick, how could a girl barely into her teens, render whole those lives broken by illness or circumstance?

'I don't know' she said, slowly. 'I don't know what I can do.'

Con thumped his hands on the table. 'And this brings me to the matter of the child.'

'You can't deny the child, Con.' Dolores placed a warm hand on Amelia's belly. The baby burped in response.

Amelia blinked rapidly. The feeble light emanating from the single bulb shimmered in a bright haze making the tablecloth dazzle. The faces of her family were blurring, as though they too had been covered in white cloth. Every time her heart pounded, another wave of pain broke on the shore of her brain.

'I can't deny the fact she's pregnant. I've examined her myself,' Con said. His voice sounded strained and his face, when Amelia looked up, was lined and drawn. 'But as for this Goddess … this Saviour idea, then it's a delusion, the product of an over-active imagination …' He buried his head in his hands. 'Rubbish. Maybe I can't deny the child, as you say …'

'Con …?' Edith, for once sounding sympathetic, put a comforting hand on his arm. 'We didn't mean … there's no way on God's earth Amelia has known a man. And if she has … then it was against her will. But, what am I saying? I believe, truly believe, that she is carrying the new Messiah.'

'I keep thinking … trying to remember. But it's the drink. I find everything is gone dim,' Con muttered, standing up so quickly the tea things in front of him were knocked flying. 'And then I think, what if? But I'm sure I've never touched her. I've never even thought of her …' He rubbed the heel of his hands into his eyes. 'There was an incident months ago, at about the right time. I can't think. I was drunk, drinking. I remember thighs, white thighs and … The child has a condition. Oh, God, what have I done?'

'What have you done, Con?' Dolores demanded. 'Surely not. Not with your own, your great niece —'

Con began to sob. Amelia stared at the table cloth, thinking of Grandma and her lilies.

'Con?' Edith's voice was sharp. 'What are you talking about? Amelia has seen the Virgin. The daughter of God, or whoever this new saviour is, will become a carnation of the virgin Amelia and made woman …'

'Spare us the Mass, Edith,' Dolores snarled. 'And pass us a cigarette. I've done with giving up.'

Edith fired a fag and collected up the dirty plates, tutting to herself. 'It's the Pope I'm worrying about,' she said. 'It's time we got the Vatican involved. They need to know what is happening round here.'

Con made a strange animal noise, a cross between a bark and a bellow. He had sunk into one of the chairs beside the fire. His features contorted in a manner far more alarming than the twitching of earlier. He gripped at his head, as though trying to tear some memory free.

'That's just it,' he moaned. 'What has been happening? A girl, a minor, says she is pregnant. She says she is carrying the "New Messiah" that her condition has been brought about by supernatural means. There are no supernatural means. You know it, we all know it. She is ill. There are only men and their carnal desires. Young men, old men, men in the family ...'

'Stop it,' Dolores said. 'You're beginning to give me the creeps. Anyone would think, listening to you, that ... There's no way. No way. Bet you haven't got it up in years. You never raped her, Con.'

Con emitted a loud bellow of pain.

Amelia closed her eyes. She had heard of people being raped. There was an old lady, ninety-two who lived near her school. Everyone knew her and the nuns would send in parcels of food. She was raped and robbed by a boy of barely sixteen. The shock waves lasted for weeks. But rape itself? What did it consist of? There was a violence about the word, it was a secretive thing, a hidden force, referred to by adults but never understood by children. Why was that word, that dirty word, being uttered now?

'I am having a baby,' she said, vehemently. 'A baby born of —'

'Oh, shut up, Amelia,' Dolores said. 'We know. The question is, do we go with the divine intervention explanation or Con's?'

Edith finished with the dishes and settled herself beside Amelia. She made a revolting sucking noise. 'What has turned you, Dolores? Evil is at play here,' she muttered. 'Everything was all right until Marguerite brought that man into the house. He's the devil carnation, brought to tempt us all with his ways of the world.'

Con gave another sigh. Dolores puffed furiously on Edith's cigarette. They all stared at Amelia whose face grew hotter by the minute. How dare they say all this stupid stuff about rape and thighs? How dare they try to pretend the Goddess wasn't real? She screwed her eyes up. Even the gloom was becoming unbearably bright. The baby was resting, she could feel her soft movements deep within her womb. The turmoil was outside of her body. Inside was all serenity.

'There is no other explanation but Irena,' Amelia whispered. No one heard. Irena, Irena, the one who had been moving mysteriously within her, causing tennis racquets to appear in duffle bags and miracles to be performed, it was She to whom they should address their doubts, not Amelia. She clenched her hands together in prayer. Proof was what they needed. It was not enough that she conceived of the child, they needed to witness, with their own eyes, the glory of Irena.

'I suppose,' Dolores began slowly, 'that we should decide what we're going to do, now. Before Marguerite really starts … believe me, we ain't seen nothing yet. I remember when Ken bought that …' She pulled nervously at the frill on her blouse. 'Has our Amelia been tampered with by some local n'er-do-well or the Angel Gabriel or whoever …? Whatever we decide on, we'll have to stick to. All of us. Oh, God. I think I'll give Father M a ring and see what he —'

'Leave that damned crow out of it,' Con snapped. 'We don't want him pushing his beak into everything. The bloody clergy, they're all alike.'

'It was you invited the nuns,' Dolores reminded.

A strange twinge of pain flickered across Amelia's abdomen. She breathed in sharply and hunched over.

'What's the matter?' Edith asked, concerned. The pain was so strong that Amelia couldn't answer. 'Are you well?'

Con stood up, his eyes were wild. 'A miscarriage now could be the end to our troubles,' he shouted.' 'Amelia, are you —'

Amelia tried to smile. Everything in the room was flickering, jumping. The pain began to recede.

'I'm fine now,' she managed. She knew that if they would leave her alone, leave her to be with her child and the Goddess, then all would be well.

Con put his hand onto Amelia's stomach, shook his head.

'It would be for the best …'

'I'm okay now, Uncle Con.' And Amelia did feel fine, washed in the aftershock of pain, a pleasant, dreamy numbness.

'Are you feeling dizzy?' Con demanded, grabbing her wrist and feeling for her pulse. 'Your heart's going like the clappers. Are you having …?'

At that moment, the parlour door was flung open and a strong gust of stormy wind dispersed some of the cigarette smoke in the room. A large, black clad bottom eased its way into the room, followed by a pair of hands clutching two well-turned ankles.

'Make way, make way,' Sister Polycarp gasped as the ankles fell from her grip. 'This is an emergency.' A loud thud ensued, followed by a heart rending sob.

'I thought you were on the plane to Dublin,' Dolores said.

'Dead, he's dead, there's no mistaking it. And not even Extreme Unction. Oh, my soul will burn in the fires of hell for eternity!'

Three other nuns pushed into the room. They looked very cold and dishevelled. The nameless one, who had been completely silent all week, found her voice. She stepped into the room and stared at Amelia.

'You have to help,' she said gravely. 'The priest is gone.'

Dolores was shocked out of her concern for Amelia. 'What priest? Tell me! Who are you talking about?'

The nameless nun stepped aside. Amelia stood up. Her back was hurting, though the pains across her stomach had completely gone. Lying in the doorway, his legs apart, his cassock rucked up to reveal thick black socks and a pair of jaunty red longjohns, was Father Murphy. His usually pallid skin was pale blue and his lips had turned a frightening shade of mauve. Dolores gave a loud cry and threw herself onto him, covering his impassive face with kisses and licks.

'What happened?' said Con, standing, and making his way to the doorway. 'How long has he been like this?'

'Oh, not long, oh, I don't know, honest I don't, it could be minutes or seconds or hours. When we heard the airport was closed with the weather, we didn't know what to do. We came back here ... In situations like this you have no idea how much time is passing. I think it was not long ago, though others may say different. Oh!' The nameless sister was silenced by Sister Polycarp's hand reverberating across her cheek.

'Shut up,' said Polycarp. 'It was about two minutes ago. This stupid woman was walking around with the bronze cast of the Holy Head when she dropped it onto poor Father Murphy. He didn't stand a chance. Neither did the head. It cracked open —'

Con knelt down, shoved Dolores out of the way and placed two fingers on Father Murphy's neck.

'Dead as a dodo,' he said gloomily. 'There have been more dead bodies in this house over the last few weeks than the bloody Co-op.'

'There's nothing you can do?' Polycarp demanded. 'What about the kiss of life? You're a doctor.'

'But she's done miracles before ...' the nameless one began. Sister Polycarp slapped her a second time.

Con shook his head and stepped over the body. 'You said it was a head injury. Chances are, even if we brought him round, he'd be a vegetable the rest of his life.'

Amelia, watching Father Murphy closely, thought she saw his arm twitch. She looked away. Was it a Sign? Or was she imagining things? Irena was still around, hovering faintly near the pile of tennis racquets. She looked again at the priest. Again, his arm moved, the fingers seeming to flicker across the carpet. But everything in the room was twitching and dancing and shuddering. She stared at him, saw his eyelids flutter. This was nothing imagined.

'He's alive,' she shouted. 'Look, Father Murphy isn't dead!'

The nuns, Con, Dolores, stared. Father Murphy lay as still and cold as before.

'I hope this isn't more of your nonsense,' Polycarp said.

'No!' Amelia was wedged behind the table, trapped in a swathe of embroidered lily. 'Just look.' She unwound herself and staggered across to where Father Murphy lay, his face concealed beneath Dolores' prostrate form. She tapped Dolores with her foot, was answered with a wrenching sob.

'Can you move before you suffocate him,' she said at last.

Dolores wrenched herself away. Mascara and shiny fuchsia lipstick covered Father Murphy's chin. Amelia knelt beside him and touched his face. It was still faintly warm though there was no sign of any breath. Acting instinctively, she pushed his body onto its side. The priest emitted a noise that was almost a burp and almost a sigh. Amelia looked up at the adults. No one had noticed. They were too busy consoling each other. Father Murphy gave a gargling sort of gulp. His body jerked forwards, the veins on his neck were bursting blue. He jerked, convulsed. A round and bright object shot across the room from his mouth and pinged against one of the glued-together remains of Edith's heirloom vases. It remained where it stood on the mantelpiece for a moment, then shuddered. The vase disintegrated.

'Jesus, Mary and Joseph, all the saints and Prince Andrew himself,' Edith said, crossing herself. 'Amelia has banished an evil spirit from the man.'

Father Murphy sat up. The colour flooded back into his face. His cheeks were suffused with mauve. He coughed a couple of times, ruffled his hair and attempted to stand up. His eyes shone with a strange luminosity.

'Thank God,' Dolores wailed, kneeling down and wrapping her arms around him. 'You're alive.'

'It's another miracle,' Edith said. 'Amelia, the little saint, the little virgin! She has performed another miracle.'

'I don't understand it,' Polycarp muttered, inspecting the priest and looking as though she might seize him to her own bosom at any moment. 'That statue must weigh at least two pounds. Anyone who can take that kind of weight on his head and come out alive must have a very thick skull.'

'Friends,' Father Murphy gently pulled away from Dolores and began to lever himself up using one of her substantial legs. 'A great thing has happened today.' He turned to Amelia, held his hand out to her. She caught it. His skin was cold and rather clammy, which wasn't surprising considering that only moments before he had been dead. 'Today, I have experienced the power of God, working through the hands of this innocent child. Friends, we are in the presence of a miracle from God.'

'Irena,' Amelia corrected. All this talk about God was very well, but it was Irena who was responsible. No one else had appeared to her and made her pregnant with the New Messiah.

As the adults mused the wonderful happenings, she picked her way over to the mantelpiece, to where Father Murphy's strange emission had landed. From the debris of broken vase, she rescued a silver Saint Francis pendant, still slimy with the priest's saliva. She remembered Edith presenting it to Dolores on the day she left Ken. She had worn it every day since. How it had ended up down Father Murphy's throat was a mystery.

CHAPTER 32
19TH DECEMBER 1981

The following morning, Father Murphy was knocking at the door before the post had arrived. He had managed to contact the Archbishop and demand an emergency audience for Amelia.

'A miracle such as this cannot be ignored,' he said, gazing glassily at Amelia who was finishing off her porridge in the kitchen. 'Let us convince the Archbishop together!'

Outside, the snow had frozen solid and the few faithful who had remained overnight were passing thermos flasks of tea laced with strong liquor to one another. An impromptu 'Away In A Manger' was filtering into the kitchen along with an icy chill. Amelia wondered if they would have Christmas decorations this year but no one had even mentioned a tree. She swallowed the last of her tea and waited for her mother to storm in and intervene. Father Murphy whispered a Hail Mary. It sounded like an invocation. Marguerite remained in bed with Pádraig.

Con arrived shortly afterwards. Despairing about his business, he had closed his consulting rooms, usually open on a Saturday morning, to "deserving cases", and offered to drive them to the Archbishop's house in his old Jaguar.

'May as well arrive in style to tell your preposterous story,' he blurted.

Amelia was forced to wear one of his old coats and a homburg as disguise. She was bundled out of the house like a mass murderer hiding from a TV crew. Con wanted 'no truck' with the devout followers carolling on the slushy lawn.

As they made their way through the whitened streets of Liverpool, along the red brick terraces of Aigburth Vale, past the leafy, well-off Otterspool prom and nearer town towards Sefton Park, Amelia worried that perhaps her mother was ill after all the trouble of yesterday. She had not been seen since retiring to bed before supper which was not normal. Marguerite was usually up before anyone, if only to make toast before Edith got her chipped claws on the job. But there was little time for speculation. They arrived at the Archbishop's residence, Con slowly pulling into the impressive rhododendron-lined drive towards the magnificent doors of the Lutyens-inspired Victorian mansion.

'Probably built on slavery,' he muttered, enigmatically. 'The Catholic church condones anything so long as it gets a cut. Think of the Nazis.'

Ushered into the majolica-tiled hallway by a tiny, scuttling creature of indeterminate sex, Con and Amelia were asked to wait on a bench until the Archbishop had spoken to Father Murphy. The priest was in with the Archbishop for over an hour before Amelia was summoned. Con didn't accompany her, he remained resolutely smoking, his huge backside dinting the plush red seat.

'I'm not going in there with you,' he intoned as he flicked through a battered copy of the National Geographic.

'Don't you want to hear what he says?' Amelia asked. A clerk, another small and shuffly personage, a wooden rosary weighted around his neck, came to fetch her. Con shook his head wearily, his eyes never left the article on the flora and fauna of the Andes.

The Archbishop's office was as imposing as his title. He sat behind a mahogany desk in the centre of a huge, marble lined room. There were a few statues around, not the kind Amelia prayed to at home or lit candles beneath in the local church, but great tall things with coloured faces and cloaks of gold and sapphire blue. She didn't know who they could portray as they were each studded with precious stones. She decided that they must be saints depicted in their heavenly majesty, rather than any earthly raiment. After all, saints were known for starvings and beatings, burnings and torture, not for their jewellery. The Archbishop looked far too ordinary for the grand room. He was middle-aged, old to her. His face was lined and rather depressed looking. He wore glasses and a grubby looking shirt. Beneath the desk, his legs were clad in blue denim. But it was a Saturday and he probably had other plans.

Amelia entered the room and stood before him, trying desperately to remember what she had learned at school about calling him your worship or your grace. He didn't speak, only sat there staring at her thoughtfully, tapping a silver pen on one of his buttons. She bowed her head a little, thought that "Your worshipful Archbishop" would be all right and was about to address him when a tiny Chinese man came in with a silver tray heaped with coconut macaroons, a bottle of Iron Bru and two glasses.

'My favourite,' the Archbishop said, winking at Amelia. 'Though I'm told it's not good for your teeth.'

Amelia shrugged and grinned at him. Perhaps he wasn't so miserable after all.

'That's what my mum says.'

'Does she know you're here?' he asked, pointing to a chair near the desk. She helped herself to a glass of pop and a macaroon and sat down. Unlike Father Murphy who scuttled out of the room after a dismissive wave from the Archbishop, she was glad that she wasn't to be interviewed on the other side of his desk; rather, she would sit beside him like an equal.

'No.' She looked up, guiltily. 'She was asleep this morning. She had … a bit of a shock yesterday.'

The Archbishop took a long swig of Iron Bru. 'And why do you think your parish priest wanted you to meet me?'

Amelia shook her head. 'Because of the miracle?'

'Ah, yes. The miracle.' He rose, frowning, and returned to his desk where he rummaged through the heap of papers in a little wire basket. He selected four or five and held them out to Amelia. 'It seems to me that you are quite the little miracle maker. A boy, a dog and now a knocked-out priest.'

She bowed her head. Put like that, her miracles seemed rather paltry. And the way the Archbishop was talking, with that smile twisting up the ends of his mouth, his eyes twinkling with merriment, made her think that he wasn't taking her very seriously anyway.

'The priest, Father Murphy, is very impressed,' he continued. 'He said he saw a heavenly light and experienced the wonder of the hand of Jesus push him towards consciousness and life. Apparently, the boy was dead too and you brought him back to life. Now, tell me what you see, what you feel and hear when these miraculous events take place. The holy souls, is it, or maybe it is the choir of angels with a couple of cherubim hovering for good measure.'

Tears pricked Amelia's eyes. The Archbishop was laughing at her. So much for the pop and the pally attitude, he didn't believe anything, and probably only agreed to see her so that he could humiliate her by mocking everything she believed in. She didn't want to tell him about Irena appearing to her in the attic, nor about the swirling vortex of dark that now accompanied her presence. All she wanted was to escape, to be at home with her mother who she still hoped would make everything come right. She shrugged her shoulders, hardly looking at the Archbishop.

'And the baby, you are actually expecting a baby, I take it? Though you're very young.'

Amelia shrugged and turned her head away. What could he know about the child growing inside her womb, the Saviour of all mankind? She felt her heart beating faster. Her breath came in quick gulps. She could not cry, not here, not now. He already thought she was a stupid kid who invented miracles for her own amusement.

'My dear girl, you are not the only schoolgirl to have conceived of a child at such a tender age. Nor, it must be said, are you the first to come up with the virgin birth idea to explain it.'

This was quite enough. The Iron Bru was nice and so were the macaroons but she was not going to stick about to be insulted. What had her grandmother said? Be true to yourself, never trust the government and keep your bowels open. The first of these dictates could not be upheld if she remained in the room with the Archbishop for another moment. Amelia stood up, knocking her drink flying and spraying the marble floor with crumbs.

'It is not an excuse,' she said calmly. 'It is the truth. I'm going home now.'

The Archbishop looked faintly alarmed. 'But we haven't finished our chat. There is a serious problem, little girl. You can't make claims that can't be substantiated. To pretend to be some sort of a saint is not only a lie in the eyes of God, it is also a wicked deception of other, more vulnerable people.'

'It's not a lie,' Amelia said. 'It's not a lie, or an excuse or —'

'These people, all those poor souls believing in you!' Again he held out the sheaf of papers. 'Letters,' he shouted. 'Letters from pathetic creatures who are dying and hopeless and terrified. They believe you are the new Bernadette. This is dangerous, immoral ... It is wrong!'

Amelia was halfway to the door. Vaguely, she wondered if archbishops could put you in prison or exact some other kind of punishment if you were rude to them. She thought of Mrs Gorgon at school, the way she never believed anything Amelia said, and put her on detention for the smallest thing. The

Archbishop was like her, only with more power. Amelia continued towards the door.

'I must say,' the Archbishop called after her, 'you're good. Convincing. You've a career on the stage ahead of you.'

Amelia froze. His voice was a horrible sneer, echoing around the cold room.

'How dare you!' she shouted. 'You know nothing of the Goddess Irena. She is good and kind and gentle. She gave unto me this child. The Saviour will be a girl and when she is older she will have priestesses. She will never have priests or archbishops or any other stupid men. The only people who can work in her church are —'

The Archbishop sighed. It was a long whistle of a noise that reverberated inside her skull. He rose slowly and followed her to the door, putting his arm around her shoulders which were shaking uncontrollably.

'You're a brave girl, but we have heard all of this before. Virgin births are impossible. More important to get to a doctor very soon, and a midwife. If necessary, the child can be taken by the Catholic Foundlings Association.'

He placed a cool hand on her forehead which she knew was hot with fury. 'You are either a good liar or deluded. Whichever, you are ill …' He opened the door for Amelia. She walked away, towards Uncle Con, without looking back.

Her Uncle rose stiffly from the bench and held his hand out to her. Behind her, the Archbishop's door slammed shut, rather too quickly to be altogether polite.

Chapter 33

Con was silent all the way home. He drove with his head fixed firmly forward, his hands, clad in half-cotton, half-leather driving gloves, gripping the wheel. Father Murphy, by his side was no more talkative, but his face beamed with a zealot's pride. They left the city and entered the snowy suburbs, the rows and roads of terraces and semis, shops and parks, schools, libraries. The low hum of the Jag engine lulled Amelia, but she could not rest. Going round and round in her head was the cruel sneering of the Archbishop. She dared not tell Con. It would only confirm his poor view of the clergy.

As they glimpsed Gethsemane Road, it was evident that the once quiet street had been hijacked by the faithful. The queue stretching around to Eighteen Calvary Crescent was still growing. The deputation from St Gerard Magella's church were pushing forward, the parishioners flashing gold jewellery and black mantillas. The church itself was adorned with a huge banner, sporting the slogan, AMELIA O'DOWD: OUR NEW BERNADETTE, as though she were a candidate for prime minister. Con saw the banner and groaned. He tried to increase his speed, but the street was jammed. Father Murphy clapped his hands when he saw the Bernadette sign. Amelia noticed that the knuckles were covered in long black hairs.

'We'll have to walk,' Con said. 'Bloody ridiculous. The world has gone mad.'

He stopped the car, opened the door, and glanced back at Amelia, who had donned the homburg. He shook his head.

'Oh, no, girl, you'll need more than that. This lot are baying for miracles. One whiff of you and there'll be blood and crutches all over the shop.'

Amelia looked around for some material to conceal her features. Now that the car had stopped, she felt slightly sick and a headache was beginning over her left eye. The only thing in the car was the striped canvas awning Con took away to Blackpool with him once a year when he went on his 'jolly' with three eminent psychologists. It wasn't the ideal cover up, but it was all they had. She threw it over her head and ducked out of the car.

Con hadn't bargained on Father Murphy. Still in his trance, he too stepped onto the pavement. He looked at Amelia and his eyes glazed over. Immediately he sank to his knees, almost falling into the gutter.

'Amelia, Amelia, I am but a humble servant. My life is at your disposal.'

Con gave a low growl. 'Get up, man, people will notice.'

'Let them notice,' Father Murphy said. 'Let them throng, for through Amelia, Christ's words will be known.'

A few stragglers at the end of the St Gerard Magella's queue began to look. Amelia started to walk homewards, her head bowed like many of her followers. Con, hurried to reach her.

'The man's unhinged,' he said, panting.

The first tears welled up in Amelia's eyes. 'What's going to happen?' she asked, squinting against the whiteness of the snow, and the pain over her eye. 'All this … the Archbishop, the people.'

Con too began to weep. 'I don't know,' he sobbed. 'I don't know anything except that I am done for.'

Father Murphy caught up with them. He scooped Amelia up in his arms, groaning a little under her substantial weight. He marched solidly towards Calvary Crescent, bearing his load. Amelia struggled to break free but he was surprisingly strong, considering his slight frame and his recent meeting with the grim reaper. We must look a funny lot, she thought, smiling to herself despite everything. The priest, all skin and bone, carrying a great lump of a girl in canvas and Con, red in the face and panting with the exertion of walking. It was hardly a suitable way for the Saviour to be announced.

They were met by Mr Lawless, whose blue Zephyr was parked across the entrance to the cul-de-sac. Mr Lawless and his wife were sitting on the bonnet, which, Amelia noticed through a haze of orange canvas, was rather grubby. There was also a long scratch on the front passenger door.

'No more!' Mr Lawless shouted, springing from the bonnet. 'Maximum twenty. There are police in there, counting.'

'Keep your hair on, old man,' Con said, taking Mr Lawless by the shoulder. 'What the hell's going on now?'

Mr Lawless shrugged. His small eyes were almost lost beneath rolls of wrinkled flesh.

'You mean you don't know … this morn —'

'That's enough, dear,' Mrs Lawless said, leaving the bonnet with more difficulty than her husband. 'You never get anything right. Four people were killed this morning. Two more hospitalised. A man committed suicide from the window of Number Eighty-Four. Number Eighty-Four didn't know him, of course. He was one of them.' She jerked her elbow in the direction of the queue.

'People killed?' Con repeated slowly.

She nodded. Amelia, hidden behind striped awning, thought that Mrs Lawless could have been talking about anything. Her joy was in being the imparter of news. The news itself was irrelevant. She might have been discussing Doreen in the Co-op.

'There was a surge in the crowd,' their neighbour continued. 'A load more turned up from the other side of Liverpool, by the sound of them. And some from over the water, though what they're doing coming from Birkenhead, I don't know. Can't they get their own miracles? Anyway, someone said they'd seen Amelia and that was it, they all lunged forward and there were screams and shouts and all sorts and then it all went quiet and they had to get the ambulance in and we later heard that apart from those who were trampled in the rush, there are others in hospital with broken bones and concussion. One poor man had a heart attack.'

'God almighty,' Con muttered. 'This is completely out of control.'

'God works in mysterious ways, his wonders to perform,' Father Murphy intoned as he lowered his arms to allow Amelia to slip gently to the floor. 'If He decrees that men must die in Amelia's name, then so it must be.'

'That's awful!' Amelia shouted, finally wriggling from his grasp and emerging with relief from the rather smelly awning. 'I don't want people to die because of me. Not even because of Irena. I want everything to go back to how it was, before Grandma died, before any of this …'

A terrible pain, the worst so far, ripped across her forehead. Winded, she sank down onto the kerb, almost bringing the parish priest down with her.

'Uncle Con, Mr Lawless, you can't let this happen.'

Con nudged her bottom with his foot. 'Amelia, are you all right?'

Her mother's voice joined in, sounding more urgent. 'Amelia, what is it? Wake up. I've been worried sick …'

Again the pain came, stronger now, she was surrounded with flickering brightness. Her heart fluttered. She stared at Father Murphy's scuffed shoes, noticed his shocking-pink towelling socks. The earth began to throb. The shoes vanished. Sparkling beads of colour threaded their way through the increasing darkness. Irena was coming, whooshing through time and space to be with her. She wasn't happy.

CHAPTER 34

The anger in the room was palpable. Marguerite clutched her hair; she looked much older with her cheeks hollowed out by the grim overhead light. She was screaming at Con but Amelia could barely understand the words. They exploded into the stuffy room like gun-cracks, to be absorbed by the soft furnishings. Con reclined on the chair by the fire, his trouser legs smouldering. Edith cowered and smoked, huddled into herself like a sick old pigeon as she prayed to the uninterested Infant of Prague.

'She is a child. A kid. This is nothing to do with pregnancy, Con. These turns she's been having. Religious visions! The lot of you should be ashamed of yourselves!'

Con let out a bovine groan, the sound of a cow Amelia once heard on a school trip to the countryside, a cow crooning as its full udder was emptied by gentle stroking fingers. The resulting warm milk was revolting, but the grateful cry of the relieved animal more than made up for it. Aware of her own swollen breasts, Amelia empathised with the beast.

'I didn't know,' he said in a high-pitched whine. 'It could have been, as she thought. Some apparition. Young girls are always —'

'Bollocks!' This was the closest Marguerite's language had ever come to emulating Julian's. Amelia sat up and listened with interest.

'That was an epileptic fit she had. I saw it with my own eyes, for Christ's sake. I'm no doctor but I know when a kid's sick. And you lot, gazing at her like she's some relic from Rome when you should have been doing all you could to bring her back into the house and make her safe. You're disgusting, every one of you. My little girl could have died … she still could.'

'Epilepsy often diminishes with pregnancy, either that, or disappears completely,' Con said quietly. 'Another reason I didn't think to —'

'You didn't think. You didn't bloody think! Well, you thought enough to bring that bunch of witches over from Ireland, didn't you? Or was that all to cover your back? The great Con O'Dowd, psychiatrist extraordinaire. Could have been a priest, but, hell, how many women do you get a crack at from the pulpit?'

'Marguerite, I will not have that language in my sister's house,' Edith slobbered.

Marguerite ignored the old woman and pummelled Con with her fist. 'What worries me is how she got pregnant. This is no divine implantation. I thought at first it was Uncle Pat — he tried it with all of us. I have kept Amelia safe all these years but someone, and I will find out who, has been …' She broke down, unable to continue.

Con moaned. From where Amelia was sitting, he looked small, shrunken as his older sister. The veins on his hands stood out in knotted, wiry ropes. His chest rose and fell with rasping irregularity.

'It was him who did it,' he said in a whisper. 'Him and her between them.' His clawed index finger pointed at Edith. 'Priests. Big priests and little boys! Makes me laugh now, it's such a cliché. Al Monagle had his own peculiar tastes. Thirteen I was when he started on me. Pat, the same. Edith will have known, the frigid bitch. Me and Pat, we used to reckon it out between us. If our Edie'd opened her legs to him, we would have been safe.'

'Wash your filthy mouth out!' Edith screamed. 'Al, what you're accusing him of, could never have been true. He would never let me touch … he was pure. A celibate Catholic priest. A credit to his vocation.' She rose shakily and hurled a tea cup at her brother's massive head. It hit his temple and fell. Unaware, he coughed a little and stared into the fire.

'You make me sick, the lot of you.' Marguerite's Blue Fit seemed to have burnt out, leaving her exhausted and tearful. Slowly, she sank onto one of the hard-backed chairs.

'You're not saying, Con … you're not confessing, that you were the one who … my God, with Amelia!'

Amelia, slumped opposite Con, her eyes half-closed as the familiar pain zipped across her skull. She leaned forward, as far as she was able, took a deep breath, managed to reach far enough to touch her mother's leg.

'Mummy?'

Marguerite looked right into Amelia's eyes. Amelia saw sympathy there, some fear, the anger dissipating. 'You don't know what's been happening to you, love, do you?' her

345

mother said with a sigh. 'Beyond this virgin birth farce, I mean.'

How could her mother think of her condition as a farce? Surely out of everything else that had happened, from her grandmother's death to now, then her role as Mother of the New Messiah was the only thing that couldn't be questioned. She shook her head, confused and hurt by Marguerite's lack of faith.

'Love, you've had a rough deal. I never should have left you. I never should have ...' Marguerite began to cry, big fat tears streaked blue mascara down her face. She gulped, swallowed, and patted her own knees firmly, as though they were a pair of recalcitrant dogs, needing a chivvy. 'We're in a mess, I must say.'

Amelia touched her mother's slightly crispy auburn head.

'Do not worry,' she whispered. 'All will be well. The Goddess —'

'Darling,' her mother continued. 'That child you're carrying is no virgin conception, whatever you might think. You're pregnant, love. A normal physical fact, though not usually when you're as young as you are. And the reason you're pregnant is —' Marguerite took a deep breath.

'Because a man put his penis in you. Inside your vagina, he ejaculated his sperm, it swam up inside you, found your egg and then a baby was made. It is simple. It happens all over the world, every day. Do you understand, love? God, I wish I'd told you all this before. I never did, you were always so young ... I never even said much about your monthlies ...'

346

Amelia brushed her mother's sympathetic hand away, turned around with difficulty to stare at Edith who had brought the rosary beads around her skinny neck, up between her lips.

'Tell her,' Amelia said fiercely. 'Tell her the truth.'

Edith emitted a whimpering noise.

'What if it was Con?' Marguerite said, wiping her eyes and grabbing Amelia by the shoulder. 'If you could only remember then we could have him up for this.'

'No!' Edith wailed. 'Not Con. There must be some other explanation.'

'No,' Amelia said. 'It's not true. The Goddess —'

'The Goddess doesn't exist, love. She's some kind of dream. You've started to have fits and sometimes those can cause ...' Marguerite had reached the edge of her knowledge.

'Mum!' Amelia rose, accidentally kicking Con in the varicosed shins she did so.

'Amelia.' Con turned slowly, fixed her with his bloodshot eyes. Sweat pimpled his ruddy forehead. The gas fire blasted heat into the room. 'The Goddess is an aura. You've got epilepsy. I think, anyway. You'll have to see a doctor. It can be controlled by drugs. Barbs.' He attempted to rise, but sank quickly back into his chair. 'We'll get you sorted. I'll phone Daniel. He owes me a favour.'

'And who the hell is Daniel?' Marguerite demanded.

'Goldbloom. Consultant Paediatric Neurologist at the Royal.'

'And what about your part in all this, Con? Or were you going to let it all carry on. Because if my suspicions are correct, the miracles and virgin births and a load of religious nutters cluttering up the neighbourhood might just be preferable to the truth getting out.'

Con groaned. 'What do you want me to do?'

'Stop it. Put an end to it right now. It's a dangerous hoax. Once it gets out that you arranged it all, the nuns and the priests and the press, you'll never be able to hold your head up in Liverpool. And once it gets out that you defiled a minor, well, I doubt all those rich ladies of a certain age will want anything more to do with you.'

'You wouldn't, Marge,' Edith whimpered. 'You wouldn't ruin this family?'

'This family has been ruined for years,' Marguerite said.

'All right!' Con bellowed. 'I'll do what you say, everything. My life is over. I must atone. Only not now, please. Not this moment.'

In silence, Marguerite marched over to where he was sitting. She levered Con out of the chair and propelled him towards the window, pulled up the nets and opened the windows wide. Immediately, the room was filled with the invigorating scent of frozen vegetation and dog dirt. In the street a universal gasp preceded a headlong rush towards the garden.

'Get away, all of you,' Marguerite shouted. 'It's over. He'll tell you. Con.'

But the crowd, seduced as they were by tales of cures and supernatural births, apparitions and portents, remained, praying intently, hoping for a glimpse of their salvation. No matter how Con tried to shout over them, their voices rose and fell in a low mesmeric hum, gliding over ancient prayers from a time when belief and faith were easy.

Amelia felt betrayed by her mother. The angry conversation left her sad and confused. She thought of Con, of penises and ejaculation. She remembered nothing. And then.

The wake. Under the table, a boy's face looming, the smell of whiskey, the sound of her mother's voice and tales of the old country. The carpet rough beneath her legs. Her skirt was pulled up higher than her bottom, the scratchy pile scraping her buttocks. There was pain, a sharp pain between her legs. No way, never, no way never no more. Well I've been the wild rover, no never no more. And another voice, closer, louder, Gloria … On and on the singing, then the talking, sweet and familiar. And her head throbbing and her mother telling the story of somebody's Great Great Uncle's head being squashed by an elephant. The smell of whiskey, stronger and stronger.

Amelia screamed.

'What is it?' Marguerite demanded, at her side in seconds. 'Darling, don't cry like that, everyone will hear. I know it's all been a lot for you to take in, but soon, once the baby has come, then soon, we will —'

'You're wrong!'

'Amelia, love. Calm down.'

349

'Mum, it wasn't Con!'

'He's more or less admitted it, Darling. I know it's awful to think about, your own uncle and everything. With me it was Pat, but at least he was only five years older than me and I was seventeen at the time … You see, history repeats itself, especially in this family.'

'Mum, it wasn't Con.'

'I said that, too, though I should have shopped Pat while I had the chance, though back then they wouldn't have listened … When I started filling out and it became obvious that I was in the family way, I married quickly afterwards and when Julian was born, well, that's another story.'

Tears began to pour down Amelia's cheeks. She had no idea what her mother was talking about, but whatever it was, it was irrelevant. Con, putting his penis inside her! It was not true, not true. The very idea made her want to be sick. She only knew what a penis was because of Portly.

With the window flung wide, the room had chilled. Edith huddled in an old, cig-burned cardigan. Con, in the hall, was busily dialling the phone numbers that would finally destroy his career.

'Mum. It wasn't Con. It was a man … A boy. Honest, Con never did what you said. It was Irena, the Goddess. I will give birth to the Saviour of the World, only …' She sobbed into her hands, feeling as though her world had broken.

'Darling. Oh, sweetheart, I know it's probably easier for you to believe that version of events, but you must understand that there is only one way for a baby to be inside you. And if it wasn't Con, then who was it?'

'A boy-man!' Ignoring the fresh waves of pain, Amelia managed to prise herself out of the chair and push past her mother into the hall. 'I don't know, I …' A name; it came rushing from the mouth of the Goddess herself. A name: any name. The name: 'Julian?'

A silence and she was aware of her brother's name being pulled from the air, a lifeline.

'The drugs,' Con moaned, into the receiver. 'Of course. He didn't know what he was doing.'

'Her own brother, though,' Marguerite wailed. 'Amelia, what happened, tell us. Where are you going?'

She had to get out, to escape the stifling house, its secrets and accusations. Her hand was on the front door, the knob turned, as though by magic. She felt Irena behind her, enveloping, and hoped against hope that the Goddess had come to save her. The front door flew open. Standing on the step, a thin, willowy person opened their arms in an expectant embrace and said: 'Hello, Amelia. I'm your father.'

Chapter 35

John, or as he preferred to be known, Joan Finnerty, stalked into the house with his bewigged ginger head held high. His clothes were immaculate, a tailored navy flannel suit with a tight-fitting pencil skirt. Underneath, a pale pink blouse with flounces down the front. He could have been a wartime film star, Joan Fontaine, or Deana Durbin. A press of Amelia devotees attempted to follow him inside, but Con quickly shoved the door to.

'Well, hello at last. I thought it was about time I found out what is going on,' Joan said to Amelia, whipping off his jacket and kicking off his sling-back shoes. 'And these damned heels will be the death of me. Nearly broke my ankle on the ice in Gethsemane Drive.'

'You're my dad?' Amelia said.

'That's right. Your papa. Bundled away like a criminal in the middle of the night. Ho-de-hum. Bet she never told you that one, did she?'

'But you're a …'

The strange creature smiled and ruffled Amelia's yellow curls. His hand was shaking. 'I'm a tranny, Darling. That's the word for it, not that our little Catholic saint, Marguerite, would ever utter it. Underneath, I'm all man.'

Amelia shuddered, unable to take this in. She would rather have no father at all, keep the old dead and lauded one, than have to look at this womanish man or mannish woman and hear its whining high-pitched voice and admit that he was her dad. She watched as he placed his shoes neatly below the full-length mirror, stopping for a moment to admire his face, to wipe a long nailed but large finger, Penelope-Pitstop-style around his fleshy mouth. Pleased with what he saw, he spun around to face Amelia.

'Well, let's have a look at you, sweetie. It must be, ooh, what? Twelve years since I clapped eyes on you. Of course, Sarah sent me the odd photo, strictly off the record but there's nothing like seeing you in real life.'

Despite herself, Amelia wanted to cry. Everything was turning inside out. A few months ago, she'd been a normal schoolgirl whose dad had died when she was a baby. She had a normal mum and a grandma and a brother who had run away to London. Even her Aunt Dolores was safely married to the spooky Ken and Edith's teeth fitted and Great Uncle Con was hardly glimpsed from one Christmas to the next. Amelia looked up at her father, noted a callous curiosity in his brown eyes but also that his face was lined and sad, far sadder than her mother's.

'You!' Marguerite pushed past Amelia and confronted him. 'Haven't we had enough today? I told you never to come back. You are not welcome here. You are no part of this child's life. Get away ...'

Joan shook her head very slowly. She touched Amelia lightly on the shoulder.

'I see you're still as understanding as ever, Marguerite. At least let me talk to my own daughter. And why can she not decide for herself whether she wants me in her life?'

'Because you're a conniving bastard?' Marguerite stepped backwards into Con who was whispering down the phone. It set off a bout of coughing in him and it was a minute or so before anyone could speak. When they did, they had calmed down a little.

'Amelia is all over the Echo,' Joan said. 'And the local radio news. Everyone is talking about it. My daughter, a little saint, eh? Well we've done that right, Marge.'

'Don't you dare call me that.'

'Come on, old girl. You can't still hate me that much, surely?' Joan said, softly. 'You can tell me about it, if you want. Or not. Up to you. I came to tell you that I'm here, that I'll always be near if you need me.'

'Why now?' Amelia demanded, forgetting her desire to escape.

Joan nodded. 'I wanted to earlier, when the newspaper articles started, but I thought it better to keep away. My shrink said that coming here might destroy me but I thought ... Well, and now you're having a baby. Funny how history repeats itself, eh, Margie?'

Amelia's tears began to flow. The hall, with its gloss-painted panels, its anaglypta wallpaper, its one picture of the ascending Christ, became infused with raspberry light as the low winter sun caught the stained glass in the landing window. Con, cowering near the phone, resembled a penitent kneeling before his confessor, whereas her father with his mask-like face, was the image of a gaudy and over-painted statue. From the front garden seeped the winter aroma of hoar frost, the sharp tang of bonfire smoke, the ever present dog dirt and exhaust. It filled the narrow hallway like a dangerous incense, at once innocent and impure.

'Why did you never come before?' she demanded, between sobs. 'Didn't you care about me and Julian? We're your children.'

Joan's eyes were wet, his mascara beginning to run. 'Don't say that. Sweetheart, don't ever think I didn't care about you. And Julian, well he was never truly mine to care about.'

'It wasn't his fault,' Con explained to Amelia and the mysterious caller at the end of the phoneline. 'Your grandmother made him leave. She threatened to expose him. He was a teacher, a headmaster. And dressing up like that. It would have destroyed his career.'

'It destroyed me, anyway,' Joan said. 'I couldn't work, couldn't do anything. Driven away from home. Sarah was wild. Marguerite was cold. They'd sorted out a flat, some money. I was dead.'

Amelia wiped her eyes. 'I don't understand,' she said. 'Even if they made you leave, made you go to another house, you could have kept in touch, somehow. All these years … I thought you really were … dead.'

Joan's make-up was a mess, his skin doughy and streaked.

'You mean you would have accepted me as your father?'

He stood over her, tall, even in his stockinged feet. The pink blouse was see-through, the skirt too tight. His bosoms, under the georgette, were lopsided. One had slipped down to his waist. He reeked of cheap musky perfume. The thought of him turning up at school looking like that, in front of all her friends. She shuddered.

'You could have worn ordinary clothes. Men's clothes. You are … You are a man aren't you?' Amelia said. Her eyes were playing all sorts of strange tricks. Joan's face seemed to be melting then remoulding like a cartoon.

'I'm a man, all right, as your mother can testify. But I need to dress like this.'

'A neurotic defence mechanism against rejection by the maternal figure,' Con explained.

'You could have tried not to,' Amelia whimpered.

'He suffers from an impaired self-actualization. The clothes are a short term fix but in the long term, it only serves to redirect sexual energies that …'

The phone rang insistently and Con snatched it up. 'Yes?'

'Get out,' Marguerite's voice was cold. 'I don't know what you are doing here, John, but you're not welcome. I told you, years ago …'

Joan kept her hand on Amelia's shoulder as he spoke. 'I know what you told me, and God, I've abided by it for years, haven't I? Not so much as a phone-call, a postcard. But this, this is different, this is my, our daughter and she is in crisis. She needs both of us.'

'Who's this, honey?' The airman, immaculately groomed, glided downstairs and took his place at Marguerite's side. If Amelia hadn't been gritting her teeth through another bout of pain, she would have laughed out loud at the contrast between her feminine father and the picture of brawny masculinity portrayed by Pádraig.

'No matter, he's just leaving.' Marguerite thrust forward, and began to push Joan towards the door.

'No, Mum.' Amelia grabbed her mother's arm. 'I think he should stay. He's my dad.'

'Jaysus!' Padraig's between-his-teeth whistle sounded like air escaping from a balloon.

'Oh God,' Con groaned, still on his knees at the phone. 'Oh God.'

Joan was clutching Amelia's shoulder, but his touch was not right. It was too tight, too fierce, even with Marguerite threatening him. Amelia tried to pull away, but his grip was like a vice.

'Dad,' she said, 'you're hurting me.'

'This is a nightmare,' Marguerite said. 'A nightmare. In a few moments, I'll wake up in my own bed. This cannot be happening.'

'Mum!' Amelia gasped. 'Dad … He won't let go …'

Padraig moved forwards towards Joan who fell backwards, the luxurious wig slipping to reveal sparse white hair clinging to a pink scalp.

'Get off of me,' he hissed. 'You've no bloody right. You lot are coining it in and there is me, all those years working the bars and the clubs, nothing to show for it. The least you can do is —'

'What is happening here?' Edith said, emerging from the parlour with a tray. 'There's enough shouting and carrying on to wake the dead, and with the all dead we've got in this family, well, I wouldn't like to tempt fate.'

As though in answer, little Patti's cry could be heard gathering momentum in the back room.

'Edith, get back in there,' Marguerite commanded. 'None of this is your business.'

Edith set her disintegrating jaw. She stood, hand on skinny hip, cigarette held high by her other hand. 'Not my business. My own brother accusing Al Monagle of tampering with him. My own niece failing to recognise the Second Coming when it is happening in her own front hall. Not my business! Huh!'

'Aunt Edith, don't upset yourself. You're not a young woman.' Pádraig fixed Edith with his dazzling smile.

'Just go,' Marguerite yelled, balling her fists into her eyes. Amelia could not be sure whether she was addressing Joan or Pádraig.

'Edith,' John gasped. 'You and I always saw eye to —'

Edith began to whimper. 'It's that man. Oh, Jesus, Mary, Joseph, all the saints, Prince whatshisname of Monaco and —'

Con dropped the phone back in its cradle and edged forward, slobbering and snarling like a rabid old dog. He reached John, pressed backwards into the banister in an attempt to avoid Pádraig, and seized him by the shoulders.

'Just get out,' he shouted, each syllable sending the veins in his temple into a throbbing puce frenzy. 'All of you, out!'

With unsuspected strength, he grasped both Joan and Padraig and hurled them towards the front door where they collided. Edith, unusually quick off the mark, opened the door and the two men fell into the path of several worshippers.

CHAPTER 36
21ST DECEMBER 1981

The following two days passed quietly. The worshippers began to drift away. The dreadful weather and Con's statement to Radio City, plus the need for some last minute Christmas shopping, saw to that. The Radio City announcement, however, cast Con in the role of 'enemy of the faithful' and his own house up at Calderstones Park was now under siege. An investigation into the fraudulent acceptance of money had been mounted. A policeman was stationed outside his Hope Street consulting rooms.

Amelia, assaulted by memories of her grandmother's wake, stayed in bed and listened to the house creaking about her, her mother's hushed footfall, Edith's sobs. Con, in anger, had torn away the pendulum on the grandmother clock. Its warm tick and resonant chime no longer punctuated the day.

On what would have been the first day of the Christmas holidays, Amelia was visited by a small, dapper man, with greased back black hair and a profuse moustache.

'This is the specialist,' Marguerite said, in her most disapproving voice, as though she were introducing a criminal. 'One of Con's ... colleagues.'

Daniel Goldbloom, Consultant Neurologist in the Royal Liverpool Hospital, with his own consulting rooms on Harley Street W1, had known Con since they studied together at Cambridge. Amelia watched, dazed, as he sat at the edge of her bed, making himself at home. His long white fingers seemed wrong, probing the candlewick bedspread with obscene precision.

'So what's the problem?' he addressed Amelia.

She made herself look at his face. His eyes were those of an earnest elf, green and moist.

'She had a fit. I saw it,' Marguerite said.

Amelia smiled. The Goddess was very near. She preferred her like this, close but not overwhelming; Her heavenly form standing guard over the New Saviour, warm and radiating heat. Irena was a furnace of passion. Amelia looked up at the ceiling but her eye was caught by a Mass card tucked into the moulding on the wardrobe door, bearing a print of 'The Light of the World'. Irena was the light, but would the Saviour be a paschal lamb, meek and mild, born to sacrifice Herself? Or a warrior, standing firm against the non-believers. Amelia thought of Boudicca, of a fearsome woman atop a chariot and hoped for the latter.

'I see a Goddess,' Amelia whispered. 'They all think I am making it up but She is right here in this room.'

Daniel brushed her hair from her face. 'Does she come often?'

The Goddess was always with her now, in fragments of colour or dark voids. She could feel Her anger and disappointment at the way things had turned out. Amelia was not, after all, a worthy subject. But she would atone. She, Amelia, must win back Her forgiveness, Her love. She would be worthy of Her glory and majesty.

'Always,' she replied with conviction. 'She is watching over me.'

'And how do you feel when she comes, when you black out? There has been mention of some automatic behaviour: thefts ... of tennis racquets? Odd ... miracles.'

Amelia sighed and stretched in the warmth of her bed. She did not want to talk to this man, to any man. This was her moment to ask. She would beg the Goddess for mercy, beg. The light that emanated from the Goddess, from the new Light of the World was blinding. The baby burped. She could hear the breathing of the doctor, her mother's impatient tongue clicks. And in the background, the strains of a familiar tune returning from the void. No way never no more, I've been the wild rover ...'

'Amelia?' Marguerite's voice was distant.

Amelia screamed. 'No!' Then, from the darkness, not Irena but him. His face, close, his smell, closer still. Inside her, pushing and pushing and pinning her down and the legs of the relatives, those legs so close and Marguerite so near and ...

'Julian?' The name heaved into the cool air, breathed across her mother and the doctor and floated out into the splinters of light near the window.

'I am sorry if this is distressing to you.' The doctor opened his bag. 'It does seem ... from reports, from your Uncle Con and your mother, that you are suffering epileptic fits. Your Goddess is an hallucination. Nothing you see is real, merely a flickering image induced by a pathology.'

Amelia closed her eyes.

Julian. No, how could he …?

The baby moved. Soon it would be Christmas, a time to celebrate the birth of another saviour, long ago. What had He done but given the world another excuse to fight. Whose baby was Jesus? He was not sent by God. Everyone said there is no such thing as a divine birth. There must be a man and his penis. The doctor shone a light in her eyes and she flinched from those white exploring fingers. A boy. Julian, her brother.

'I know she's pregnant,' the doctor said in low, almost reverent tones. 'But I think, under the circumstances, I shall put her on Phenobarbitone. There may be side effects, drowsiness, that sort of thing. We'll have her in for tests once the baby is born.'

'And these drugs, they'll cure her, will they?' Marguerite demanded. 'No more visions. No more …'

'That's the general idea.' Goldbloom took a small pad from his bag and scribbled a prescription down. He ripped off the top sheet of paper and handed it to Marguerite. 'But there's no such thing as a cure-all. The child …' He looked down at Amelia's stomach. 'You know who the father …?'

Marguerite shook her head.

'Still,' he said. 'Not good, I wouldn't have thought. Not good at all. Give Con a thump when you see him.'

'I doubt he'll be round here for some time,' Marguerite said, sucking in her cheeks. 'If ever.'

Goldbloom frowned and looked down at Amelia. 'He's not all bad,' he said. 'Whatever you might think.'

'I no longer think anything,' Marguerite said. 'Amelia's asleep. Let's leave her now.'

CHAPTER 37

Months passed. Amelia slept. She slept through the coldest day since records began, through The Maid Of Orleans by Orchestral Manoeuvres In The Dark, through the start of the Falklands War and the sinking of the Argentine warship, Belgrano. Outside her window, buds unfurled, spring sprouted tendrils and weeds grew up, threatening to choke the neglected garden.

When she did wake, or was woken, the world was leached of colour and a routine had been established. She was washed and combed and clothed. Doctors pummelled and shone lights. Words slipped away from her, meanings vanished in the winter cold. The house, once so full of voices and clutter was empty save for Marguerite and poor Edith who tiptoed and whispered, miserable and cowed. Sometimes, Amelia lay in bed and thought she saw Irena. A chink of light would enter her visual field. She would wake to find the world even darker, her medication increased and the Goddess dissipated into a grey blur of barbiturates.

In the drunken haze of her new life, Amelia hated the growing baby. It was a cuckoo child, planted in her womb in an unspeakable act. She refused to think of the act itself; she wouldn't remember it. Instead, she looked down at her body in despair. It resembled nothing but the bloated carcass of a man she once saw fished out of the Mersey; grey and pallid and waiting to spew its vile contents.

And as the world, for Amelia, slowed into silence, Calvary Crescent, floodlit by spring, awaited the papal visit.

PART FOUR
THE GLORIOUS MYSTERIES

CHAPTER 38
30TH MAY 1982

'There is no way on earth that our family would miss our Pope's visit, never mind what your mother says about all religion being evil,' Edith whispered to Amelia a few days later.

Amelia, emerging from her dreams in the high Egyptian bed, smiled faintly. Her aunt was right. Crimes she knew nothing of a few short months ago, incest, rape, fraud, could not stop the O'Dowds from donning their most pious expressions along with rosary beads and mantillas and joining in the celebrations.

'Haven't we,' Edith continued, 'haven't we supported our own convent for one hundred and fifty years? We are Catholic with a capital C. And we're certainly not about to be outdone by the Lawlesses, who are only United Reform, almost atheists when all is said and done, hiring a new Cortina for the day.

'And I know, love, what they're saying. About you. About your brother. Gossips. I take no notice. That child you carry is still nothing short of a miracle and I for one am not going to judge.' She gave one of the shuddering sobs that accompanied any speech she made these days, and smoothed the sheet over Amelia's stomach. 'Not after the things Con said about Father

M … Well, enough of that. His Royal Highness is coming today. Today! Imagine! We're all going together. The McKennas are over from Donegal as well as the O'Neills. They're staying in a B&B in Garston which I can't think would be up to much. I haven't seen our Lil for over forty years … and … the Pope's going downtown, to the Cathedral.' Another sob.

Amelia allowed the old woman's grief and anticipation to wash over her in a curiously pleasurable gush. Edith's teeth had never been replaced and the flapping jowls gave a moist cadence to her voice that had previously been lacking. The old woman's veiny hand lay upon her arm, cold and dry. She smelled of death. Outside, a Russian vine had taken hold of the drainpipe and was threatening to bring it down. Amelia watched a probing tendril wave against a sky of clear cerulean. A flow of warm fluid soaked into her nightie between her legs.

'You will get up, won't you, love?' Edith disturbed Amelia's dreamy contemplation. Had she wet herself? She didn't think so. This was different, a soft, gentle flood that smelled of blood. She imagined herself flowing away, all the life ebbing from her until she would be spent, a wrung out husk upon the bed. The thought was consoling.

Edith shook her. 'And you will come to see when His Royal Majesty comes. You won't lie in bed then, will you? Not when you can watch him in person down town. It would mean such a lot to me and it might help you in your hour of …'

When Amelia tried to focus on her aunt, the old woman fragmented into two ghostly facsimiles of herself. What could mean anything anymore, to Edith or anyone, now their saviour had been appropriated by carnal acts so vile they could not be spoken. She practised saying her brother's name in this rare moment of clarity. The fluid trickled between her legs. Julian. Julian: a name she had uttered all of her life, with love and concern and pity. Now it tasted of ashes. She could never, however hard she tried, match the Julian of memory, of Mr Quiet and the Magic Roundabout, with the hollow-eyed junkie who had appeared at her grandmother's funeral. She could never, even in imagination, understand why, after defiling her the night before, he had turned up at church. She could never forgive him …

She breathed deeply, tried to concentrate upon her aunt's words. That was wrong. Julian had not been at the wake. She tried to think. The image of him clacking down the aisle of Saint Jude's was strong but her memory was jumbled. The truth came in flashes that darted away too quickly. A boy, a stupid boy crawling towards her under the table.

'And Julian,' she whispered, 'will he be there, too?'

Edith patted her stomach absent-mindedly. 'He's not well, love. Not well at all. They think he won't ever be able to speak again. You should see him, sitting there, gazing out the window with this stupid grin on his face. He won't be the same as …' She broke down, sobbing and rubbing her eyes with gnarled fingers. She looked so thin and old. 'The drugs,

so they say. They have altered his personality. Oh, please God
…'

Amelia sat up in bed. 'He will die?' The dark wooden
wardrobe loomed like a sarcophagus.

'I don't know, love. How could I? I don't know anything
any more,' Edith wept.

Amelia lay back on her pillows. Perhaps Julian dead was all
that was needed. A life for a life. His unproved innocence to
be lost with his mind.

Downstairs someone was hammering on the front door.
She heard her mother answer it with her usual crisp greeting.
She watched Edith wrench herself from the bed with
difficulty. Time was speeding up.

'That'll be them arriving!' the old woman said, her voice all
quavery and thick. Sound waves came from another place,
outside of the room, the road, outside of the time they
inhabited. Amelia stared at her aunt. Was she speaking or was
that strangely wobbling tenor emanating from another being?
The old woman moved through the room as though she were
walking through water, so much thicker, heavier than air. The
air itself was moving. Amelia placed her hands over the dome
of her stomach. Pain sliced through her womb. She tried to
focus on the border of tea roses, but it dissolved into a
wobbly, watery version of itself.

'Oh Jesus, Mary, Joseph, all the saints and Cilla Black, your
mother will have an apoplexy when she sees the McKennas
…'

Edith was gone. New voices, waves disturbed the already quaking atmosphere. Amelia rose like a wraith from her bed, propelled by some strange need. Her legs were stiff and aching, unused to activity and it took a few moments to bear the enormous weight of her pregnancy. She found her old dressing gown on the back of the door. It covered only her arms with any effectiveness. Her gravid belly, in its pale pink cotton casing, protruded hideously, like a giant mushroom emerging from the navy blue darkness of the dressing gown.

She waited on the landing, listening to the voices below. The stained glass threw its raspberry light across the stair carpet, sprinkled the anaglypta with lemon and orange flecks, reminding her of candied peel in a Genoa cake.

'Well, Margie, how's that child of yours, the one with ideas above her station?'

'Edith, I must say you've aged. But it suits you. I never bothered with teeth after 1972 and Seamus watched that film, Emmanuelle it was …'

'Will you look at the spam sandwiches and her a millionaire.'

Another streak of pain bent her double. Her womb was surely turning itself inside out.

'Is the baby not due around now?' Some other relative, some cousin, no doubt once or twice removed was chipping in downstairs.

And Marguerite's tense little laugh. 'That would just be our luck …'

The smell of drink. Whiskey. No way never no more …

The pain waned, then went altogether.

Amelia pulled down the steps to the attic. They were heavy and stiff and creaked more than she remembered. All movement was difficult now the baby was so big. It was months since she had ventured up there. The offertory flowers would be dead, the space, the altar she had kept so clean and dusted, was probably cluttered with the bodies of dead insects and other things, worse things. But none of this mattered. All was dead. Amelia had not visited the Goddess's temple since Paula's suicide. Every time she thought of it, she remembered that terrible sight, the flies, the gaping mouth, and couldn't bring herself to hook down the door.

But today the sun was bright and Amelia had changed. She no longer felt creepy at the memory of Paula. She no longer felt anything very much. She took in a deep draught of air. Ripples disturbed the atmosphere, as though another world was breaking through, some other time or space. Amelia closed her eyes. She had to see one last time; she had to look at the dress she had once thought belonged to Irena. She put her foot on the bottom rung. Her toes were swollen, her feet, puffy. She looked up.

'Amelia, get dressed and come down.' This was Marguerite's voice, her posh voice that she put on when relatives came. Today she was attempting to disguise her anger. The vibrations of her fury throbbed through the atmosphere towards her daughter.

Amelia ignored them and began to climb.

The cockloft had not been touched since the police cut down Paula's body and Rentokil dispensed with the thousands of blue bottles. A few dried-up husks remained, making a dry, crispy rasp as her fingers, groping over the entrance hatch, came into contact with them. Attempting to heave herself through the square opening, she was horribly aware of how huge she had become. The hole was impossibly smaller, as though she had taken some Alice in Wonderland potion to make herself too large for the house. Her lungs were crushed by the baby and breathing was difficult. The extra bulk weighed so heavily, her arms could barely take the strain. Eventually she pulled herself through and lay gasping on the loft floor until her heart returned to normal.

The roof-top window had been propped slightly ajar so that some fresh oxygen could mix with the stale air that collected from the rooms below. Everything had been moved around by the police. Aunt Mabel's trunk was on its side, its dark contents strewn all over the floor, the mirror was upturned and cracked down its length, boxes spewed their mildewed contents across the beams, books and files mingled with ancient clothes and obsolete household gadgets. The history of the family was in this cramped space, written into outmoded objects, fading photographs, illegible memoirs. The loft had been plundered, torn apart, violated, its mystical secrets released.

Amelia's hands trembled. She hardly dared look over to where the Goddess's mortal form once hung so magnificently. The dress she had tried on all those months ago would surely have escaped the probing fingers of the detectives, whose only real interest had been in Paula's fly-blown body. Like a robot, she set about putting the room to rights. Moses parting the Red Sea could not have affected a clearer route to his chosen land.

The pain returned, stronger and longer lasting. She sat and waited patiently for it to subside. Far away, a vibration disturbed the dusty air.

'Amelia. Amelia! Get down here this minute. We've an hour to get to town and the taxi's booked. And you never had your tablets last night or this morning …'

As the pain ebbed, some tint began to invade the colour scheme of the attic. Browns and duns became infused with a golden light.

'Goddess?' Amelia whispered tentatively. 'Are you here?'

But the cockloft remained unresponsive. Only the midday sun, having paused above the skylight, offered any illumination.

The dress, when she found it, had fallen from its hanger, and lay in a heap, caught between a giant brass bed-frame and an elephant's-foot umbrella stand. Tenderly, Amelia unhooked the bodice, smoothed the rumpled fabric, tried to reconjure the dusty smell of untold secrets. She lay her cheek on the grey tulle, remembering the day of her grandmother's death. She had believed it to be a beginning, a new world opening up to her. But that had been an hallucination. The Goddess's first appearance had been nothing more than a manifestation of her illness. She had never been real and now even the idea of her was dead. She held up the dress to the light, gripped it tightly with both hands and ripped. The sun reached its peak directly above the velux and finally banished the gloom, showering Amelia with swirling motes of gold. The sticky fabric gave in her hands. Dust flew up, to be bathed in light. She rent the dress in two. This was not enough. She took the bodice and tore at the tiny hook-and-eye fastenings she remembered attaching oh so carefully over her summer dress. They pinged across the rafters. Once begun, a maniacal glee overtook her hands as she rent sleeves and burst seams, destroying forever the buttons, the trimming around the neckline, the layers of petticoats. The dress could never again hold any power over her, it was a dress, a stupid, meaningless bit of lace and material. It meant nothing.

The pain returned. This time it ripped across her stomach. She was almost sick. It was a low down animal pain. She let out a deep moan.

'Amelia?' Her mother's voice in the distance. This time the pain made Amelia rise up on all fours like a lumbering dog, a pressure mounted inside; that could only mean one thing.

'No!' she screamed. 'No, not now.' The baby was coming.

And then all was glittering, sparkling, the attic and its clutter vanished behind the jewel colours. The Goddess had returned.

'What can I do to atone?' Amelia whispered through the searing pains. 'Please, Goddess, help me …'

The Goddess laughed. It was a horrible sound, harsh and sarcastic.

Fool that you think you would receive another chance. Fool of flesh. All is dead. All is corrupted.

She reared up, zoomed in towards Amelia's face. For the first time it was possible to decipher her features and Amelia realised that she was not, as she had thought, young and beautiful, but old and wizened. She was a crone, a hag. The hair was not golden but white and sparse, the teeth, blackened and broken. She was not life but death.

Stupid stupid little cow.

The light was so intense that Amelia had to close her eyes. Pain washed over her, bringing relief from the fear of the Goddess's anger and hatred. There was nothing to do but succumb to the birth pangs.

'Amelia?' Marguerite's head appeared inside the cockloft. Amelia, lying and writhing on the floor watched her mother struggle into the dark space.

'What are you doing up here? Oh my God, you're in labour.'

She crawled to where Amelia was lying and shoved the torn dress away. The Goddess blacked out the skylight. Her anger was terrible to behold. Amelia closed her eyes. She would not look at her, she would not, could not ... And yet, the child was about to be born.

All is dead. All is corrupted.

'Amelia. Christ, she's having a fit as well. Oh, the tablet, I forgot. Oh I am sorry. Darling your waters are broken. The bed ... We have to get you back downstairs. An ambulance.'

Marguerite crawled back to the entrance and shouted. 'Phone an ambulance. Amelia has gone into labour!'

The pain ceased for a brief moment and Amelia dared to open her eyes. No Goddess, just her mother, smiling anxiously into her face.

'Oh, you're back, sweetheart. Look, do you think you can get down the steps?'

Amelia nodded and allowed her mother to help her up. One of the fastenings still clinging to the bodice of the dress had attached itself to her dressing gown. She tried to pull it away.

'That bloody dress,' Marguerite wrenched at the bodice. 'Don't worry, sweetheart.' She put her arm under Amelia's but another wave of pain had begun. Amelia, winded, stopped and tried to gulp air, to brace herself against the monster that was forcing its way out of her body. She was sure it would rip her apart. What if it was evil, this thing she carried, this spawn of some unknowable cousin smoking by the coal bunker?

'It's all right, love. I'm here.' Marguerite held Amelia's head to her breast until the pain lessened. Amelia felt the thing move inside her, it was dislodging itself. She would never get down the steps. The child would be born in the cockloft.

'Mum?'

The Goddess swooped across Amelia.

See what you have done? See all is dead all is corrupt all is dead is corrupt is …

Amelia screamed, put her hands over her ears but the mantra continued louder and louder, now accompanied by the buzzing of insects, the flies from Paula's body which was surely still hanging there only it was … The Goddess in the dress, her mouth covered in flies and shouting at her. And the pain, worse than anything she could imagine, she was tearing in two, dissolving into the blinding flood of agony and noise and …

Amelia could feel her mother's hand clutching. She knew her panic. The blood pumped out of her.

For a moment, the Goddess was back, beautiful again, shimmering. Amelia turned her face towards Her, filled with hope, but now She was dissolving. Amelia was aware of a rattling, a trembling batting, a sensation that overtook her entire body. Where had she heard this before? A surge of pain sent her beyond the edge of thought and the thing was slipping from her, it expelled itself into her mother's waiting hands and she faintly heard Marguerite scream. A torrent of warm fluid flowed out of her and a feeling of profound peace descended. She lay for a few moments, gasping, exhausted before the batting began within her, stronger now that her body was so weak.

Goddess?

Amelia's soul disengaged itself from its earthly home and hovered for a moment over the attic room, watching Marguerite slap hysterically at the dead child among the carnage of decades. A fluttering of light and Amelia swerved up and beyond the house and paused momentarily above the rooftops of Aigburgh. Higher and she could see the crowds lining the streets, Faith making them giddy, the Popemobile easing its way through Liverpool towards the cathedral. And the cathedral itself, refulgent in the sunshine soaring upwards into the blue sky. Amelia's soul too, soared upwards into the atmosphere far beyond the earth and there in the stillness and darkness of the cosmos, she waited.

Where was the Goddess, where was the God?

Nothing. In the blackness, she waited.

Is there anybody there?